Annie McCartney is an actress who has worked on stage, TV and radio. She was also a rock 'n' roll DJ in America for five years. She's a regular broadcaster on BBC Radio Ulster and RTE, and more recently she has made h̶ plays for Irish radio and BBC Rad̶ is the author of three bests̶

Pr̶

'Stuffed with sex 'n' ̶ ̶est, it rattles along like a good rock tune shou̶ ̶er characters are both thoroughly believable and deliciously dysfunctional' *Irish Times*

'The humour, the pace and sheer curiosity keep the pages turning . . . it's all mayhem . . . hilarious' *Irish Examiner*

'A rollercoaster of a read. Hilarious, evocative and moving' *Bibliofemme*

'Smart, snappy and often very funny' *Image*

'An honest and entertaining read' *New Books Magazine*

'As effervescent as the best champagne, but with intriguingly complex aftertastes' Nuala o'Faolain

'A rollicking, no-punches-pulled tale' *Woman's Own*

Also by Annie McCartney

Desire Lines

ANNIE McCARTNEY OMNIBUS

Two Doors Down

Your Cheatin' Heart

sphere

SPHERE

This omnibus edition first published in Great Britain by
Sphere in 2009
Annie McCartney Omnibus copyright © Annie McCartney 2009

Previously published separately:
Two Doors Down first published in Great Britain in 2007
by Sphere
Reprinted 2007 (twice)
Copyright © Annie McCartney 2007

Your Cheatin' Heart first published in Great Britain in 2005
by Time Warner Books
Copyright © Annie McCartney 2005

The moral right of the author has been asserted

A CIP catalogue record for this book is available from the British Library.

ISBN 978-0-7515-4160-1

Typeset in Bembo by Palimpsest Book Production Limited

Two Doors Down

For Bernie

Acknowledgements

A huge thank you to my neighbours in Rugby Road for the inspiration, tea and sympathy – and the occasional glass of wine. I would also like to thank my long-suffering friends (they know who they are), my editors Louise Davies and Jo Dickinson, the great team at Little Brown, my agent Sheila Crawley, for her support, Judy Meg Kennedy and Naomi Leon from AP Watt. The Tyrone Guthrie Centre Monaghan for providing me with a haven of peace and, of course, Katy, Duncan and especially Iain. No thanks at all to the mad poglets.

1

At nine o'clock sharp on an unusually bright Monday morning, Sally O'Neill rode her shiny motorbike along Marlborough Road. She slowed down at the top of the street and with an expert swerve turned through a pair of high gates into a back lane, passing as she did so from urban grey to leafy greenery, and at this time of year, late May, through a profusion of blossom, birdsong and noisy children.

Marlborough Road, a wide, confident tree-lined street in south Belfast, sported on its odd-numbered side a fine example of a redbrick Victorian terrace. The row of tall houses stood proudly to attention, all but two of the neat front gardens framed by cast-iron railings. The brightly coloured front doors were a palette of yellows, blues and reds, with one a startlingly vivid purple. All sported polished knockers and letterboxes – three of them gleaming more brightly than the others, for Sally O'Neill knew how to clean brass. She cleaned three of the houses in Marlborough Road on a regular basis, and had at some time helped out in nearly every other house in the terrace, not only with the endless domestic chores, but with the endless domestic dramas too.

The terrace had the advantage of backing on to one of Belfast's finest parks. Those walking in the park might have noticed, had they been able to see clearly through the dense greenery, that a lane separated the houses from their back gardens, creating an enclosed world, a hidden little bit of Belfast. It was here that the residents played out their lives, rarely using their front doors, preferring to leave and enter by the back, enjoying the privacy the gates at the top of the lane afforded them.

In the summer months, the younger children rode their bikes up and down the lane, skilfully avoiding the occasional yapping dog, and roamed in packs from garden to garden with little to interrupt their fun but the odd tumble from the Nelsons' tree house or the wrath of Miss Edith Black when a muddy foot-ball struck her sparkling windows (plenty of vinegar in the rinsing water). All the comings and goings took place right here in the back lane. Endless visits to various kitchens, to chat or gossip, to drink lemon and ginger tea, to borrow milk or maybe beg something more exotic – a shoot of lemon grass, a pinch of cumin or a sprig of rosemary for a recipe. And strictly after six p.m., neighbours might also meet to indulge in a glass of wine or a refreshing gin and tonic. Sometimes, when an excuse could be found for celebration, a bottle of good champagne might even appear.

As she rode slowly down the lane, keeping a watchful eye out for children, Sally noticed that the McDonalds' wisteria had colonised at least two other houses, forming an arch of pale mauve blossom that stretched from number 25 to number 29 like a garland. Not for the first time, she thought how the back lane really came into its own in summer. The clematis Miss Black had planted five years ago had grown almost all the way up her lilac tree. At number 21, the McNamaras had inher-ited a large magnolia tree from the previous owners, and earlier that spring Sally had enjoyed the delicate pink flowers. Over the years she had gradually learnt the names of all the various flowers and shrubs from Miss Black, and knowing what the plants were added an extra layer to her pleasure.

She stopped outside the back door of the McDonalds' house and turned off the engine, then swung herself off the bike. She still felt a wee bit self-conscious about riding it, but each time she nearly lost her nerve she focused on how it had added a new dimension to her life. It made her feel different from the run-of-the-mill cleaning lady, and best of all, it gave the residents of Marlborough Road something to blatter on about. She smiled to herself as she imagined them saying, 'What noise? Oh, that. It's just my cleaning lady roaring off on her motorbike.'

She had won the bike in a competition. She'd filled out some form or other – *name three kinds of pasta and win a sexy Italian bike*. There was a time when she would only have known spaghetti and macaroni, but no longer: the kids in Marlborough Road seemed to eat nothing but fancy pasta, so she had simply opened Clare McDonald's cupboard, and written down *tagliatelli*, *papardelli* and *fusilli*, taking care to spell them properly. She hadn't expected to win, of course, but then ages afterwards, when had forgotten all about it, she'd got a phone call to say she'd won first prize. She simply couldn't believe her luck. At first she had fully intended selling the bike – it was a Piaggio, stylish, chic and worth quite a lot of money, something Sally didn't have much of – but when she saw it, she loved it so much she just decided to keep it. It was fire-engine red, with black swirly patterns on the petrol tank and plenty of sparkling chrome. She hadn't regretted keeping it for a minute. She stored it under a tarpaulin cover in her back garden, and every Saturday gave it a good wash and polish. Her heart filled with pleasure at the sight of it: it was hers, all hers. It conferred on her a sort of kudos that she'd never had before. Even now, after owning the bike for four months, she could recall perfectly the looks on the faces of Clare and the other women she cleaned for when she first turned up on it. For almost the first time in her life Sally had felt she measured up; she was exotic, special, like all of them in Marlborough Road with their iguanas, hamsters and macaws, and, of course, their free-range children.

'It's only me,' she called now as she entered. She took off her crash helmet, fluffed up her hair and straightened her clothes. Then she hung up her jacket and went to change into her slippers. She hoped Clare was upstairs at her desk, well out of the way. That meant she could make a good start on the kitchen before Clare came in looking for some camomile tea to calm her nerves. Awful-looking yellow stuff that tasted like hay, but it was too much to contemplate what Clare would be like without it. She drank gallons of it, but was still, in Sally's opinion, 'highly strung'.

Sally had answered an ad – *Lady wanted for light household duties* – nearly ten years ago and had been hired on the spot by Clare McDonald from number 25. 'Light household duties' was a bit of a misnomer, for there was nothing light about them. The place was totally disorganised and Sally had been welcomed into the chaos with utter relief.

Ten years ago Tony and Clare McDonald were just about thirty, a year younger than Sally herself. They had three children: Rory, eight, Evie, six, and the new baby, Anna. Their house, in the middle of the terrace, was roomy, tall (four storeys) and absolutely chock-a-block with stuff, all of it supposedly essential. At times the clutter nearly did Sally's head in. Each room was shelved from ceiling to floor, and the shelves were stacked full of books. She had never seen so many books outside a library, and she doubted anyone could live long enough to read them all. Still, apart from all the stuff, the house had a good feel to it.

Sally had grown up with the old adage 'a place for everything and everything in its place'. But then you could have

4

fitted her small rented semi in west Belfast into the McDonalds' upstairs drawing room. Nonetheless, she slowly got used to the house and to the family, and gradually her original two hours once a week grew to two hours three days a week, and then three hours on a Friday, as Clare and the other women Sally cleaned for became more and more dependent on her.

As she put the kettle on, Sally surveyed the damage in the McDonalds' kitchen. They must have had a dinner party last night. Honest to God, you'd think Clare ran a restaurant. She seemed to entertain all the time, and although she could cook, she never used one dish when she could use ten. The dishwasher had been run, that was something, and the pots were steeping in soapy water. Sally would rush through the lot and reward herself with a cup of tea before she tackled the floor. That bloody dog had peed on it again. They had a sort of nappy thing they put down for it, but Sally thought that if someone would take the trouble to train the poor thing, or let it out at night, they could do away with the pads.

For some odd reason the dog adored Sally. It sat and looked at her with a soupy expression on its face while she bustled around it. She needed it out from under her feet now, though, if she was to tackle this mess. The dog gazed at her beseechingly.

'C'mon, you, out you go.' Sally opened the door and pointed. 'Go on. Out . . . get out!'

Lola went reluctantly. The residents all specialised in weird names for their pets, and used their surnames too, so Lola was known as Lola McDonald.

Sally's shouts had alerted Clare to her presence. Down she came. Sally handed over a cup of camomile; Clare sipped it gratefully, then moved to the bench near the kitchen window, yawning as she did so. She was still wearing her dressing gown, a worn-out blue towelling thing she'd had since Anna was a baby. Sally often wondered why she didn't buy a new one. But

5

then why would she? People like Clare could get away with wearing threadbare dressing gowns, not to mention old cardigans and shapeless tracksuit bottoms; you needed the confidence and the posh voice to carry it off.

Clare McDonald was a tall, slim, naturally elegant woman of around forty. She was pretty, with thick shoulder-length blonde hair that she mostly tied back. Her green eyes were striking and she had sharp, regular features, redeemed by a warm full mouth and lovely teeth. She had that particular ease of people who know they are attractive. She put little effort into her appearance, except when she was going out. Sally, on the other hand, fixed herself up every morning, even for just coming to work.

In the dining room the candles had all burnt down; it looked as if they had had a power cut. There were more candles than you'd see at a high mass, but this was par for the course. They were all very fond of candles in this terrace. Electric light seemed to unsettle them. Sally surveyed the damage. They had used those massive wine glasses again, like goldfish bowls on sticks; you could fit a bottle of wine in each. No wonder the bottles in the yard were piling up. All their back yards were stacked with empties for recycling. At home Sally put her bottles in the bin; she doubted that recycling her one wine bottle a week would save much of the planet anyway. She lifted the glasses gingerly; they had to be hand-washed as well, which was a pain. She was always terrified she'd break one. Not that Clare made much of a fuss about the occasional breakage, but Sally hated to be beholden to any of them.

Happy as she was in her job as cleaner and counsellor to the denizens of Marlborough Road, there was always a part of her that longed for something more challenging. But there was little chance of that; she had to live, didn't she? From time to time she thought of leaving, but they paid her well, and gave her holiday pay and birthday and Christmas presents, and since she was qualified for nothing, it seemed as good as she could get. After all, she had a house to keep, and no husband. Not that she lost much sleep over that. Getting rid of Charlie had been one of the more positive things in her life. She didn't mention him to her employers; no one asked, they were all too preoccupied with their own lives. They just assumed that she was divorced, which suited her fine.

She had married Charlie O'Neill twenty years ago. He had had dark brown curls, a lithe figure, a great smile, and blue eyes that really twinkled, like bits of coloured glass. He had delivered bread every day to the Spar where Sally worked, and was great craic, just full of devilment. He would spend ages teasing and joking with the shop assistants, who were all mad about him and flirted with him like crazy. All except Sally. She was in love with him, but didn't join in because she didn't think she had the slightest chance of getting him. So when he asked her out, she could barely contain her joy. Of course she said yes, and that was it. In no time at all they were inseparable. Charlie seemed to adore her, and couldn't keep his hands off her. But Sally was a good girl, and Charlie had to set a date before he could get her to sleep with him. Not for Sally McManus a shotgun wedding. They would do things right and wait till they had somewhere to live before starting a family. She stuck to her guns, and they married the day after her twenty-first birthday. At first she thought it was so romantic to fall asleep every night and wake up every morning in Charlie's arms. She had yearned for a place of her own, growing up as she had as one of eight kids. But it wasn't long before she found out that there was more to life than romance.

Sally sighed and went back into the kitchen for a tray. She'd have the wine glasses washed in a few minutes, and then she'd tackle the ironing. She hated ironing, but it was part of the job description. She sensed Clare couldn't be pushed too far on this one, since she hated it too, so she suffered it, but Clare

7

wasn't stupid and over the years had gradually whittled down the unruly pile so that now, instead of a huge crumpled mountain that just kept growing, Sally ironed only Tony's shirts and the children's school uniforms. She had been delighted when Rory, Clare's eldest, left school and went off to uni. At least Clare allowed her to use spray starch. Saffron McNamara, who lived at number 21, was convinced it was destroying the ozone layer, so Sally had to rely on steam there, and if anyone's shirts could have used a bit of starch it was Trevor's. God love him, he never quite looked the part of a successful solicitor. To make matters worse, Saffron had a habit of putting all the laundry in together at the wrong temperature. Very few things in the McNamara house stayed their original colour.

Sally set up the ironing board near the kitchen window; that way she could get a good view of the comings and goings in the lane. While she ironed, she listened to Gerry Anderson on Radio Ulster. She thought he was a scream, as sharp as a tack. He was so insulting to some of his listeners, but it didn't seem to bother them, or stop them ringing him up. If Clare was in the kitchen, Sally had to put up with *Woman's Hour*, and Jenni Murray talking about the problems of working mothers or obscure female medical conditions. Arranged marriages were a favourite topic. Sally had her own opinions about marriage, but she kept those to herself. Her troubles with Charlie had started after their daughter Bronagh was born. Charlie was not, to put it mildly, an ideal father. After he had worn out his lines about his little bundle of joy, he more or less left Sally to it. She had saved for years and had quit the Spar with the intention of having three children, but their second attempt ended in miscarriage so she resigned herself to having only the one. Charlie increasingly spent most of his time out with his mates, drinking heavily and hanging around in the bookie's. Every time Sally tried to talk to him about the lack of housekeeping money, or the loneliness of sitting in alone night after night, he would promise her faithfully that he was going to change. His eyes would light up as he shared his pipe dreams with her. He had plans for them, big plans. That was one of the reasons she had married him. She had truly believed him when he said he didn't see either of them spending their lives in a housing executive property in west Belfast. He had wanted them to move over to south Belfast, to a big roomy house. Well, Sally was in a big roomy house in south Belfast right now. The only problem was, she was cleaning it.

2

Wednesday was one of Sally's long days. After the morning spent at the McDonalds', she went to number 21, the McNamaras', for the afternoon. She had a quick sandwich at Clare's before she left. She didn't trust most of the things Saffron cooked. That vegetarian malarkey was all very well if you were a natural cook, but Saffron most definitely was not.

The colour purple sprang to mind immediately Sally thought of the McNamara home. She often joked that if she stayed still long enough, Saffron would spray her lilac to blend in with the background. Saffron loved the colour; she even had a purple toilet seat in the downstairs loo. Her house made the McDonalds seem like minimalists. Sally had overheard Evie saying this to her mum and thought it was right on the button. Saffron threw nothing out; she was much worse than Clare. Several of the children's grubby drawings were displayed about the place. Half-used candles were kept, elastic bands, string, unread copies of the *Guardian*, read copies of the *Guardian*, and all the children's birthday cards. Postcards from various exotic locations accumulated over the past ten years were stashed in piles here and there, or stuck to the fridge with magnets.

As for the drawers — well, there were no words to describe the state of the drawers. Sally daydreamed about holding a massive jumble sale and clearing out the entire contents of the house. In the meantime, she cleaned as best she could, but for all the hard work she put in, she felt she hardly made a dent in the place.

Saffron was sitting looking dishevelled, with Posy on her knee sucking away. Saffron gave a helpless shrug.

'Oh, Sally, thank goodness you're here. She won't stop feeding, and she had such a big lunch.'

'Saffron love, is it not time you stopped that? She's three years old. You know it's just for attention. C'mon, you,' she said to Posy, 'I'll get you a nice drink of juice.'

Posy came obediently. Sally glanced at Saffron's breast hanging there, looking abandoned.

'You need to get yourself some new underwear. Most of your stuff is in ribbons, and you've had that bra for years.'

Sally knew the state of the underwear of everyone in the terrace. Didn't she wash it often enough?

'You're right. Evie said she'd go with me to Marks any time. She says they have beautiful stuff there.'

'Well, the sooner the better.'

Unlike some of the women in the lane, Saffron didn't take good enough care of herself. For a start there was the vegetarian lark. Not a bad thing, Sally knew, but if there was anyone who looked as if they needed a good steak, it was Saffron. She spent hours cooking strange meals like mung bean stew, or couscous with aubergines, or stuffed vine leaves, all tasteless-looking concoctions made with vegetables Sally had never heard of. Now and then she relented and sent out for a pizza, but Sally was convinced there was no nourishment in most of the stuff she ate. She couldn't have weighed more than seven stone, and then she'd just sit for hours letting Posy suck the life out of her. Posy was getting all the goodness. She was a big, hefty child, more her father's build. It would have to stop. Sally was on a crusade.

She gave Posy a drink and turned to survey the state of the kitchen. Immediately she noticed two saucepans streaked with wax sitting on the draining board.

'Ach, Saffron, you haven't been making candles again?'

'Oh Sally, don't worry, I'll clear it up, I promise.' Saffron caught Sally's look. 'It's just that Edith is having her special barbecue and I thought it might be lovely to have some citronella candles. They keep the insects away without killing them, and of course we don't have to have all those awful sprays damaging our lungs.'

Saffron drove Sally bats with all this nonsense, but then she had the zeal of the convert, and Sally knew they were the worst. She had been brought up in east Belfast as a good wee Protestant girl named Enid, but had met some fellow who took her off to India, where she changed her name and became a vegetarian Buddhist. He eventually ran off on her, so she returned home and got a job temping as a legal secretary. One of her first placements was at McNamara & Son Solicitors. Even though he was some twenty years her senior, Trevor fell head over heels for this exotic waif, and within a month, much to everyone's surprise, had married her. Sally thought the marriage a good one. Trevor doted on Saffron, and that was how it should be, the man being the one beholden. Women got more attention that way. It was plain Saffron adored him too, though lately she seemed a bit too absorbed in the children. Treasure, she called him. When Sally first started working in this house she had found it all a bit strange, especially after the dynamism of number 25 and the austere peace of 29. This was like landing on another planet. Trevor had owned the house for years – his father had bought it for him while he was a student – but things had changed dramatically since 'the invasion', as he called it. His quiet bachelor residence, livened only by the discreet visits of lady friends, had turned into a family home teeming with children and animals. Within a year of their marriage, Simon was born. He was nine now. Posy came along six years later. Sally often wondered why it had taken Saffron so long to get pregnant again. She figured it had something to do with all that breastfeeding. She didn't like to ask what age Simon was when Saffron stopped.

Sally hadn't breastfed Bronagh; no one had suggested it. Everyone gave their babies bottles where she came from. You would have to be very sure of yourself to breastfeed. All the same, now she'd been around it so much and heard Clare and Saffron rave on about how good it was for the babies, she hoped Bronagh would do it when she had her own children. Clare had managed eight months with Anna – that was long enough – and Patricia Thompson from down the lane had stopped as soon as she got her figure back. But three years was far too long. Sally would have to have a word with Trevor. He needed to tell Saffron that enough was enough. Surely he didn't want her to waste away?

'Well, d'ye want me to do the kitchen?'

'As a matter of fact, I wondered if you could just do the children's rooms, mainly Simon's. I thought if his bed was changed he might get a good night's sleep. He has his Grade Two piano exam tomorrow.'

Sally hated cleaning Simon's room, or even changing his bed, because in order to do either she had to face his pet iguana. Saffron read this in her hesitation.

'Don't worry, Iggy is in the front room with Simon, and we've taken his cage out too.'

Sally nodded her approval and headed upstairs. In less than an hour she had the room spotless. She came back down to the kitchen to find Saffron stirring some vile-looking yellow gloop on the stove. It smelled like a curry. Saffron still had a yen for all things Indian. The house always reeked of incense, and she draped the lamps in scarves, and of course she dressed in that hippie gear as well.

Sally began to put the lids back on all the wee spice jars. She was halfway through when Evie McDonald came strolling in. Posy immediately ran to her, arms outstretched. Posy adored Evie, and the feeling was mutual. Sweet and Sour was Sally's private nickname for Evie. She was a delight outside her own home, but these last few years Clare had borne the brunt of all her vitriol, with Sally as an occasional witness.

'There was a phone call for you, Sally, to our house, someone with an American accent from a place called Maids to Order. She couldn't get you on your mobile.'

Saffron's ears pricked up, but she didn't say anything.

'How did they get *your* number?' asked Sally, inwardly cursing Bertha McClure.

Evie didn't know.

'Did she leave a message?'

'She would like you to call about a time for your appointment.' She handed Sally a piece of paper.

'Thanks, Evie, and just while you're here, when are you taking Saffron shopping for her new clothes?'

Sally needed to distract them. She didn't want them knowing her business, and she could sense Saffron was intrigued.

'Would you not take a wee run into town, Saffron?'

'I could go with you now,' said Evie. 'I'm not doing anything.'

'That sounds great. Why don't the two of yis get going? I'm here till five. I'll look after Posy and Simon. You could be back in two hours if it's only Marks you're going to.'

'But Sally, I wasn't even thinking of shopping. Good Lord, what about all this tidying?'

'To tell you the truth, I'd get more work done without you under my feet. Away you go, you've been threatening to go shopping for months.'

'Yes! C'mon, Saffron,' whooped Evie. 'I was born to shop!

14

I'll just tell Mum I'm off', and she was out the door like a bullet.

Reluctantly Saffron got up to get ready. She really needed to invest in some new clothes as well as underwear. Today she was wearing a purple kaftan sort of shirt with billowing sleeves and a bright lemon skirt covered with lots of wee mirrors. She had on a pair of industrial-looking sandals, and large gold hoop earrings, and she hadn't shaved her legs. She might as well be carrying a crystal ball, Sally thought. But she was a pretty girl, and with her beautiful creamy skin, dark brown eyes and thick curly hair, she could get away with dressing like someone daft. Besides, as Evie was fond of telling Sally, boho chic, whatever that was, was in.

'What is your appointment about, Sally? Anything exciting?'

'Ach no, nothing important.' Sally tried to sound casual.

'Why don't you use the phone? Go ahead.'

'No, I'll ring later, I have my mobile.'

Bertha McClure, a neighbour of Sally's, had recently been recruited by a new cleaning firm called Maids to Order. When she heard they needed an extra supervisor, Sally had sprung to mind. Bertha had been nagging at her to apply for over a month now. She knew that Sally would be an asset, and she thought she was starting to take the bait because Sally had humoured her and gone along to a meeting. Now it seemed that wasn't enough: Bertha had set up an appointment for her with Miss Maybeth Weston, the woman who ran Maids to Order.

Sally went quickly to her bag in the cloakroom, fished out her phone and dialled. She kept her voice low, for she didn't want Saffron to overhear.

Sally had formed her own opinion of Maybeth at the talk for potential recruits about a week ago. It wasn't really a favourable one. Maybeth reminded her of one of those evangelical TV preachers enlisting people into the army of the Lord.

But all the way home on the Piaggio, her bony fingers digging into Sally's back, Bertha had pleaded with her to just go and talk to Maybeth alone. Now Sally was wishing she hadn't agreed.

Knowing Saffron wouldn't be too long getting ready, Sally kept the call as brisk as possible. She agreed to go in and see Maybeth the following morning. She might as well find out exactly what she was being offered. It would do no harm. She wasn't committed to anything yet. And in truth she was flattered by Bertha's insistence that she could have the job if she wanted it. It was good to be in demand, and not just as a cleaner, but as a supervisor.

Evie was back within minutes, with Posy perched on her hip. The little girl was grinning with delight and carrying a DVD. Evie was never surly to Sally. She had inherited her mother's green eyes and blonde hair, and her height, with the bonus of her father's curls, warm smile and perfect teeth. Despite all this, she did everything in her power to make herself look unattractive, plastering her lovely clear skin with make-up, straightening her long curly hair and wearing clothes about four sizes too big.

'Straighten your shoulders, Evie, and stop slouching.'

'Oh Sally, you sound just like Mum!' Evie shot back, but she clearly didn't mind Sally telling her off. She regarded Sally as part of the family – well, almost; Sally was the cleaner after all. And despite the obvious attempts of the various families to make her feel part of them, Sally knew her place, though she didn't always like it. She tried not to dwell on the fact that she could have made much more of her life. She yearned to feel she mattered as much as her employers. She wanted to have the same self-confidence, the casual ease with which they took their place in society. She still felt intimidated by them. If she had had the support and background of these kids, there would have been no stopping her.

Evie settled Posy in front of the TV with her Pingu DVD.

'There, she can watch that for a while.'

Saffron severely limited her children's TV watching. She was convinced too much of it stunted their emotional development. Naturally Posy was gleeful at this rare treat. She loved Pingu. Sally could cope with cartoon penguins. They didn't leave foul waste everywhere like the awful Iggy.

Saffron came downstairs wearing violent purple eye shadow. She looked like a wee girl; she was so excited at going into town.

'Are you sure you don't mind, Sally?'

'Not at all. You need to get away more from this set-up, it'll do you good.'

'You're a darling. We'll be back by four thirty at the latest, and don't worry about the house, just watch Posy for me. Simon is in with Anna and the hamsters.'

'Just make sure you get some sexy underwear. Evie, don't let her buy anything too sensible. No more bras with flaps!'

'Don't worry, Sally, we'll do Ann Summers as well!'

'There's no call for that!'

'Chill pill, Sally, just a joke.'

And off they went, giggling like two teenagers. Sally got back to her work, and pushed all thoughts of Maids to Order out of her head. While she was finishing up scraping the wax off the pots, Edith Black popped her head round the door. She lived at number 29, and Sally did a few hours a week for her too. It was unlike her to drop in. She was looking frail, and Sally thought again that all those recent trips to visit her sister Ellen had certainly taken it out of her. Though a widow, Ellen, like Edith, was childless.

'Oh Sally, you're here! Ah yes, of course, it's Wednesday, isn't it? Do you know if Trevor is popping home for lunch?'

Sally looked at the pot of curried garbanzo and mung bean on the stove. She felt it would be safe to say that he wouldn't be.

'Saffron has gone into town with Evie to do some shopping, so I don't think so. Can I leave a note for him?'

'No, I wanted to talk to him about the barbecue. Don't worry, I'll see him this evening. Hmmm, interesting smell.' Her gaze swept the kitchen. 'Heavens, Sally, it's really terribly cluttered in here. Does Saffron ever throw anything out?'

'Not enough, if you ask me.'

'Yes, quite . . . Oh well, must dash.' And she whirled out as quickly as she had entered.

Sally watched Edith pass the kitchen window. She cut an unusual figure. She was a tall woman, big-boned, with broad shoulders, imposing and well built despite her recent weight loss. Her thick white hair was swept into a grand chignon – or a bun, as Sally would have been inclined to call it had she not been informed otherwise. Edith had few wrinkles for a woman of her age, having always avoided the sun. Her mode of dressing was old-fashioned; her clothes would have been in vogue thirty years ago. However, they were so out of date they were coming back in again, so much so that Evie was starting to take an interest in them. Sally had come to realise over the years that Edith's imperious manner was partly an act, although she was so in the habit of it now that she would have been hard pressed to find another mode of behaviour. The children mocked her a bit behind her back, but they were scared of her and behaved like little angels to her face.

In a couple of weeks' time, Edith was having a barbecue. She was not the sort of person you would naturally associate with outdoor activities of any sort other than gardening, but she had watched the barbecue culture develop in Marlborough Road over the last few summers, and oddly enough had found it exhilarating to dine alfresco. It reminded her of trips abroad. So she'd decided to have a barbecue built. She didn't favour those metal ones run by gas that the others had. They were much too common. Hers was a brick one, with a proper chimney. She had driven the unfortunate man trusted with the arduous task of building it – not to mention everyone in the lane – completely mad with all her attention to detail. Having decided that the Victorians had not specialised in barbecuing, she had gone for a rococo style, built entirely from old brick. She was looking forward to the evening. It was far and away the biggest event she had ever considered. She had her reasons for holding it. Firstly, she wanted it to be a showcase of sorts for Otis, one of her lodgers. He was the son of some close friends of Ellen, who had taught him English, and he was apparently a talented young man, despite his scruffy appearance. She also thought it would be an opportunity for people to meet Fintan Fanning, the well-known opera singer, and appreciate that she only took in the finest-quality lodgers. Perhaps he'd even treat them to a song. There was nothing more thrilling than the sound of a fine tenor voice soaring upwards in the clear air on a summer evening. She made a mental note to check the weather forecast as well. Sally had agreed to come along as a guest. She sometimes helped at these occasions, but Edith felt the time had come to include her on the guest list. After all, she was part of the Marlborough family.

Sally had accepted Edith's invite to the barbecue with some trepidation. She might be referred to as one of the family, but everyone knew that she was not their social equal. She hoped it would not be too much of an ordeal and that she would feel comfortable. She aimed to look casual, not overdressed, and she wanted above all to blend in. She had mentally run through her proposed outfit about a hundred times so far. She hoped she could manage it, especially now that Fintan would be there.

The phone rang, interrupting her thoughts.

'Is Trevor there?' A female voice; sounded like an English accent.

'No, he's at work. Who's speaking?'

'Oh, just a colleague of Trevor's. I saw Saffron in town and thought he might be home – not to worry.' The woman hung up abruptly.

Sally couldn't quite place the voice, but she was sure it was someone she knew; it sounded strangely familiar. Very odd that the caller hadn't given her name.

Sally was at the kitchen table trying to keep Posy occupied when she heard the front door open and Evie and Saffron came in laden with shopping bags. Evie had managed to persuade Saffron to buy not only lots of new underwear but a couple of lovely summer dresses and a jacket as well. Sally sat patiently through the impromptu fashion show, glad to see Saffron in such good form. Now that she thought about it, she hadn't been quite her usual self recently. Sally wondered why. There must be something up with her; Saffron was usually such a contented soul. Could it be anything to do with the mystery caller?

3

In west Belfast the eye is lifted from the urban sprawl to the familiar bright green shape of Divis Mountain, the highest in the ring of hills that surround Belfast. The legendary Hatchet Field, halfway up its gentle slopes, is well known and revered for the fact that it is home to the fairies. During the late fifties and early sixties, before television and cynicism claimed them, all children growing up here were well schooled in folklore. Sally's own childhood, pre-Troubles, was filled with visits to the Hatchet Field in vain attempts to see these fairies.

Nestling in the shade of Divis was the housing estate in which Sally lived. Practically all of her family, including her parents, lived within walking distance of her house. Hers was a small semi with a compact back garden, big enough for the odd few days of sunshine that Belfast caught throughout the summer months. Sally took pride in her garden; she kept it weed-free and had replaced the grass at the front with gravel. Over the last ten years she had slowly accumulated some plants from the garden centre, and had planted some wee bushes round the fringe. Miss Black had given her various cuttings, and Sally found to her satisfaction that she had green fingers. But for all her care, she didn't own her house. Many people in her neighbourhood were homeowners, and that remained Sally's dream; meanwhile she paid her rent on time and got on with things.

Some of her neighbours had really gone overboard with their gardens. Sally blamed Alan Titchmarsh for turning their heads. The gardens were littered with Davids, Venus de Milos and Cupids, and every second house had a water feature. The real gardeners grew flowers and impressive rose bushes, but many were content with trellises of fake roses in every shade including blue. Reality wasn't an issue. Sally knew better than to make her views known, for it would serve no purpose. Before she worked in Marlborough Road she had never really paid much attention to her neighbours' gardens, but now she often saw things through her employers' eyes. Miss Black, who had never ventured over this end of town, would have lost the run of herself entirely if she had seen these gardens. Mind you, her rococo barbecue would have been a big hit round here.

As for the inside of Sally's house, although she rarely invited the neighbours in, she kept it spotless. Over the years she had disposed of all the frills and fancy things. She went in for the plain, uncluttered look now; it suited the house. She had a couple of framed posters of flowers Clare had given her by an artist called Georgia O'Keefe, one in the living room and one in the hall. In the living room she had a copy of a William Conor she had bought in the Ulster Museum, and above the fireplace hung a painting of a bowl of fruit that Rory McDonald had done for his A level art. Clare had had that framed for her because she had liked it so much. They really brightened the place up. She would have loved to own a real painting, but unless she won the lottery, there'd be little hope of that.

Sally had only just got in from work and was getting the supper together when Bronagh breezed in the door. She had had her hair done pink and blonde this week. It had been deep red the week before with black underneath. Sally had given up worrying about it. She couldn't keep up with all the different colours these days. Bronagh had a pretty wee face and her father's blue eyes and could get away with it. She didn't make a lot of money at the hairdressing, but she worked for a fancy salon in town and she was getting well trained. One day a week she went to college, which meant she would have proper qualifications. She had big ideas of opening a hairdressing salon of her own, but she'd have a long wait. Sally just agreed with her when Bronagh told her of all her plans; she put Sally in mind of her daddy then.

'Mammy, I met Bertha McClure on the bus. She says she offered you a job as a supervisor for a new cleaning company.'

'She did. I told her I wasn't interested.'

'Maybe you should go along and check it out.'

'I might, but sure, one cleaning job's the same as the next, and I'm in a routine over there.'

'You'd be a supervisor, you wouldn't have to clean. Do you never get fed up cleaning?'

'Of course I do, but I'm used to Marlborough Road. They're good people really.'

'I think they're snobs.'

'What do you mean, snobs? Weren't they always very nice to you when you came over?'

That was true enough, they were always very nice to her, but Bronagh had still felt different. Sally had occasionally brought her along with her during the school summer holidays. She always wore her good clothes. The McDonalds ran around in grubby clothes she wouldn't be seen dead in, but they didn't seem to mind at all. It confused her; she thought rich people would be all dressed up. On one of her trips over

23

there, she had worn the lovely new pink sandals she was so proud of, but Evie, who was wearing torn sneakers at the time, said 'You're wearing heels. That means your feet won't grow properly,' and Bronagh had suddenly hated her new sandals.

Bronagh had brought home some free vouchers for the salon. She was starting her hair-cutting; women's hair first, then men's.

'Mammy, would you do me a favour? Could you give these out to some of the ones over in Marlborough Road? Alan has been nagging us to get some new customers in.'

'I thought they were snobs? What about some of your chums? Couldn't they use them?'

'Alan says we aren't to give freebies to our mates. He wants people who might come back and pay. And none of my friends can afford our prices. He's put them up again. He just bought a Porsche.'

'Well give them to me then and I'll ask over there. Evie might like a haircut.'

'She probably wouldn't come.'

Ever since the remark about her shoes all those years ago, Bronagh had always felt intimidated by Evie. Sally was aware of this; she knew the feeling well. It was a class thing, of course, and Bronagh needed to get over it.

'I bet you she would be delighted to go. Her mammy's always giving out about how much her streaks cost.'

'These are just haircuts.'

'Well I'll take them over anyway. How many have you?'

'Six . . . they have to be used over the next six weeks. And they have to call first to make an appointment.'

Sally took the vouchers. Someone would use them, she felt sure. Maybe not Edith, for she just rolled her hair up into the bun thing, but she'd offer her one anyway. Clare loved a bargain, and definitely Trevor, he could do with a trim. His hair was a

24

mess. And she was sure Bronagh would do a good job. She took her work very seriously.

Bronagh helped her clear up and then they watched *EastEnders* together. Sally loved it when Bronagh stayed in and kept her company, though she was careful not to be too possessive; the child had to have her own life. She and Bronagh were close. She thought Bronagh was a great girl, very sensible, and there was none of the old nonsense from her that Clare had to take from Evie. Maybe it wasn't such a good thing to have all your needs catered for; it left you with nothing to strive towards.

Sally still fretted at times that she had deprived Bronagh of a father by leaving Charlie, but he had given her little choice, and technically *he* had left her. She thought back to all his promises; moving to south Belfast had been just one of his dreams. He often regaled her about all the foreign holidays they would take. In reality, Sally had only one holiday during her marriage. When Bronagh was four, she was lucky enough to get a week in a caravan in Port Ballintrae with her brother Liam and his wife. Charlie was to join them for the weekend; he didn't arrive, of course. Something came up. He was so repentant on her return, hugging her and Bronagh and telling them how much he loved them, that despite her misgivings Sally forgave him. She was to forgive him a lot over the years. Somehow she made it through by absorbing herself in her child, but bit by bit she found the love she had for Charlie dying in her. His easy charm finally wore thin. There were too many broken promises, too many nights alone in bed wondering where he was, listening for the sound of his key in the door and waiting for him to stumble upstairs looking for forgiveness yet again. But she was in no position to leave. Apart from the shame and the gossip, where on earth would she go? She had no qualifications. If she got a job, she would need to leave the baby somewhere, and all her family had plenty of kids of their own.

She found out the true extent of Charlie's gambling when she went to the credit union to get the money for Bronagh's First Communion dress. At first she thought they had made a mistake. She had had two thousand and forty-three pounds in there, her life savings, set aside for a deposit on a house of their own. The thought of it had buoyed her up during the endless rows and screaming matches with Charlie. But it was all gone; every last penny of it. Well, he had left two pounds in to keep the account open.

Sally didn't know which was worse: the hopelessness of losing her nest egg, or the pity in the woman's eyes when she told her there was no money left in the account. How had he found out about it? And why had she been so stupid as to open the account in both their names? She could barely make it home, her legs were so weak. She cried for hours, and by the time he came home that night, reeking of drink, she didn't even have the energy to argue with him. She just told him she would be borrowing a First Communion dress for Bronagh because they couldn't afford to buy one. And then she quietly asked him to leave. He didn't really believe she meant it. He moved out that night fully expecting to be reinstalled in her good books when she calmed down. But his luck had run out this time. Sally stuck to her guns and ignored his charm offensive. She went back to work part time in the Spar and prayed fervently that she would never set eyes on Charlie O'Neill again. She did, of course; there were a few occasions when, full of the drink, he came round to the house promising he had changed and tried to get her back. But Sally was weary. She hardened her heart. She needed a better life for herself and her daughter. Then, out of the blue, Charlie was arrested and put away for armed robbery. For all his flaws, Sally couldn't believe he had had a gun. It was out of character, but she supposed it was a desperate attempt to pay off his gambling debts. She was shocked and embarrassed, feeling that Charlie's actions reflected on her. How could she have been so stupid as to marry such a weak man?

A week later one of her sisters told her about the ad for a cleaning lady – and Sally's life turned the corner.

4

Sally struggled into her waterproof coat and trousers. It was Edith Black who had suggested she buy them. The first few wet days she had arrived on the moped she had looked like a drowned rat.

'Heavens above, Sally, you are drenched!' Edith had exclaimed. 'If you are going to keep that motor scooter you have to get kitted out properly. Otherwise you'll catch your death, and we can't have that.'

Edith was right: the weather here would put years on you. As likely as not it was raining either on the way there or on the way back. After a few soakings Sally gave in. She had got the jacket and trousers in a sale in the bicycle shop near Marlborough Road. They were very practical and well made; they'd never wear out. Mind you, they were far from flattering, so if there was the slightest chance it wouldn't rain she left them off, for she felt like a right eejit all geared up in them.

Arriving at Miss Black's, she struggled out of her wet-weather gear, hoping she wouldn't bump into the new lodger just yet. His name was Fintan Fanning, the well-known tenor. He'd arrived a few days ago. Sally had let him in and showed him his room. He was really friendly, not full of himself like some of them.

When Sally first started working for her, Miss Black had just retired from her job as secretary to the managing director of some important company or other. She spent a lot of time telling Sally how invaluable she'd been. Retiring had left her at a bit of a loose end. Sally found this understandable. After all, it couldn't be that easy for her to fill her days; there was a limit to the number of charity shops she could volunteer for, and Sally thought there was little point in her wandering round the house with her two arms the one length. Then out of the blue Miss Black was contacted by the Grand Opera House, and asked if she would put up a singer for six weeks. And so began her rebirth as landlady to the visiting talent, or at least some of it. She was very particular who she took in. Her lodgers were of a higher order altogether, people such as dancers from the ballet, opera singers, set designers; the more cultured types, of course. And Miss Edith Black enjoyed her bit of culture with a vengeance, there was no doubt about that. Last Christmas she had refused to take two of the dwarfs from *Snow White*, and there were mutterings from her more liberal neighbours about this being politically incorrect.

'It has nothing to do with their size. I never take pantomime performers,' Edith confided in Sally. 'Believe me, I wouldn't have taken Snow White herself. Now if they had been in the ballet or the opera it would have been a different matter.'

Sally suspected there weren't many operas that featured dwarfs, but you never knew.

Sally had worked for Miss Black for almost nine years. Having heard glowing reports from Clare, Miss Black had begged her for one day a week to do some 'light dusting'. By now Sally was wise to the true meaning of the word 'light', but she agreed anyway, and so on Tuesday and Thursday mornings she went to number 29.

She often marvelled at the variations in the interiors of the houses. From the front of the terrace it seemed the only difference was the colour of the doors. She liked the decor of number 25 best. Clare had a good eye, and obviously the money to indulge it. Sally loved the colour scheme. It was bright and airy, all yellows, pale blues and creams, and many of the windows had Roman blinds instead of curtains. The upstairs drawing room and the living room had big squishy linen sofas, and there were wooden floors throughout, except in the bedrooms. The house was full of real paintings, not prints from Boots or the like. Tony and Clare collected Irish art. New stuff too, some of it hard to make out, but colourful, and apart from one odd-looking painting of what appeared to be a nude man on a cow with two legs, Sally loved it all. Number 25 was a happy home. People tended to drop in a lot, and were always made to feel welcome.

Miss Black's house, on the other hand, was a wee bit too old-fashioned for Sally's taste. It was dark and quiet, carpeted throughout, with deep red walls downstairs and chintzy wallpaper in the bedrooms. The furniture was ancient, all antiques Sally supposed, which suited the house. These walls too were covered in paintings, though not modern ones like the McDonalds'; mainly rural scenes with gilt frames. There was a William Conor that Sally loved. It was a portrait of an urchin with a cheeky half-smile. In Edith's upstairs drawing room there was a very large painting that almost covered an entire wall. It featured a skinny, crabbit-looking man in a dress coat and top hat. Apparently he was some relative or other of Edith's. There was a brass lamp on the wall above it just to light that one painting, and of course that needed to be polished regularly. When Edith discovered how much Sally appreciated the paintings, she encouraged her to go to the museum, which was just across the park. So on her way home now and then Sally did go, just to look at the art collection. She knew that before she worked for Edith, the idea of traipsing round a museum would never have occurred to her.

Miss Black had two china cabinets full of crockery and lots of silver with twiddly bits, which were a bugger to clean. She insisted too on real Irish linen napkins, which she required to be starched and ironed. Her house retained a lot of the original Victorian features. She had been careful to let Sally know this, pointing out all the intricate carving round the cornice and the ceiling rose. More dust-gatherers, Sally thought, but then what would she know? She wasn't refined like Miss Edith Black. Mind you, her lack of refinement had been no barrier to a real warmth and understanding developing between the two women over the years. But Sally was still aware of her position, and didn't for a minute feel she was Edith's equal.

Fintan was sitting at the table having breakfast when Sally walked into the kitchen. He was a broad-shouldered, solid man, and would have put you in mind of that French film star Gérard something-or-other, although luckily he didn't have the big nose. Edith had only a small kitchen table, and somehow this accentuated Fintan's size.

He stood up when Sally came in and greeted her warmly. He was wearing a pair of fancy pyjamas; Sally felt immediately embarrassed but he had noticed her gaze.

'It's my karate suit,' he smiled. 'I wear it for t'ai chi.'

Sally nodded. She felt a bit wrong-footed, so she lifted his empty cereal dish and took it to the sink.

'Leave that, Sally, I'll do it. Can I pour you a cup of tea?'

She would have felt slightly uncomfortable just sitting down beside him at the table, especially were Edith to come in, so she thanked him and said she had a lot to get done, so she had better get started. All the same, it was nice of him to offer, she thought, as she went up to strip Miss Black's bed. She normally did the kitchen first, but she didn't like disturbing Fintan.

He was still sitting there with a music score in front of him when she came back down. She supposed she'd just have to work around him.

'I met Clare yesterday. Very nice woman, she's asked me to drop in for coffee any time.'

'Oh? I suppose she had you regaled with Maud.'

Clare lectured in Irish studies, and was writing a paper about Maud Gonne, some famous Irishwoman who was a great friend of Yeats. Sally still knew all the words to 'The Lake Isle of Innisfree'. Nearly twenty-five years ago her English teacher had offered a bar of chocolate to the first girl to learn it by heart, and Sally had won. She still thought of Miss Beckett with deep affection.

'Her thesis? Yes, she was indeed telling me about it. What an amusing title, "The pre-menstrual mood swings of Maud Gonne". I'm sure her tongue is very firmly in her cheek.'

Sally said nothing. She had an idea what the expression meant, but she didn't want to agree in case it gave him the impression that she was critical of Clare.

'I might call in tomorrow when you're there, how about that?'

'I'll be far too busy to stop for a chat. And I have to go somewhere from work.'

'Gosh, Sally, do you ever sit down?'

'Sure they don't pay me for sitting.'

Fintan laughed; he had a warm, throaty laugh.

'I suppose not. Well, I'd better not keep you back then.' He picked up his music and left.

After he'd gone, Sally felt sorry she hadn't had the tea, for wasn't he only trying to be friendly? But to tell the truth, she felt uncomfortable with some of Edith's lodgers. That other fellow, Otis Flaherty, the rock poet, she couldn't stand him. Fortunately he confined himself mostly to his room, but for some reason today he was downstairs. Sally gave the Hoover a vicious stab underneath his chair. She had asked him to move, but you'd have thought his arse was welded to the seat in front of the television. He was watching some loony daytime chat show: lots of shapeless, badly dressed people with big doughy faces. Miss Black was out, otherwise he'd have been up in his room smoking out the window and pretending he was writing a song for his band. Sally was on to him. She thought he was a leech. He had fooled Edith with his unctuous ways and all his chit-chat about poetry, but he hadn't fooled Sally O'Neill; she knew the type.

'Look, I'm watching this because I'm in the middle of like writing a song on the theme of daytime TV, so could you like clean someplace else?'

'Right then,' Sally said, 'I'll just leave Miss Black a note to say you were watching TV and didn't want to be disturbed – she'll want an explanation if I don't clean in here.'

She pushed her foot down on the button of the cleaner and watched the cord wind up with a snap. Then she lifted the Hoover and headed towards the door. Otis was up like a shot.

'Right, man, like take a chill pill, I'll go upstairs.'

Sally felt triumphant. Really, she had never met anyone so annoying in her life. Why didn't he get a place of his own?

Miss Black's lodgers stayed for differing periods of time. Some of them were performing for one week only. Others arrived for rehearsals and the performances, staying for as long as six weeks. Fintan would be here for ten, as his show was on for a month. Otis – a fake name if Sally had ever heard one – was supposedly writing a rock opera, so God knows how long that would take him.

Sally had begun to think that Edith should stop taking the lodgers; she believed it was all too much for her. She was worried about Edith's health.

Ellen, Edith's sister, had been ill for almost a year and was now in a hospice. Since Ellen lived in Portadown, this meant

Edith was driving back and forth three or more times a week. It was a long drive as well, almost an hour each way, longer given the speed Edith went at. It couldn't be good for her. She was losing weight and looked a bit peaky. Perhaps it was time Sally mentioned her concerns to Clare or Saffron. But she wasn't sure if it was her place to do that.

At times Sally felt like a therapist. You'd need a degree in psychology to cope with the lot of them, but Sally made do with common sense and lots of patience, and it got her by very nicely.

5

Sally was at the McDonalds' the following Monday when Clare spotted Fintan doing the t'ai chi thing in Edith's garden. She was out like a shot, and five minutes later was back with Fintan in tow. He was wearing his karate suit and looked slightly uncomfortable. However, Clare noticed none of this; after all, didn't she spend a lot of her time in the blue dressing gown?

'Put the kettle on, Sally, would you. I'll make some coffee.'

And away she went, grinding beans and chatting endlessly at the same time. The coffee would have her up to high doh in no time. She should stick to the camomile; she was hyper enough on that.

'Oh, I forgot, excuse me. Fintan, this is Sally; Sally, meet Fintan Fanning.'

'Oh, Sally and I have already met,' Fintan said with a smile. Clare looked surprised, then collected herself.

'Of course you have, at Edith's, silly of me. We're all desperately dependent on Sally over here. She keeps us in order, don't you, Sally?'

Clare gave her flirtatious laugh, which meant she wanted Fintan to fancy her. She did this without thinking; Sally had watched it often enough. Of course once he showed the slightest interest she would start talking about Tony, or the children, or her thesis. Then whoever the man was would start feeling uncomfortable until he got over his initial misapprehension and appreciated her amazing mind and her domestic goddess qualities simultaneously.

But Fintan was talking to Sally, his lovely blue eyes attentive. He really was a very handsome man. Sally reckoned him to be in his early forties.

'How many houses do you work in?'

'Just the three: here, Miss Black's and the McNamaras' at number twenty-one.'

'And all very different inside?'

'Yes, that's right.'

He looked around appreciatively.

'They are really lovely big houses. You'd pay a fortune for one like this in London. Edith tells me they are listed buildings.'

'Yes,' Clare chipped in, 'we all love it here, and it's such a great place for children to grow up, what with the back lane to play in.'

'Yes,' said Fintan wryly, 'there do seem to be quite a number of children.'

'Oh, Edith thinks they are all monsters, doesn't she, Sally?'

'I wouldn't say that. She just thinks they are allowed to get away with far too much. And she could be right.'

Clare nodded vigorously.

'She has a point. We are all too soft on them.'

She poured the coffee; you couldn't see through it.

'Sally?'

'No thanks, I'm all right. I'll do your study now while you're down here.'

Sally left them chatting. She was beginning to find Fintan a bit disconcerting. She couldn't remember the last time she had felt so attracted to a man. He was so open and friendly, but maybe all famous people had that ease with them. That was why people liked them so much. Just because he looked at her when he spoke didn't mean he fancied her. Once upstairs, she took a deep breath. Clare's study was always a challenge, and it was good to get her out of the way when she tackled it. That way she could chuck more out. What was the point of Clare having a computer if she filled her study with papers? It was a good job no one smoked in this house; one spark and it'd all be up in flames.

Sally worked steadily and had the study in a semblance of order when she heard the sound of raised voices. She rushed downstairs. Evie was standing in the middle of the kitchen holding a glass of water. She was pale, bleary-eyed and wearing only a long crumpled T-shirt. She'd obviously just got out of bed.

'Evie, answer me! Why aren't you at school?'

Clare was shouting accusingly at Evie. Fintan was sitting looking distinctly uncomfortable. Sally felt sorry for him. He was trapped.

'I feel sick. Doh! I texted you earlier, Mum. I was up all night throwing up,' Evie shrieked back even louder.

'You texted me? From your bedroom? Honestly, Evie, you redefine the word lazy!'

'You see? I knew you would throw a psych if I told you in person, and I was right.'

'I am not throwing a psych; you're not sick! You've a hang-over, and little wonder, going out on a Sunday with that layabout and getting up to God knows what.'

'Mikey is not a layabout. You're a snob, and *you* can talk about drinking – just look at the yard, it's full of empty bottles. You'd think this was a home for alcoholics.'

'Evie, we were entertaining last night, and I certainly don't need to explain to you why there are bottles in the yard.'

'Anyway we only have history this morning and it's of no use to anyone.'

'History – no use?'

'Yes, taught by that saddo who thinks she knows everything.'

'She certainly knows more than you ever will at this rate.'

'You should never have had children; you have no maternal instincts.'

The voices rose even higher.

'Will you two stop for a second, please?' Sally broke in. 'How am I to get my work done with all this screaming? Evie, why don't you go and get ready for school? I'm sure your mammy will write you a wee note to say you weren't very well this morning. Would you be in time for your next class if you left now?'

Evie's school was just a ten-minute walk from Marlborough Road.

'Yes, I suppose so.' Evie looked sheepishly at Sally, then turned to go back upstairs.

'And Clare, you have a cup of camomile tea and calm yourself. You and Evie can have a chat later.'

'Yes, you're right. Sorry,' Clare added, noticing Fintan.

'Oh, don't mind me, I have work to do. I'd better go.' Fintan got up to leave, glad of a chance to escape.

'I'm sorry. That was very rude of me, but Evie is driving me crazy at the moment.' Clare fixed her face in a rueful smile, expecting forgiveness. 'Poor Sally, I'm sure we drive her nuts with all this bickering. I know I should try to stay calmer with Evie, but she is so provoking.'

Fintan still looked a bit shell-shocked.

'Aren't you lucky you have Sally to sort things out for you?' He moved quickly to the door. 'Maybe I'll see you tomorrow, Sally – you're at Edith's then?'

'Yes, in the morning.'

Sally felt embarrassed that he had asked her in front of Clare;

she hoped Clare wouldn't think she had been making up to him. But Clare said goodbye to him as if nothing had happened. Sally would have been mortified in her position.

'Oh, Sally, she's dreadful, isn't she?' Clare shook her head sorrowfully.

'Sure they're all the same at that age. She'll grow out of it, they all do.'

'I hope you're right. Well, Fintan's not the only one with work to do.' Clare sounded a bit uncomfortable, as if she had suddenly realised that all the screaming in front of Fintan had been a bit too much. She made her way up to her newly cleaned study.

Clare and Evie did have a difficult relationship. Clare flew off the handle too quickly with her. But then she had little or no support from Tony. In Sally's opinion Clare's husband spent far too much time at work. Even now, ten years on, she still wasn't quite sure what Tony did, except rush off to work with a bulging briefcase looking stressed. He was something high up in the Civil Service, and knew a lot of important types who kept coming to dinner. He was very friendly to Sally, though, and always looked pleased to see her. Sally suspected she eased his conscience a bit. He probably felt guilty that he left all the domestic matters to Clare, so he willingly paid for Sally.

Sally's own daughter, Bronagh, two years older than Evie, had gone through this rebellious stage too, but then Sally was used to being a single parent and had learned to handle her alone. She didn't go in for shrieking. She'd found out the hard way that it didn't work. All the yelling and screaming at Charlie had just ended in heartbreak.

6

Sally's appointment with Maybeth was at ten a.m. She was prompt; it wasn't in Sally's nature to be late for anything. Maybeth ushered her into her office. No secretary, Sally noticed as she sat down. The office looked as if it had been quickly cobbled together. Sally had developed an eye for quality in her years of working for the Marlborough Road gang. In her own home she had learned to go for plainer looks: no patterns, and nice toning colours. This office was a clash of peach and turquoise, with really tacky curtains. The carpet was synthetic; she felt the static as she walked across it. Maybeth obviously had no taste – that is, if she had been the one responsible for it. Maybeth came straight to the point.

'Can I ask your present salary?'

Sally had it worked out precisely. She was unsure whether to tell Maybeth the exact figure. She wasn't paying tax on it. However, she took the chance, stressing the fact that it was tax free.

'And your hours?'

Sally told her.

'Well,' Maybeth said, 'that seems an extremely generous

amount.' She made a note on a pad. 'That is more like US wages, but I'm sure we can match it. Bertha – who as you know is a dynamo – seems to think that you will be worth every penny.'

Bertha a dynamo? From what Sally understood, dynamos were lively, sparky people who moved fast, not fat dour grumps like Bertha McClure. The only muscle Bertha moved with any regularity was her tongue. Sally wondered briefly if Bertha had told Maybeth she was a dynamo, or whether Maybeth had decided that herself. If the latter, then there was more wrong with Maybeth than her taste in decor.

Sally sat and rearranged her face in a smile and listened to Maybeth chitter on about the number of hygiene technicians she would be hiring and the impressive advertising campaign she had planned. She told Sally that they would be getting a photographer in to photograph Bertha and Sally dressed in their gear for billboards all over the town.

'Gear? What gear?'

'Well, you'll just love these.'

Maybeth opened a cupboard, and with a flourish pulled out a peach-coloured polyester jumpsuit with the logo 'Maids to Order' embroidered on the left-hand pocket. It was vile; Clare would have had a taste blackout on the spot.

'Surely if I'm not cleaning I won't have to wear those?'

'Well, we would like all our hygiene technicians to be instantly recognisable, so yes.'

'But Bertha told me I would be driving round just super-vising all the other cleaners; I could hardly wear that on my bike.'

'I know, but there would be times when, say, another hygiene technician did not make an appearance, and then I guess we would hope – in the spirit of company congeniality – that you would fill in for him or her. So we would issue you with two pairs of regulation cleansing apparel.'

41

'Him or her?'

'Why yes, we are hoping to recruit both sexes.'

Sally snorted with derision; she couldn't help herself. Most of the men she had had anything to do with were totally useless in the home, and that included the ones she worked for. When she was married to Charlie, he seemed to think that every little bit of domestic nonsense was her job. He even used to boast to his mates that he never lifted a hand in the house – it was women's work. And as for Tony, Trevor and the likes, well they just paid up and shut up. Now and then Sally would watch Trevor as he walked aimlessly round the kitchen trying to work out which handle to pull down to find the dishwasher. When Posy was born he was next to useless, at one stage flooding the living room as he blundered into the birthing pool while Saffron was mid-contraction. Tony allegedly could cook, but then he was never there, and in Sally's opinion, hurling steaks or chops on to a barbecue was hardly cooking. If Maybeth was looking for male cleaners, she'd have a long look.

'Would you not have to change the name if yis had men?'

'Why Sally, we haven't considered that just yet. But that indeed is a point. Now, when would you be available for the photo shoot?'

'I'm not sure I want to take part in that. I'll need time to think it over, and of course I'd have to wait until the residents could get replacements.'

Maybeth's mouth tightened, but she smiled; well, it was a sort of smile.

'Why Sally, I do declare you are playing hard to get! Listen, why don't you let me know by next Monday? We would like you to start by the beginning of next month.'

Sally was already feeling sure she wasn't going to take the job, but somehow the words wouldn't come out to say no. Instead she thanked Maybeth and left. On her way out she turned and asked, 'Oh, who decorated the office?'

'Why, I did it all by myself. Don't you just love those colours?'

Sally nodded. That wasn't a lie: the colours were fine, only not there and not in that order.

Normally Sally was up and showered and on her way out the door by eight o'clock. Today was a rare day off, so she took her time over breakfast, even allowing herself the luxury of a boiled egg. She was at the kitchen table, finishing a piece of toast and reading a magazine, when her sister Eileen's face appeared at the window.

Sally's heart sank. She got up to open the door. Eileen only called round when she was after something.

'Hi, what's up? What do you want?'

'What's eating you? I don't want anything. Did you get out of the wrong side of the bed this morning?'

'No, but how did you know I was here? I don't normally have Fridays off.'

'I phoned the McDonalds and they told me.'

'Eileen, you have no right . . .'

'Well you should turn your mobile on then.' She paused dramatically. 'I just thought you should know – Charlie O'Neill got out yesterday.'

For a minute Sally thought she was going to faint.

'How do you know?'

'He was in Milligan's last night. He's put on a ton, and he's lost most of his hair. His waves have waved him goodbye.' Eileen related these facts with relish, as if in some way they would be compensation for the fact that Charlie was out of prison.

'Oh God, what am I going to do?'

The almost forgotten rush of dread hit her. What would happen now, with Charlie out of jail? What if Clare – or even worse, Edith – found out? Although Sally had implied to Edith that she was separated, and had been the one to instigate it,

43

she had left out the detail that Charlie was in jail. She had been afraid that in some way this revelation would contaminate her; make Edith think less of her for being foolish enough to marry Charlie in the first place. Edith frequently complimented Sally on her good judgement and common sense. If she knew about Charlie she would revise her opinion, and Sally couldn't bear the thought of that.

'Well? What *are* you going to do?' Eileen looked at her, patently excited by the whole thing. Eileen's life was dull. She was the youngest of the McManus clan, still in her early thirties, and was married to a loser whom she avoided by spending lots of nights out on the town with her mates. They had no kids. Sally thought she should get a life and leave him. But Eileen wouldn't have thanked her for her opinion so she said nothing. She couldn't be bothered getting in the middle of it all.

Sally's overwhelming feeling now was panic. During the last ten years she had successfully banished Charlie from her life and thoughts. All that the Marlborough Road lot knew were the simple facts. She was separated; he was away. They didn't ask where and she never told. The very idea of him being free was sickening. She would have to let Bronagh know. She couldn't take the risk of him showing up at the house. Bronagh was going out with her mates tonight directly from work; she'd phone her at lunchtime.

After a while, having delivered her bombshell and not getting the response she'd hoped for from Sally, Eileen left. Sally's plan of taking a wee run into the town didn't seem enticing any more. She tried to busy herself round the house, but ended up sitting watching daytime TV – something she never did. She was half-heartedly looking at *Richard and Judy*, and feeling sorry for herself, when her phone rang. She thought she might as well take the call. Her day was ruined now anyway. It was Bertha McClure, sounding delighted with herself. She was outside Sally's house. Eileen had told her Sally was off today.

Sally opened the door to Bertha with bad grace. Bertha barged in and plonked her big fat arse on the sofa, barely able to contain her delight.

'Oh Sally, wait till you hear. Maybeth just loved you. She thinks you – hang on a wee sec, I wrote it down.' Pulling a piece of paper from her pocket, she read out:

'"Radiate efficiency". She'll be writing you a letter offering you the job. Isn't that brilliant?'

'Look, Bertha, I am not sure about the job. You told me that going along to see her didn't commit me to anything. I mean, I haven't made up my mind if I even want to leave Marlborough Road. And even if I was going to, I'd have to give in my notice.'

'Notice, whaddya mean, notice? How much notice?'

'I'm not sure, maybe a month. I couldn't just leave them all in the lurch.'

'A month? I don't think so! She wants you to start as soon as you can.'

Then Bertha's eyes narrowed, she looked like a snake, or even worse, like Iggy McNamara. Sally felt like punching her in the mouth. She said nothing. A sleekit grin spread over Bertha's big ugly face.

'Here, Sally, is it true that Charlie is out?'

'Who told you? I don't know anything about him.'

'I heard he was in Milligan's last night. I thought you'd better know. I wouldn't think all them snobs in Marlborough Road would like it if they knew you were married to a jailbird.'

'I'm not married to him any more. We are officially separated, and anyway they wouldn't be interested.'

'Sure if you left now and took Maybeth's offer, they would never have to know about him at all.'

Sally had a sickening feeling in the pit of her stomach. Maybe Bertha was right. If she handed in her notice before anyone

45

in Marlborough Road learned about Charlie, she could leave with her head high.

Bronagh arrived home directly from work to see how her mother was. She had appeared to take the news calmly when Sally had called earlier to tell her about her father being out of jail, but then she had been in work.

'I just wanted to check on you before I went out. Have you seen him?'

'No, but our Eileen has, she came round this morning to tell me.'

'Leave it to Eileen, can't wait to spread the bad news.'

'I'll understand if you want to see him; after all, he's still your father.'

'I'm not ready to see him. I hate what he's done to us, to you.'

'You never said . . .'

'Sure why would I? You had enough to cope with and I didn't want to make it worse for you.'

Sally could hardly swallow. The lump crept up her throat. She nodded her emotion and Bronagh squeezed her hand.

'I spent years in school with people telling me my da was a jailbird. If he'd been in the RA or something it would've been cool, but he was just a rotten oul' criminal. It was shite. I hate him.'

But Sally knew that she didn't mean that; perhaps she was saying it out of loyalty to Sally, or more likely because the news confused her. Nonetheless, she was grateful for Bronagh's apparent desire not to get in touch with Charlie right now.

7

Sally was on eggs all weekend. Every time the door creaked or the phone rang she got tense. She hardly slept a wink, and eating was out of the question – she couldn't chew, her mouth didn't seem to function – but thankfully there was no sign of Charlie. She refused Eileen's offer to go out with the girls to Milligan's on Saturday night. It was a ridiculous idea, being the last place Charlie had been sighted. No, she thought, avoidance tactics were best. She put herself under house arrest for the rest of the weekend, afraid she would bump into him on the street or at the shops. Her ex-in-laws lived nearby, as did two of Charlie's sisters. By Monday she was so worn out that she wondered if it was worth calling Clare and saying she was unwell. They could hardly complain; she rarely missed work – maybe twice in ten years – struggling in with colds and sniffles rather than let them down. But prudently she realised that staying at home would achieve nothing, so she got on her bike, so to speak, and by nine o'clock was in Clare's kitchen wading through a stack of pots.

About eleven o'clock, she was just about to have her cup of tea when a tentative knock on the back door startled her. It was Fintan Fanning.

She felt odd seeing him after the weekend she had just had. She was sure she looked as wrecked as she felt.

'Clare's out,' she told him.

'Oh well, never mind that. I came to see you. I saw the bike.' He indicated the kettle. 'Am I just in time for tea?'

'What kind?'

'Real tea, of course.' And he sat down quite naturally at the table.

Sally wasn't sure what to say, but Fintan had no such qualms.

'Well, Sally, I hope you had a restful weekend.'

'Ach, I was just futtering about, didn't do much. Have you no rehearsals today?'

'No, just a costume fitting this afternoon.'

Sally told herself to get a grip and act normally, but she felt paralysed. The events of the weekend had stunned her, and she didn't have Fintan's ease of conversation in the first place. She had been glad this morning that Clare was rushing off to the library and a lecture. Just herself in the house, unless you counted Lola, who was in her basket in the corner of the kitchen, her worshipful eyes trained on Sally.

'You seem a bit distracted, Sally. Is everything all right?' His blue eyes were fixed on her, compelling her to confide in him.

'Well, I've been offered another job.' Best to tell some of the truth, she felt. 'It's a new cleaning service and I'd be a supervisor, you know, have more responsibility.'

Fintan laughed. 'Good Lord, Sally, you couldn't possibly have more responsibility than you have around here. Heaven knows how they'd manage without you.'

'I wouldn't just be a cleaner.' The words were out before she could help it.

Fintan looked at her thoughtfully.

'Is this what you really want? I mean, are you fed up with Marlborough Road?'

'It's hard to be sure. No, I don't think I'm fed up with

Marlborough Road so much as I'm fed up just being a cleaner. I mean, I always thought I'd be . . .'

Sally trailed off. What did she think she would be? Realistically, what else *could* she be? She had quit school just before she was due to sit her O levels, so she'd left without a single qualification. As the eldest of her family she was expected to contribute financially as soon as she could. The money was needed, with so many children to feed. It wasn't that she was stupid – she'd always been in the top half of the class – but absolutely no one from her street went on after leaving age. Plenty of the neighbours thought Sally's parents had given her notions of herself by allowing her to go to the grammar school in the first place. Sure didn't the uniform alone cost a fortune?

Fintan interrupted her musings.

'Yes? You thought you would be . . . ?'

'Well, not a cleaner. I mean, I worked as a manager of a shop when I first left school. I only took the cleaning job because it allowed me to work fewer hours for more money.'

'What has changed?'

'I suppose housework is so . . .'

'Repetitive?'

'Yes, and I sometimes feel like I'm a servant.'

'I understand, but they do respect you, Sally, and they love you. Anyone can see that. And they are very dependent on you.'

'Ach, don't worry about me, Fintan, I'll get over it. Maybe I'm getting ideas above myself.'

'Well, let's think,' said Fintan. 'There might be other options open to you, you know? How many hours a week do you work?'

'Three days here, that's nine hours, two mornings at Edith's and two afternoons at Saffron's. Although sometimes I do extra hours if they're stuck.'

'So you would have time to go to classes?'

49

'Classes?'

'Yes, Sally — classes. Get some qualifications and you'll be able to get a better job. You know everyone here would support you. I'm sure they would all love for you to further your education. Don't you think?'

'I don't know. I suppose Clare is always banging on about the benefits of education. And I didn't even take my O levels.'

'Why not think about doing some GCSEs? The basic ones first.' He smiled at her. 'A few at a time, see how you get on.'

'I've never thought of that. Maybe I could.'

After Fintan had left, Sally thought over what he had said. He was probably right, but it would take some effort on her part. It was years since she had done any studying, but doing some course or other might be a good idea. Maybe she would pick up a syllabus from the tech. As for the other job, well, she wouldn't say yes or no ... not just yet. She had almost told Fintan about Charlie, but something made her hold back. There was no reason for anyone over here to know. Unless, God forbid, Charlie O'Neill reared his ugly mug and they found out about him. There was no way she could stay on if that happened.

'Sally, do you think Trevor still loves me?' Saffron asked later that day.

'Ach, Saffron, of course he does. Why on earth would you think that?'

'He's just different these days. He doesn't come home for lunch any more and he seems to criticise everything I cook. And I'm sure he's been eating meat on the sly. I found a receipt for a lunch and it was for two people and two steaks.' Saffron looked on the verge of tears.

'Well that hardly means he's stopped loving you. He's never made much of a secret of the fact he finds it hard being a vegetarian. If he didn't love you, he'd never even have tried.'

Now that Sally thought about it, Trevor had been in odd form this last while back, but he was working extra hard, and Saffron didn't make things easy with her incessant pandering to the children. Sally had watched him fidget while Saffron spent an hour nursing Posy. It wouldn't have surprised her if Trevor felt a wee bit neglected now and again, but she didn't say this to Saffron.

'I'm so tired these days, Sally, I have no energy.'

'Saffron love, you worry far too much. Why don't you have a nice bath and light one of your aromatherapy candles? I'll take Posy down to the McDonalds'. I've got to do an extra hour there, and there's no one in today. She can watch a DVD.'

'I was going to read her French storybook to her.'

'Well sure isn't Pingu French? She can watch him instead.'

And before Saffron could protest, Sally took Posy's hand and led her out. She knew Saffron needed the break and would be a lot calmer when she brought Posy back.

Saffron was indeed in much chirpier form on Sally's return. She asked if Sally would take a suit of Trevor's to the dry cleaner's. Sally had hung it up earlier whilst tidying the bedroom. It had been lying crumpled on the floor. She nipped up and got it, promising Saffron she'd drop it in on her way home. She put the suit in her pannier and closed it, and was starting up her bike, thinking she couldn't wait to get home to put her feet up, when she was startled by a tap on the shoulder. It was Fintan.

'Are you going through the town, Sally?'

'Yes, I am.'

'I don't suppose I could have a lift?'

Sally was speechless. 'I haven't got an extra crash helmet,' she stammered eventually.

'Oh, I'll take my chances, I've always fancied a ride on one of these.' And he climbed up behind her and wrapped his arms around her waist as if it was nothing at all.

Sally dropped him outside the opera house. He gave her a cheery wave and shouted, 'See you tomorrow!' and she rode off feeling distinctly light-hearted. It was amazing what a bit of attention from a good-looking man could do. It was only when she arrived home that she remembered she had forgotten to stop at the dry cleaner's.

8

Sally finally remembered to call in at the dry cleaner's with Trevor's suit on her way to work. The assistant was a young girl who could hardly be bothered looking up at her. After searching the pockets aimlessly, she handed Sally a few pieces of paper.

'Here,' she said, 'are these any use?'

There were a couple of old receipts and a note with a message: *Can't wait to see you. I'll be outside if the weather's good.*

Now what was that about? Sally crumpled it with the receipts and threw them all in the litter bin outside. The note made her feel uneasy. The writing looked familiar; she'd seen it before, but it wasn't Saffron's. Then she had a thought. The call, the note, Trevor's odd ways – could he be involved with someone else? She told herself she was imagining things, put the thought out of her head, and set off for Marlborough Road.

Sally always made more headway in any of the houses she cleaned when she had the place to herself – no chat and no interference. She was a fast worker, and normally didn't even sit down for her cup of tea. Today she was taking advantage of Clare being at work to give the McDonalds' fridge a good clear-out. Finally a chance to bin all the stuff that was past its 'use by' date. Why on earth anybody needed five different jars of mint sauce was beyond her – especially when they made such a big deal of making the real thing from a garden overrun with fresh mint.

She was manoeuvring the glass shelf back in, trying not to break it and not quite getting it straight, when a voice said, 'Here, let me do that for you.'

She was so startled she almost dropped it. It was Tony, home from work in the middle of the afternoon. Now that was a rare sight indeed.

'Tony? What's up? Did you lose your job?'

Tony laughed good-naturedly. 'I know, Sally, I'm a terrible case. I had a meeting this end of town and decided to drop in. Is Clare here? '

'No, I'd say she'll be back shortly. Would you like some tea?'

'No, don't let me interrupt. I'll get it myself – would you like one?'

Sally refused, and just as Tony was sitting down to drink his, Clare arrived through the back door.

'What's happened, Tony? Did the office burn down?'

'There's no need to be sarcastic, Clare. I had a meeting end earlier than I thought, so I came home.'

'Really? Well I hope you manage to finish that tea before you remember something of vital importance and rush off.'

'I've a favour to ask, love.'

'Oh, I knew you wouldn't be here for the good of your health.'

Sally felt uneasy stuck in the middle of this sniping, but all the various jars of mayonnaise and God knows how many out-of-date cranberry sauces were on the counter, so she felt she couldn't just walk out and leave the mess. On the other hand, she didn't feel she should hear whatever it was Tony had to say. She excused herself and made to leave the kitchen, but the pleading look on Tony's face told her he needed a witness.

'No, Sally, don't go, really it's nothing important. Clare love, I've invited Harvey McLeod to dinner.'

Harvey McLeod was Tony's boss, a junior minister in the Northern Ireland Office.

'Ah Tony, you're not serious! You've invited the minister to dinner? Here? In this house?'

'Yes, we've had people from the office before.'

'Yes, but not the minister.'

'He's a really decent fellow. He was saying he was fed up with eating out in restaurants night after night, so I thought it might be a nice gesture.'

'When have you asked him for?'

Tony looked uncomfortable. 'He said he was free on Thursday night.'

'Thursday? But that's tomorrow.'

'I know. I'm sorry, love, I wasn't expecting him to be free so quickly. I thought maybe we could just throw some steaks on the barbecue.'

'Hardly – I thought you told me he loved his food?'

'I'm sure he'll appreciate whatever you cook.'

'Thursday night . . . no one goes out on a Thursday. Who will I ask, or is it just *en famille*?'

'What about Shane from the office?'

'God, no! I'll ask a few of the neighbours. Now I'll have to spend tomorrow trawling through the cookbooks. But don't worry. I have nothing else to do all day.'

'Listen, love, don't put yourself out, anything would be great . . . I mean, anything you cook usually is. I'll sort the wine out. I know he likes Fleurie. And I'll try to get home early.'

'Brilliant, I can't wait.'

'Erm . . . He'll have two minders with him.'

'Ah Jaysus, do I have to feed them as well?'

'I'm not sure. Maybe they just wait in the car.'

'Well *do* they wait in the car? Or do I feed them?'

'I'd better call and check.'

'Oh honestly, Tony!' wailed Clare. 'Talk about being dumped on.' She turned to Sally, who knew instantly what was coming.

'Sally, is there any chance you could come tomorrow instead of Friday? I'll need you here if I'm going to be cooking all day.'

Sally felt a brief stab of resentment. It was typical of Clare to do this, ask her with Tony looking at her beseechingly as well. No doubt she'd overpay her, but Sally had been looking forward to seeing Fintan tomorrow and she needed a bit of peace – far more likely at Edith's than in the chaos of number 25.

'I suppose if you can sort it out with Edith – if she doesn't mind me coming to her on Friday.'

Clare beamed delightedly. 'Oh thank you, Sally. I'm sure she won't mind and we can always ask her along to dinner.'

'Do we have to?' Tony said. 'I mean, she could bore for Britain.'

'Given his position, I'm sure Harvey McLeod is well poised to cope with the occasional bore. He must meet loads of them at work. Had you given me advance warning, I could have trotted out some interesting people. But it's a Thursday night and I have had one day's notice. So unless you want to send for a carry-out, shut up. Plus Edith will be doing us a favour letting us have Sally.'

Sally thought there was something ridiculous about that idea, Edith allowing Clare to have her. It was almost like she was a vacuum cleaner or something. But she knew Clare didn't mean it like that.

'I think Edith might appreciate a night out, Tony,' Sally said gently.

'Her sister is very ill and she doesn't look great herself with all the running up and down to Portadown. I've been worried about her.'

'You're right, Sally – that was a bit unkind of me. It's just that she can be an awful snob and she can rattle on a bit. Doesn't she know someone Harvey's related to?'

'I think she used to work for his uncle.'

'Is there any chance of your staying on a bit longer to help with the wines, Sally?' Tony and Clare both looked at her hopefully. 'Help with the wines' was code for clearing up all the dishes.

'Well I suppose I could manage it this once. Bronagh has a late night at the salon on Thursdays.' After all, she figured, she only had to do these extra nights about twice a year, and she usually enjoyed them. She didn't mention that she was glad of an excuse to get out of the house in case Charlie O'Neill came calling.

Clare and Tony both looked relieved.

'Oh, Sally, you're an angel. I may start looking through the cookery books for a pudding.' Clare was fuming inwardly at the whole deal, but she didn't want to start on Tony now in front of Sally.

'What about that lemony chicken thing you make? That's very nice.'

'You're right, Sally. Maybe I will make the Moroccan chicken; let me see if I have all the ingredients.'

'I can take you to the supermarket, sweetheart.' Tony was anxious to please now that Clare had calmed down.

'Well let me check what I have first.'

'In that case I'll just nip upstairs first. I've a few calls to make. Give me a shout if you need me.'

As Tony left the kitchen, Clare started to rummage through various cupboards. Sally hoped she hadn't just binned a vital ingredient. She was finishing off the fridge when Fintan strolled past the back window.

'Oh, there's Fintan Fanning,' Clare said. 'I must ask him if he'd like to come tomorrow night.'

She went running out the back door and called down the lane. Fintan came walking in after her, looking slightly trapped.

'Now you will have a cup of tea?' She indicated all the cookery books on the kitchen table. 'I'll just move these. Fintan, this is awfully short notice, but would you like to join us for dinner tomorrow night? About half seven? Tony has rather landed me in the middle of things by inviting his boss, and I need some interesting guests.' She beamed at him. 'I'm asking Edith as well,' she added hastily.

'That's very kind of you, Clare. I'd like that. I do have a rehearsal tomorrow, but I would be finished by then.'

As he made to leave, Anna came rushing in from school with Simon in tow.

'Mum, can I go to Simon's, please? He's going to help me with my maths.'

'Anna, where are your manners? Fintan, this is Anna, our youngest, and Simon McNamara, her friend. Fintan is an opera singer, you two, isn't that wonderful? He is staying with Miss Black.'

'Oh?' Simon's earnest little face perked up. 'Mum is taking me to *Tosca* at the opera house. We are reading the libretto.'

'Really?' Fintan seemed impressed. 'I am playing Cavaradossi.'

'Does that mean you are a tenor?'

'It does indeed.'

'I'd like to be Scarpia, he's an evil villain.'

'Would you now?'

Fintan and Clare exchanged amused looks. Wasn't it well for them, Sally thought, knowing all about opera? She had been to an opera, years ago, while she was still at school. Sister Maura, the nun who taught music, had asked if there were any girls keen to go on a trip to the opera house to see *La Bohème*. They had listened to it in class and Sally thought it the saddest

58

story ever and the singing just wonderful. She brought in all her pocket money to buy a ticket. There were only twenty places.

She had left something behind in the music room, and as she rushed back to get it she overheard two of the nuns talking. She caught her name and her breath and waited outside the room. Apparently twenty-one people had brought in the money and they were deciding who shouldn't go.

'What about Sally McManus, Sister Maura? You could leave her off the list. Why on earth would she want to go? No background whatsoever.'

Sally's heart was in her mouth, but Sister Maura had stood her ground.

'Well I have to disagree with you there, Sister Agnes,' she said. 'Sally has followed the libretto avidly and produced the most wonderful work on the opera. If she hadn't managed the ticket money I would have used the school funds and taken her myself. Now Suzanne Savage pays no attention in class and wouldn't be at the school if her father didn't give so generously to the building fund. I'll suggest to her that she go with her parents. Lord knows, a bit of culture might do them good.'

Sally couldn't do enough for Sister Maura after that, but the phrase *no background* had stuck with her ever since. She knew what it meant – poor, not the right accent, second class.

On the way out the door, having refused a cup of tea, Fintan turned to Sally.

'Oh Sally, in case I don't see you tomorrow, I was going to mention that I get some complimentary tickets for the run. I thought perhaps you would like a pair.'

'Oh, I'd love to go to the opera. We've been meaning to book,' Clare said eagerly. Fintan looked a bit taken aback. Really, thought Sally, the nerve of her. She could obviously afford the price of a couple of tickets.

'Well if they offer us any more, I'll certainly get you some.'

59

He turned back to Sally. 'I thought you might want to wait till near the end of the run. Till we find our feet, as it were.'

Clare was looking at Sally intently, probably hoping she'd say no. Sally quickly made up her mind, rather pleased that Fintan had chosen her over Clare – it was like the time with Sister Maura all over again!

'That's very nice of you, Fintan, I'd love to go.'

'Good, we can sort out which night later on.'

And off he went. Really, Sally thought, as she put the last of the jars back in the now gleaming fridge, the effect that man was having on her, she must be losing the run of herself entirely. He was hardly George Clooney. Clare, looking slightly miffed, went off to talk to Tony. Anna came into the room. She had changed out of her uniform to go to Simon's.

'Oh Sally, guess what? When I was coming home from school I saw Evie in the park. AND a boy was lying completely on top of her.'

'If he was completely on top of her, how do you know it was Evie?'

'Oh Sally, you know what I mean. They were snogging, like in the movies. You know, all soppy like. It's so embarrassing. Everybody knows she's my sister. And he has purple hair! I saw them.'

Clare came rushing into the kitchen.

'What did you say, Anna? You saw Evie with a boy on top of her? In broad daylight? What were they doing?'

'Nothing, Mum, I was just joking.' Anna had thought Clare was safely out of the way.

'Oh my God! Sally – call Tony. He needs to go and get her out of the park.'

Sally felt another situation coming on. She headed for the kettle.

'Clare, calm down, she's sixteen. I'm sure they were just having a cuddle.'

At that moment, Evie, who, despite being engaged in her romantic gymnastics, had seen Anna peering at her, stormed through the back door and grabbed her sister by the arm.

'Well, you grotty wee spy. Have you told everyone, then?'

'Mum, she's hurting me.' Anna began to wail loudly.

'Honestly, Evie, could you not curtail your behaviour in public – and in your school uniform too.'

'You know, Mum, it's really perfectly normal behaviour for teenagers. At least it wasn't a girl. So you can be glad I'm not a lesbian. Especially since Anna is probably one.'

'And he has purple hair.'

Evie pushed Anna aside contemptuously.

'The colour is aubergine, you little saddo.'

'Does the school allow him to have hair that colour?'

Clare was pitching for a fight; Sally could hear it in her voice.

'He doesn't go to school. He's left.'

'Oh my God, how old is he?'

Anna, bored with it all now, left with Simon in her wake, and Sally began to fold the laundry. It was relentless, this endless sparring between Clare and Evie.

'He's nineteen – maybe twenty. I don't know and I don't care, and before you start getting all snobbish about him, he's in a band and he works at a bar in town and there's nothing wrong with people who don't go to university. Isn't that right, Sally?'

'Leave me out of this one, Evie. I'm just putting the laundry away before I go'.

But the noise had brought Tony downstairs, and as Sally excused herself and left, she could hear him trying to calm Clare down, with Evie now in floods of tears.

'Clare, for heaven's sake! Why do you always have to make an adversary of her?' Tony sounded exasperated.

'I do not – you don't know the half of it. You are never

61

here. You're only home now because you needed a favour! She's not studying at all for these exams. She has a forged ID, she's drinking, and I don't know who this boy is – or where he's from.'

'He's lovely, just because he's not a snob like you. Dad would like him.'

Sally left quietly. This row would go on for a while. She was glad to get on her bike and home. Sometimes Marlborough Road would wear you out.

When Sally arrived home, Bronagh was in the kitchen and had put the dinner on. She had just poured one of those jars of sauce over some chicken and cooked some rice. Nonetheless, Sally was delighted.

'Well this is fantastic, love, just what I needed.'

She went upstairs to get changed. The dinner was on the table when she came back down.

'Evie McDonald is coming in to the salon next Wednesday to get her hair cut.'

'Is she? That's great. I told you she was delighted with the free voucher.' Sally had done as Bronagh asked and distributed the vouchers round the three houses. Everyone had been pleased. It didn't seem to matter how much money people had; they all liked getting something for nothing.

Sally tucked into her meal. Things tasted great when someone else had gone to the bother of cooking.

'Clare's asked me to help out tomorrow night. She's having some fancy dinner party. Would you do my hair for me?'

'Aye, no problem. Who are they having this time?'

For all her sour opinions on them, Bronagh loved the tales of the famous people who visited the houses in Marlborough Road, even if they were just minor celebs.

'Harvey McLeod, the politician, some of the ones in the lane, and Fintan Fanning the opera singer.'

'Oh, nobody cool then?'

'No, unless you count Fintan.'

'But you said he was an opera singer.'

'Well he is, but he's lovely. Very polite and thoughtful.' Sally hoped she wasn't blushing. 'I'm just doing it for the extra money, and you'll be out.'

'Why not? You spend too much time in this house alone.'

They ate quietly for a few minutes, and then Bronagh put her fork down.

'I saw my daddy in the town today. He was waiting for me outside the salon at lunchtime. He said he'd like to see you.'

Sally felt her knees turn to jelly. She suddenly had no appetite for her meal.

'You would still know it was him, but he's awful quiet-spoken, and he looked really sad.'

'I don't want to see him. I wouldn't care if I never set eyes on him again.'

'I know that, Mammy; he said Eileen told him that. But if you change your mind, she has his mobile number. He's staying with Carmel.' Carmel was Charlie's sister. 'He said he might be getting a job in London.'

'I hope to hell he does!'

Sally got up to clear away. She was shaking. On the one hand she could understand Bronagh being curious about her father, and she hated herself for sounding so bitter. But even after all these years, Charlie's betrayal still hurt. She just wasn't ready to let him back into her life in any shape or form. He had done enough damage in the past. All the same, that was no reason to keep Bronagh from seeing him. Sally had always felt guilty about depriving her of a father.

Bronagh had moved into the living room to watch TV. Sally followed her and sat down beside her.

'Bronagh love,' she said gently, 'I told you before, I don't mind if *you* see him. He's your father.'

'I know that, Mammy, and I'm going to think about it, but I haven't made any arrangements.'

And they left it at that.

9

Total chaos reigned when she arrived at the McDonalds' the following day. Clare was wailing round the house like a banshee. Evie was sitting listening to her iPod whilst painting her toenails a sort of metallic green and sticking wee diamonds on each finished one. There was glue on the table, and about ten saucepans, some full, some empty and dirty, strewn around the kitchen. Hamlet the hamster's cage was on the draining board. He had forsaken his afternoon nap for a whirl on the wheel. Radio 4 was on full blast. Classical music was wafting from the front room, the TV was on somewhere, and from upstairs the strains of that rap music Evie liked drifted down. Anna and Simon were on the kitchen floor with Ophelia the other hamster and about six little pink bald creatures on a towel. Sally took a deep breath. Clare saw her and smiled with utter relief.

'Oh Sally, thank God you're here. It's crazy today.'

'So what's new?'

'Sally, Sally, come and see! Ophelia has had six wee babies!' Anna was ecstatic.

'Would you like to hold one?' Simon asked, cupping one of the little things in his hand.

'Ugh, no, I certainly would not. Now put them all back in the cage or they'll die. You're not supposed to handle them.' The children obediently did as Sally told them. 'Now take them up to Anna's room and keep them there. They probably need a nap, and I have a kitchen to clean.'

Sally surveyed the scene. Clare was in Nigel Slater mode, or should that be Nigella Lawson? Nigel and Nigella, honestly you couldn't make it up, Sally thought. One thing was for sure, those TV chefs must have an army to clean up the mess they made. Unfortunately for Sally, she was Clare's army.

'I'm doing the Moroccan chicken as you suggested, Sally. It's always popular and I have all the ingredients.'

Sally filled the sink and started on the pots. It was going to be a trying afternoon, and to think she had agreed to stay on and help this evening. While Clare thanked her lucky stars, Sally wondered if she had any.

Usually the residents of the lane kept their social lives and their neighbourly life fairly well separated. But in emergencies they tended to call on each other. So Bill and Laura Nelson from number 31 had been asked, Patricia Thompson from the last house on the terrace, with her partner Dave, and of course Edith and Fintan. Despite several heavy hints, Clare had resolutely refused to ask Edith's other lodger, the ghastly Otis. She didn't like what she knew of him. All he seemed to do was spend a lot of time smoking out in the back lane – and by the smell of it, not always tobacco.

When Harvey McLeod had been appointed as junior minister for Northern Ireland, the local press made quite a thing about his Northern Irish connections. This had especially delighted Edith, since one of the directors of the firm she had worked for was an uncle of Harvey's. She appreciated the fact that she was finally getting to meet him. She had phoned Sally last night and told her not to worry about coming on Friday, because she would be away from Saturday till Tuesday.

'Somewhere relaxing, I hope?'

'Oh, just to my sister. I'll see you next week as usual.'

Trevor and Saffron were going to drop in for a drink later, after everyone had eaten. Clare couldn't cope with a veggie meal as well. By six o'clock things were almost under control. Laura Nelson brought round a large raspberry pavlova, assuring Clare and Sally that they were 'all the thing' again. How desserts could be in and out of fashion was a puzzle to Sally, but it looked amazing. She put it well out of the way; she didn't want Evie or Anna to poke at it or pick the raspberries off. Clare would have a fit.

Tony and Clare were using the dining room tonight. Sally looked at the table appreciatively; it was beautifully set, with flowers, candlesticks and all the best wine glasses. Clare had a real flair for that sort of thing. Evie and Anna were eating first in the kitchen, though their parents encouraged them to mingle with the guests and chat to them. Sally supposed that that was how they built up their confidence. She couldn't have imagined Bronagh being able to chat to a government minister at ten years old; even now, at eighteen, she would have found it difficult. No doubt about it, it was a different world entirely. Sally had spent a lot of time at evenings like this just observing. She found that provided she kept in the background and just got on with her job, no one really took any notice of her, which suited her just fine. Perhaps she had a slight inferiority complex. She found it hard to chat to people she had just met.

Her sister Eileen had no such qualms. In the past she had come with Sally to help out on a night like this. She had been a great success because of her chat and the way she flirted with the men and teased the women. But Sally had always felt a bit ashamed of her. She couldn't really pinpoint why, exactly. Maybe it was Eileen's 'working class and proud of it' demeanour. Her sister didn't feel the ones over here had anything more going for them than luck, and accident of birth. She was right, of course, and Sally wished she could feel like that, but she couldn't; perhaps her ten years working for them had made her more keenly aware of the disparity in their lives.

Eileen hadn't been remotely intimidated by any of them; she was very free with the chat and too free as well in helping herself to the drink. Later that same evening, when she was supposed to be clearing up, Sally had found her deep in conversation with Saffron. Alarm bells rang when she caught the word 'Charlie' and saw Saffron's eager little eyes fixed on Eileen, waiting for some crumbs of gossip. Sally grabbed Eileen firmly by the shoulder and marched her into the kitchen. Fortunately it was empty.

'Don't you be gossiping about me to any of them!' she said furiously. 'I don't want them knowing my business.'

'I wasn't gossiping,' Eileen said feebly, but Sally could see she was lying.

'What have you told her?'

'Nothing,' Eileen said sullenly. 'Sure you pulled me away before I could get a word out.'

'I heard you mention Charlie.'

'She mentioned him; she asked how long you had been separated from him.'

'And?'

'I told you, I didn't get a chance to say anything.'

'Good, it's got nothing to do with her.'

'She's nice, Saffron; she said I could drop in to see her any time.'

'Well I don't want you dropping in; she's my employer, and you can't mix work and pleasure.'

And that had been the last time Eileen had been over in Marlborough Road. Sally saw to that.

Harvey McLeod was an amiable sort of a fellow and very low key for a government minister. He couldn't have been more than his late forties; in fact Sally had some recollection of reading his age in one of the papers and being surprised, for he had that settled look about him that made him seem older. He also had the self-confident manner of someone who was used to giving orders. He was unmarried, supposedly gay. Clare loved gay men; the way she behaved with her friend Padraig was shameless. She took their sexual preferences as a sign that she could flirt safely all night long, a chance to practise the wiles and cute looks that the years of marriage had dulled.

The dining room with its high ceiling looked imposing in the dying sunlight. Clare had just lit the candles. There was a large gilt mirror that sat above the fireplace; it stretched almost to the ceiling. Sally had a full view of the table and could see herself reflected; standing by the door, looking a bit ill at ease, whilst the dinner guests, now well oiled by wine, gesticulated and laughed loudly and confidently. Fintan was talking animatedly to Patricia Thompson, who seemed to be hanging on his every word. Sally felt a wave of jealousy, followed immediately by an inner voice telling her to get a grip. After all, he was a single man, and he would hardly be looking for someone like her – a cleaner – to rescue him from his bachelor state. She smiled at him and moved quickly round the table, lifted some nearly empty dishes and went back into the kitchen. Trevor and Saffron were just arriving as she entered. Evie had agreed to sit with Posy whilst they were here. Simon was upstairs with Anna and the brood of hamsters.

Trevor was in good form; there was nothing like an evening away from the children to cheer him up. Saffron, on the other hand, looked a wee bit lost. Sally poured her a drink at once; she could see there was something troubling her, though she had worn her new outfit and looked well, and Evie had been up earlier to do her make-up. Trevor, needing no coaxing, was emptying a bottle of red wine into a glass he had lifted from the counter top.

'Have they finished eating?'

'No, I'm just about to bring this in.' Sally indicated the raspberry pavlova.

'Ah, great stuff, just in time for pudding, then.'

He took a gulp out of his glass and led the way into the dining room. Sally busied herself in the kitchen. She would leave after the last dishes were cleared.

Her mind ran busily as she washed up. She needed to find something to give her some self-worth. Cleaning other people's kitchens wasn't going to do it any more. Earlier on, when Edith and Fintan had arrived, Anna had asked Sally, 'What is your cleaner called, Sally?'

'She's called Sally O'Neill.'

'Is she? The very same name as you? That is really funny.'

Clare interrupted. 'Anna, off you go if you've finished your meal. Sorry, Sally, I'm sure she didn't mean any harm.'

'Don't be silly, Clare. Sure all the kids round here think that houses come with cleaners attached,' she joked.

Maybe that was the only way to go: think big. If you expected that someone else would come and clean your house then perhaps you would be likely to marry someone who could afford to pay for it. Thinking of Anna, she remembered it was time the child went to bed. She went into the TV room to tell her. As she did, she noticed that the front door was slightly ajar and went to close it. In the nick of time she realised that Laura Nelson and Trevor were standing outside. Laura was having a cigarette. Trevor must be keeping her company; he sometimes smoked cigars. They were huddled close together, and something about the look of them gave Sally a feeling of unease. Then she saw Trevor lean towards Laura and kiss her on the ear.

'Don't worry,' he said, 'it'll all work out.'

It suddenly hit Sally like a thunderbolt. That voice on the phone – it had been Laura, of course; the English accent gave her away. Why hadn't she realised? And the note; that was why Sally recognised the writing. On the few occasions she had bailed Laura out, she had left her a list of things to do. Oh dear, poor Saffron. Sally's heart went out to her. That was all she needed.

Sally backed away, not wanting to be seen. Clare called her, asking where the cream was, and Sally didn't have time to think about Trevor and Laura as the rest of the evening passed in a torrent of dishes. She didn't leave till the kitchen was sparkling and the guests were settling down to brandies. Tony had offered her a drink, but she refused, protesting that it would make her fall off the motorbike.

She had got to the top of the lane before she noticed somebody standing at the gate. He was a small bald fellow, and she didn't recognise him, but he was barring her way so she stopped the bike.

'Sally? I just wanted a wee word with you.'

Her heart stopped. Oh, he was changed, there was no doubt about that. The last ten years hadn't been kind to him. He was grey and bald and worn-looking, an air of defeat hanging about him like a shroud, but she'd have known those eyes anywhere. It was Charlie O'Neill.

'How did you find out where I worked?'

'I met Bertha in Milligan's.'

'Bertha? Oh God, just wait till I see her. How dare she?'

'Don't get mad, Sally. I made her tell me. I didn't like to go to the house. Look, I just want a wee chat for old times' sake.'

'Old times' sake? I'd rather forget the old times if you don't mind.'

'Please, Sally. Sure did Bronagh not tell you I was going away for good?'

'I have nothing to say to you, Charlie. Now would you please move?'

And she started up the bike and rode off, leaving him standing with his mouth open.

10

Bronagh was apprehensive about Evie McDonald coming in to get her hair done. What if she made a mess of it? Aside from the idea of giving Evie something to complain about, Bronagh took her job very seriously. She wanted to be a good hairdresser and she knew from her limited experience that the good cutters got all the clients. Alan, the owner, had really pissed her off by insisting she find some fancy new clients. How could she manage that? But she was hardly in a position to complain. The problem was, she didn't know any rich people. The Marlborough Road ones were as close to rich as she could come up with, but Alan's idea of wealthy was people who drove Porsches, wore Ebel watches and dressed like Posh and Becks. She was raging that Kelsey, another trainee, had told Alan that Bronagh's mum worked in millionaire homes, although she supposed she had sort of exaggerated Sally's job a bit to Kelsey on their day release to the tech.

Some other fellow had rung up for the free haircut as well, a Mr Flaherty. He was coming in for her last appointment today. She vaguely remembered that her mother found him irritating, so she wondered why Sally had given him the voucher. She hoped he didn't have a wire about himself.

Just then, Evie walked in. She turned heads. The thing was, she didn't seem to notice the effect she had. Bronagh watched Joe, the only male trainee, gaze in open admiration at her.

'D'ye want me to shampoo for you, Bronagh?'

He smiled sickeningly at her as if he liked her; he was a nasty wee shite really, full of himself. Usually Bronagh had to fight with him to get him to shampoo her clients, though he was her junior so he'd no choice on that one. He'd only been at the salon for six months.

Evie was all smiles and chat, and obviously delighted to let Bronagh loose on her hair. Bronagh began to relax. Maybe Evie wasn't so bad after all. And she sort of looked rich; she was tanned and confident. She had a posh voice. Even Alan looked over approvingly.

Bronagh wasn't sure what to say to Evie at first, but she was really easy to talk to. She had picked up a magazine with yet another article on Posh and Becks and so they started to chat about David Beckham's tattoos. Evie wondered if he would have room for the names of any more children he might have. She didn't approve of tattoos. Then they got into a mild disagreement about Kate Moss. Was she gorgeous or not? Evie thought yes, but she wasn't Bronagh's type. They then discovered they both had the same handbag (from Topshop), so the time flew.

It was obvious Evie was well satisfied with her haircut; she even let Bronagh persuade her to have a fringe. As she was getting ready to leave, having thanked Bronagh profusely a million times for cutting her hair so well, Bronagh said to her:

'Someone else from Marlborough Road is coming in to have his hair cut today. A Mr Flaherty.'

'You are kidding me?'

'No, do you know him?'

'Not really. He stays at Miss Black's. He's a rock poet or

something. My boyfriend Mikey sort of knows him. He's quite old, like about thirty something.'

'Does he have hair?'

'Yes, absolutely loads of it.'

'Well that's all that matters.'

'But . . .' Evie paused dramatically, 'it's bright red. He's a ginger minger!'

They both burst into uncontrollable giggles. It took Bronagh a few minutes to stop. Evie McDonald was a laugh. She offered to put Evie's name down to have her highlights done in two weeks' time. You could get them done at the training night for a tenner. Evie left a £3 tip, hoping it was enough, and suggested to Bronagh that she come to Edith's barbecue with her mum, though they both knew she wouldn't.

The minute Otis Flaherty walked in the door, Bronagh knew it was her client. They didn't get many like him. What a wild-looking guy. Evie certainly hadn't lied about the hair; he was a real carrot top, like Ronald McDonald. He was, as Evie had said, older – about thirty at least – and not a bit attractive; still, he had loads of hair, which he wore the Bob Geldof way, a bit unkempt and looking like he needed a shampoo. She couldn't wait to cut it off.

Otis surprised her by being very chatty and pleasant. Bronagh didn't say who she was, and obviously Sally hadn't said anything to him about her, so they just chatted generally. He did have a bit of a wire about himself, though. He told her he was an Ulster Scots poet as if it was some kind of big deal. He said he recited his poems with the backing of a rock band. Bronagh had never met a poet, at least not to her knowledge. But she'd heard somewhere that Belfast was full of them, so she'd probably walked past a few dozen in town without knowing it. It wasn't as if you could exactly pick one out in a crowd. Still, there was a part of her that thought it a romantic profession. Otis was currently writing a book of poems all about love. She was the kind of girl, he said, that poets would find inspiration in.

'You have beautiful blues eyes,' he said, 'like limpid pools.'

She felt a bit offended at that. All she knew about limpets was that they were sea creatures and clingy, but he had nice thick hair so she concentrated on that. It was a good head to train on. She just smiled and chopped away.

He wanted to look good for next week, he told her. He had a gig at the Empire. 'I can leave your name on the door if you like. It should be good craic.'

'I'm not sure it's my scene, but thanks anyway.'

'How do you know if you don't check it out? You can bring a friend if you like. I'll put plus guest.'

'Okay then. I'll see if Tiffany will come with me.'

She thought about it after he had left. Perhaps she would go. It would be something different; she got fed up going out to the same clubs every week. And he was a poet after all. She'd phone Tiffany when she got home. She decided not to tell her mum, though, especially since Sally had said Otis got on her nerves.

11

Miss Black was in the kitchen in a bit of a flap when Sally came in to work on Tuesday morning.

'Ah, Sally, good to see you. I have been looking for the voucher you so kindly gave me. It's good for six weeks, is it not? I thought I would have a trim at some stage. It is very good for the hair, you know, to trim the ends every now and again. My late mother, God rest her, used to singe the split ends of our hair as well to keep it strong, and if I may say so it really worked. Both Ellen and myself have a good head of hair. Don't you agree, Sally?'

Sally did indeed agree; who was she to argue? So she admired Miss Black's thick tresses and told her she'd have a look for the voucher and if she couldn't find it she would talk to Bronagh and see if she could give her a replacement. Reassured, Miss Black left for her charity shop. Sally hung up her coat and listened. The place seemed to be empty. She was glad. She wasn't in form for either a chat with Fintan or a run-in with Otis, and if by any crazy chance Charlie came to the door, at least she would be able to deal with him without an audience.

Of the three houses she cleaned, Edith's was the only one

with drawers that remained in a semblance of order. Her cutlery was neatly in the appointed drawer, though not the good stuff of course, the family silver. To her eternal delight, Edith had inherited that. Her sister Ellen hadn't been interested. She had gone for the more contemporary look, which meant she and her husband Derek actually had stainless-steel cutlery, designer of course, but stainless steel nonetheless. It vexed Edith, but as she told Sally, it had turned out lucky for her. Not so lucky for Sally, though, who had to clean the silver and put it all back carefully in the walnut box with individual little drawers.

Sally pulled open one of the drawers in the kitchen dresser. She had given the salon voucher to Edith in the kitchen; perhaps she had put it away here. She carefully sorted through the contents. Bits of tidily rolled string, paper napkins – Edith disapproved of them, but used them from time to time in an emergency – cocktail sticks, and the warranties for all the electrical goods. It was also full of cards for plumbers, electricians and various services, even though Edith always used the same people, and the occasional flier for a Chinese restaurant or the local Indian, as well as the napkin rings of course, the everyday ones made of African walnut. The silver ones were kept in the dining room sideboard.

Sally's eye was caught by a hospital appointment card. It was for Miss Edith Black and gave the name of the consultant, Mr Brian Smedley, Department of Oncology, and the date, two weeks away. Oncology? Sally couldn't quite remember what that was, but she had a feeling it wasn't a cheerful department. She could hardly ask Edith what it was about, but she hoped for her sake it wasn't anything serious. She had enough to contend with. Sally tried to dismiss it, and rummaged in the other drawer, but there was still no sign of the voucher.

She was polishing the mirror when it came to her, shockingly. Of course! Her sister Sheila had had breast cancer, and she was attending the oncology department. Oh no, surely Miss Black couldn't have cancer? Sally thought about it. Maybe the word meant something else; she'd look it up. Miss Black kept a large two-volume dictionary, complete with magnifying glass, on the shelf in the den. She used it sometimes when she got stuck on the *Times* crossword. Sally got it down, opened it, and checked. Yes, there it was – oncology . . . that part of medical science that relates to tumours. How bland it looked, the definition. Her heart froze. Surely not? Maybe it was just a scare . . . it frequently was.

'Is everything okay, Sally? You look like you've seen a ghost.'

Sally dropped the book.

'Ach, Fintan, I didn't hear you come in.'

'I came down the back. I'm thinking of phoning the police, actually. There's a dodgy-looking character at the top of the lane; he's been there all morning. I asked him what he wanted and he said he was waiting for someone, but . . . Hey, are you okay? Is something up?'

Sally had gone pale. Was it Charlie out there again? She made a fuss of putting the dictionary back.

'Here, let me do that. Goodness, this is heavy. Have you been doing the crossword?'

'No, I've been looking up the meaning of the word oncology,' she blurted out, shaken by her suspicions about Charlie.

A flash of alarm crossed Fintan's face.

'And you know what it means?'

'Yes, I had figured it out, but I wanted to be sure.'

'Do you want to talk about it, Sally. Have you had bad news?'

Sally shook her head. 'No, not me, it's this.'

She went to the drawer in the kitchen; Fintan followed her. She took out the card and handed it to him.

'Edith?'

'Yes, I was looking for her free voucher for the hairdresser's and I found this.' She didn't want Fintan to think she was a snoop.

'The hairdressing voucher?'

Sally nodded.

'I still have mine, but the other was sitting on the table last week. I think I saw Otis lift it.'

So that was that mystery solved, she should have thought of that. Still, he mustn't have used it. Bronagh hadn't mentioned anything. Fintan moved to put the kettle on.

'Can you take five minutes to have a cup of tea?'

Sally nodded and sat down. She felt quite shocked.

'Perhaps it is something simple, like a mole, or a smear test.'

He wasn't even embarrassed saying that to her, she noticed.

'No, I have had both of those and you just go to the outpatient departments.'

'Well let's hope it isn't anything serious. I'm sure she would have said.' He poured two cups of tea. 'I wonder should we say anything to her? She's such a private person.'

Sally didn't think they should. If Edith had wanted anyone to know, she would have mentioned it. They'd just have to keep an eye out for her.

They were sitting drinking their tea when Evie came in through Miss Black's door, knocking carefully. Edith was adamant that no one should just barge in. Her back door was kept closed most of the time.

'Hi.' Evie said, smiling winningly at Fintan. 'I'm selling ballot tickets, only a pound each. Are you interested?'

'Sure I couldn't win an argument.'

'Don't forget your gorgeous motorbike, Sally.'

'That was a competition, but I'm happy to buy a ticket.'

'I've sold twenty so far. Isn't that good?'

'How many have you left?'

'Just five. It's for breast cancer research. It's very important work. This cancer affects everyone, even Kylie.' She held up a multicoloured wrist. 'Look, I'm wearing a pink band for it as well.'

'I'll take the last five,' Sally said impulsively.

'Are you sure?'

'Yes, why not?'

She exchanged a look with Fintan. It seemed such a co-incidence for Evie to have come in just at this moment.

'What's the prize?'

'A holiday for two in Crete.'

'Crete?'

'Yes, we've been there, to a villa, last year, don't you remember? It's lovely. Dad thought it was too hot, though.'

'Well I could use a bit of heat; the weather here would put your head away. If we have one more rainy day, I'm selling the bike.'

'No, Sally, the bike is cool. Good for your image.'

'I'd like to buy one as well, Evie,' Fintan said. Hang on. Let me get my wallet.' He went out of the kitchen.

Evie looked after him.

'Gosh, he's dead good-looking, Sally, isn't he? I mean for someone old.'

'I wouldn't know.'

'Well he is. Mum wants us all to go to the opera to see him, but I'm not really the opera type, y'know.'

Fintan came back in waving a fiver.

'Here, Sally, let me treat you.'

'Don't be daft.'

Sally took out her purse and tried to get Evie to take her fiver.

'Here, Evie, I'll treat Fintan.'

Fintan pressed his own fiver on Evie.

'I'll have three; Sally, you have two.'

Evie laughed. 'Okay okay, don't fight over it. Look, I know

what. Each of you have two in your own name and one joint one. I'll put both your names on one of the tickets.'

And negotiations over, she left. She was off school at the moment and obviously had got fed up revising. This way she could go in and out of all the houses and see what the vibes were.

Fintan looked at Sally.

'Oh Sally, I hope Edith is okay. It's very worrying. I've got so fond of her over these last few weeks.'

What a nice man he was, Sally reflected. He fitted in so well in Marlborough Road. She finished her work, bade him a cheery goodbye and went up the lane to number 21. She had a good look for the strange man Fintan had mentioned, but thankfully there was no sign of him.

12

Sally let herself in the back door of the McNamaras' with a cheerful smile on her face and a bright hello, Charlie and her troubles pushed firmly to the back of her mind. She came upon Saffron, sitting woebegone in the kitchen. Posy was perched on the long kitchen table painting eggshells. Saffron was a quare one for the mosaic collages, ever since she had done a children's art course last year that featured them heavily. The house was practically papered with them. Beside Posy was a pot of wallpaper paste, sheets of paper, several brushes and a mess that suggested that the excitable three-year-old had spent quite some time mashing the lot together. The cauldron was bubbling away on the Aga, some foul smell wafting upwards, and the iguana was sitting motionless on the shelf above it.

Jesus, you couldn't make this up, Sally thought. Iggy stared at her through his heavy-lidded eyes, and shifted his long tail as if he knew she had it in mind to kill him. With a bit of luck he'd fall into the curry gloop when no one was looking.

'Well, Saffron, are yis nearly finished with this?' Sally indicated the mess with a fixed smile.

'Oh Sally, I'm so sorry, it's just been hard to occupy her. I'm not feeling in the best of form these days.' Saffron sighed heavily in case Sally thought she was insincere.

'Is Simon here?'

'Yes, he's upstairs in his room.'

Sally marched purposefully to the bottom of the stairs and shouted at the top of her voice: 'Simon, you come down here this minute.'

Simon came running down the stairs two at a time. He always paid attention to Sally, even though poor old Saffron could be screeching like a banshee for him to come down all day long with little result.

'Yes, Sally?'

'That Iggy McNamara one is sitting on the shelf on top of the Aga. Now if you want me to go out that back door and never come back again, you can leave him there.'

'Oh, Sally, I'm very sorry. I forgot all about him. You see, being an arboreal lizard he likes to sit in trees, so I thought he could sit up there and watch Posy painting, and as a matter of fact, he rather likes the heat.'

Simon had a precise, clipped little voice, like he had swallowed a dictionary and it was coming up in chapters, Sally thought.

'Well he gives me the heebie-jeebies, so if you don't mind, I'd like him to go upstairs and watch you instead. That's higher up, isn't it?'

Simon lifted the thing off the shelf and carted it upstairs. It glared at Sally on the way past. She didn't meet its gaze. It would turn your stomach just to look at it.

It took Sally about twenty minutes to clear the table, put all the mess away and make Saffron a cup of herbal tea. Then she brought Posy upstairs and ran her a bath. Posy looked as if she hadn't seen water for a week. Sally bathed and dried the child and went to find something to dress her in; that done, she plonked her in front of the TV with the Pingu DVD. It would do her no harm to watch it again and it kept her quiet. She went back down to the kitchen and found Saffron still sitting immobile at the table, flicking listlessly though a book. Sally just got on with her work. She figured Saffron would talk when she was ready.

Eventually, when the kitchen was clean and tidy, the dishwasher going and a load of clothes on, Saffron spoke.

'Oh Sally, what on earth am I going to do?'

'About what, Saffron?' Sally didn't think there was anything particularly different about today, except that Saffron's usually upbeat mood had been replaced by this air of doom.

'I know Trevor has stopped loving me.'

'Ach, Saffron love, you said that last week and I told you it's nonsense. Of course he loves you.'

'Do you think he could be having an affair?'

Sally's heart sank. She thought back to what she'd seen at the McDonalds' the other night. Could there be anything serious going on between Trevor and Laura Nelson? No matter if there was; Sally wasn't going to be the bearer of bad news, and besides, it was probably nothing. Laura and Trevor were both lawyers and saw each other professionally, and Trevor doted on Saffron; they had been married over ten years. Sally always thought it a good match.

'Why would you think something like that, Saffron?'

'Oh, I told you he's stopped coming home for lunch almost completely, and then when he does come home in the evening he's taken to popping out for drinks to any house in the lane that'll have him, and he was so rude this morning when I mentioned the barbecue . . . he said he didn't care what I marinated, I could grill Iggy for all he cared. I'm glad Simon was still upstairs.'

Sally thought of the pot bubbling on the stove. The smell would have knocked you out of the house. Many a man would have left for better cooking.

'Well, Saffron, maybe things aren't going too well at work. He does seem a bit distracted. Have you tried to have a chat with him?'

'No . . . and there's something else. Sally, I think I might be pregnant again.'

'Think? Have you had a test?'

'No, but I haven't had a period in about four months and I feel really queasy in the mornings.'

'Mother of God, Saffron, that sounds fairly convincing.'

'But I have an IUD in.'

'Sure two of my sisters got pregnant with an IUD in; in our Nora's case the baby was born with it on its head. It was okay, though. A healthy wee boy.'

'Gosh, Sally!' Saffron looked horrified.

'You need to get them checked regularly; they can work loose. Would you like me to go round to the chemist on the bike and get you a test thing?'

'Oh Sally, if you don't mind, that sounds like a good idea.'

Saffron was indeed pregnant. Sally couldn't believe she hadn't realised it sooner. She was surprised Evie hadn't noticed it when they were out shopping. Sally looked closely at her; she was more bosomy than usual and her tummy was quite pronounced, definitely a few months at least. On anyone else it would have been obvious before now, but Saffron was so thin and wore all those shapeless kaftans. Sally got her to call the doctor and make an appointment, which she did without protest, glad to have someone else take charge.

'How am I going to cope?' Saffron started crying.

'You'll have to take it easy for a while. Maybe you'd think of putting the children into school in September; stop teaching them at home.'

'Perhaps you're right; it'll be hard to manage a third. I'll talk it over with Trevor tonight, though he has a late meeting.'

She stopped and swallowed hard. Sally felt sorry for her; she looked utterly miserable.

'I hope Trevor doesn't mind my being pregnant.'

'I'm sure he'll be delighted.'

But both of them wondered if indeed that would be the case.

When Trevor finally got home, late again, Saffron had dinner ready. She'd made a vegetable curry – it was one of her better efforts – and she had also opened a bottle of wine, real wine, not the organic vinegar they usually had. A feeling of alarm washed over him. He gulped heavily on his glass. The place seemed quiet, ominous. There were just the two of them, either ends of the kitchen table. The children had already eaten and were over with Anna.

'So what is it, my pet? You have something to tell me?'

'Treasure, darling . . .' Saffron looked tense. 'I don't know quite how to say this.'

'Give me a clue . . . Is it about the children?'

'No . . . Have you noticed anything different about me recently?'

Trevor thought rapidly. Was this a trick question?

'Different in what way?'

'Well, we haven't been making love much recently, and so you might not have noticed that I am a little plumper—'

'Haven't we?' he interrupted. 'I'm sorry, my pet, I suppose I've had a heavier than average workload, and you've been somewhat distracted . . .'

'Yes, I know, darling, I'm not complaining. I haven't been feeling well, but now I know what is causing it.'

Oh Christ, she wasn't going to tell him she was ill, was she? She was dying, and he was being punished . . . Oh no, and he really did love her. The curry rose in his throat. He felt sick.

'What *is* causing it?'

'I'm pregnant.' She looked at him almost pleadingly.

'What? Surely not? Haven't you got a coil thingy fitted?'

'Yes, but they sometimes can work loose, I think.'

Trevor couldn't quite get his voice to work. This was the last thing on earth he had expected, and the timing couldn't have been worse as far as he was concerned. But Saffron expected him to be pleased, so he tried to smile. It was okay for her, she had had all day to think about it and she had accepted it, and anyway, she had always wanted a large family. Trevor couldn't believe he had got away so far with only two. Oh God, what a nightmare. He finished his glass of wine and poured another, then looked at her. She was sitting there quietly, the tears about to flow. He got up and went round to her and took her in his arms. He did love her really; it was just so hard being married all the time.

'Don't worry, make an appointment with Dr Jones and I'll come with you.'

'Oh thank you, Treasure. I have already phoned. I'm seeing him tomorrow. I knew you'd understand.'

Somehow they made it through to bedtime without Saffron bursting into tears again.

Trevor lay in bed tossing and turning and hoping that it wasn't true – Saffron, pregnant, he couldn't believe it! Perhaps when they went to see Dr Jones tomorrow they would find out she wasn't. This was all he needed; his life was complicated enough.

Saffron liked Dr Jones a lot. He was a lovely man and had been very supportive of her when she had decided to go for a home birth with Posy. Trevor sat nervously reading the paper while she went into the consulting room. After the doctor had examined her and questioned her about her last period, he reassured her that the coil was well and truly missing but that all looked fine. Then he did a scan, and there clear as anything were two little babies, wriggling round top to toe inside her.

'Aha!' he said with a big beam. 'Well, well, well. Two of them. That's a big surprise, eh?'

And he sent the nurse out to get Trevor, who came in looking distinctly uncomfortable. Saffron felt sick. She was apprehensive of Trevor's reaction; something in her waters made her feel he would not be delirious with happiness. Even the idea of a third child had seemed to plunge him into gloom. And she was right.

'Twins?' he squeaked at Dr Jones in disbelief. 'Are you sure? Surely she can't be having twins?'

13

Bronagh took a lot of time over Sally's hair, wanting her to look her best. Her mother needed a good night out. The whole business with Charlie had been upsetting for her. She wasn't going to dress up too much because she was sure everyone but Edith would be casual. Despite having already decided what to wear she tried on about three different outfits before she settled on a pair of turquoise linen trousers she had bought in the sale and a pale cream cotton sweater. She decided against dangly earrings and just went for the little pearl ones Bronagh had bought her for Christmas. She wasn't taking the bike. She wanted to have a glass of wine and you couldn't be too careful these days. Drink went straight to her head anyway. She called a taxi and waited outside the door in case the driver missed the house. He was there on the dot of seven.

Sally arrived at Edith's front door and wondered whether to ring or let herself in, but she was a guest tonight after all, so she chose the former. They would all be out the back; maybe she should have walked down the lane. But no, she heard footsteps coming down the hall. Someone was in. Fintan opened the door and smiled at her. He was wearing a blue polo shirt tonight. It matched his eyes. He seemed very relaxed.

'We're all out the back. We weren't sure if you would come down the lane or not, so I said I'd wait.' His gaze swept her appreciatively. 'You look great, Sally.'

'Oh, I clean up well,' she said with a smile. But she was delighted with his compliment.

They walked through to the kitchen, where Edith was finishing off a pasta salad.

'Ah, Sally, how nice to see you. We're almost ready, I've just a few more things to bring out.'

'Let me give you a hand, Miss Black.'

Edith paused, about to hand her the bowl, and then said, 'No, not at all, Sally, I can manage. After all, you are our guest of honour.'

Sally hoped as she followed Fintan out the back that Edith hadn't overcooked the pasta. It would be just like her.

Many's the barbecue in these isles that has been ruined by bad weather, but tonight both luck and sunshine shone on Marlborough Road. Edith's garden had a full profusion of summer flowers at the moment and looked delightful. Saffron's citronella candles, some a little lopsided, provided extra perfume. There were three large wooden tables placed together and an assortment of chairs. A selection of bowls containing various salads were already sitting out, covered for the time being in clingfilm. Sally noticed they were mainly using plastic glasses, though Edith had also wine glasses laid out. Not her best ones, of course.

Tony had managed to make it home in time for once. Just as well, because he was the designated chef for the evening. He and Bill Nelson were currently bent over the barbecue sipping beers and turning steaks and chicken fillets. Patricia Thompson was talking animatedly to them, dressed in shorts and a backless top. Trevor was lurking behind, also drinking a beer, looking as if he was afraid to get too close to the meat in case he went wild and grabbed it all in a frenzy. On a separate gas barbecue Saffron's organic vegetarian offerings were cooking accusingly.

Everyone was indeed casually dressed. Clare was wearing an outfit not dissimilar to Sally's own, but you could tell her linen trousers were expensive, and her sweater was most definitely not Marks and Spencer. Fintan led Sally over to one of the wooden chairs and found her a cushion. She was relieved to see there was no sign of Otis. Laura Nelson wasn't there either; she would be along later. It seemed she had some important meeting or other.

'Now, Sally, you're not to lift a hand tonight.' Fintan smiled at her, making her melt. God, he was gorgeous. 'Let everyone look after you for once.'

A drink was placed in her hand, a glass of sangria, which was red wine and lemonade and tasted quite pleasant. Edith came back out and was chattering away, filling glasses. Saffron sat quietly, not saying much, with Posy clamped to her as usual. Sally had noticed as soon as she arrived that Saffron's down-in-the-dumps mood didn't seem to have lifted at all. She wondered how the doctor's appointment had gone, and if all the others had been told yet. As Edith reached her with the jug, Saffron refused a glass.

'Oh Saffron, *do* have some, dear. This sangria is wonderful, very refreshing, my own recipe, although I myself love Pimm's at this time of year.'

Saffron shook her head. 'No thanks, Edith, I'm fine, really. I have some juice here.'

Clare, overhearing, brought over another large glass jug filled with sangria and fruit.

'Here, Saffie, have some of this, it's very weak. I made it. It'll only give you a slight buzz.' She leaned over conspiratorially. 'Avoid Edith's. I think she's put a ton of gin in it.'

Saffron bit her lip and looked into Clare's face.

'I can't have anything to drink, Clare. I'm four months pregnant.'

'You're not serious?'

'Yes, I'm afraid so.'

She looked towards Sally for moral support. Sally smiled at her reassuringly. She had been hoping for Saffron's sake that the 'do it yourself' kit might have been wrong. She moved and sat on the garden seat beside Saffron. She wanted to hug her, but instead patted her on the arm. Saffron seemed on the verge of tears. Clare, open-mouthed at the news, plonked the sangria on the table and herself on the bench beside them.

'My God, Saffron! Gosh, you sly old thing! You never said a word. Are you delighted?'

She gave her a hug, and Saffron smiled wanly.

'I only found out for sure today. Sally got me a kit. I mean, I've suspected since last week, and I was sort of coming round to the idea. I've always wanted three, I could have coped with that, but it looks like I'm having twins.'

'Looks like?'

'No, it's definite. There were two on the ultrasound.'

Twins? Poor Saffron. That was the last thing she needed; a frail wee thing like her. Sally nearly choked on her drink.

'Twins? Gosh!' Clare rolled her eyes.

'Yes, twins,' Saffron echoed miserably.

'But it'll be fun. You'll have to talk to Laura when she gets here.'

Sally thought of Jack and Eric, the Nelson twins. With luck Saffron would have girls.

'When are you due?' asked Clare.

'November. I have to go for a second scan next week. I think poor Treasure is still in shock. Aren't you, darling?'

Trevor looked over. He was standing with Bill and Tony, looking distracted, but he had heard.

'Yes, we're pleased of course, but it was unexpected,' he ventured lamely.

Bill Nelson smiled encouragingly at him.

'Twins are great, good company for each other.'

His two were now seven-year-old monsters who had managed to see off about four au pairs in the last two years. Sally thought it was just as well they had each other – no one else could put up with them.

As the party went on around her, Saffron thought of the scene in the doctor's office. She sipped her juice quietly and watched her husband, remembering his horror when the doctor said it was twins. Trevor was darting looks here and there. His mind seemed elsewhere.

Bill Nelson called one of the twins to go and see if his mother was back yet. All the food was ready. The children lined up to be served. Simon dutifully took his quorn kebab, then announced to the assembled company:

'We must be expecting one more person. There's an extra steak, even counting Mrs Nelson.'

'You should work for MI5, Simon,' quipped Sally.

'Actually, Sally, I am considering it as a career option.'

'I've been half starved all year at uni, Simon, and I'm having two steaks, so there.' Rory McDonald, who had just arrived home today from university, was obviously in on the plot. Sally saw immediately what was up. The steak was for Trevor. Maybe that was why he was acting so shifty. At least she hoped that was the reason.

'You do realise that you are increasing your chances of CJD – aside from murdering a defenceless animal, of course.'

'Thank you for the info, Simon, I appreciate your concern.'

Rory patted Simon on the head and laughed good-naturedly, and the matter was dropped. Sally had a few more glasses of the sangria. They were pouring it out like there was no tomorrow. She was starting to feel relaxed. Evie arrived with

Mikey, who aside from the famous purple hair seemed to have pierced several parts of his face at random. She had got permission to go out with him later on, provided she endured the barbecue first and brought him along so Clare and Tony could meet him. Sally could tell Clare found him outrageous but was trying, for Evie's sake, to play down her disapproval. Tony, who had made a face when Mikey's back was turned, was keeping quiet. Mikey seemed uncomfortable; he was doing that shifting thing, swallowing too much and smiling too brightly. Sally's heart went out to him. These people were great, but they had no idea how off-putting they could be to outsiders.

Eventually all the children were fed, and dispersed to charge up and down the lane and annoy the rest of the inhabitants. Other residents had been asked to join the gathering later on for drinks. Sally thought that Edith was in good form, positively sparkling, and flirting outrageously with Fintan, who seemed to take it all in his stride. She thought back to the hospital appointment card she'd found in Edith's kitchen. Perhaps there was nothing wrong with her. After all, anyone could have a bit of a scare.

The idea of having the barbecue on Midsummer's Day had been Edith's. And she had to be given credit for choosing well. On the longest day of the year it simply didn't get dark in Belfast, particularly on a warm night with a clear blue sky such as this. It was almost nine and the sun was still shining. It would be light almost till midnight. As Edith pointed out to Evie and Mikey, who were sitting listening (a captured rather than captive audience), the reason for this was that Belfast was situated at fifty-four and a half degrees latitude north.

'Oh yes, we are very far north and no doubt would not have our lovely cool temperate oceanic climate were it not for the happy fact that the Gulf Stream wraps itself round the island of Ireland and prevents the worst excesses of winter.'

Sally didn't want to argue about the worst excesses of winter bit, but she didn't think the Gulf Stream helped much when she was battling though icy rain on the bike summer and winter alike.

'Oh yes, remarkable, don't you think?'

Miss Black smiled brightly whilst gazing roughly in the direction of Mikey's pierced eyebrow. Evie had a glazed smile fixed and Mikey just looked baffled. Sally suspected that the Cokes they were drinking were at least fifty per cent vodka. She thought the sangria had certainly loosened Edith up. She was in magnificent form. She had missed her vocation; she should have been a teacher.

Her lesson was interrupted by the arrival of Laura Nelson, looking trim and tanned and glamorous in a lime-green linen dress. She sat down, accepted the proffered glass of sangria, and waited while Bill got her a steak and a plate of salad. Sally watched Trevor; she was interested to see how he would handle this, but he used Laura's arrival as a distraction to sneak off into the McDonalds' kitchen for his large sirloin steak. He had watched Rory carry it inside on a plate, saying he'd have it later. He hadn't intended the meat issue to become such a major one, but he just couldn't resist every now and then. He felt guilty; he felt like he was always cheating on Saffron – in more ways than one.

When he returned from the kitchen, Saffron stood up to excuse herself; all the excitement had been a bit much for one night.

'I think in view of my condition I can leave early. Trevor, would you round up Posy and Simon, darling?' And off she went.

'What condition?' Laura had turned to Trevor, who appeared not to hear her question. 'Trevor, did you hear me? What condition? Is Saffron okay?'

'Oh, you missed the announcement earlier, Laura.' Clare laughed. 'Saffron is pregnant and expecting twins!'

'Yes, I think poor Trevor is still in shock.' Tony patted Trevor on the back jovially.

Laura placed her drink on the table, faced Trevor and said in an icily cold voice, 'How on earth could she be pregnant?'

Tony leaned smilingly over to Laura – all the men flirted with her a little, thought Clare.

'I guess Trevor must have been misbehaving himself!'

Trevor stood there frozen, like a little boy about to be slapped.

'Yes, I suppose you must have been misbehaving, Trevor. It seems you are somewhat of an expert on that.' Laura almost spat the words out at him. Then she reached over and patted him on the head. 'Well congratulations *are* in order then, aren't they? You clever old thing. And with twins – a double whammy! I'm sure you're thrilled to bits. Imagine you becoming a daddy again, and at what? Fifty-two? No, almost fifty-three. That'll make you seventy-one when they go to college. Gosh, what a big challenge for you. I wonder if you are up to it. I doubt it very much.' And to everyone's astonishment she slammed her drink down and stormed off.

14

Bronagh had listened to Tiffany nagging all the way over in the taxi to the Empire. She had already necked a half-bottle of vodka before they left the house and sounded like a parrot on speed.

'Why are we going here? What is a rock poet? I've never heard of one before. I bet you the drinks will be twice the price.'

All this whingeing was unsettling Bronagh. She wasn't exactly sure what a rock poet was either, but she certainly didn't want Tiffany to know that. So she explained patiently for the tenth time that they could always leave early if it was no good, and offered to buy the first two rounds just to shut her up. She had her fingers crossed that their names were actually on the list. She could imagine Tiffany's reaction if they had to pay in. But they were there, right at the top: *Bronagh plus one*. She relaxed a bit. That was one less thing for Tiffany to bitch about.

It was really stuffy in the bar, and smoky as hell. The band weren't on yet. The crowd was weird – lots of Goths and student types. All the tables were full. Bronagh pushed her way up to the bar and tried in vain to catch the eye of a barman.

Tiffany stood beside her, arms folded and a venomous look on her face. Bronagh was having no luck, and was about to change her mind and go when she saw Otis in the crowd. He caught her eye and waved, then worked his way effortlessly through the crowd.

'You made it.'

'Yes.'

'We're on at ten.' That was an hour away. He leaned over and caught the barman by the sleeve. 'Put this drink on our tab, will you, Declan? Cheers. I have to go and get ready. Catch you later, doll. Okay?' And he gave her a big cheesy grin.

Bronagh felt pleased he had bothered to come over. She ordered the drinks – double vodkas with cranberry juice – and handed one to Tiffany.

'That's the fella whose hair you cut.'

'I know.'

'That's how you got the free tickets,' Tiffany said accusingly.

'Yes, so what?'

'He's dead old; he must be at least thirty. Here, do you fancy him?'

'No I do not! I just thought it would make a change to see a live band.'

Bronagh suddenly saw a free table. She pushed her way over and sat down, keeping the other seat for Tiffany. They'd stay for the first half anyway; it might be okay.

Back in Edith's garden, Laura's outburst had been forgotten and Clare's pudding – 'something wonderful with plums' – was being served for the adults, the children having had ice creams. A few of the other neighbours had joined them, and the wine was flowing. Sally was glad she had come. She was enjoying herself, and Fintan was sitting by her side acting as if she was the most beautiful woman there. She was almost starting to believe it herself.

Suddenly the children came running en masse into Edith's garden, babbling about the strange man who had climbed into the Nelsons' tree house and right now was spying on everyone.

'A strange man! Where? Show me – what strange man?' Clare was up like a shot, shrieking down the lane. The others followed in a straggle. The children were delighted they had created such a rumpus.

The Nelsons' tree house was about eight feet from the ground. Bill had built it a few years back into the largest tree in his garden, which was a horse chestnut. It was in full bloom now, the candles pointing upwards and the leaves thick and green. The children loved it in summer for the shelter it gave them, and of course in autumn for its rich harvest of conkers.

Before the residents and Sally reached the garden, they could hear someone giving an extremely loud and drunken rendition of Van Morrison's 'Brown-Eyed Girl'. A rather dishevelled balding man was sitting precariously on the edge of the platform, clinging on with one arm and fortifying himself with sips from a can of beer between lines. To Sally's mortification and horror, the singer was none other than Charlie O'Neill.

Several pairs of eyes gazed up at him. Charlie immediately spotted Sally, and carolled drunkenly at her in a loud voice: 'Yew ma brown-eyed gurl . . . Sally, oh Sally, why did you leave me? I loved you, so ah did, I loved you, Sally.'

All eyes swivelled in unison to Sally. She felt her head swim, and stood rooted to the spot as he continued to address her.

'Why will you not even talk to me, Sally? All those years I thought about you, all those wasted years. You're the only woman I ever loved. What God has put together, let no man pull asunder.' And with this pronouncement he fell backwards into the tree house and passed out.

There was a kind of stunned silence, and then everyone began to talk at once. Patricia Thompson was looking at Sally as if she had a bomb under her arm and was about to detonate it.

'Who on earth is he? What is he doing here? How does he know your name, Sally?'

Sally shook her head. She had totally lost her voice.

Fintan moved protectively to her side.

'I've seen him before. He's been standing at the top of the lane a few times recently. I told him to move off.'

'Do you know him, Sally?' asked Clare, eyebrows arched.

'I . . . No, I don't know him . . . I used to know him,' Sally whispered, almost in tears. She couldn't bring herself to say he was her estranged husband.

'Shall we call the police?' Edith assumed her headmistress voice.

'No, don't be ridiculous. We'll just ask him to leave, unless of course he's been bothering you. Has he, Sally?' Tony asked.

Without replying, Sally turned on her heel and ran down the lane. She went straight into Edith's garden and picked up her handbag, then made her way through the house and out of the front door. As fast as she could, she ran out of Marlborough Road and on to the main road to get a taxi home. She would never be able to face any of them again. Her whole body was trembling violently. The bastard, the stupid bloody bastard! Hadn't he done enough to ruin her life years ago? It was sickening, his turning up and making her look like a total eejit in front of everyone. She would call Maids to Order first thing on Monday and accept Maybeth's offer. They'd hardly want her back here after this scene. She could still plainly picture Patricia Thompson's sneering face. She would take a week's leave and start the following week in her new job. She was distraught. Why tonight? And just when she was relaxed and getting on so well with Fintan. It was all ruined now.

She got to the taxi rank and there was a cab sitting waiting.

She gave him her address and sat back in the seat. The Friday-night rush hadn't started yet, and the streets were full of young ones out enjoying the good weather. The taxi had her home in no time. The house was empty. Bronagh would be out till late. She went in and plonked herself down on the living room sofa, and then, unable to hold out any longer, allowed herself to cry. She thought she wouldn't be able to stop. When finally she calmed down, she knew sleep was out of the question. The sight of Charlie serenading her from the tree house was playing over and over like a clip from a ghastly newsreel in her mind's eye. Each time it scrolled past, her humiliation deepened. She felt as if her entire body was blushing. Why could he not just leave things well alone and let her get on with her life?

The band had been going for nearly an hour. Bronagh, on her third drink now, was beginning to chill out. Tiffany, on the other hand, was getting surlier by the minute.

Otis was at the microphone, wailing like a demon. The band was playing softly behind him, gazing expressionlessly at the crowd. Bronagh listened carefully; you could make out the words despite the noise of the crowd.

'Your love curls round me, ties me, chokes me, it spins me. I am left reeling. It sets me free, makes me dizzy.'

Otis began whirling around. The drumming intensified.

'God, he makes me dizzy. No wonder they're called The Reelers,' Tiffany said sourly to Bronagh.

Privately Bronagh thought the poems were nonsense, but she wasn't going to admit that to Tiffany. The band was good, though.

'What would you know about poetry?' she sniffed.

'Nothing, but I know that's shite. Anyway, he looks like Mick Hucknall.'

Tiffany had a point. Perhaps, Bronagh thought, they'd do better to cut their losses and go. She was about to suggest this, but just as they were finishing their drinks, Evie McDonald walked in with a fella with purple hair. She spotted Bronagh and waved.

'Hiya, Bronagh, great crowd, isn't it? This is Mikey.'

Bronagh introduced Tiffany, who affected nonchalance.

'Yeah, Bronagh said you came to the salon; you had the free coupon.'

Bronagh was mortified, but Evie laughed.

'Too right. Let me know if you get any more. Mikey needs to get his hair back to normal if he's going to get back in our door.'

Mikey looked at Evie adoringly and nodded.

'I don't think they liked me round there.'

'Is it still going on?'

'Yes, we left early; some madman started singing in the Nelsons' tree house, so we legged it and left them all to it.'

Bronagh hoped Sally had had a good time at the barbecue, but she had no intention of asking in front of Tiffany, who was on the defensive now that Evie had joined the company.

The band stopped and Otis came over to them. Bronagh noticed a lot of the girls nudging each other and looking at him. Honestly, the way people behaved if you put yourself forward at all. You'd have thought he was Robbie Williams; sadly Bronagh figured Tiffany's assessment of his talent was closer to the truth. Bronagh was distracted by Evie's presence. Throughout her life, all she'd heard from Sally was Evie McDonald this, Rory McDonald that, and then the wee one, Anna; what a pet she was, and how clever. Sometimes she felt jealous of them; they seemed to have it all. Good looks, brains, a daddy with an important job; plus *her* mother around to slave for them. She knew the real reason Tiffany was grumpy was that she felt out of her depth. Bronagh didn't feel entirely comfortable either, but she was determined not to show it. Evie was treating her like a mate. She joined in the banter and said she'd probably wait around for the second half. In reality she planned to leave and put Tiffany out of her misery, but she would choose the moment.

As soon as the band started and Otis began another of his poetic raps, she whispered to Evie that she was leaving. She nodded towards Tiffany and mimed as if to say her friend was about to be sick. Evie waved goodbye and the two girls went outside. It was still light, so they decided to walk into town. They might go for a few at the club all their mates favoured. Bronagh relaxed. She was glad they'd left. At least she could be herself now.

'You were talking all posh in there,' Tiffany said accusingly.

'Don't be ridiculous. I was just making myself heard above the crowd. Our English teacher Miss Walsh used to say to us, "Don't mumble, girls, enunciate!" Well that's what I was doing.'

'Hmm, it looked like showing off to me.'

When Bronagh arrived home a few hours later and a little the worse for wear, she noticed the light on in her mother's bedroom. She didn't go in. She answered Sally's 'Is that you, Bronagh love?' with 'Yes, Mum. Night night, see you in the morning.'

It was just as well, because she would have seen at once that Sally's soft brown eyes were red and swollen from crying.

Sally spent the entire weekend in a limbo of indecision and upset. She had turned her mobile off and unplugged the phone. Extreme she knew, but she wasn't ready to face any of her employers. There was no way she could go back to Marlborough Road now. Friday night had been the last straw, for she had no guarantee Charlie would stay away. She had to leave her job; she couldn't cope with Clare, Saffron and Edith thinking badly of her. They would wonder why she hadn't come clean about Charlie earlier, and if they heard that he'd been in jail, they probably wouldn't want her anyway. It was unbearable to think about it. Eventually she decided it would be best if she wrote rather than phoned. She found a notepaper and envelope set that Edith had given her last Christmas, and wasted three pages before she was finally able to compose something that satisfied her, aware of her grammar, her spelling and her handwriting. In the end she wrote:

Dear Clare,

I am addressing this to you since I have worked for you the longest. I am sorry after all this time to have to tell you that I have got a new job and will be starting it next week, so I won't be coming back. It is nothing personal. I enjoyed working for all of you in Marlborough Road. I hope this will not put you out too much. I am sorry not to give you more notice, but there are plenty of cleaners out there. I would be glad if you could please tell Saffron and Miss Black.

Yours truly,
Sally

That was the best she could do. She'd post the letter first thing on Monday, right after she'd called Maybeth and accepted the job with Maids to Order.

15

Monday morning at nine o'clock, Clare shrugged herself into her blue dressing gown and yawned. What a weekend. No wonder she wasn't feeling at all rested. Friday night had ended in chaos. It had taken four men all of half an hour to wake Charlie and get him down the ladder. They had sent him packing but the party was over. Sally's disappearance and Laura's outburst had put a dampener on the evening, and Edith had suggested everyone head home. Fittingly, it had rained all of Saturday and Sunday.

Clare had a paper to prepare, but first she needed a strong cup of tea and a piece of toast. She went downstairs, glancing into the TV room on her way to the kitchen. Honestly, the place was a tip. Rory and Evie just took so much for granted. She noted the discarded cans and juice cartons piled in the wastepaper basket, the empty cereal bowls and spoons on the floor. She would have to tell them both to shape up. She wasn't having a summer like last year, with two big lumps dossing around eating her out of house and home, up all night and sleeping away the days. Rory was home for the rest of the summer now and he needed to find work soon. Tony was firm that there was to be no more freeloading. And for that matter Evie needed to get a job; the end of term was about a week away and she couldn't live on the money she made from babysitting Posy. As for Mikey, pierced and tattooed Mikey, well she hadn't the energy to even go there. Evie had been in at some ungodly hour on Friday, but since Rory was just home and Tony was around for most of the weekend, Clare had decided in the interests of family harmony not to make an issue of it.

The kitchen was another disaster area, so she decided to do a bunk upstairs before Sally came – if she came at all. Clare dismissed the uneasy feeling she had about Sally running off on Friday night. Too much drink had been taken, she reasoned. So what if some old tramp had taken a fancy to Sally? Still, poor Sally had been totally overwhelmed by the incident. Clare had had no luck calling her over the weekend. She was crossing her fingers Sally would show up as if nothing had happened, but she was late, and that was most unlike her. She had kept great time since winning the motorbike.

The *Guardian* was on the table; Clare lifted it and tucked it under her arm. She'd just have a quick flick though it while she ate her toast. Then she'd shower and begin her work.

In a very tidy kitchen on the other side of town, Sally O'Neill sat feeling dejected. She had posted the letter earlier with a first-class stamp, but of course it wouldn't arrive until tomorrow so she was awaiting with trepidation the inevitable phone call from Clare. She had been rehearsing the words in her head all weekend. Her tea had gone cold; she got up and rinsed the cup. It was almost ten o'clock. Maybe she'd take herself out of the house, but somehow she felt unable to move.

Predictably, at ten thirty, the phone rang. It was Clare, of course.

'Ah, Sally, you ran off on Friday, we couldn't believe you'd gone. We got rid of the drunk; he left with no bother at all. Fintan said he's been hanging round before, but he's been told in no uncertain terms . . .' Clare trailed off. 'Sorry for rabbiting on. Are you okay? Are you not coming in?'

'No, I won't be in today.'

'Oh Sally, you're not sick, are you? Don't worry, Rory can just pull his weight. Sure we'll see you on Wednesday. Do you need anything? Is it a tummy bug?'

Clare knew it was nothing of the sort, but she hoped that maybe by going through these formalities she was giving Sally a chance to opt out of a final decision.

'I don't feel myself, Clare.' That was true enough, she didn't. 'I've written you a note.'

'A note? About what?'

Sally didn't answer; there was nothing she could think of to say. She felt wrung out, quite unable to explain.

'You'll get it tomorrow. Sorry, Clare, I have to go.'

She put down the phone dejectedly and decided to take herself into town; there was little point in staying about the house, for she knew she would find it hard to put in the day. Her heart was too heavy.

In the end it was a sort of lost day. She couldn't get her mood up at all. So after a half-hearted wander round the shops, she came back home. Bronagh was lying on the sofa watching daytime TV, *Big Brother* or something. What a waste of time, lying around doing nothing watching other people lying around doing nothing. It couldn't be good for you.

'You're home early.'

Sally nodded agreement.

'Bertha called, she said she'd drop round later.'

'Great, I can't wait. Are you just going to lie there all day?'

'It's my day off; I'm not doing any harm. What's eating you?' Bronagh felt a brief stab of alarm. Maybe Sally had found out about Friday night and Otis. From the little Sally had said about him, Bronagh knew she disliked him. She had heard her give out about what a waster he was, and Sally was rarely unpleasant about anyone in Marlborough Road.

Sally went into the kitchen and decided to wash the windows. She thought maybe a bit of work would liven her up. Sitting about all day just bored her.

As soon as Clare McDonald saw the envelope, she knew at once what the contents of the note would be. Sally had sounded so cold on the phone. After all these years being treated as one of the family, she was going to leave them without so much as a by-your-leave. Good God, she hardly thought they blamed her for the behaviour of some drunken old workman, did she? Did she think they had no soul? It was all too much for Clare. She had had the deadline on her thesis extended twice and was really feeling the strain. Now with the summer in full swing, Rory home, the girls off school next week and Tony still being a selfish bastard about his working hours, all she needed to complete her misery was this — Sally doing a bunk. She wanted to cry. It simply wouldn't do. They would have to persuade her to come back.

Clare went immediately to see Edith; she didn't want to stress Saffron out just yet. Edith had also called Sally and heard a dejected voice on the other end of the phone telling her she wouldn't be back. Edith had persevered and finally Sally told her that she'd accepted another job. Edith wasn't going to let this deter her. Sally must be brought back. She decided to call a residents' meeting for that same evening. Naturally it wouldn't include every household, only those for whom Sally worked full time. And certainly not Laura Nelson, who, Edith felt, had behaved worse than the drunk on Friday. Clare agreed: definitely not Laura. What was eating her? Clare wondered. Did she have some sort of crush on bloody Trevor? Clare wouldn't be in the least surprised. Laura flirted shamelessly with all the men in the lane, but no one had paid much attention to it. Perhaps it was time they did.

At eight o'clock, Clare, Tony (yes, this was an emergency even he understood), Trevor, Saffron and Edith sat round the kitchen table to decide on their next move. The mood couldn't have been more serious if it had been a meeting of the Cabinet. There was little doubt that this was a major crisis. Each household involved had gradually over the years become more and more dependent on Sally. Aside from the implications of finding another cleaner, she would be a hard act to follow. Psychologically they were all used to her cheery, no-nonsense view of life and the affection she had for the children.

Edith had made out an agenda of sorts.

1. Wages: do we pay her enough?
2. Holidays: is two weeks a year plus Christmas enough?
3. Has she been asked to do too much recently?
4. Why did she run off on Friday? Was everyone nice enough to her?
5. What on earth is her new job?

The first question they could answer easily enough: Sally was paid twice the minimum wage by all, and occasional gifts were given as well. As for holidays, they paid her in full for two weeks and Christmas; she rarely went abroad, preferring to visit one of her sisters down south. She had gone to the Canary Islands a year or so ago and had come back declaring they could keep it: the heat had been too much and the beer-swilling fellow holiday-makers had annoyed her from the moment she left Belfast International Airport. As far as the work went, both the amount and the hours were entirely dictated by Sally. There were of course extra beds to change when Edith had a new lodger, and extra dishes when Clare had a dinner party, and of course none of the children was much use at helping, but it had always been thus. There were other issues, such as Lola and Iggy, and Chutney, the Nelsons' macaw, but she had always seemed relaxed if abusive about these pets.

Friday night seemed to hold the key. Who was the drunk?

'Could it have been a workman from number thirty-nine?' Clare suggested. (Patricia Thompson was having her kitchen redone.)

'He seemed to know Sally; he certainly knew her name,' added Tony.

'Maybe it was her ex-husband?' Saffron suggested. 'Sally's sister Eileen told me a few years ago that he was fond of the drink.'

'I thought he lived in England?' Edith said this as if living in England was the equivalent of living in Tierra del Fuego.

'There is fairly free travel between England and here, Edith.' Tony tried to sound good-humoured, but this whole thing was pissing him off. How had they let themselves get so dependent on one person? He liked Sally a lot, and he knew she kept Clare under control – well, relatively – but for that kind of money, surely they could get anyone? He suggested this tentatively. Clare almost exploded at him.

'No, we can't get anyone else. How could we? We trust Sally, you can leave anything lying around; she's discreet; she knows the houses, the children, even the pets, and it would take ages to get someone else into her routine.'

'Maybe if we struggle through the summer, get the two big ones to help a bit more . . .' Tony knew immediately that this sounded limp, and he was right. Clare's voice shot up about twenty decibels.

'I have agreed to an extra class next year because Anna will be at big school. At least with Sally I know that two and sometimes three mornings a week the house will be manageable.'

'Your house is always lovely, Clare. I mean, compared to mine,' Saffron volunteered, feeling sorry for Tony.

But Clare was off on a tangent. 'This is what happens, I suppose, when we take on too much and need other women to help us out.'

'Clare, your mother has had domestic help all her life.' Tony couldn't ever understand Clare's issues. The way he saw it was Sally did a job, they paid her, end of story.

'Yes, but my father was a GP, she had to have help. She needed to be available to answer the phone.'

'Precisely! That is why you are more entitled to domestic help than your mother.' Edith sounded brisk. 'I don't think we have time to agonise over the philosophical aspects, Clare, just the reality of the situation. We need to get Sally back.'

But Clare was in self-flagellation mode. 'Maybe I should have been friendlier to Sally, treated her more as an equal, but that's so unrealistic; in the final analysis, I'm her employer. Although I do have issues about another woman working for me, I can't just stop work. Aside from the money being useful, I couldn't stand being at home all day. I mean, when Anna was small, I thought I would be found suffocated in a pot of home-made playdoh.'

'I quite enjoy making playdoh,' Saffron chipped in, 'although Sally hates the way it sticks to the pots.'

'Ladies, could we forget about the playdoh and get back to the business in hand?' Working for the Civil Service as he did, Tony had got fed up with meetings rambling on for hours with no conclusion.

'Yes, we really need to get her back again. Even with the two older ones at school, it's going to be hard.'

Edith hadn't pleaded her own circumstances – her house was more ordered than the other two – but she felt that at this particular juncture in her life, she should be doing less not more. If Sally left, she would have to stop the lodgers, and then what would there be to do? The house was far too big for one. And there was the other matter of her health, though she was staying positive on that. It would be very lonely without Sally. Her neighbours were lovely, but they all had such busy lives and such big families.

Tony surveyed them all.

'I think a delegation over to her house is in order. No point in sitting here chatting.'

'Don't be ridiculous, Tony. We can't just barge over there and demand an explanation.'

'She seems very fond of Fintan; perhaps we could ask him to contact her,' Edith suggested. She thought Clare was very snappy with Tony; all he had done was made a suggestion.

'Good idea, Edith.' Trevor nodded enthusiastically, and downed a second glass of Tony's wine, even though the others were all pointedly on tea.

Edith had thought things over carefully. She had seen Sally develop a thing about Fintan over the past few weeks. It seemed an unlikely match, an opera singer and a cleaner, but Sally had a quick mind; she didn't have to stay a cleaner. Edith Black suddenly saw herself in the role of fairy godmother, but she wouldn't rush things. She would bide her time.

The consensus was to leave things for a week; they could blunder on without her. There was always the hope that she would hate her new job – or even miss them. All fingers were crossed.

16

Evie had just a few days to hand in her history project. It would form a large part of her mark. She needed one further interview for her Blitz on Belfast section. Clare had suggested Miss Black, who was apparently a small child during the Blitz and therefore qualified as an 'actual witness'. Hundreds of people had been killed then, because of the Harland and Wolff shipyard, which the Germans were trying to bomb. Evie was bored with it all; why didn't people just get over it? It seemed to keep them permanently annoyed. Mikey had the right idea, leaving school and working in a bar. Her own parents were obsessed with education. Clare was even doing a PhD. Imagine, Evie thought, at *her* age. It was totally ridiculous. What was the point of knowing loads of stuff about Yeats and Maud Gonne? Who cared?

She went downstairs and into the kitchen. Clare was in there, sighing a lot and cleaning in a way she hoped everyone would notice. She'd been in a foul mood since Sally left. Evie was really sorry Sally wasn't coming back. Sally was like part of the family, she'd been coming here so long. Evie hoped she might change her mind. She would ask Bronagh when she went in to get her highlights done.

'Mum, would you ask Miss Black if she would tell me what it was like living in the Blitz?'

'Honestly, Evie!' Clare snapped. 'I thought that project was meant to be handed in months ago!'

'Yes it was, but I got an extension.'

'On what grounds? That you were too busy going out drinking to do it?'

'God, Mum, you are so tuned to Moan FM these days.'

'What?'

'Just moaning twenty-four seven.'

'Well maybe if I had someone to help out in the house a bit more, and your father paid us an occasional visit instead of living in that bloody office of his, I might not have quite so much to moan about.'

'Whatever. Are you going to ask Miss Black for me?'

'No, go and ask her yourself! I'm busy cleaning this filthy house.'

Evie stormed out of the back door.

One didn't just stroll into Miss Black's; her back door wasn't always open anyway. Evie was about to go round the front, but then she noticed Miss Black in her garden. She was kneeling on a little pad, weeding. Her garden was easily the nicest in the lane. It had neat flowerbeds either side of the lawn and they were a riot of colour at the moment. There were clusters of tiny deep blue flowers planted along the border, and taller flowers of different colours, and beautiful velvet crimson roses like something off a chocolate box. A little path made from hexagonal stones ran down the middle of the lawn. The small conservatory was furnished with iron garden furniture and of course the famous rococo barbecue was tucked away in a corner at the back. It was the only garden the children avoided; that was why it still looked good, Evie thought as she tiptoed up the paving stones.

'The flowers look absolutely gorgeous, Miss Black.'

'Ah, Evie! Thank you so much. I am glad you appreciate them. They are a joy at this time of year. It's such hard work keeping them weed-free. Now, can I do something for you?' Edith knew Evie was hardly there to talk about flowers.

'I'm doing a project on the Second World War, on the Blitz on Belfast, and Mum thought you might have some stories I could write down.'

Edith put down her trowel and regarded Evie.

'I was only a babe in arms then, Evie, you understand.'

'Oh. I know that, Miss Black, it's just our teacher told us we'd get more marks for reality stories. Mum's Auntie Mary told me some things, but she's way older than you, almost eighty.'

'I see. I'll bring some lemon barley out to the conservatory and we can talk there. You have a pen and paper? Good.'

To Evie's satisfaction, Edith Black told her a long story about being carried up Divis Mountain as a small child to escape the air raids and how she was dressed in a little suit called a siren suit. She also told how her father had had a cousin killed and his body had been laid out in the Falls Baths with hundreds of others. Edith's father had to go along to identify him. She seemed to enjoy talking about it all and Evie didn't have to pretend to be interested. It was a great story. She wrote it down verbatim. Maybe history didn't have to be boring after all.

When Miss Black had finished, Evie carried the tray back into the kitchen for her. Otis was there, sitting at the table. Even with all his wild-looking red hair cut off, he was still a minger; a ginger minger. Evie smiled at the idea.

'Oh, hullo, Evie,' he said, mistaking her smile for a friendly one. 'Great craic on Friday, sorry you couldn't stay till the end.'

'No, I had to be home, my mum throws a psych if I'm back late.'

116

'I see your wee friend Bronagh left early.'

Evie could tell Otis was trying to sound dead casual. He obviously fancied Bronagh, though he was really old. He could be her da, or not far off it.

'Oh yes, the other girl, Tiffany, was feeling sick. She had to go.'

He looked pleased at that.

'Well if you see her, tell her we might be opening for some of the big bands at Oxegen. She might like to come.'

Evie was impressed. Oxegen was a great rock gig, held each year outside Dublin in Kildare. She wondered if he was really going to open for a big name or if he was only boasting. She had wanted to go but her mum had said she couldn't go to a concert away from home unless she was with Rory. Maybe her mum might let her go with Bronagh. *She* was eighteen, after all.

'I'll let her know. I may be seeing her next week.'

'You wouldn't have her mobile number, would you?'

'Sorry, no. You could always call her at work.'

Bertha rapped on Sally's window about six o'clock while Sally was finishing her meal. Bronagh had bolted hers down and was upstairs getting ready to go out. Sally opened the back door with a heavy heart.

'Well, Sally, only a few days now till you are a Maid to Order.' Bertha beamed at her with satisfaction.

'I thought the whole point was that I'd not be a maid, I'd be a supervisor.'

'No, you are deputy supervisor, I'm the chief supervisor.'

'There's no cleaning involved, is there? Have you been cleaning?'

'Ach, a wee bit, you know. Maybeth says it's just till we have the full quota of staff. But you needn't worry. You go to a different house every day, and the people aren't even there.'

'Maybeth told me I'd be driving round inspecting the cleaners and making sure they finish the typed lists.' Maids to Order had job sheets that itemised the various tasks required in each household.

'You don't seem to be looking forward to it much,' Bertha ventured.

'No, I'm not. I wish to God I hadn't agreed to take the job.'

'Well you can hardly back out now. I mean, how would that look for me? After me getting you the job, doing you the favour.'

Sally didn't rise to the bait; you could never win an argument with Bertha anyway. She was far too thick. There was no point in changing her mind now and going back to Marlborough Road. What was done was done, and she'd have to live with it.

Miss Black had not had an opportunity to talk to Fintan about Sally till now. Fintan had been preoccupied. *Tosca* had opened on Tuesday, to extremely flattering reviews in his case. He had three performances this week. Possibly he hadn't even realised that Sally had not been in to work.

Edith waited up especially for him; she was sure he would oblige and use his winsome charm on Sally. It was almost midnight when he got in. He was surprised to see her.

'Ah, Edith, you're up late.'

'Yes, I wanted a chat, and besides, I haven't been sleeping well recently so there's no point in my going to bed to toss and turn. How did the show go tonight?'

'We had a great audience, very appreciative, gave us a standing ovation. It should be in good shape by next week.'

Edith planned to go the following week. Her friend Isabelle was going to accompany her. Fintan sat down on the chair opposite her.

'So what did you want to chat about?' He forced himself

118

to sound bright. He hoped it wasn't anything to do with the hospital appointment card. He was tired. 'Is something wrong?'

'I'm afraid Sally is not coming back.'

'Oh no! I had a feeling that would be the case. How awful for everyone. I have tried to phone her. Are you quite sure?'

'Yes indeed, she wrote a letter to Clare – well, a note really – to say that she has another job.'

'Has anyone tried to talk her out of leaving?'

'Well that's why I wanted to talk to you, Fintan.' Edith stood up and moved to the sideboard. 'I was just going to have a small whisky. Would you join me?'

She poured two malt whiskies and sat down again. She looked at Fintan intently.

'We had a meeting, and all of us felt that you were the very person who would be able to talk her into returning.'

Fintan took a gulp of the whisky.

'So – no pressure, then,' he said.

'Well,' Edith said with a beseeching smile, 'it's just that you have made such an impression on her, and of course you are the perfect mediator, not being in either camp.'

'I can try,' Fintan said, not sounding convinced.

'Isn't she coming to a performance next week? Perhaps you could have a drink afterwards.'

They sipped the whisky quietly. Edith liked to drink good Scotch malt, and always decanted it and served it in crystal glasses. One had to have standards, after all.

Fintan was sad that Sally had left. The timing was dreadful, what with the opening night and that. He had meant to call her, but hadn't. But he also thought Sally needed to have some space, and he remembered what she had said about wanting more for herself than just cleaning. He had grown enormously fond of her in the short time he'd stayed at Marlborough Road. She was refreshing and down to earth, and he liked her lack of sophistication. The world of opera

119

could be bitchy and highly competitive. As in many other professions, the petty jealousies got to him now and again. He'd call Sally tomorrow.

17

Sally had been down to the offices of Maids to Order and had had a very unsatisfactory meeting with Miss Maybeth Weston. It seemed Bertha was right on the nail. Sally would be expected both to clean and to supervise. Not at all what she had been told when Maybeth had first offered her the job. She pointed this out to Maybeth, who was busy trying to deflect her questions by offering her three peach jump suits in 'medium'. They looked like rejects from Guantanamo.

'Well, honey, this is just a temporary situation. I sincerely hope that eventually you will be touring our client dwellings and checking they are cleaned to perfection, but until we have enough recruits, we would hope, in the interests of company harmony, you would agree to do some of the cleaning. You will still be paid at the rate we agreed.'

Sally left in a rage. She would take the job and meanwhile look for another. What choice did she have? She felt she had queered her pitch regarding Marlborough Road. She just didn't have the nerve to crawl back there and say she had made a mistake. She rode home on the bike feeling hollow and stupid. It wasn't the one incident with Charlie that had forced her decision. It was the certain knowledge that he would keep coming back. After they had split up, he used to come to the house each time he was drunk (every night) and make a scene. He'd wait for her outside her work as well, making a holy show of himself. She had had to take out a restraining order. It only stopped when he'd gone to jail.

Fintan finally got hold of Sally. She was taken aback to hear from him. He had never called her before. It took her a minute to find her voice.

'Is everything okay?'

'Well, apart from the fact that you've left us.'

'Ach, Fintan, it's too complicated . . .' She trailed off. What was there to say really?

'I have some good news and some bad news . . . Which first?'

'Good.'

'Well, you've won Evie's ballot – the trip to Crete, remember? The bad news is it was the ticket with both our names on, but I'd really love you to have it. I'm not sure when I would be free to go, and I know you'd love Crete. I've been there twice, it's wonderful.'

Sally couldn't think of a single thing to say. She was still stunned by the fact that he'd called. Eventually she managed 'How are they all?'

'Well, no point in lying. Everyone is very upset, and hoping fervently they can persuade you to change your mind.'

'I can't now, Fintan, even if I wanted to. I'm too far into this other thing, and I couldn't face them all.'

'Is it because of the drunken fellow?'

'Well I suppose that was why I left on Friday, and now I feel I can't go back. But before that . . . I was beginning to feel taken for granted. And I had been offered the other job

– the supervisor one. So I . . . I couldn't face explaining all about him to everyone.'

'You know him?'

There was no point in pretending. 'Yes, he's my ex-husband; we've been separated for ten years.' There, she had said it out loud. What would Fintan think of her now?

'I had a feeling it was. It was patently a good idea to get rid of him. Has he bothered you since?'

'No, and I'm hoping he'll go away off to London soon.' She hoped Fintan would assume Charlie was just over on holiday or something. She couldn't face telling him every single detail just now.

'It must have been extremely upsetting for you, but you must understand that no one here blames *you* for his behaviour.'

Sally said nothing. She was trying to stay composed.

'I think they all thought it was a bit of a laugh really.'

'I didn't.' Sally sounded on the verge of tears.

'Of course not. I'm sorry, Sally; I didn't mean to upset you.'

'You haven't.'

There was another awkward pause.

'Look, if the new job doesn't work out . . .' He trailed off.

'Fintan, please don't tell them just yet that it was my ex-husband. I would be mortified. I never lied about him, but I never really told them about him either.'

'Don't worry, I won't.'

They chatted aimlessly for a few more minutes. Fintan asked if she still intended to use her tickets for the opera. She said she did, but he had a strong feeling she would either not show up, or cancel at the last minute. He hung up feeling he had achieved little.

Edith arrived home exhausted from Ellen's and found Fintan ensconced in the kitchen. He was cooking something that smelled delicious.

'Dinner will be ready in half an hour; why don't you go and have a nice restful bath?'

She didn't need to be told again. She practically ran upstairs. Fintan's interest in her health touched her, and she realised that the only other soul who'd shown so much concern for her had been Sally. If truth be told, she thought ruefully, she had not appreciated her enough when she had had her.

Fintan had been shopping earlier. There was a good farmers' market in Belfast, and an excellent Asian supermarket, both within walking distance. He decided to try a bouillabaisse. He pointedly did not include Otis in the pot. Otis never seemed to replace any of the food he ate. He was out somewhere, and judging by the smell permeating the kitchen, he had fried up half the contents of the fridge before he left.

When she came downstairs, Edith's sole task was to lay the table in the dining room. This she did with great relish, giving Fintan the history of the cutlery and the napkins and all her pet theories on entertaining. The meal was superb. He had bought some good bottles of Meursault, which he had chilled, and after a few glasses Edith was behaving as if she was on a date.

'Well, Fintan, this is so lovely, we could be in a five star restaurant. What a delicious meal.'

'I enjoy cooking, and I enjoy the company of beautiful women.'

Edith positively dimpled at this, but Fintan wasn't lying. She did look lovely. She was contented, happy and eating good food. He was so glad he had made the effort. He resolved to cook for her again soon.

'You know, Fintan, I haven't felt so relaxed in months.'

'Well that's hardly surprising, Edith, you've had a lot to bear . . . what with Ellen and all that.'

'Yes, poor Ellen. Still, Fintan, she did enjoy her widowhood.'

'Oh?' Fintan was intrigued. Had Edith had too much to drink? 'Enjoyed her widowhood?' he echoed.

'Oh yes, she had had such a happy marriage too; she and Derek seemed so close, so we were all surprised. Most people expected her to go to bits.'

'But she didn't?'

'No, she coped remarkably well. She gave up bridge, which she claimed she had never liked. She took to playing golf, and most surprisingly she changed their very comfortable car for a snazzy sports car of all things.'

'I think I like the sound of Ellen.'

'Yes, she would like you too, Fintan. She loves handsome men. I even heard a few rumours of close friendships in her last few years of good health.'

'Good for her!' Fintan roared approvingly.

Edith smiled. 'Yes, I was a bit taken aback at the time, but I must say I'm glad now. We never know the moment, do we, Fintan?'

18

Saffron was overwhelmed. She had no one to turn to with her problems. Until recently she had regarded Trevor as her best friend. She reflected sombrely on Shakespeare's apt words: 'When sorrows come, they come not single spies, But in battalions.'

Two more babies, *two more babies*, what a terrifying thought. She hoped they couldn't feel her panic in the womb. It might transmit bad vibes to the poor darlings, and she didn't want them coming out nervous wrecks. And Trevor? She hadn't expected him to be thrilled, but whilst being reverential enough to her, and coming home dutifully on time, he had been flat and unenthusiastic. She thought he had seemed overwhelmed by the pregnancy. He wasn't home yet, and he'd been out late last night as well. He had some sort of business engagement – a legal meeting. It had taken her ages to get Posy to bed and read her story. When she finally got into bed herself, she was wrecked and tearful.

If Sally had still been around, she could have talked it over with her. She felt sad; she missed Sally shockingly. Marlborough Road was not the same without her. Posy missed her too –

she had asked about her several times last week – and Simon had even offered to give Iggy to the zoo if it would help bring Sally back to them. She shifted in bed, trying to get comfortable. She was alarmed at how fast her tummy was growing. It seemed that now, their existence having been acknowledged, the twins had decided to stretch and push out. She was also hungry all the time, and far too exhausted to cook. They had all become rather rather dependent on pizza and even, heaven forbid, chips and vegeburgers for the children. This was making her feel incredibly guilty and inadequate. Posy had been exceptionally difficult all week, as if she realised that her days as the baby were numbered, and Evie had been so busy with her school project she hadn't been available to help out. Saffron, who was normally quiet and placid and answered all her children's questions with infinite patience, had taken to fending them off with the first answer that came into her head. She allowed them virtually unlimited access to the TV. Neither of the children could quite believe their luck, and Simon had asked her a few times if she was feeling well.

It was well after midnight when Trevor came in. He smelled of drink, so she lay and pretended to be asleep. Two minutes after he got into bed, he began snoring loudly. Saffron realised that it had been some weeks since he had been amorous with her. Perhaps her pregnancy was putting him off, though it hadn't with the other two; quite the opposite, in fact. Maybe she should make the first move? She snuggled closer to him and nuzzled the back of his neck. Trevor was a light sleeper and normally he would have responded to her at once, but he muttered and moved away, and Saffron realised that he was simply pretending to be asleep. She felt hurt and rejected. What was happening to them?

19

Sally left for her new job on Monday morning with a heavy heart. Maybeth was effusive in her greetings, then handed her a checklist, and three addresses. One of them, the last on the list, had one maid short. Since they were only being paid for three hours, Sally might need to give the woman a hand, but hopefully when they had the full quota of staff this wouldn't be usual. Sally set off on her bike, taking careful note of the mileage; she was to be reimbursed for that. The first two houses were okay. She didn't have much to do, just point out a few things to the maids that needed redoing, and show one of them how to polish the big stainless-steel fridge with a drop of baby oil on kitchen roll to make it shine. She left her to finish the job even though she was tempted to do it herself because the woman was going so slowly. Two speeds she had: dead slow and stop.

The third job was up the Malone Road. Sally experienced a bit of a pang as she drove past her usual turn-off for Marlborough Road, but that was natural enough, she reckoned. She needed to get over herself, as Evie was fond of telling Clare. The house was in a gated street. It was a massive double-fronted Victorian with a long driveway. A large black shiny 4x4 was parked outside the front door. Sally smiled as she remembered Clare and Saffron's rants about what they would like to do to the sort of people who drove these destroyers of the planet. She rang the doorbell. The owner of the house was home. She opened the door to Sally and swept her with a supercilious glance. She was a young woman in her early thirties, very made up, Barbie doll type. She was wearing perfectly coordinated gym gear.

'I'm Sally O'Neill from Maids to Order,' Sally said.

'Oh, and about time. I take it you are the other cleaner? I have been on the phone twice to Miss Weston,' she snapped.

Sally opened her mouth to reply but the words didn't come; the woman's rudeness had taken her breath away. She indicated for Sally to follow her into the kitchen.

'I usually have two women come, and I'd need three today to make up for this one.' She nodded towards a shapeless woman of about fifty who was slowly drying a bowl at the sink. 'This is Molly; she has been doing the kitchen for the last two hours. I think you are *almost* finished, aren't you?' she said acidly.

Sally smiled at the cleaner, and said to the young woman, 'Sorry, I didn't catch your name?'

'I'm Rosamund Henderson; I prefer it if you call me *Mrs* Henderson,' she said abruptly. 'Can you follow me? I need to show you the bedrooms. I want you to change the beds and vacuum and dust. This way, please.'

Sally followed her up a large carpeted central staircase. Paintings adorned the walls. It was painted all soft pastels. It was obvious no money had been spared in the decoration. Mrs Henderson opened the door into what was obviously the master bedroom. She nodded towards a door leading off it.

'This is the en suite, it needs cleaning, and then you can hoover and dust the room and change the bed.' The fresh bed linen was sitting in a neat pile on the bed. 'The dirty linen goes in this basket and is taken straight down to the laundry room off the kitchen.'

'Cleaning materials?' Sally kept her voice sharp to match, but inside she was churning with humiliation.

'Downstairs in the utility room off the kitchen.'

'Vacuum cleaner?'

'We have central vacuuming, so you just plug this hose into the wall.' She indicated a long tube lying on the ground, and a flap thing on the wall. 'I am already late for the gym.' She glanced at her watch. 'I'll be back in two hours. Ask Molly if you need anything. I've already explained everything to her more than once. With luck maybe some of it has gone in.' And off she swept.

Sally heard the front door slam and the car start up. She went back down to the kitchen; Molly was putting away the bowls. She smiled half-heartedly at Sally. She looked dejected.

'I was here last week as well. She's full of herself, that one. Nothing to do all day, you see, the kids at school and the husband out making the money. It would make you sick. The last firm I worked for seemed to specialise in cleaning houses for grumpy wee girls who married up. They've a lot to learn as far as manners go.'

'You can say that again. I'll not be talked to like that by the likes of her. I'll finish whatever there is to be done today and that's it. I shouldn't even be cleaning, it's not part of my job description. I am normally a supervisor.'

'Oh? Do you know Bertha, then? I worked with her last week; isn't she a supervisor too?'

Sally nodded, stung. But Molly smiled at her, she wasn't being sarky.

'Sure just give me a shout if you need me. I'll be in the drawing room. She wants that big mirror cleaned; I may get on with it.'

'Well I suppose I'd better get upstairs and get the beds changed.'

130

Sally didn't know why she had been so pathetic as to drop the supervisor number on poor Molly. It had only made her feel like a sad git. And it was already only too obvious that her big, important title was meaningless anyway.

Otis had called Bronagh at work and she had agreed to go to QFT, the university film theatre, with him. She wasn't sure why she had agreed, and she certainly hadn't told anyone. The film was French, with subtitles. He said he really rated the director.

The foyer was buzzing, with lots of people talking at each other at the tops of their voices. They all appeared to know each other, or were pretending to at any rate. Bronagh looked nervously around for Otis. She had told him she would meet him here. She quickly spotted him standing at the bar. He was hard to miss; that carrot-coloured hair was like a beacon. He was with a couple of people around his own age. Taking a deep breath, she walked over to them. Otis appeared delighted to see her and introduced her to his friends. She spoke as quietly as she could in case her accent was too broad Belfast. She could tell they were giving her the once-over, wondering what she was doing with Otis. Hardly surprising; she was wondering herself. He asked her what she would like to drink, and she was about to ask for a vodka and Red Bull but then saw they were drinking wine, so she had a wee bottle of white wine. It was very strong and slightly sour, but she drank it anyway.

The film was okay, actually. She could follow it easily enough. Afterwards they had another drink in the bar. Otis chatted easily; you'd have thought he owned the place, he was that full of himself, but he was very nice to her, and kept patting her arm, in a fatherly way really. For a moment Bronagh wished she'd had a daddy when she was growing up, not some drunken jailbird who'd ruined her mother's life.

★

Sally came home to an empty house. Bronagh was out again tonight with some friends. She watched something useless on TV and tried not to think about the job. Maybe it had just been a bad day. It couldn't be like that all the time. She wondered where Bronagh was. She didn't usually go out much during the week. She had been acting a bit secretive recently, giving Sally evasive answers as to where she had been. Last night she had snapped off her mobile phone when Sally had come into her room.

'Bye! See you tomorrow night, then.'

'Who was that?' Sally had asked her. 'Tiffany?'

'Mmmm, yeah.'

'Where are you off to then, love? Anywhere nice?'

'Oh, nowhere special.'

Sally knew she was lying, and wondered why. But then she worked it out. Bronagh was off to see her father and didn't want to upset her feelings by letting her know. It did hurt, but part of her also understood. She had done her best for the child while she was growing up. Nonetheless, the cliché remained: girls always loved their daddies. When Bronagh had been a little girl she was the apple of Charlie's eye. She was almost eight when he was put away, and Sally had shielded her from his bad behaviour so that she would only remember the good times.

She lay awake waiting for Bronagh to come in. She didn't mean to be neurotic; she couldn't help herself. Finally she heard the front door.

'Bronagh, is that you, love? I'm still awake.'

Bronagh came into the bedroom. She looked flushed.

'Well, were you out anywhere nice?'

'No, I just went to the pictures with Tiffany.'

'Oh? What to see?'

'It was a French film; about school kids in a wee country village – it had subtitles.'

'And what did Tiffany make of that?'

'She wasn't that fussed on it, but I liked it. Mum, I'm really tired. I'll see you in the morning.' And she kissed Sally good night and went into her own bedroom.

Imagine her making up she was at a French film, and with Tiffany. As if! She was lying, of course. Tiffany had called the house looking for Bronagh at nine o'clock. She told Sally that Bronagh wasn't answering her mobile. Sally was convinced she'd been with her father. She wondered where Charlie had taken her. If it was anywhere local, Eileen would let her know. Sally normally wouldn't have minded, she would even have expected it, but coming on top of her new job, it was a bit much to take. She had looked after Bronagh alone all these years. Why should Charlie O'Neill just waltz back into their lives and ruin everything?

The only crack of light amidst the clouds in the following days was a text from Fintan asking how things were going. On impulse when she got home one evening she dialled Miss Black's. Her thoughts were in turmoil; she wasn't sure what she would say if Edith answered. As it happened, Otis did, and didn't recognise her voice.

'Is Fintan there?'

'Sure, man, hold on a sec.'

Fintan didn't have a performance every night. He had explained that the opera was in repertoire; it was running with *La Rondine* and he wasn't in both.

'Hello?'

'It's Sally.'

'Oh Sally, how lovely to hear from you. How are things?'

'I'm grand. I was wondering how Edith is?'

'Well, not any worse, but still looking frail. She misses you, of course. How is the new job going?'

'Ach, Fintan, I have to give this other thing a try. Sure they are probably too mad at me to want me back.'

'I should think they'd leap at the chance. Have you made your mind up about the opera?'

Sally didn't answer at once.

'You are coming?'

'Yes, if that's still okay.'

'Of course. The tickets will be in your name. Look, why don't we meet afterwards for a drink? Say the Crown bar?'

'Are you sure? Have you nobody else you need to see?'

'Absolutely not. It takes me ten minutes or so after the curtain comes down. I'll look forward to it.'

And before Sally could protest, he said his goodbyes and hung up.

20

Charlie O'Neill had been seething with indignation for over a week. He kept having action replays of the scene over at Sally's work. The indignity of falling over in the tree house, and then those patronising shits telling him to go quietly or they'd call the police . . . Who did they think they were? He knew what they were all right: smug bastards, with their fancy houses and posh voices.

He had been in the pub having a few drinks when the urge to see Sally had overwhelmed him. He had been trying to have a chat with her since he got out. Fuelled by Dutch courage, he had taken a cab to Marlborough Road. Bertha had told him she was at some fancy do over there. He had finished his six pack sitting in the tree house. From where he was, he could hear all of them high-falutin' types chatting away. They were laughing at the tops of their voices. And Sally was there too, right in the thick of it. He could still pick out her voice. All he wanted was a wee chat with his brown-eyed girl. That wasn't a lot to ask. Sally could at least have heard him out. He was hardly going to do her any harm.

It had been the same with Bronagh, his own wee daughter.

She wouldn't talk to him that day outside the hairdresser's. It was hurtful. You'd think she would love her daddy; all girls were supposed to love their daddies. Sally had probably poisoned her mind. He wasn't a bad man. He wasn't a real criminal; he'd just been unlucky all those years ago, when Bud Rafferty had had the bright idea of robbing the bookie's. He had been against the idea at first, but then Bud and Bottler McCann had talked him round. Why was he broke in the first place? Because he had spent most of his money in the bookie's — well, a bit in the pub too, but mainly the bookie's, and sure didn't everyone know that the races were rigged in their favour? For God's sake, you couldn't win if you tried. So it wasn't really robbing; all he and the lads were doing was getting their own money back. If it hadn't been for Bud bringing the bloody gun and that eejit of a teller having a weak heart and dying a week later, they'd all have been out in three years. And Sally should have known the entire gig was just to get a better life for her and the wee girl. He would have taken them all off to Disney World. That had been his dream, but try telling Sally that. Sure you couldn't win with women. You were on a hiding to nowhere. Everything you did annoyed them. He would take a run round to Sally's house now, he thought, and try to have a reasonable wee chat with her, make her see sense.

Bronagh was sitting in on her own; not that she'd be out tonight anyway. Tiffany usually called round most nights, but Tiffany had fallen out with her because she wouldn't admit she'd seen Otis again. Her ma had gone up to her granny and granda's. She usually made dinner for them on Tuesdays.

Tiffany would get over it. Bronagh had no intention of giving her all the dirt on Otis; she'd probably think Bronagh was off her head going out with the likes of him. 'That Mick Hucknall lookalike', Tiffany called him. But strangely, Bronagh had enjoyed the few dates she had been on with Otis. The guys she usually went out with had only one thing on their minds, but Otis hadn't tried to lay a hand on her yet, which was just as well. She didn't feel *that* way about him.

The doorbell rang. Probably Tiffany had decided it wasn't worth falling out over a man; their rows never lasted long. She opened the door and there stood Charlie.

'What do *you* want?'

'Ach, Bronagh love, that's no way to speak to your poor oul' daddy, now is it?' Charlie gave her his version of a winning smile. 'Is your mammy in?'

'No, she's up at my granny's.'

'Are you not going to ask me in?'

'All right, but you can't stay, my ma will be back at nine.'

Charlie followed her in, taking a good look round him as he did so.

'She has the place lovely, hasn't she? Very posh, looks like one of them places you'd see on the telly.'

'Hardly, it's a housing executive house.'

'What about a wee cup of tea?'

Bronagh hesitated, and then said, 'No, I don't think so.'

'Ach, love, don't be so hard on me.'

'Well okay then, but you'd better be quick. I don't want Mammy coming in on us.'

Bronagh pushed the button on the kettle and chucked a tea bag into a mug. She didn't ask Charlie to sit down, but he perched on one of the kitchen chairs anyway. He stared hard at her, and then when she met his glance looked away.

'You're looking lovely, Bronagh – honestly, you've turned into a gorgeous girl. I missed you when I was . . .' he looked awkward as he tried to find the right words, 'a guest of Queen Lizzie. I'd have loved the odd visit.'

'Well you should have thought about that before you robbed the bookie's. It wasn't easy for us, you know, on our own all those years, and Mammy working all the hours God sends.'

Bronagh glared at him. She was finding this very upsetting. But Charlie didn't respond; he just looked at her like he was going to cry. It was hard to resist his pleading look.

'I hear you're doing great at the hairdressing.'

'It's going okay.'

'You'll be opening your own salon next, what?'

'Aye, right. Where would I get the money for that?'

'Well maybe when I get myself settled, and get a wee job, I could help you out.'

'I can't wait.' She had recovered herself somewhat. 'Look you'd better finish your tea; my mammy will be back soon.'

'Can I see you again, love? Please?'

'I don't know . . .' She was about to say 'Daddy', but the word wouldn't come out. She walked to the door and opened it, and dejectedly Charlie left.

Bronagh was shaking. She wished she smoked, but Sally had done a good job on her. She had found her with cigarettes when she was thirteen, and had made her smoke an entire packet. It had put her off for life.

She couldn't get herself together after Charlie left. She felt so torn. She had forced herself to be cold and cruel, while a part of her badly wanted to hug him. She had felt so sorry for him tonight. He seemed such a lost soul. He was pale and a bit overweight, but you could still tell he'd once been a good-looking man. It was easier to hate your father when you didn't have to look into his eyes and do it.

When Sally came back in later, Bronagh didn't mention that Charlie had called round. Her mammy had enough to cope with. She looked tired and drawn. She told Bronagh that she was off to the opera next week, and was going to bring Eileen along for company.

'I hope she behaves herself.'

'You hope! How do you think I feel?'

'Why did you ask her then?'

'I had no one to go with, so I mentioned it to her. She wasn't keen at first, till she found out the tickets were free.'

To Sally's surprise, Bronagh said, 'I'll go with you.'

'You? To the opera? That's not like you.'

'What do you mean, not like me?'

'You know what I mean, love. You've never shown any interest in opera.'

'Neither have you, and I'm sure my auntie Eileen wouldn't know what opera was if it bit her in the neck.' She stopped and looked at Sally pointedly. 'What's wrong? Do you not want to take me?'

'Don't be silly, I'd love you to come. Sure you know our Eileen does my head in. I just didn't think it would be your cup of tea. It'll be great. I'm dying to hear Fintan sing, and he says it's one of the easier operas and has titles in English above the stage so we'll be able to understand it all.'

So it was settled. Bronagh would come to *Tosca*. Sally thought it was a lovely gesture on her daughter's part. She felt a lot cheerier about the trip to the opera now; she rarely went out anywhere with Bronagh these days. Maybe she'd buy something new to wear; she could always check with Clare how people dressed. And then she remembered: she couldn't ask Clare any more; she'd just have to guess.

21

The curtain came down and the audience rose as one to cheer. Bronagh and Sally were sitting in the front row of the dress circle and had had a great view of the whole show. Sally had forgotten completely her insecurities about her dress, and even Bronagh, who had been slightly fidgety at first, had been carried away by the whole drama. Fintan was right: the words had appeared along the top of the stage and had been ridiculously easy to follow. As for Fintan . . . Oh, his voice, what a beautiful voice he had, and how tortured he had seemed. Sally's heart was in her mouth listening to him. He sang like an angel, or how Sally supposed an angel would sing if given the chance. She couldn't remember feeling emotion of this sort before. She had a lump in her throat and the tears started when she heard the screams of him being tortured. And that awful twist at the end just as it looked like they could be together, when the awful Scarpia tricked Tosca with live bullets, and she loved Mario so much she leapt to her death. It was so romantic. Sally had been thrilled; yes, that was the word, thrilled.

At the first interval they had sat on, although most of the audience had made their way out to the bar, but then there was a second interval and so they got up to stretch their legs. Bronagh had bought them ice creams; the queue for the bar was ridiculous.

'I think you have to order drinks for the interval and then it's left on one of them wee shelves with your name on it.'

'Oh,' Sally said, impressed that Bronagh knew that; she didn't ask how. She just ate her ice cream and they made sure to get back to their seats as soon as the bell went. She had caught a glimpse of Miss Black and her silly old friend Isabelle coming out of the bar, and she wasn't ready to see her.

Bronagh agreed to go over to the Crown with her and leave the minute Fintan arrived. She had never met him, because he hadn't got around to using his voucher, preferring to leave his hair long for the show. The Crown bar was jammed full; it tended to be when there was a good show on at the opera house, and they were unsure where to sit. Suddenly Bronagh saw Otis sitting in one of the snugs, chatting earnestly with a couple of his mates. Her face paled, but luckily he hadn't seen her; she needed to get out fast.

'Mum, I feel a bit faint. Can we wait outside?'

Sally agreed – it was stuffy and noisy anyway – and they stood in Great Victoria Street and waited for Fintan. He wasn't long in coming. Sally made the introductions. He was most polite to Bronagh and delighted that she had enjoyed his performance so much. He was very modest about it, as Sally would have expected.

Sally didn't feel at all like going back into the Crown, so she said to Fintan, 'It's bunged in there; would you mind if we went somewhere else?'

He didn't mind at all; he always thought the place too smoky, and bad for his throat. They decided to walk to a wine bar round the corner, and after telling him once more how good she thought he had been and thanking him for the tickets, Bronagh made her excuses and left.

141

Fintan went up to the bar and came back with two glasses of white wine. He sat beside Sally and took a sip and smiled at her. He had just the slightest trace of eyeliner round his lashes – he obviously hadn't removed his make-up properly – but Sally thought it made him look even more appealing.

'It's so good to see you, Sally.'

She shifted in her seat. 'It's nice to see you too. I loved the opera. I didn't think I'd enjoy it so much.' She hoped she didn't sound too gushing.

'I'm so glad. It's a good one to start with. Now tell me all about the new job. How's it going? Nice people?'

Sally immediately thought of Rosamund from the big house. She wished the bitch could walk in and see Sally O'Neill now, sitting with the star of *Tosca*. She'd be sorry she'd treated her like dirt. She recollected herself. Fintan was waiting for an answer.

'Not nice people, to be honest, but I'm getting into the way of it. It's nothing like Marlborough Road. I think a lot of the people who use Maids to Order are people who don't want to have to deal with a cleaner, or ones who can't keep a cleaner.' She was quite sure Rosamund fell into the latter category. She related the story to Fintan.

'Oh, Sally! How awful for you. That is the height of bad manners. I hope you complained to your boss?'

'Sure what's the point? She wants the business and she doesn't have to listen to the likes of her, but if she asked me to go back there I wouldn't go.'

'You wouldn't think of going back to Marlborough Road? You are sorely missed.'

'I think I've burned my boats, Fintan.'

'Of course you haven't, not at all, but let's leave it for now. I think Clare is going to get a service in the meantime, and Patricia Thompson – is that her name? – she thinks her cleaner might take Saffron on temporarily. But it's really Edith I worry about.'

'Is she okay?'

'She seems frail, hasn't said much, but her sister looks to be on her last legs. She's still running up and down to Portadown, and of course I'm leaving in a few weeks. My next job is in Glasgow.'

Sally felt her heart plummet all the way to her toes. She'd forgotten Fintan wouldn't be here for ever. Her wine turned sour in her mouth, but she swallowed it anyway and wished for the ninetieth time that they had thrown away the key when they had locked Charlie O'Neill up.

They finished their drinks and then Fintan walked with her to the taxi rank and she went home. He had a performance the next evening and didn't want a late night. She wondered if she'd ever see him again. He hadn't mentioned the holiday to Crete, and Sally hadn't the nerve to introduce the subject herself, though it had been on the tip of her tongue. She'd enjoyed her evening very much; it had been a memorable one. She hoped with all her heart that it wouldn't be the last she'd see of Fintan Fanning.

22

Clare glared at the computer screen. It looked back blankly. She screwed up her eyes and challenged it. Think of a new thought on Maud, Maud Gonne. No, Maud was well and truly *gone* – she had lived up to her surname. She clicked on solitaire and tried not to weep at the aptness of the bloody game. Never mind Maud being gone; more to the point, Sally was gone and the kitchen looked like a food fight competition headquarters. Forget the kitchen, she told herself. Get over it. It is not my responsibility. I am more than a hausfrau. She was, wasn't she? She didn't crochet her own muesli, she didn't make patchwork quilts out of the children's old rugby shorts; why should she? For fuck's sake, she was a happening woman. She had her work. She had deadlines, quotas, images. Promises to keep and miles to et cetera, and Tony, the bastard, still wasn't home. He was supposed to have a day off today, having been in Dublin on business last night. The garden beckoned, the overflowing bins beckoned, plus the wonky light fittings that he alone could reach. The smoke alarm had no battery; they could be burned to a crisp in their beds for all he cared. Where was he? She would bet he'd gone straight into work to sort out a bit of paperwork. Jaysus, it was so unfair. He got away with murder. When she nagged him, the kids all took his side, even Anna, and Evie treated him as if he was the coolest dad on the planet.

She paused for a moment and let the froth of resentment stop bubbling through her addled brain. Logically she knew in her heart and soul that she had a lot to offer. No, she was not George Eliot or even Jane Austen, but in her own way she had gifts. Yes, gifts! She had a talent of sorts. She could write, she could teach. The students didn't fidget too much in her lectures, so why did she feel so swamped at present because her cleaning lady had left?

In her marriage she was the one with the showy degree, but despite that, for a long time she had assumed her biggest gift had been her ability to snare Tony and give birth to his children. Much as she loved them, they had recently developed the knack of making her feel that she was an inadequate mother and everything that went wrong was totally and completely her fault. At least Evie did. Clare tried desperately to think of something positive. And of course it was a no-brainer . . . at least she wasn't expecting twins. She'd go down to Saffron and have some of her vile fruit tea and her wonderful lemon cookies. That would do it.

Edith was tired. Her appointment with Brian Smedley was this afternoon at two o'clock. She had been wide awake listening to the radio since five forty-five. She listened with an earphone, out of courtesy to the house guest who slept directly above her . . . Fintan at present. Though if truth be told, there was something very comforting about a radio in the ear. It lulled one to sleep. It had to be talk; music didn't do it. Music excited her and made her feel like a participant. Voices were different; she could tune out voices, and besides, this rolling news on the World Service was an affront. It deserved to be tuned out;

whyever would one want to listen carefully? The quality of programming had dropped severely. Sometimes she changed to Radio Five in the middle of the night; she found the announcer, Rhod Sharp, soothing. He had a nice gentle Scottish burr, and a courteous and intelligent form of questioning, reminiscent of her late father.

She had better get up and have her bath. It was a sunny day and almost nine o'clock; she was wasting God's good weather, as her mother would have said. And there was the washing and ironing. She supposed she would have to tackle that herself, now there was no more Sally. She might pop along to Clare later and suggest they all have a go at luring Sally back. It had been two weeks now, surely long enough to make her point, whatever point she had intended making. Clare had made some vain attempt to get another woman, but it had proved fruitless and it looked like they would have to resort to agencies, and the thought of that made Edith shudder. Apparently you couldn't even be certain of getting the same person two weeks running. No, a pow-wow was definitely in order. Invigorated, she threw on her robe, went to the bathroom and drew her bath.

Saffron sat despairingly in her less than perfect kitchen, gazing in mild panic at her ever-increasing bump. Suddenly the back door opened and Clare came in.

'Hiya, what's up? Fancy some tea?'

'Oh no, I should be offering you, Clare. Sit down, let me put the kettle on.' Saffron waddled out of the chair – at least it felt like a waddle – and lifted the heavy kettle on to the Aga. 'Sorry about the state of the kitchen.'

'God, you should see mine. It's a midden.' Clare looked around her. Well, perhaps this was worse. 'Sure why don't we take it outside? It's a lovely day.'

Between them they carried biscuits, tea pot, cups and Posy

out to the garden. It really was a beautiful day, and so much nicer outdoors. Edith passed them, scurrying up the lane, and was hailed to join them.

'You have to see the funny side of it,' said Clare when the tea had been poured. 'Here we are sitting like the three witches trying to work up a spell to lure Sally back.'

Edith sipped her lemon and ginger tea carefully and nodded. 'She was at the opera last night, but I'm afraid I didn't spot her.'

'Oh?' Saffron's curiosity was piqued. 'I wonder who she was with.'

'Had I done, it would hardly have been appropriate to approach her. It was a full house, so many people there. I was with my friend Isabelle. What a performance. Fintan was mesmerising.'

Saffron nodded enthusiastically. 'Yes, Simon loved it. He went last week and thought Fintan was fantastic. Of course he was thrilled to know one of the cast.'

'And did you enjoy it?'

'Oh Edith, I didn't go. I couldn't face it. And Trevor was keen to take him. Simon said the Nelsons were there as well.'

Later that afternoon, as Sally drove off for her latest supervisory duties with a long list from Maybeth shoved into the pannier of her bike, Edith set off for her hospital appointment in a positive frame of mind. After all, she reasoned, Mr Smedley the surgeon had been reassuring on her last visit. She had had a colonoscopy and he had spotted a polyp and removed it.

'We'll send this off and see what the lab makes of it. Now, I don't want you worrying yourself needlessly. How should I put this, Edith? At our age the cell growth slows down, so even if it were malignant it might be easy enough to contain.'

It had been kind of him to say 'our age' – she knew she was at least ten years older than he – but he was a kind man and she played bridge with his wife. She had consulted him privately; she could easily afford it, so why not leave the National Health to those not as fortunate as herself? She had noticed him at the opera last night with Betty, his wife, and he had given her a cheery smile. That surely was a good sign. She wondered if Fintan had managed to meet up with Sally and have a chat with her as planned. He had been home quite late. She had heard him, but had resisted the temptation to get up and quiz him. He was still in his room now, probably exhausted from his performance last night. Edith had thought him wonderful as Cavaradossi and was very pleased indeed to let Isabelle, who could be such a snob, know that he was a house guest of hers. Perhaps Fintan would have a coffee with her on her return from hospital, if he was around.

She thought it would be quicker to walk to the hospital; the traffic was a nuisance at this time of day. She strode briskly through the park, noting how well kept the flowerbeds were; the rhododendrons and azaleas were in full bloom too, and the palm house sparkled in the sun. They were very lucky to have such an asset on their doorstep, so to speak. Life was worth living, though poor Ellen wouldn't have much longer now. Edith swallowed the lump in her throat; there was no point in being maudlin. Ellen wouldn't want her to be. She had made all her arrangements to be admitted to the hospice without the slightest hint of sentiment or self-pity; she was admirable, an example to all.

After arriving at the hospital, Edith only had to wait a few minutes before she was shown into Dr Smedley's office.

'Ah, Edith! That was a wonderful production of *Tosca*, wasn't it?' Brian Smedley sat back in his chair and regarded Edith levelly.

'Yes indeed. Fintan Fanning happens to be staying with me at present: a truly lovely person, such a gentleman.' Edith smiled proudly. The doctor looked suitably impressed.

'Oh, he was very good indeed, though I did have the honour of seeing Pavarotti perform the role some years back.'

Edith revised her opinion of Brian Smedley somewhat. She hadn't taken him for the boastful type.

'Now, Edith, I had a look at your lab results and I fear we might have a little problem.'

Why on earth did doctors always say *we*? Edith felt immediately nervous, but she tried to remain composed.

'What sort of problem?'

'It seems the polyp we removed from your bowel is malignant. I would like to operate and remove a small section of the intestine as soon as possible, and afterwards you will probably need chemotherapy.'

'My sister has bowel cancer; in fact she is dying from it.' Edith surprised herself at how unemotional she sounded. She had taken her cue from Mr Smedley. Inside she was paralysed with fear.

'Yes, that would fit in. Having a relative with bowel cancer doubles your chances of getting it, I'm afraid. But on the bright side, this looks containable. It seems we have caught it at an early stage, and the chance of a full recovery looks good. I would like to have you in next week, though, if you can organise that. Now, do you have anyone with you?'

Edith shook her head.

'Would you like to call someone?'

'No, it's all right, I'm fine.'

'I'm so very sorry, Edith, but I honestly think we have caught it in time. It won't be pleasant, because there is a chance of hair loss from the chemo, and you will have to take things very easy for a while, but with the right attitude I think we can beat this.'

He stood up and walked with her towards the door, patting her gently on the back as he led her out.

'I'm sorry,' he repeated, 'very sorry, but let's be positive.

Christine will be in touch as soon as we can organise a bed for you.'

Walking back through the park, Edith felt on the verge of tears. She looked again at the flowers and plants, this time with new meaning. Surely she didn't have to die yet, and leave all this wonderful profusion of colour? The sun shone almost mockingly at her, making the colours of the flowers brighter. No, she most certainly did not want to die yet. There was so much more for her to do. Heavens, she had planned to go to China next year with Isabelle. She hoped fervently that Mr Smedley was being straight with her, but then she had consulted him as soon as her symptoms had appeared; subconsciously she had realised they were similar to Ellen's, and Ellen had been careless, ignoring her weight loss for ages, pathetically feeling pleased that she was slimmer. It was only when she happened to mention a change in her bowel movements that she had listened to Edith's advice and gone to her doctor. Of course consequently her cancer had been very advanced when she finally went into hospital. Imagine, two sisters with the same illness within a year. It must be some defective gene, Edith thought. Her dear mother had died from cancer, although people didn't use the word so freely then. She wouldn't tell Ellen about hers; there was little point, though she would have to let her know she was going into hospital. She would think of some white lie to cover the reason.

All her life Edith had minded her feelings. Her father and mother had been pillars of the church, morally erect, controlled people; people who had little time for the untidiness of emotion. Even as small children Ellen and Edith were never allowed to laugh too much, or cry too much, or eat too much, or play too much. 'Too much of anything is a bad thing' was her mother's mantra. Edith could remember the occasional time when her father, coming home from his work and finding her alone, would hug her tightly and swing her round till she screamed with delight, but he would stop immediately and put her down with a gentle 'there, there' and a smile should her mother come in. Over the years the restraint had built so firmly into Edith's soul that she felt now that were she to give vent to it, and let the lid off, the outpouring of emotion would devour her.

She walked slowly down the lane, mulling over her news. She was in a state of mild shock, and so preoccupied she hardly noticed Lola, the McDonalds' dog, peeing on the lemon balm in her herb garden. She saw that Fintan was under the tree in the garden, doing his t'ai chi. She knew not to distract him, so she went into the kitchen and filled the kettle. She would make some tea and take it out into the garden, and chat with Fintan as soon as he finished. She considered telling him her news, but thought on balance she wouldn't. After all, although she was extremely fond of him and felt they had bonded, he was hardly a close friend. But then who was? Edith suddenly felt very lonely.

23

Trevor McNamara and Laura Nelson sat in one of the corner snugs in the Crown bar. It would not be overstating things to say that Trevor was not having a good time. For a start he felt very conspicuous; you could run into anyone here. But on the other hand it was usually so busy that there was also the chance of relative anonymity. Wordlessly, and with the same scary expression she'd been wearing for the past hour, Laura held out her glass. Trevor got up to buy her yet another gin and tonic. He ordered another glass of Guinness for himself. He had made the first one last over an hour; he needed to stay sober. As he steered through the noisy crowd back to the snug, he thought he caught a glimpse of Otis, Edith's loony red-headed lodger, with a girl of about seventeen. The girl glanced at him. She was a pretty young thing. It didn't surprise him in the slightest to see Otis with her; he'd always figured there was a touch of the perv about the man. Mind you, he was one to talk, considering the mess he'd got himself into. His heart was down in his boots at the very thought of it. How he had managed to get things to this state was beyond him. It was so random, as Evie might say.

Laura and Bill Nelson had lived in Marlborough Road for nearly seven years. They had been good neighbours, and their children played with the McNamaras' children. Trevor had always thought Laura an attractive woman. She was a barrister; he'd first noticed her in court, and they'd met at a drinks party the first Christmas after she and Bill had moved in. But tonight Trevor was here for one reason alone, and that was to tell her that he would never be able to see her again. Her outburst at the barbecue had been the final straw.

The affair – if that was the correct description – had begun a few months back, in April, at a cross-border law meeting in Dublin. They had met on the train on the way down – both were in first class. They had a drink and a chat and it seemed perfectly logical to share a taxi, since they were also, by chance, staying in the same hotel. Well, not really by chance, since all the Northern crowd were staying there. The dinner had put everyone in great form. They had served a simply wonderful standing rib roast with trimmings, and many bottles of good claret. Later on, back at the hotel, after a few rather excellent glasses of Calvados, Laura and Trevor had ended up being the last two guests in the residents' bar. They bantered a bit, talked about their children and exchanged the odd grumble about their respective spouses, although Laura seemed to have more gripes about Bill than he had with Saffron. Trevor thought her very attractive, easy company.

The barman was getting restless, but manners and regulations meant he had to stay up until they chose to retire. So since both rooms were equipped with minibars, and more drink tended to seem like a good idea at two a.m. when one had already had rather a lot, they had repaired to Laura's room. Trevor hadn't thought anything of it; that is, until they were actually in the room and Laura decided she would be more comfortable in a nightie. Well, a version of a nightie – it barely covered her and made her alarmingly more attractive than ever.

Before he could talk sternly to himself and tell himself that the last thing he needed was to behave like a reckless idiot, they were in bed together.

Laura Nelson was something else; Trevor had not experienced anything like this, even in his bachelor days. She appeared to have no sexual boundaries, and even though they had consumed vast quantities of drink, she kept him aroused for over two hours. He had left her room for his own in a state of sexual euphoria and passed out exhausted as soon as his head hit the pillow. The following morning there was a talk on European law in Trinity College during which he had barely been able to keep his eyes open or his throbbing head up. Throughout the tedious meeting, he had a sort of roll of fear in his gut when he thought of his romp with Laura last night, but he reasoned that she would feel the same. After all, they both had a lot to lose, and people behaved all kinds of silly ways when drink was taken. He tried to avoid her during the rest of the meeting, until his brain had processed things.

On the way back to Belfast, she sat opposite him. They couldn't discuss anything – the train was packed and the other seats were occupied – but she had, he thought, an extremely dangerous look about her. When she spoke there was a steeliness in her speech that he had never noticed before. That was when it hit him that this was not going to be brushed aside as a drunken escapade. He was right. Laura did not intend to let him off lightly. She was not going to be used. She told him this as soon as they were off the train and out of earshot of the other passengers. He was grateful at least that she had waited. They shared a taxi home, and during the ride she extracted a promise from him that they would meet for a drink during the next week.

Trevor carried his infidelity like a coating of lead in his heart; he was sure he would just blurt it out to Saffron. He desired absolution, but he also knew that was the most selfish thing to do, so he suffered quietly. Occasionally, though, unbidden thoughts of the sexual pleasure he had experienced with Laura drifted to the front of his mind and he had to concentrate on whatever task he was involved with to immediately banish the picture.

He didn't see Laura for the rest of that week, or the next. Perhaps she had wised up, he thought. Gradually he began to relax again and the intensity of the experience lessened. Life returned to its normal humdrum state. Saffron seemed a bit off form and not amorous, but this was a relief to him in a way. Then, out of the blue, Laura left a message asking him to meet her for a drink. He had to admire her nerve. He called her mobile and agreed to see her at a pub on the river, Cutter's Wharf. This particular venue tended to be frequented by a younger crowd, so he hoped they would not be spotted. He wasn't sure what to say to her. Perhaps he would just reassure her that he found her attractive and all that but point out that they were both married and that he'd prefer it if they reverted to their platonic friendship.

But as soon as he arrived, he realised he wasn't going to get away with any such thing. Laura had been waiting outside, sitting on a bench overlooking the river. It was a mild evening and most of the drinkers were outside, a noisy, rowdy lot. As soon as he approached her, Laura downed her drink in one and stood up.

'Let's get out of here,' she said, and led him briskly to a row of flats across the road from the pub. They were more like maisonettes – each had a regular tidy front garden. Laura walked to the door of one and opened it.

'Why are we here? Who owns this?' Trevor felt utterly out of his depth. 'I thought we were going to have a chat about . . . you know . . .' His voice faltered.

Laura walked into a room, while Trevor stood frozen in the sort of living-cum-dining-room. For a full five minutes he literally couldn't move.

'Aren't you coming in?' she called out.

He went slowly into the room, and Laura was sprawled naked on the bed.

'No, Laura, we . . . I can't . . . I can't . . . Whose place is this?'

'It belongs to a friend; she's out for the evening.'

Trevor felt as if his legs were made of lead, but he was totally aroused too. Laura was tanned, trim, and oh God, she was so sexy.

'Look, this is crazy.'

'Only if they find out.'

'But we can't . . .'

'Don't you fancy me then?' she said.

Of course he did, but he was afraid too, and then suddenly he was undressing and in bed beside her. And of course it was thrilling and erotic and terrifying.

After that evening they had met for the occasional drink, nothing more, though he had a feeling she would have liked more. But there was no reason why they couldn't be friends; he enjoyed talking to her. She was refreshing. Lately he had begun to feel overwhelmed by both fatherhood and marriage. The relentless catering to the whims of the children had begun to irritate him. They were so demanding and energetic, and he was feeling anything but. Middle age had hit him with a vengeance. He wanted to have fun, but he was smothering in domestic bliss. He and Saffron had little or no social life beyond the lane. His thing with Laura gave him a little extra frisson, helped him cope with his chaotic home life.

His complaints about Saffron were minor, if somewhat disloyal. Laura was sympathetic; she found Bill infuriating at times. Trevor told her of his desire for a foreign holiday, and Saffron's unbending opposition. Her sojourn in India all those years ago seemed to have convinced her never to leave Ireland again.

'She feels air travel is ruining the children's legacy by destroying the environment. It really pisses me off.'

'I don't know why you don't just stand up to her. Where are you going on holiday this year?'

'Donegal again,' Trevor said glumly.

Each year, towards the end of July, they rented a house in Donegal. His suggested compromise, of renting a house somewhere like Italy or France, had been rejected yet again, and now all he could envision was three weeks of pure torture.

'I have suggested Club Med or even a gîte in France, you know. I mean, it might be fun to meet some new people and actually have a good time, see a bit of sunshine, drink some chilled rosé, that type of thing . . .'

When he had arrived tonight, he had his speech about how they needed to stop all this nonsense well rehearsed. But he had hardly sat down with the drinks when Laura presented him with a solution to his holiday woes.

'Why don't you and I go to the South of France for a week? You can tell Saffron you have a business meeting.'

'I can't, Laura, especially not now.'

'Well a weekend in Paris, then.'

'I can't. Saffron is pregnant, I can't leave her. It's totally out of the question.'

'I'm not asking you to leave her.'

'I know, but even for a few days. Look, Laura, I asked you here tonight to explain that I can't really see you again.'

'God, why are men such cowards?'

Trevor was on a damage limitation mission. He knew he was being a coward. It wasn't that he suddenly found Laura sexually unattractive, but surely Laura herself realised that it was all a big mistake and couldn't continue? Trevor had never been unfaithful to Saffron before. He loved her, and until recently had seen few faults in her. He wished he had never gone on the trip to Dublin in the first place. No one in Marlborough Road ever had affairs. Or did they?

'Does Saffron know about us?'

'Er, no, she has rather a lot on her plate at present, and I thought we had both sort of come to our senses.'

'I've asked Bill for a divorce.'

'Oh God, you haven't. Have you told him why?'

'Why . . . why?' Her lip curled contemptuously and she looked at him with utter distaste. Trevor had a feeling for a moment that he was in a movie – a surreal one at that.

'Don't flatter yourself, *Treasure*. This isn't to do with you. Although I think you should at least be honest about our fling. You don't deserve to get off scot-free. I didn't exactly do it all by myself.'

Trevor buried his head in his hands. There was nothing to say. They finished their drinks in silence.

Trevor finally poured Laura into a taxi and walked towards home. His head was spinning from the whole experience. He called Saffron as he walked, and let her know he was on his way. He'd told her he had had to have a drink with a legal colleague. At least it wasn't an outright lie. She was going to bed fairly early these nights, even though it was bright until late. The twins, Posy and the house with no Sally were proving too much for her.

I am a total bastard! Trevor repeated this to himself like a mantra. He hoped tonight had finally put the lid on things. Laura had Bill and her children to think about as well, even if she was sick of the whole business of motherhood and being a wife, and she hated her career.

As he walked down the back lane, he passed Evie and her strangely tattooed boyfriend on their way out for the night.

'Hi, Trevor! You'll not be popular coming home at this hour. Posy's just gone to bed.'

'I had a business meeting.'

'Aye, right!' called Evie.

God, she was getting very cheeky that one, but Trevor smiled anyway. He knew Saffron depended on her for babysitting, so he had no choice. Anyway, he liked her too.

'Laura Nelson is in our house right now and she's absolutely rinsed! She almost fell in our front door. You should drop in and help Mum and Dad out with her.'

'Ah, I won't bother, Evie; I'd better get on in now.'

Trevor's hand shook as he turned the key in the back door. Oh God, oh God, please, Laura, don't say anything to Tony and Clare. Please, oh please.

'Hi, sweetie!' he called out. 'I'm home.'

24

Mr Smedley was as good as his word. Within a week, Edith had a phone call from Christine, his secretary. They had a bed for her and she was to go in next Thursday evening; her operation would be on Friday morning. The time had come to make a few arrangements.

Ellen first: she was ensconced in the hospice and was getting wonderful care, and fortunately she had a few good friends who visited her daily. Before her own diagnosis Edith had been going three days a week at least to Portadown. Obviously this was now out of the question; she hoped Ellen could hold on till she herself was on her feet again. She pushed away the thought of Ellen dying without Edith beside her. It was too heartbreaking to contemplate. She decided to phone Ellen's best friend Marjorie, and tell her she was going in for something minor for a couple of days, and not to say anything to Ellen – explain it as a cold or something. Marjorie understood perfectly, and said she would call in more often.

'Try not to worry, Edith. You look after yourself. Ellen is so much stronger these last few days. Honestly, it's hard to take it in sometimes that she is . . . you know.'

Edith gave Marjorie her number and told her to phone in an emergency. With luck she wouldn't need to. She went to bed that night and slept reasonably well.

She saw Fintan next morning at breakfast. Otis wasn't around; she saw very little of him these days, but was too preoccupied to dwell on it.

'Fintan,' she began, 'I have to go into the hospital . . .' She stopped. This was difficult for her. But Fintan had misunderstood.

'How is Ellen?' He sounded concerned.

'She's very unwell, to be honest, though she's being very brave about it. But this is . . . it's . . . me; I have to go into the hospital on Thursday evening. I have to have a small operation.'

'Why Edith! Is everything all right?'

'Yes, it's just a routine op, nothing to worry about, but my surgeon thinks it can't wait.'

'Is there something I can do?'

'No, I'll be fine. I'll be out before you leave, so perhaps a few cups of tea in bed then would be nice.' Fintan sensed that whatever was wrong with Edith, she was not in a mood to discuss it at length.

'I am not quite sure how long I shall be in, but I shall telephone you after a couple of days.'

There, she thought, she hadn't really lied, just spared him some of the more personal details.

Fintan simply didn't believe Edith was telling him the whole truth. He recollected the card Sally had found in the drawer. It obviously had something to do with that. He couldn't say anything, of course, but he was saddened by her news.

'Edith, you've be so kind to me, and really made me feel I was staying with a friend, not a landlady. That has meant a lot to me. So if there is *anything* you want me to do, please tell me.'

161

'I'm sure I shall be fine.'

'May I visit?'

'But you are so busy.'

'Yes, but the opera is up and running now. I have much more free time.'

'Well perhaps on Sunday.'

'Right, Sunday it is. May I tell Clare and Saffron?'

'I don't want to worry them unduly; perhaps you could tell them if you run into them.' And she wrote down the ward and hospital.

On Friday afternoon, as Edith was prepped for her operation at Belfast's City Hospital, feeling lost and alone, Sally O'Neill was several miles away in County Down, thinking that she'd like to kill both Maybeth and Bertha McClure. She just wasn't sure of the preferred method of death, or which one she would like to kill first. She was going mad in this job; the balance of her mind must have been disturbed when she agreed to it. She was working as a maid yet again, in another big house, out in Cultra this time. This was Northern Ireland's 'Gold Coast'. Oh, there was money around here, little doubt about that. The last few weeks had opened Sally's eyes. She had always thought the Marlborough Road ones a wealthy lot, but they weren't in the same league as some of the people she had cleaned for since. Today she was in a modern house with the most beautiful long, elegant sofas in muted beiges. There were low glass tables, and leather and chrome chairs artfully placed throughout. Huge dramatic paintings of women with scowling angular faces covered the walls. The light fixtures were an array of gold discs that seemed to float in space, bathing the entrance hall in shimmering light, like perpetual sunshine. The hall was huge, as big as a normal room. She was polishing its wooden floor now, with a special machine. Then she had to clean the lights. The owner of the house, yet another skinny, over-made-up girl, had told her before she drove off in her fancy sports car that they were all bought in Milan so she had to be extra careful dusting them. The place was making her nervous.

Mary, the other maid, was busy in the kitchen. It was gleaming stainless steel, and multiple Marys were reflected throughout: red, anxious and out of breath, polishing as if their lives depended on it. It was massive and looked like a restaurant kitchen, though one that hadn't been used. The entire house had seemed spotless when they had arrived. But they had stuck rigidly to the checklist, changing bed linen that looked as if it hadn't been slept on, dusting and vacuuming imaginary dust, and shining windows that looked as if they weren't there, so clean were they. They had been at it for three solid hours. Sally preferred dirt; there was something more satisfying about getting rid of it.

Suddenly something exploded in her head. She had had it. Enough was enough. If she had to sign on the dole on Monday morning she would do it. She was fed up to the back teeth with this awful job. She'd wanted to better herself, but this was worse than before!

'Mary!' she called to her fellow maid, who was still grinding away in the kitchen. 'Let's get out of here. I can give you a lift into town on the back of the bike. I think this place is clean enough.'

As they rode into Belfast past all the lofty mansions with their manicured lawns, Sally fumed. Maybeth Weston hadn't kept her part of the bargain, so Sally didn't feel obliged to keep hers. She'd look for something else; she was far too good for this sort of abuse. She would drive to the tacky headquarters of Maids to Order and tell Miss Maybeth where to put her job, *and* her peach-coloured jumpsuits. She was so pleased with this thought that she unconsciously speeded up, and it was only when she heard Mary's frightened squeak from the back of the bike that she caught herself on and slowed down. She couldn't afford to have an accident now. She had things to do.

When she arrived at the office, she handed her check sheets back. After looking through them, Maybeth smiled her false smile and addressed her in her bright fake voice.

'You know, Sally, that all our teams have almost completed their training in hygiene management. In a few weeks we will not strictly need you in a supervisory role. However, we are putting together a "dream team" of top maids like you who will only go to certain houses. I am sure you know the houses I'm speaking of . . . our wealthier clients.' Her fake grin widened. 'We need people we can truly depend upon for those clients. I thought you and Bertha would make a perfect team.'

Maybeth gazed at Sally confidently, as if she was bestowing some great honour on her. The condescending bitch! Sally couldn't believe her ears. Maybeth was completely moving the goalposts. And pairing her with Bertha, of all people! Sally's original attraction to this job had been purely the fact that she wouldn't be cleaning. She had put up with the fill-in days because there had always been some reason for it. Someone hadn't shown up, or it was a new job and there was no time to find extra maids. God! How Sally hated the term *maids*. It was so demeaning. She used to laugh at Edith introducing her to people as her housekeeper, but pretentious as that was, at least it wasn't insulting.

'We are getting paid today?' Sally asked.

'Yes, of course.' Maybeth opened a drawer and handed Sally an envelope, as if she was the Queen awarding her a gong. Sally took it.

'Thank you, Maybeth. I'm sorry to tell you that I won't be coming back. You'll have to find another partner for Bertha. I have decided that I have nothing left to give to Maids to Order.'

Maybeth's brightly glossed mouth opened wide, but before

she could utter a word, Sally turned on her heel and left the office.

She got on her bike with a light heart. Finally she was doing what she felt was right for Sally O'Neill.

25

On Saturday morning, Fintan decided to drop in on Clare. He would be gone soon, and Edith needed all the support she could get. He knew she could depend on her neighbours. It was odd, he mused, just how quickly he had become entangled in the lives of all these people. He would find it hard to leave.

When she saw Fintan pass the window, Clare wished she had bothered to run a comb through her hair. She heard him knock lightly on the back door and open it – she had unlocked it earlier to let Lola out.

'Coffee?' she called.

'Yes please.'

Clare wondered briefly why he had dropped in; she hadn't seen much of him these last few weeks. He was obviously quite a private person. Really, all they knew about him was his public face.

'We loved the show on Wednesday. You were amazing.'

'Thank you, we had a great audience, and of course Tosca is magnificent, as is Scarpia.'

Clare poured two cups of coffee and sat down at the table opposite him.

'I'm sure you are wondering why I'm here?'

'You don't need a reason. It's lovely to see you.'

'Edith is in hospital.'

'Oh my God, what happened?'

'Nothing serious – she told me she was going in for a routine operation.'

'She hasn't mentioned anything to me.' Clare looked taken aback.

'The trouble is, I don't believe her. I think she is down-playing it.'

'Do you know which hospital she is in?'

'The City Hospital. She wrote the ward number down for me.'

'That's very near here. Perhaps we should visit her this after-noon. When did she go in?'

'Thursday evening; apparently her operation was yesterday.'

'Oh poor Edith. I hope it is nothing serious. You know her sister Ellen is very ill?'

Fintan nodded.

'Look, I'll call the hospital and find out how she is.'

'Surely they wouldn't give that information out?'

'If you let me know the ward, I'll say I'm her niece or some-thing. Maybe Bill Nelson could call; he works there.'

'No, I think we'll just keep it between us for now, though I'm sure you could tell Saffron. I said I'd visit on Sunday.'

Fintan finished his coffee and left, promising to leave in the details later. Clare would let Saffron know. But perhaps Fintan was right; she'd not tell the Nelsons. Laura had dropped in last week, outrageously drunk and behaving worse than Evie. They couldn't get rid of her. She had ranted on for over an hour, telling Tony and Clare how much she loathed Bill and how she was going to leave the fucking bastard as soon as possible. It had been highly embarrassing, and as luck would have it, it was one of the rare occasions when Clare and Tony had been sitting alone, watching *Newsnight* and enjoying a glass of wine. Tony practically had to carry Laura back down the lane.

Edith toyed with her unappetising lunch. She didn't feel hungry. She hadn't slept a wink last night. Of course no one could in hospital. That was why they came round each night and offered sleeping pills. She had refused. She didn't want to get dependent. She was in a private room, but the door was left ajar and the place was a hive of activity, with phones ringing and bleeps going off. Mr Smedley had been in to see her early this morning before he left for the weekend and pronounced himself pleased with her operation. The prognosis looked good, he told her; they had managed to get all the affected part of the bowel, and she wouldn't miss a few inches, he joked, not with all those yards and yards of it. He was going to start her on chemotherapy purely as a precaution, but they would wait until she was up and on her feet first. She could barely walk today. Perhaps she would be feeling better tomorrow; she had the prospect of Fintan's visit to cheer her.

She had become greatly attached to Fintan; he really was a lovely man. She felt as if she had known him for ever. Otis, for all his way with words, was not exactly practical or dependable. She had begun to revise her opinion of Otis somewhat. Perhaps she had been too quick to allow him a room without a lease.

Earlier, with the help of a lovely young Filipino nurse, Edith had managed to place a call to the hospice to enquire about Ellen, and was told she was holding her own. She sent her love and asked if they would please tell her sister that she would visit next week. She felt sure Clare, or Trevor even, would be kind enough to drive her down once she was out of hospital. That would be in a few more days. There seemed to be no such thing as long stays in hospital any more, what with beds at a premium. Maybe tonight she would allow herself the indulgence of a sleeping pill; one could hardly get addicted in a matter of days.

As Edith lay there contemplating her life, with the racket in the corridor as background, her thoughts turned to Marlborough Road. How she missed her home and her neighbours, and Sally too.

26

For more than an hour, Sally had listened to an overwrought Bertha banging on about how she had ruined her chances of a brilliant career and turned her back on the chance of a lifetime. Sally had patiently explained that she didn't care to clean for clients such as Maybeth's. She'd rather starve.

'It's them ones over in Marlborough Road; sure they turned your head. Made you think you were something. Sure when did anyone over our way ever go to something like an opera?' Bertha's ugly red mug glared at her.

'I *am* something,' Sally said, in a voice that sounded a lot calmer than she felt. 'Bertha, why don't you listen? The reason I'm not going back to Maids to Order is *one*, I am not a maid, and *two*, I won't take orders from the likes of Maybeth's clients.'

Bertha roused herself to reply, but before she could, the phone rang. It was Fintan. Sally told him to please hang on one second.

'Excuse me, Bertha, would you mind going? I have to take this call.'

Bertha gathered her shapeless self up to go.

'You've got too big for yer boots, Sally O'Neill,' she said.

'Charlie's right, them oul' snobs have filled yer head full of rubbish.' And she stormed out, slamming the door as she went.

'Hello, Sally, I hope I'm not interrupting you?'

'No, it's just a friend leaving.' She wondered if he had heard Bertha. 'Is something up?' There was something about the tone of his voice that made her feel this was not a call for a cosy chat.

'Well I'm afraid there is. It's Edith; she's been admitted to hospital. She had an operation yesterday. She's told me it's merely routine, but I don't quite believe her.'

'Which hospital?'

'The City.'

'The City? Oh heavens, that card . . . I was worried it was more than a check-up. I should have asked her about it, but I didn't like to be nosy.' Sally had an odd sort of feeling in the pit of her stomach. She missed Edith Black, and the thought of something happening to her was not a pleasant one at all.

'She did say I could visit Sunday. Perhaps you'd like to come with me?'

'I'd love to, Fintan, but she's probably still mad at me for leaving her.'

'Oh Sally, don't be silly. I bet she'd love to see you. I'll phone tomorrow morning. We can meet and go together to the hospital.'

'That would be great. Whatever time suits.'

Sally put the phone down dejectedly. Poor Miss Black, she had abandoned her in her hour of need, and all for what? It was a good job Bertha had left. Sally would have been up for manslaughter.

Clare had had her shower and was just on her way out the back door when Saffron, accompanied by Posy and wearing a forlorn expression on her face, came in.

'Is something wrong?'

Clare watched helplessly as Saffron dissolved into tears, followed seconds later by Posy, who was obviously out in sympathy. She boiled the kettle and made a pot of strong tea, and poured Saffron a cup, which she drank without a word. Posy was bought off with a chocolate biscuit. Clare fed the dog and waited until Saffron was ready to talk.

'It's Trevor; I think he's having an affair!'

'Oh Saffron, I'm sure you're wrong! Trevor? It seems so unlikely.' She resisted the temptation to add that she couldn't imagine anyone having an affair with Trevor. He was hardly an attractive prospect; he didn't exactly score high in either the looks or the charm department.

'I hope I am, but he's been so different, even before he knew I was pregnant. I can't think of another reason why. There must be someone else.'

'But who on earth could it be? He's always home, unlike Tony!'

'Someone at his work? They did get a new secretary last month. He says she's nice, and she's probably very young.'

'But you're young!'

'I feel old and fat.'

'You're pregnant with twins.'

'I know, and he's resentful.'

'Saffron, this has all been quite a shock to Trevor, as well as to you. He's over fifty, probably thinks he can't cope. I think the whole thing has been too much for him. Have you asked him straight out?'

'No, I can't bear to. I'm afraid he'll admit it.' She seemed a lot calmer now. 'You see, he hasn't been coming home as much, not for lunch anyway, and he came in late last week and he had been drinking. And then with Sally leaving . . . well, the place is—'

'Saffron, I'm sorry things are a mess for you, but you need to know that Edith has gone into hospital.'

172

'Oh Clare, you must think me selfish, rabbiting on about my problems. When?'

'Thursday. Fintan just called in to tell me. She's having some routine operation, and obviously didn't want to bother anyone. Poor thing, what with Ellen so sick.'

'Oh heavens! We should go and see her.'

'Yes, but let's give her till tomorrow. We can walk round. Evie can mind Posy.'

They chatted generally after that, but Clare was intrigued with the idea of Trevor having it off with someone else. He wouldn't, surely? Saffron was at least twenty years younger than he was, and for all her eccentric dressing she was still awfully pretty, and kind too. But after Saffron, much calmed, had left, she suddenly had a flash: Laura Nelson – it couldn't be! But that scene at the barbecue when Saffron had announced her pregnancy? That was outrageous. And last week, when Laura had poured herself into Clare's kitchen full of the drink, she announced she had been out with a colleague. Would Trevor qualify? They were plying the same trade, and this place was a parish. It was none of her business, of course, but all the same she wondered whether, if she dropped in for a drink at the Nelsons', Laura might give herself away.

Next morning Clare sat in her kitchen, flicking listlessly through the pages of the *Observer*. Everyone else was still in bed. Evie had come in really late last night, and Clare could never sleep easily until she knew she was safely back at base. What was more, she had been drunk, dead drunk. Clare had heard her trying to open the front door for about five minutes, before she had thrown on a dressing gown and gone downstairs to let her in. Her eyes were glazed over and she was slurring her words, but Clare had resisted the temptation to bawl her out. Tony was fast asleep, of course. He could sleep through anything; besides, he figured one person worrying about the kids was enough.

'You're being ridiculous, love; you never worry whether Rory is in safely each night when he's in Edinburgh,' he had said before he fell asleep.

'Of course I do, I wonder constantly, but there's nothing I can do about it.'

'Evie is quite sensible; she'll be fine. Just get some sleep.'

But Clare had lain there fretting. She didn't like this Mikey much. Evie thought it was for snobbish reasons, of course, because he was a barman, but that had nothing to do with it, well not really. Clare just felt that someone with the same goals – exams, for instance, and a college education – would be a better example for her. Leaving aside his tattoos and piercings, which made her queasy, he appeared to spend most of his money on drink. You'd think working in a bar would put him off the stuff. There were so many articles in the papers about the perils of binge drinking. Evie's liver would be in a sling before she was twenty.

Saffron called in about two as promised. Trevor had offered to mind the children. Clare wondered if he had a guilty conscience. Just as well he had agreed to babysit; there was no sign of Evie yet. She was still in her pit, and Clare hadn't the energy yet for a stand-off. Tony was pootling in the garden, pretending to be a regular stay-at-home guy. All her rants made little impression on him. He'd hardly change now. He was just a workaholic, or a perfectionist as he preferred. She wished he'd apply a few of his standards to his marriage.

They walked round to the hospital. Saffron was huge, so they made slow progress. The twins were kicking like fury, she said. She had already chosen the names: Ariel and Calypso; from the latest scan it appeared they were having two girls.

Edith was on a surgical ward, in a side room. Clare thought she looked very poorly indeed; although she made the effort to sit up to talk, it was obvious to both women that she was quite weak. She was pleased they'd made the effort, but they didn't stay long; they more or less said hello, left her some flowers and sidled out.

'Oh God, Saffron, she's looking terribly ill. What kind of surgery do you think she had?' Neither had liked to ask.

'I wonder if she has someone to look after her when she gets out?'

'I don't know. She made so little of it, saying it was routine, but a routine operation doesn't leave you looking like death.'

They had just reached the exit when they encountered Fintan and Sally, no less. All four regarded each other uncomfortably. Sally was most ill at ease. Fintan took charge of the situation.

'I take it you've been to see Edith? I've dragged Sally along.'

Clare nodded. 'She doesn't look a bit well, though she said it was nothing, just a small operation. We only stayed a minute.'

'Maybe we shouldn't go in, Fintan,' Sally said dubiously.

'No, I said I would come. We'll just pop our heads round the door to let her know we're thinking of her.'

Clare and Saffron left the hospital feeling uncomfortable. They were both wondering what exactly the relationship between Sally and Fintan was. Neither spoke for the first few minutes. Finally Clare couldn't contain herself.

'You know, Saffron, I'm just raging with Sally. After all those years she keeps in touch with Fintan and not us, and leaving that pathetic note . . . She should be ashamed of herself.'

Sally felt sick to her stomach. It hadn't occurred to her that she might meet anyone else from Marlborough Road, though she realised now that had been very silly of her. She wasn't at all sure any more she wanted to see Edith. It seemed a bit cheeky, to visit her after all that had transpired. She said as much to Fintan, but he brushed her protests aside.

'Look, Sally, stop worrying. You've come all this way. We'll literally just say hello. I can pop back later if needs be.'

He knocked politely on the door and heard a weak 'Come in.'

Edith looked up at her second lot of visitors in ten minutes. Really, people were very kind, but she wasn't in great form for them. Then she realised Sally was with Fintan, and felt a deep surge of contentment. She suddenly realised everything was going to be fine.

'Oh Sally,' she said, 'you've come back to me! How lovely.'

Sally looked at Miss Black lying there, looking in deep need of her, and to her own surprise she found herself nodding.

'Yes, as soon as you're out of hospital, I'll be there to look after you.'

Edith nodded and lay back in her bed.

'How very kind of you, Sally. Yes, I look forward to that. It takes a weight off my mind. You know, I'm feeling better already.'

Fintan left a *Sunday Telegraph* and a plant beside the bed. Sally added her box of chocolates, dark chocolates, which she knew Edith preferred. They left and made their way down to the lobby.

Sally didn't know what had come over her. She had found herself just agreeing to Edith's statement, acting from pure instinct, and now she was feeling somewhat apprehensive.

'Gosh, Fintan, I don't know what happened there, just agreeing like that to come back.'

'Admit it, Sally, you hate the new job and you miss them nearly as much as they do you.'

'As a matter of fact, I gave in my notice on Friday.'

'Well, what perfect timing.'

'But what about Charlie? What if he shows up again?'

'That's the least of your worries. I honestly don't think they give a stuff about Charlie.'

'I don't know that I'm ready to just go back to things the way they were.'

'I understand completely. Look, why not just see Edith

176

through her convalescence, and then if you feel like going back to Saffron and Clare, you can decide when would suit you, and how often. Remember what we talked about before? You sounded keen on the idea of doing some studying. Get a prospectus for classes in the autumn. There's nothing to stop you doing both.'

'I'm not sure, Fintan. It's been years since I studied. My brain doesn't work.'

'Do something easy to start with.'

'Such as?'

'I don't know – what interests you?'

'Well, I like paintings, and English.'

'Art appreciation maybe, that type of thing?'

'But perhaps I should think about business studies, or computer studies. You need that for everything these days. I could run my own cleaning company, give Maids to Order a run for their money.' She started warming to the idea, imagining Maybeth's face. Then reality struck. 'I do need to make some money.'

'We all do . . .' Fintan paused. 'Sally, I don't mean to embarrass you, but I can help out . . .'

Sally turned bright red and immediately got flustered.

'Oh, no way, Fintan. I can manage. I have savings.'

He quickly changed the subject, seeing that he had indeed embarrassed her, and they walked to where she had parked the bike and parted.

Clare and Saffron walked back chatting nineteen to the dozen about Sally and Fintan. They had both been gobsmacked at seeing Sally.

'You know, Clare, she wasn't in touch with Edith,' Saffron ventured. 'Maybe Fintan is still keeping in touch with *her*. She did look really embarrassed.'

'Yes, so she should.'

'I wonder if there's anything going on between them.'

'Hardly. I mean, I don't want to sound like a snob, but he's a well-known opera singer, and she's, well, a cleaner.'

As she said the words Clare thought that she did indeed sound snobbish, but it was a fact. They were an unlikely combination. She had wondered when she first met him whether Fintan was gay, but she had dismissed the idea quickly. He was definitely straight. She had good strong gaydar. She prided herself on it.

'Poor Sally, it probably upset her meeting us like that. I might phone her tonight, and tell her we'd still like to be friends.'

'Yes, you're right, Saffron. We should keep up the connection. She was part of all our lives for so long.'

'She might even come back to Edith to help her convalesce.'

'Yes, we should ask Fintan to suggest that to her.'

27

When Clare arrived back, Tony was still in the garden. She went to tell him about Edith. Evie finally got out of bed at almost three o'clock. One look at her made Clare mad as hell.

'I have had enough of your behaviour, Evie; last night was the final straw.'

'What behaviour? You nearly knocked me over, pulling the door open like that, and then slamming it shut in Mikey's face . . .'

'Mikey wasn't even there. I heard you fumbling with the key for ages; you were absolutely drunk.'

'I was not drunk. I only had a few vodkas. Anyway, you can talk! You can hardly get in our back door for wine bottles.'

'That is not the point! When we were your age we did not drink. Anyway, I've had enough. You are not leaving this house for the rest of the week.'

'No way! I'd rather be in prison than in this dump. I'm thinking of moving out anyway and moving in with Mikey.'

'Yes, why don't you? He looks like he'd be just the right one for you, a tattooed layabout. He'd certainly keep you in the style to which you're accustomed.'

'He isn't a layabout!'

'I just hope if you are up to anything you are using condoms.'

Evie was outraged. This was so unfair. She'd hardly even kissed Mikey, let alone had sex with him. Her mother was a hateful old bitch.

'Oh thanks a lot for trusting me, Mum. It must be great to have a slag for a daughter. Maybe I will move in with him and have a baby and then I could be a teenage mum. That would really give you something to bang on about.'

Clare was sure her blood pressure was sky high. She stormed out the back door, aware that she was yet again losing control of the situation, and cornered Tony, who was sanding one of the garden seats and talking to Bill Nelson. She nodded to Bill.

'Tony, can you please come in here and talk to Evie at once. I have had enough of her!'

Tony sighed and shrugged his shoulders at Bill as if to say, women – all the same, eh?

'Clare love, why do you get yourself into such a state? What has she done now?'

'Well in case you haven't noticed, it is almost three o'clock and she is just this minute out of bed. She wasn't in till almost two last night and she was totally drunk. She is only sixteen, and she is your daughter as well.'

Tony went slowly into the house, not relishing for a minute a confrontation with Evie. Clare followed. Evie wasn't in the kitchen. Tony called upstairs to her. Anna answered.

'Evie has just gone out the front door, Dad. She slammed it really hard. She scared my hamsters.'

By dinner time there was still no sign of Evie. Clare had called her mobile repeatedly but had just got voicemail. Tony had also called and left a message, but whereas Clare was frantic, he was laid back.

'There's no point in getting yourself into a state. She'll come back when she's calmed down.'

'I hope you'll ground her for the rest of the week.'

'Yes, love. Look, we've been through this a dozen times. I'll have a chat with her about her behaviour.'

'A chat!'

'Here, have a glass of wine and relax.' Tony took a bottle from the fridge and opened it. 'Listen, why don't we barbecue? It's a lovely evening. Have you anything?'

Of course Clare had loads of stuff – she usually shopped on Saturdays – and so she occupied herself by making some marinades and a salad, trying not to think about all the things that could happen to a teenage girl alone in town, and attempting to convince herself that Evie would be home soon.

28

Evie totally hated all these run-ins with her mother. But her mum just whinged about everything she did. And she took all her bad moods out on Evie. Maybe she *had* been a bit drunk last night, but what was wrong with that? A lot of girls she knew got wrecked three days a week. Her mum so had an attitude problem. Evie thought it was because her dad worked so hard and obviously her mum felt she was just as smart as him. Evie was fed up listening to her go on about how she got the best degree and she needed to stretch her mind more. Who cared? She didn't pick on Rory; he seemed to be able to do what he liked, and of course Anna was the baby, so she was just a spoiled little brat. And she knew Mikey was regarded as not good enough, which infuriated her. Evie liked him – they were just pals really – but he was crazy about her, and couldn't do enough for her. He was very generous too; he wouldn't let her buy a drink. He had had a rotten life. His dad had left his mum when he was only six, and Mikey had hinted that he used to hit him and his older brother. His mum lived with some other guy now; Mikey didn't like him, and so he never saw her. He had left home at seventeen. He was different from all the boys at her school. They were all either boring swots or rugger buggers.

She phoned Mikey's mobile the minute she slammed the front door. When he answered, he sounded fairly wrecked. He had had a lot to drink last night too. She asked if he would meet her in the park. It was a lovely afternoon.

'Ach, Evie, I don't feel like moving. I'm knackered. Why don't you come round here?' he said.

Evie agreed, though to be honest, she didn't really care much for Mikey's place. She had only been there once before. It was a total kip, and smelly too. And all Mikey's friends were real dopers. They dropped E's and smoked pot. Evie didn't think pot was a bad drug; a lot of her friends had tried it, and it was practically legal. Mikey smoked it a lot. He had let her try it once, and it had made her head spin and her heart go too fast. She hadn't tried it since. She preferred vodka.

He opened the door to her looking as if he had slept in his clothes.

'My mum is so totally pissed off with me for last night.' She brushed past him, and he followed her in, rubbing his eyes. The place stank. 'I'm starving. Do you have anything to eat?'

She opened the fridge. There was a rotting lettuce, a jar of dried-out pasta sauce and some rancid bacon. She tried the cupboard. Great. Here she was starving, and all he had was two stale Pot Noodles and a rusting tin of chopped pork.

'Why don't we go out and get something?'

'It's Sunday.'

'So? People have to eat on Sundays. We don't have to go anywhere expensive. We could try the pizza place. It's open on Sundays.'

Mikey's best mate Andy was lying on the horrible stained brown sofa. Evie couldn't believe they were stuck indoors on a day like this, but then she herself had been in bed until half an hour ago.

'You go and have a shower; I'll wait.'

Mikey looked at her as if she was mad.

'Go on, it'll wake you up.'

Obediently, he did as he was told. She sat and watched TV with Andy, who was smoking a joint. She refused his offer to share it.

'I don't smoke,' she told him.

'Whatever. This is good stuff, though, it chills you. You seem majorly stressed to me. You should have a toke. Here.' He held it out to her. 'It'll relax you.'

He was right: she was stressed. She really hated all that stuff with her mum. It was so out of control.

'Well, maybe just one puff, then.'

Evie took the joint and tried to inhale. Almost immediately she began coughing like crazy. She went into the kitchen and looked for a clean glass to get a drink of water. Then she went back into the room, which she supposed doubled as Andy's bedroom. He handed her the joint and she had another go at it.

'Hold it in this time and swallow the smoke,' he ordered.

This time she didn't cough. She felt a bit floaty, but definitely more relaxed, and her head wasn't spinning. Pot smelled funny. Well, maybe it hid even worse smells, like boys' socks and stuff. Evie thought the smell of a house important. Clare liked scented candles and bunches of lilies. Marlborough Road always had a lovely smell of flowers and food.

Eventually Mikey came into the room, looking a lot better. His hair was wet.

'Let's go Evie. Later, man,' he said to Andy, who by now was totally chilled.

Part of Evie's plan in getting Mikey to take her out to eat was to waste time. She intended going home later, when they had all gone to bed, though she was beginning to doubt if she could manage that. She figured her mother wouldn't be

184

feeling much like sleeping. She'd only been gone an hour and she had had five missed calls from home. She thought of phoning Rory, but then he was probably out with all his rugby mates doing his boy things, and he'd just tell her to go home anyway. But why should she go home and listen to her mother raving about how ungrateful and useless she was? She'd heard it all before. Maybe she'd stay at Mikey's tonight, even if it was a bit smelly there. He didn't exactly go in for fresh sheets, but she'd keep her clothes on. At least by tomorrow everyone would have calmed down. Deep down she felt this might not be quite the right plan, but she pushed her niggles to the back of her head.

They went to the pizza restaurant near the BBC. It was practically empty, except for a family and two other couples. One of them was Bronagh and Otis. Evie's jaw dropped. What was that all about? Surely Bronagh wasn't dating him? Bronagh looked a bit uncomfortable when she saw Evie. They acknowledged each other with a smile, but fortunately she and Otis were at a table for two. Mikey headed over to a seat by the window; he liked watching traffic. He was talking to someone on the phone.

'Right, mate, that sounds all right, we might be up for that. I'll phone you back.'

Evie waited for him to finish.

'That was Andy. He and his mate Brian are driving down to a gig outside Dublin, Oxegen; they have free tickets for the last two days. Some brilliant acts, d'ye fancy it? His other pal Jimmy's already there. They're leavin' now, back tomorrow night. They'll pick us up here.'

'No, I can't. I don't think Mum and Dad would let me go.'

'You know, Evie, you need to start doing things for yourself. They treat you like a kid; you're nearly seventeen.'

'I know, but they'd be dead upset. I was supposed to be grounded for a week.'

'Grounded for what? Going out with me? They don't think I'm good enough for you, isn't that it?'

Mikey sounded hurt, and bitter too, Evie thought. Perhaps she should go to the gig; after all, it was the school holidays, and it would put an end to her dilemma: she wouldn't have to face another bollocking from her mum and dad, at least not for a while. There was nothing worse than her mum's rage in surround sound. She didn't need it right now. The more she thought about going, the more it seemed like a good idea. She was strangely calm. Andy was right. Pot was okay really. She thought she'd text Rory and say she was fine and to tell the parents not to worry. She'd be back tomorrow night. Put a bit of space between them.

'Okay then, I'll go. You'll have to buy me a toothbrush, though.'

Mikey looked delighted. 'Brilliant. Jimmy has a tent set up and all. We can kip there.'

'Just one thing, is Andy driving?'

'No, he can't drive. His mate Brian is. It's okay, he's not into blow or drink. He's got his mum's car for the night.'

Evie went to the loo when she had finished eating. Bronagh was there too, fixing her make-up. She looked a bit put out to see Evie.

'It's not what you think,' she said. 'I'm not going out with him or anything. I mean, I have been out with him, but I don't fancy him. There's nothing going on. He's just nice to talk to and that. He knows all about poetry.'

Like Evie cared about poetry. But whatever, if Bronagh liked it.

'Don't worry, I think he's okay really, apart from his age. I thought he was going to be playing at Oxegen, y'know, the rock festival outside Dublin this weekend.'

'Oh yes, that one. I don't think it worked out.'

'We're going down tonight, just for the last acts. We're leaving in a few minutes, actually.' Evie suddenly felt very friendly towards Bronagh; maybe she reminded her of Sally. 'I wish your mum hadn't left us,' she blurted out. 'I really miss her, she was so good at calming my mum down.' And she started to cry.

Bronagh was a bit taken aback. Evie seemed such a together girl. Could she be stoned? Her eyes were red. Surely not? Maybe she'd had a few drinks, although Bronagh had noticed they had just ordered Cokes. She found a tissue and helped Evie dry her eyes and fix her make-up.

Once Evie had calmed down, she assured Bronagh she was fine. It was just that she had had a row at home, she said, and was not quite herself. Bronagh waited until she was sure Evie was all right, and then excused herself.

'Evie, honestly, I'd better go,' she said. 'Otis will be thinking I've climbed out the window. I'll give my mum your love.'

Bronagh and Otis watched Evie and Mikey leave. They had only had a pizza, which they appeared to have inhaled.

'How do you know them?' Otis asked.

'Evie gets her hair done in the salon.'

There was no point in letting him know her business. He still hadn't made the connection with Sally. Her mum had been telling her just last week that she missed everyone in Marlborough Road – everyone, that is, except Iggy McNamara, who was an iguana, and Miss Black's ginger lodger. Bronagh had said nothing. She wondered what exactly Otis had done to annoy Sally.

29

By eleven o'clock Clare was utterly distraught. She had been crying since Rory came home and showed her the text from Evie saying she would be back tomorrow night. Evie still wasn't answering her phone. Tony was doing his best to calm her.

'Clare love, she will be all right. There's no point getting yourself into a state. She says she will be home tomorrow.'

Despite his even tone, Tony was extremely worried too. He felt powerless. His inability to do anything about the situation was overlaid with a heavy dose of guilt. He realised now that he had been too dismissive of all those spats between Clare and Evie. He should have intervened earlier. He looked at his wife. She was the picture of misery: a competent, intelligent woman reduced to a weeping wreck. He hugged her close. He should have been able to protect them.

'This is what comes of leaving me on my own with the children so much. Children need a father; it gives them a sense of security.'

'Clare, it's not as if I have left home or I'm out on the town. I am working, for God's sake, providing the money so we can live in a house like this and have nice holidays!'

'Yes, but your work means far more to you than your family.'

'That's nonsense, and you know it.'

'You're never here.'

'I'm here now.'

'Yes, but we eat without you most nights. You should be here. Evie doesn't play you up the way she does me.'

'You shouldn't let her.'

'She pays no attention to anything I say. I have far too much to do. I run this house; I haven't got Sally any more. I am like a single mother with three kids, a dog and a demanding job. Anyway, you spoil Evie when you are here.'

'I spoil her?'

'Yes, you always take her side. You believe every single thing she says, her version of the truth. You never stick up for me. It's no wonder I lose my temper with her; she's impossible at times.'

Tony was flummoxed. He had never seen Clare quite so worked up, but there was no consoling her. He tried anyway.

'Clare sweetheart, please try not to fret. I have a feeling she'll be okay.'

'What do you mean, you have a feeling? I'm frightened she won't be. You should call the police and say she's under age. She could be passed out on drink and drugs for all we know. Someone else could have used her phone to text Rory.'

Rory came back into the room. He was feeling awful. His parents never had rows this bad. He tried to reassure Clare.

'Mum, I don't think someone else would have used her phone – how would they know who I was? And she doesn't even have me in under Rory; she has nicknames for everyone.'

'We should call the police,' Clare said stubbornly.

'Clare love, there's no point in going to the police. I don't think they would pay a lot of attention, unless she had been abducted.'

189

'She might well have been. Who is this Mikey anyway? All we know about him is that he's a barman with tattoos. We don't even know his surname.'

'It's Brown, I think.'

'Brown? That sounds like an alias.'

'Mum, please try to chill a bit. I'll go round to his flat now and see if they are there. They've probably just been in a bar in town.' By now Rory had phoned Evie dozens of times, but she wasn't taking his calls either. She was such a selfish brat at times. He'd choke her when she finally showed up. 'Don't worry, they're probably back by now. It's Sunday night. Everywhere closes early.' And Rory left.

Tony didn't know what possessed him to make his next move. He had come into the kitchen to make Clare some tea, and was standing beside the phone waiting for the kettle to boil. He was vaguely thinking it might be an idea to call Sarah, Clare's best friend. She could talk to her and try to calm her down. He pressed the first speed-dial button; *Sa*, it said, though the letters were worn. The phone was answered at once.

'Hello? Sarah?'

'Eh . . . no, this is Sally O'Neill speaking . . . Hello . . . Tony?' Both of them were equally thrown.

'Sorry, Sally, I was trying to get Clare's friend Sarah . . . I must have pressed the wrong button.'

'No problem . . . I thought you were Bronagh.'

'Sally – Evie's run off . . .'

'What? When?'

Tony filled Sally in on the whole sorry saga.

'Oh God, no, that's terrible news. Poor Clare, I bet she's demented. Please phone me and let me know when she comes back. It doesn't matter how late. I won't sleep now worrying about her myself.'

Tony agreed, and then phoned Sarah, but got no response. Perhaps she was away for a few days.

190

Rory's visit to Mikey's place proved fruitless; there wasn't any response at all. It was after midnight when he returned. Tony persuaded Clare that even if she was upset, she'd be better in bed, and resting. It looked like they were all in for a sleepless night. Rory had got into Evie's page in Bebo and was checking out her mates. He began to call all the numbers from her last phone bill, but no one had heard from her. Periodically they dialled Mikey's place – to no avail.

At about one thirty, the phone rang. Even though no one was asleep, it was shocking. Everyone froze. It rang about three times. Clare cried out and Tony picked up the receiver.

'Tony? Sorry to ring so late, it's Sally. Bronagh has just come in. I was telling her about Evie, and she said she saw her earlier today, about three o'clock. She was with that boyfriend of hers, Mikey. She told Bronagh they were driving down to a festival outside Dublin called Oxegen.'

'Oh, Sally . . .'

'Bronagh says it's well patrolled and Evie said they were going with a few others.' Sally paused and then said, 'Eh . . . could I speak to Clare for a second?'

Tony handed over the phone, while relaying the news to Clare.

'Oh, Sally,' Clare wailed. 'It's all my fault. I lose my temper with her too quickly. Suppose something happens to her. I'll never forgive myself.' And she started sobbing.

Sally's heart went out to her. She couldn't bear to think of Bronagh running off. She waited till Clare had calmed down a bit.

'Would you like me to call in tomorrow afternoon? I'm going to see Miss Black in hospital about three; so I'll be over your way.' Her heart was in her mouth for the split second it took Clare to say:

'Oh Sally, that would be wonderful. I'd really love to see you.'

30

Throughout that long night, Clare's emotions ranged from panic to worry to fury and then back again. Lola, sensing upset, began a strange sort of high-pitched whining that was driving Tony bats. Normally it would have sent him up to the top of the house in an attempt to escape the noise and get some sleep, but he couldn't leave Clare. His exhortations for Lola to calm down were having no effect whatsoever, and it wouldn't be fair to the neighbours to put her out the back. He barely closed his eyes the entire night and went to work on Monday morning absolutely wrecked. He knew he probably should have stayed home with Clare, but he had an important meeting. He told Clare he would keep his phone on and would be home as soon as the meeting finished. He also told her, with a lot more conviction than he was feeling, that Evie would be back by dinner time. It didn't help. Clare didn't have any classes on a Monday, and housework, although it was piling up, seemed very low on her list of distractions. So at midday, partly to take her mind off things, she went to the hospital to see Edith.

Edith was looking much better and was sitting up reading the paper. Mr Smedley had told her she would be out in three days. She noticed that Clare seemed agitated, and managed with little difficulty to coax the story of Evie's flit out of her. She was very reassuring. She realised she didn't often see this vulnerable side of her neighbour, and liked Clare all the more for it. Being surrounded by achieving women in Marlborough Road wasn't always an easy cross for Edith to bear.

'Don't make it too hard for her to come back, otherwise you could scare her into staying away for longer than she intends.'

'Oh Edith, I couldn't bear it. Perhaps I should text her and say I am missing her and she won't be in any trouble if she comes home.' Clare sounded wretched.

'Yes, dear, I think that might do the trick.'

So Clare sat and sent off the message; laboriously, since despite the efforts of both Evie and Rory, she had not yet learnt to do predict text.

'And about the boy: try not to nag her. We all go through that stage, you know. I walked out with some most unsuitable young men in my time, by my parents reckoning, that is. You know I've often thought over the years that I would have been much happier had I not paid quite so much attention to their opinions. Perhaps I wouldn't be just a lonely old woman lying in hospital with no family to visit me.'

'Oh Edith, that's not true!'

'Well, dear, it is really. I know I have many friends in the lane, but delightful as they are, they are not family.' She smiled warmly at Clare. 'You know, I am awfully pleased that Sally is coming back to me. She's really the closest thing to family I have. I shall have to cherish her more this time. We can't have her running away again, can we?'

'She's coming back? When?' This was news to Clare.

'Well she said she'd be there for me as soon as I got out.'

Clare felt a sharp stab of jealousy.

'That's great, Edith. How did you manage to convince her?'

'I simply asked and she said yes. I know, it is so reassuring.'

'What about the other job?'

'I'm not sure. Perhaps she intends to do both.'

Clare tried to calm herself. Okay, Edith was sick, but after all, *she* had been Sally's first employer. Edith wouldn't even have had a cleaner if not for her. But she wisely said nothing more and changed the subject. Perhaps she could sound Sally out when she saw her this afternoon.

'I assume the operation was a success, Edith?'

Clare was curious about the nature of the operation, and was biting her tongue not to ask, but to her surprise, Edith told her briskly exactly what was wrong with her, and confided how bad things were with Ellen too. Clare offered to drive her down to see Ellen as soon as she was on her feet again. Poor old Edith; imagine having to cope with no family at all. Clare suddenly felt thankful for what she had. She decided she would try to sort things out with Evie and stop nagging Tony so much. Her own dissatisfaction was turning her into a whinger. Perhaps Tony was staying at work for a reason. She left the hospital feeling curiously uplifted, and a bit more confident that Evie would be back soon.

At three o'clock, Edith had her second visitor of the day. Sally knocked timidly on the door, peeked round, and was greeted with a friendly smile. She was looking very smart, not being in her working clothes.

'Ah, Sally, how lovely to see you! I was beginning to get bored. I would so love to have a radio; all they've got here is that ghastly TV. It is on twenty-four hours a day. I had to make a fuss to get it disconnected.'

Sally grinned. 'I see you're beginning to feel a bit better. Will I phone Fintan and ask him to bring you a radio?'

'Yes, what a good idea. The small transistor from the bathroom would be ideal. It would be so soothing to listen to Radio Four.'

'And are you comfortable otherwise? You're not in too much pain?'

'Oh no, whatever they're giving me seems to be doing the trick.'

Edith's voice, bled of its usual commanding tones, seemed to carry an extra warm quality to it. Sally felt welcomed; she smiled in return and placed a copy of *Homes and Gardens* down on the locker.

'I thought you maybe had enough chocolates.'

'Really, you shouldn't have bothered, but it's just what I need. I shall look forward to reading it.' Edith indicated a heavy, important-looking book by her bed. *Anna Karenina.* 'I'm afraid I haven't much felt in the mood to revisit Tolstoy.'

Her tone changed; she sounded almost anxious.

'Have you told your organisation you'll be working for me? I hope you haven't changed your mind.'

Sally reassured her that she would be there waiting when Edith was discharged. She told her she had left her new job and recounted the saga of Maids to Order, hamming it up a bit for Edith's benefit, and interspersing it with stories of the rudeness of the spoilt young things she had been working for this past month. She even did a passable imitation of the ghastly Maybeth, and Edith lay back and enjoyed all the gossip. It struck Sally that this was the most comfortable she had ever felt in Miss Black's presence in all the time she had known her. And she liked the feeling.

Sally's next stop was the suggested visit to Clare. She passed Simon on her way down the lane, and of course he hotfooted it up to tell Saffron she was there. Saffron had planned on calling down anyway. Trevor had just phoned to say he'd met Tony and that Evie was missing.

Sally sat down in the kitchen, keenly aware that she was in the visitor's role, but feeling welcome nonetheless.

'Would you like some tea?' Clare asked.

'That would be great.'

Clare busied herself setting out mugs. Camomile for her, and good strong afternoon tea for Sally. They had hardly had their first sip when Saffron and Posy arrived in the back door. Posy headed straight for Sally's knee and climbed up.

'Where Ebee?' Posy wanted to know at once. She still expected Sally to have the answer to everything.

'She'll be back soon,' Sally said, with a lot more conviction than she felt.

'You know I can't settle myself at all,' Clare confided. 'I took Edith's advice and sent her a text saying I just wanted her back and I wouldn't be cross, but she hasn't replied yet.'

'I'm sorry, I didn't even know she was away, Clare, or I would have been up earlier,' Saffron said anxiously. 'Trevor just phoned to tell me.'

'Well at least we knew where she was, thanks to Sally,' and Clare recounted the saga to Saffron.

'Gosh, I couldn't bear anything to happen to darling Evie; I do hope she knows how much we all love her. Don't we all love Evie, Posy?'

'Yes, I love Ebee.'

'They're all the same at that age. Sure Bronagh and I were at each other's throats for a couple of years. She'll settle down, Clare. She knows she's loved.'

Clare looked gratefully at Sally. 'Oh, I hope she does.'

'I suppose you've heard I'm coming back to Edith?'

'Yes, she told me earlier.'

'I must let Fintan know. I'll need a key. I sent mine back.'

'Are you in touch with him often, Sally?' Saffron couldn't resist imbuing the word *touch* with meaning.

'If you mean is there anything going on, well that's hardly likely, is it? He is a famous opera singer, after all, and I'm, well . . .' She trailed off. 'He's been very kind to me, and I suppose he seemed to just take me as he found me. Maybe it's easier to talk to people you don't know so well.'

Clare and Saffron immediately felt ashamed. They had always been just a wee bit aloof from Sally, but that was only to be expected. Their circumstances were poles apart. Both women liked having Sally in their lives, though. Each was dependent on her and was genuinely fond her. Of course it was easier for Fintan to just slide in and make a friend of her. He would be gone next week. Besides, Clare thought, there was just a hint of a project about his thing with her.

'How is the new job? Will there be a conflict between that and Edith?'

'I've left. I couldn't stand the way I was talked to.' She told yet again the story of Rosamund. The two women were hanging on her every word.

'Oh Sally, we were never that bad, were we?' Saffron said almost pleadingly.

'Well now, I would hardly have stayed ten years if you had been.'

'I suppose you wouldn't consider coming back here as well? Even for one day a week?' Clare crossed her fingers under the table.

'Yes, Clare, I'm sure I might be able to manage that, and of course to you too, Saffron. But let me just see to Edith this week. The other thing is . . .'

'Yes?' both women chorused.

'Well, I was thinking I might like to go back and study, get a few qualifications maybe.'

Clare cleared her throat. 'I've been thinking about that too. Fintan told me you were keen to catch up. I've checked the adult education prospectus at the tech. You are eligible to do an access course.'

'When would I have the time?'

'It's two evenings a week, and takes two years. You would

197

then be able to go on to university afterwards.' She handed Sally a page. 'It's all in here. I printed it off the web this morning.'

Sally felt light-headed.

'Have a read through. It's fairly straightforward; you're just the sort of candidate they're looking for.'

'Am I?'

'Yes, and of course I can't wait to help you with your choice of subjects.'

Just then Clare's phone beeped. It was a message from Evie: *Luv u mum very sorry for upsetting u on way home now.* Clare was almost crying with relief as she read it out to the other two women.

'Well,' Sally said, 'I suppose that makes two of us who are coming back.'

Posy couldn't understand what was going on when her very tubby mama and Ebee's mama suddenly started dancing with delight around the kitchen. But she thought she would join in anyway.

31

Evie turned her phone on. She had kept it off to prevent roaming charges over the border, which was why the message from her mother had only just beeped through. She read it a few times before she really took on board the fact that Clare was so frantic with worry that maybe she wouldn't get a bollocking if she went straight home. In truth, she was a bit worn out from it all. Her mother's plea convinced her that a prodigal return was in order. She texted back at once and said she was on her way home.

The concert should have been great, but she had felt strange because of the pot – and very frightened too. At times she felt her head wasn't attached to her body. It hadn't been a great experience. She and Mikey had argued because she didn't want to get in the same filthy sleeping bag as him, and he had called her a stuck-up bitch, although he apologised later. She had spent the entire night awake, wondering what on earth had possessed her to come along to the gig. She hadn't even enjoyed the bands, being as she was so overcome with guilt. She blamed her madcap decision on the fact that she had smoked the joint, but it hadn't really been that. She was just fed up having rows with her mum. She didn't know why they couldn't get along. Clare was cool really. She just exaggerated the importance of education.

Evie arrived home late afternoon. She didn't feel she could face a screaming match, so she avoided the front door and crept down the lane and in through the back door, but Clare saw her, and much to Evie's relief, with a whoop of delight simply took her in her arms and hugged her really tightly.

'Oh sweetheart, please don't do that again. I was so afraid something would happen to you. I'm so sorry I said those things to you. I honestly don't know what I would do without you.'

Evie couldn't believe she was getting off this lightly; it made her feel twice as guilty. Her mother looked wrecked as well, and on the verge of tears. Evie snuggled up to her. It felt good. Maybe her mum did love her after all. She expected her dad would have a 'wee chat' with her later when he got home from work, but she could handle that. She apologised to Clare about a hundred times and then went to have a very long bath. Rock concerts were too smelly.

When she came back down, her mum was in the mood to chat, and for once Evie was in the mood to listen.

'You know, darling, I'm just not managing my life very well. Perhaps I shouldn't have gone back to work when Anna started school.'

'But Mum, you love your work, you'd go bonkers here all day.'

'I know. It got so boring when Dad and I were out at a party or something, answering the endless "And what do you do?" with "Well I'm a stay-at-home mummy, actually, but I used to be a person."'

'I definitely want to have a career when I'm married.'

'I expect you'll have to work for those A levels then, won't you?' And they both laughed.

★

Clare felt more relaxed after her chat with Evie. She would indeed go bonkers stuck here all day. She had read and reread in the broadsheets the arguments each way, and had concluded that something in her remained unsatisfied without a career. She had a need to be defined. But of course, once she returned to lecturing, even though on a part-time basis, it had to be grafted on to full-time motherhood. This resulted in her becoming more discontented than ever. If truth be told, she was a bit lukewarm about her career. She knew she would never scale the dizzy heights now, even should she finish her long-overdue thesis. She had missed the boat. She watched enviously as younger, more ambitious colleagues soared past her, full of self-belief and vitality. But the money was useful; children were expensive. They could live well enough on Tony's salary, but hers afforded an extra security blanket. The upkeep of the house was a big expense – older houses always seemed to have something falling off or down – and of course the children going off to college would be quite a drain.

Tony drove home that evening having spent the day rethinking his own working practices. He did take on far too much, and being a civil servant, he was not paid any extra for it. The job expanded according to the amount of hours he was prepared to put in. He was effective, though, and got things done, but he found it difficult to delegate. He'd have to sort that out.

Clare was on her own in the kitchen making dinner when he got in. She had already phoned him to let him know Evie was back.

'She's in her room.'

'Maybe I'll just have a word with her before dinner, but I've been doing a bit of thinking, love, and I feel the house and the kids and your thesis is all just a bit much for you, and I know I don't help matters. You need a break. so I thought, since Evie and Rory are both here, that the two of us could fit in a long weekend somewhere nice. What do you think?'

'I'd love a break actually, and I suppose they could manage all right, especially now that Sally's coming back.'

'I'll check out some places, then. Maybe somewhere in Donegal.'

He was not relishing his proposed chat with Evie, but she had really crossed the line this time. Until she was in a position to keep herself, she'd have to obey the house rules. He and Clare had been very laid-back as parents, perhaps too liberal; that was part of the problem. Evie wasn't a bad girl really. She was just testing the boundaries, and the time had come to show her exactly where they began and ended.

32

Otis had a plan. The more he thought about it, the more it appealed to him. He would ask Bronagh to dinner. He would have the house to himself for one night before Edith came out of hospital. He had overheard Fintan tell someone on the phone that he was going down to Dublin overnight on Wednesday for some sort of a recital.

Otis had been a bit flummoxed to realise that he actually fancied Bronagh. He'd held back a bit, because she seemed to treat him as if he was her uncle or something. Last week he gave her a lift home and nearly kissed her as she was getting out of the car, but she had sort of shifted her cheek and it had ended up a half-hearted peck. He wasn't sure why he liked her; she was only a wee hairdresser.

Even though he'd be thirty-three on his next birthday, he'd only had one long-term relationship. She had upped and left him earlier this year. He wasn't that fussed. Women ended up bossing you about and looking for stuff. She had run off on him with some flash Harry, a guy who made his money selling insurance polices, or so she claimed. Otis thought he was probably a drug dealer. He sold the small semi they had shared, split the money with her, and left Portadown. It was a dump anyway, full of nothing but dour oul' gits, tacky roundabouts and Chinese restaurants. He had put his half of the money in the building society.

After she had cleared out, he decided to quit his teaching job. His heart had never been in it. The money was shite anyway and the headmaster was full of himself. Thought he knew it all. As for the parents, well, they were a constant source of irritation. Half of them were daft enough to think they'd produced a genius and were never done cornering him to ask about wee Jimmy's progress, and the other half seemed totally uninterested in what their kids were like. The latter were mostly from broken homes and behaved like savages. They paid absolutely no heed to Otis when they came to school. Otis figured they'd end up as paramilitaries, and hoped grimly that eventually they'd all shoot each other.

He decided on a move to Belfast to start his new life. He had certainly lucked out with Marlborough Road. Edith's sister Ellen knew Marjorie, his mother. She'd told Edith he was a poet, and Edith had offered to put him up. He let her think he was broke, so she went really easy on him with the rent and that. He used to get meals too, before that opera eejit moved in, then she transferred her affections.

When Bronagh agreed to come for dinner, his initial thought was to get a takeaway. Now he figured, since he would have the place to himself, possibly for the last time, that it might be better to cook for her. It would be much cheaper than a takeaway and she might be impressed enough that she'd be willing to go upstairs afterwards. The plan of action was to sort out a menu. He wasn't quite sure what sort of food she liked – they'd only had a pizza together till now – but he suspected she was just used to basic fare. Maybe he'd buy gammon steaks, and boil a few spuds. There was a packet or two of frozen peas in the freezer; Miss Black seemed to stockpile them. She was forever telling him they were as good as fresh ones. He'd noticed people put a slice of pineapple on top of gammon. He'd buy a tin; surely that would impress her – gammon with pineapple. Another thing, he'd not stint on the wine. He'd buy one each of red and white; there was an offer on round the corner, two bottles for eight pounds. He would get it early so the white would be cold, and there was some decanter thing he could put the red into, that would impress her. There was a bottle of sherry in the fridge. Sherry went off, so he'd be doing Edith a favour by finishing that. He'd use the silver too. It was a pity the wee cleaner hadn't been, for it looked in need of a polish, and even though he'd not been too struck on Sally, she was good at the polishing. But then he thought, sure it's far from silver Bronagh was reared, so he decided he'd use it as it was, and get out the crystal glasses while he was at it.

Bronagh was starting to feel slightly panicked. It was mental of her to accept Otis's invitation. Suppose somebody, like Evie for example, walked out of their house and saw her going into Miss Black's? What would she say? How could she explain it? Having a meal in Pizza Express was different from going to dinner. Would he have told Miss Black? There was a frightening thought. Just say Miss Black suddenly arrived home from hospital. Bronagh's granny had been sent home without warning last time. Sally had answered her enquiry about Edith earlier, telling her she would be home the day after tomorrow. Her mother seemed happier now she was going back to them all. Bronagh felt it just hastened the moment she would have to tell both Otis and Sally the truth; unless tonight was the last time she would see him. He told her he had lots of books he wanted to give her, and that he was cooking for her himself. No one had ever invited Bronagh to dinner before. She was looking forward to that bit; all the same she hoped he wouldn't cook anything too fancy. She had started to pretend that this was what things would have been like if Charlie had been someone cultured like Otis; she'd be going to him on weekends for a meal. Bronagh reckoned Otis was about thirty-five. Tiffany's dad was that age.

Otis straightened his clothes and took a last look around the dining room. He thought it all looked quite impressive. The table was one of those big mahogany ones and at first he had laid a place at either end of it, but then he thought that looked a wee bit pompous, not to mention too far apart, so he moved the place settings together. He had used the crystal wine glasses, and placed the candles in Miss Black's silver candelabra. He had managed to find two linen napkins, and as a final touch he had gone out to the garden and picked a small bunch of flowers, which he had arranged quite artistically, if he said so himself. Oh yes, he thought, she would be impressed; how could she fail to be? Sure wasn't she from west Belfast and what would she know about fancy tables and the like?

The doorbell rang, and there she was, smiling away and looking a wee bit bashful, but sure wasn't that why he liked her?

'Glad you could make it. Let me take your jacket; you go and sit down in the drawing room.' He nodded upstairs. 'We'll have a wee sherry first.'

Bronagh walked gingerly up the stairs. She remembered the drawing room was the one at the front. It was huge and old-fashioned, and all the walls were covered in paintings, scenes of mountains and lakes. There was one rather large one of some old fellow with a very stern look on his face; probably one of Miss Black's ancestors. There was some sort of classical music playing, and the overall effect was like a scene from a movie. She hovered in the middle of the room, unsure of what to do. A moment later, Otis bounced into the room and lifted a crystal decanter off a small table. There were two glasses sitting beside it. He filled them both. Bronagh was tempted to say that she didn't like sherry but she decided that wasn't a good idea; he had set it out so nicely. So she settled uneasily on one of the chairs and took the glass with a smile. She sipped slowly, for it was very sour, not a bit like the sherry Sally bought at Christmas; this was more like vinegar than wine. She decided to drink it all in one gulp, like medicine, then put her glass down on the little table beside her. Otis immediately poured her another one. Her heart sank. Maybe she should take this one a bit more slowly. She smiled at him again.

'Well,' she said, 'how is the poetry going?'

'Not bad, not bad at all. I've nearly finished the book. I'm hoping to hand it in to the publisher soon. I was thinking I might dedicate it to you.'

'That's really class; will you be able to buy it in the shops?'

'Oh definitely.' He didn't seem to want to go into detail. 'I've been cooking all day, so I hope you enjoy my efforts. Knock that sherry into you, and we'll go downstairs.'

Almost holding her nose, Bronagh tipped the second sherry down and followed him. Her head was reeling a bit. Funny, she had always thought that sherry was an old ladies' drink and not really alcohol. But Otis was knocking it back like there was no tomorrow.

They went into the dining room; it was an intimidating room, all dark and Victorian. Otis ushered her to her seat and made a fuss of opening her napkin for her. It was a large white linen one, not paper.

'Now you sit here, this is just the first course. How about a wee drop of wine to start?'

He poured quite a generous amount of white wine into her glass. He had two plates already laid on the table.

'We're having smoked salmon to begin. Do you like smoked salmon?'

Bronagh nodded. She'd had it before; it was raw, and you squeezed lemon on it. She took a bite. It wasn't bad actually. She washed it down with the wine. Otis sat opposite her. She noticed he practically inhaled his.

He poured her another glass of wine. Then he lifted both the plates, and scurried off into the kitchen. Bronagh was facing the window. It was still light, and she could see out into the back lane. There were children running up and down. She recognised one of them, as Anna McDonald. She had grown; she must be nearly eleven now.

Otis came back carrying two meals; he placed one in front of her with a flourish. It looked fairly unappetising: mashed potato, a huge heap of peas, and a bit of gammon, which looked raw. There was a ring of pineapple perched on top of it. Bronagh took a deep breath and another gulp of wine.

'Tuck in!' Otis said with a grin as he started to wolf his.

Bronagh realised that Otis had not got very good table manners; you would have thought he hadn't eaten for a week.

As Otis cleared away the plates, he declared that he was sure Bronagh wouldn't want to ruin her figure by having dessert. He hoped he'd guessed correctly, since he hadn't bothered to buy anything. Bronagh, having forced the gammon and rather a lot of the lumpy potatoes down, was feeling a wee bit queasy and agreed with alacrity.

'I wondered if you'd mind if I read you some of my latest poems?'

'Why not? Sure I'll sit here and you just bring them down.'

'Well I haven't printed them out yet, so they're still on the computer. That's in my room,' he added.

Bronagh was by now feeling quite drunk.

'Can't you remember them?'

'Ach, not every single word. I'd rather read them to you.'

'Could I have a cup of coffee first?' She thought she had better sober up before she went home.

Otis beamed at her and took her by the arm, leading her into the hall.

'No bother. I'll put the kettle on. Just come up and have a wee look first.'

Reluctantly Bronagh allowed him to guide her upstairs. She felt a bit apprehensive; she knew instinctively this wasn't a good idea, but her head was reeling and she couldn't quite summon the strength to protest. Otis couldn't resist a smirk as he led her upstairs. He hadn't had a decent shag in ages, and surely the drink would have loosened her up. He had invested enough time and energy in her; it was time for a little dividend. She probably fancied the knickers off him and was just playing hard to get.

'Here you are, Bronagh, this is my room,' he said, and he followed her in.

33

Otis scrolled down the few lines he had written. His room was very untidy, Bronagh thought, and somewhat stuffy; it smelled of stale smoke. She was feeling queasy. Otis coughed and cleared his throat.

'Listen, Bronagh, I wrote this especially for you.'

Bronagh tried to concentrate, but her head was spinning. The only chair was in front of the computer. She sat stiffly on the edge of the bed.

'It's a love poem.'

Bronagh felt like throwing up. She lay back on the bed in an effort to stave off the feeling; within seconds, Otis was practically on top of her and covering her with slobbery kisses. His hands were everywhere. Bronagh tried her best to push him off, but he was really strong.

'Ach, c'mon now, sure you must have realised that I fancy the knickers off you? I want to make love to you. I know how to please a girl.'

'No,' Bronagh cried. 'No, get off me! I don't want to, please just leave me alone.'

Otis's mood changed.

'What do you think you're up to, coming over here smiling and eating my food and drinking my wine? And now flinging yourself on the bed in that short skirt?'

He sounded half deranged. He was attempting to kiss her and tugging at her skirt. Bronagh sat up and tried with all her might to push him off, but he was so much stronger. He was holding her tightly by the wrist and he was scarily determined. Suddenly, before she could stop herself, she threw up all over him. Otis sprang up like a scalded cat.

'Ah, for fuck's sake, there was no call for that!'

Bronagh ran downstairs. She tried the front door, but it was locked, so she ran to the back and the key was in the lock. Her hand was shaking, but she managed to open the door and run out into the back lane. She was sobbing now, and still feeling sick, and so ashamed of herself. She straightened her clothes. Most of the vomit had landed on Otis, but she looked a sight. She suddenly remembered she had left her bag there, and her phone, but there was no way she was going back. She made it a few doors down the lane and then was violently sick again.

Evie walked Mikey to the back door. She had been looking after Posy and Simon, and had invited Mikey round to keep her company, as they hadn't seen each other since Oxegen, but now she wanted him gone before Trevor and Saffron got back. She was kissing him good night when she saw a girl staggering up the lane. She watched as the girl stopped at the Nelsons' back door and threw up. Suddenly she realised it was Bronagh.

'You go on, I'll call you later,' she said to Mikey.

Mikey shrugged. Sometimes Evie puzzled him, but then girls were like that. Anyway, he was dying for a smoke, so he shuffled up the lane. He glanced back to see Evie with her arm around the girl, talking earnestly.

Evie couldn't work out what had made Bronagh so upset.

She was crying her heart out. It had obviously been something fairly traumatic. Evie was at a loss what to do, so she just patted her on the back till she calmed down a little.

'Where were you? What happened?'

Bronagh shook her head; her voice came out in sobs.

'It doesn't matter, I'll be okay.' She dabbed round her eyes, and took a deep breath. 'Don't worry, Evie, I'm fine.'

'I'm babysitting for Trevor and Saffron. Why don't you come in here for a minute?'

'No, I'd rather not.'

'Look, the kids are in bed, and they won't be back for over half an hour.'

Bronagh let Evie lead her into the house. It was quiet. Evie went into the kitchen and poured her a glass of water.

'Here, maybe this will help.' She indicated a chair. 'Sit down.'

Bronagh obeyed.

'Can I call a taxi?' she asked.

'No, wait a bit, they come very quickly. Anyway, you need to stop being sick first.'

'I think I have.'

'What happened? Did you have too much to drink?'

Bronagh said nothing.

'Would you rather not talk about it?'

Bronagh nodded. 'I'm okay now.'

Suddenly Evie had an insight. 'You were with Otis, weren't you?'

Bronagh nodded, and then started to cry again.

'What did the bastard do to you? Oh no! He didn't?'

'No, no. I didn't let him, honestly. I ran away, but I've left my handbag there.'

'Do you want me to get my dad to go down to him?'

'No, please, please. It's my fault. I didn't fancy him or anything; I just thought he wanted someone to talk to about his poetry.'

'Aye, right, poetry, I don't think so. Sure he's a mad bastard.

What would he know about poetry? Look, you wait here, I won't be a minute. Don't worry, no one will come down.'

Bronagh sat and waited. Why on earth had she been so stupid? Why had she believed that Otis just wanted to teach her about poetry? Surely he knew that she had just thought of him as a father figure? She felt sick at the thought of him fumbling all over her, and tearing at her clothes. Sure he was not even a bit attractive or sexy. Why would he think she fancied him in the first place? She had never flirted with him or anything like that, had she? He had said that she had, but he was lying.

Evie marched purposefully down to number 29. She could see Otis in the kitchen, sitting at the table. She rapped the window loudly. He looked up, startled.

'Evie! What are you doing here?'

'Can you let me in, please?'

He swung the back door open and smiled broadly at her. After Bronagh left, he had had a quick shower and changed into a grubby tracksuit, but he still smelled strongly of sick.

'Well, Evie, this is an unexpected pleasure. What can I do for you?'

'Bronagh left her handbag in your bedroom. She's in my house, and my dad sent me down to get it, so can I have it, please?'

Otis paled. 'Is she okay? I think she got the wrong impression; I didn't mean to upset her. I mean, we'd just had such a great meal. I went to a lot of bother.'

'To upset her?'

'Is she upset?'

'Hello? Yes, she is! She's in absolute hysterics. I might have to call a doctor. So could you please go now and get me her bag?'

Otis disappeared upstairs in a flash and came back and handed the bag to Evie. Evie checked it for Bronagh's phone.

'I think she got the wrong end of the stick.'

'No, I don't think she did somehow.'

'Should I come up and apologise to her?'

'I don't think an apology would make much difference at this stage. You'll be lucky if my dad doesn't call the police.'

Otis looked as if he was about to faint. Evie turned on her heel and left. She was quite pleased with her performance. Serve the nasty bastard right.

When she got back, Bronagh was sitting quietly in the kitchen. She had obviously gone into the cloakroom and washed her face. She seemed more composed.

'Thanks very much, Evie. I need my phone to call Mum. She'll be wondering where I am.'

'Do you want to stay the night in my house? We have a spare room. I think the bed's made up.'

'No, I'd rather get home. Mum will be starting to worry. She doesn't know I was with Otis.' Bronagh pulled an anxious face. 'Evie, you won't tell anyone about this, will you?'

'Not if you don't want me to, but he shouldn't be allowed to get away with it.'

'Nothing really happened; I mean, like, you know ...' Bronagh trailed off.

'Yes, but if you hadn't managed to run away, it might have. He's so old – and a ginger! No one in the lane likes him, but then no one likes Mikey, and he's young.'

Bronagh smiled. 'You can't win.'

Evie laughed. 'I know. Listen, I phoned the salon like you told me, and Jimmy is doing my streaks next week. I'm the last appointment. Do you want to go for a coffee after?'

'Yes, that would be nice. And Evie, thanks for sorting things out for me. It was really good of you.'

'Don't be silly. I just got your handbag – oh, and I told Otis my dad was thinking of calling the police.'

'Oh my God, you didn't! What did he say?'

'I didn't wait to hear, but I bet he's worried sick, and it serves him right, the disgusting pervert.'

As Bronagh left in her taxi, she was looking forward to going for coffee. Evie was great fun, nice, and dead ordinary. She suddenly felt really glad her mum was going back to work in Marlborough Road. It would be a perfect place as soon as Otis moved out, and somehow she had a feeling that wouldn't be too long.

34

Fintan had another job to go to after Belfast; a production in Glasgow of *Don Giovanni*. Rehearsals didn't start for three weeks. He planned, therefore, to stay an extra week with Edith; see her back on her feet, as it were. It would be relaxing to stay around and not have to rush off to work or rehearsals.

Edith was being discharged from hospital today. Clare had been up to the house yesterday before Fintan left for Dublin and selected a suitcase of clothes. She was picking Edith up after lunch, as soon as Mr Smedley had finished his ward round.

Fintan arrived back about nine thirty. Sally was coming at ten to give the place a good cleaning and make sure everything was to Edith's satisfaction. Clare had offered to cook a casserole and send it down, but Fintan thought a nice omelette might suit Edith better, and of course he could do that easily, so he suggested Clare do something next week, after he'd gone. Edith would need more support then.

The kitchen was a total disaster. Bloody Otis must have had a party. He called upstairs but got no reply. Otis had buggered off somewhere. Fintan didn't understand how Edith tolerated the man. He cursed him inwardly. He couldn't let Sally arrive back to this. He cleared a space and made a pot of coffee.

Sally arrived on the dot of ten, feeling more light-hearted than she had in weeks. She parked the bike smartly outside Edith's back door and came in to the smell of freshly ground coffee; Fintan had timed things perfectly. For a second she felt a bit embarrassed, but recovered quickly.

'I went to see Edith yesterday; she looked great, and she said she had good news from her surgeon.'

'Yes indeed. She'll just have to take it easy for a while. Sadly her sister has taken a turn for the worse. Her friend rang as I got in this morning, so I told her we'd try to bring Edith down to visit this weekend. I hope it doesn't upset her too much.'

'Poor old Edith. I know she's been expecting it, but it'll be hard for her when Ellen goes. She has no other family. God love her, she hasn't her sorrows to seek, has she?'

'No, she certainly does not. I'm afraid the kitchen is in a bit of a state. Otis must have had people in.' He indicated the pots and glasses. 'I'll give you a hand.'

'No, don't worry, I've coped with worse.'

'At least let me get all the dishes together.' He took a tray and went into the dining room, where the table was still full of dishes, two of everything. Obviously Otis had had a romantic dinner à deux. He'd used the best cutlery, silver and crystal.

Sally and Fintan worked in tandem until they had restored the ground floor to pristine condition. As they worked, Sally told him of her plans to take the access classes.

'I called the Belfast Institute and they've invited me to an open day tomorrow. Right enough, they sounded very friendly.'

'Good for you. I bet you'll make an excellent student.'

'Clare has said she'll help me to select subjects. Though you have to do the basics again.'

'Good, and you'll be able to combine it with working in Marlborough Road?'

'Yes, I think so. I'll know after I've been to see them, though this house is a breeze compared to the other two. God knows what Posy will have stuck on the walls, and Saffron, honestly, have you seen the size of the poor girl? She can hardly get about; those twins will be born walking. And I have to face Iggy the iguana again. I'm dreading the thought of that baggy oul' face staring back at me.'

Fintan threw back his head and laughed. 'Sally O'Neill, I don't believe for a single minute you are dreading any of it. If I'm not mistaken, you are positively looking forward to it all. Well?'

Sally laughed. He was right, of course, but she did feel a trifle apprehensive. It would take a while for her to settle back into the routine.

'Now,' he said, 'I'm afraid I have to go; I've an appointment in town. I'll maybe see you tomorrow morning.'

After he'd left, Sally washed her cup and Fintan's and put them away carefully in the cupboard. She would do Edith's bed next, and use her good Egyptian linen. Then she would cut some flowers from the garden. She wanted Edith to arrive home to a perfect room with everything in its place.

The idea of taking the classes had excited Sally. She was looking forward to the open day. If she could stick to her resolve and see it through, it would make a lot of difference to her life. It was just the sort of challenge she needed. The following morning at ten, she made her way to the tech and was shown into a room and asked to take a seat. There were three other women waiting. Two were about her own age, and one was possibly around fifty. A woman who told them she was one of the tutors popped her head round the door and said she'd be back in five minutes. She handed out some forms for them to fill in. Sally felt somewhat intimidated, but began to do as she'd been told. Then the older woman spoke.

'Heavens, this reminds me of being back at school waiting for the headmistress.'

The others laughed, and the ice was broken.

'I'm feeling a bit scared, actually. I have hardly had time to read a book since my last child was born, and she's sixteen now.'

Sally smiled back in solidarity and then the tutor returned. Her name was May. She was helpful and gave them some general information, then she showed them the library and the lecture theatres and fixed a day for enrolment. It was all surprisingly easy, at least that part. Sally still felt unnerved when she thought about actually getting down to it, but Joyce, the chatty woman, walked out to the car park with her and confided that she was feeling much the same.

'Oh,' she said when she saw Sally's bike. 'I'm impressed. I'd say you must be somewhat bohemian. You'll take to social studies like a duck to water.'

Sally left for Marlborough Road feeling gratified.

Things had been a little better in the McNamara household of late. Saffron had gradually come round to the idea of twins; they had always talked of having four children, and at least now she was getting off with just three pregnancies. Trevor seemed to have gone from belligerence and annoyance to stoicism. There had been a shift in their relationship.

Laura hadn't been around recently. She had taken the children on holiday to her parents. With her departure, Trevor's mood had lightened considerably. Bill planned to join the family for a few weeks before school went back. Trevor had chatted to him a few times in the lane and concluded that he knew nothing of his dalliance with Laura. Either that or he was a very good actor. Trevor had an uneasy feeling that it might all rear up again, but for now he was just mightily glad of the respite. If he could get to the end of the summer – better still, the pregnancy – with no further contact from Laura, well that would suit him just fine.

By about lunchtime both Saffron and Clare had separately found excuses to drop in to Edith's. Now that Sally was back in business, they were checking that she wouldn't run away and leave them again. To their immense satisfaction, she was bustling about Edith's house hell-bent on restoring it to its former glory. She indulged them when they arrived within minutes of each other by stopping for a quick cup of tea to catch up on the goings-on in the lane. Besides, she needed to consult with Clare about the arrangements to get Edith home from hospital.

'Oh, Sally, did you hear that the Nelsons are separating?' Clare settled down with her cup of tea.

Saffron looked at her amazed. 'Gosh, Clare, even I hadn't heard that.'

'Yes, apparently they're splitting up. Laura called me. She's spending the rest of the summer with her parents in Devon, and then when the law and school terms start again she'll come back. She says they'll probably put the house on the market.'

'Oh dear,' Saffron said, 'that's awfully sad, especially for the children. I thought they were quite happy.'

'To be honest, I thought something was up. She came into our house a few weeks ago absolutely plastered, and sat yacking on about men being bastards.'

'Well a lot of them are.' Sally had already finished her tea and was back bustling round.

'Trevor is friendly with her, I wonder if he knows about it.'

Saffron had a vague expression on her face. Immediately a look flashed between Sally and Clare, as if suddenly they both knew without a doubt that Trevor was somehow inextricably connected to this news.

'I was so looking forward to having her around after the twins are born, what with her experience.'

'Ach, Saffron, we'll all chip in with the twins. Sure it's only two of the one baby. You need to look after yourself and enjoy being the mother of two for these next few months.'

Sally took their cups, put them on the draining board and shooed them both out the door.

'I can't sit around chatting all day. I'll see you at nine tomorrow, Clare, and I'll be into you at lunchtime, Saffron.'

The two women left, but lingered outside in the lane.

'Gosh, Clare, that is fairly awful news about the Nelsons. It's so out of the blue. And selling the house – why?'

Clare shrugged; she had no idea. 'I expect they can't afford to run a house this size and another one as well.'

'Heavens, I do hope they don't sell to a property developer. He'd fill it with students. That would be all we need.'

'Stop, don't even go there. Maybe it'll not happen and they'll sort things out.'

'I hope so; it would be so awful for the poor children.'

Saffron walked home feeling inexpressibly sad, but also strangely relieved, and she didn't want to think why. She was very glad, however, that she hadn't voiced her suspicions about Trevor's friendly behaviour towards Laura; it would have served no purpose. Laura had always been a bit discontented with her lot in life. She had never liked Northern Ireland. Perhaps she'd be happier away from here.

There is a saying in Ireland, 'If you don't like the weather, just wait five minutes.' Trevor was mulling this over as he walked home in the pouring rain. He had left the car at home this

221

morning, since the sun had been shining brightly. The downpour had started seconds after he left the office. He had no umbrella and he was soaked. He looked longingly at each passing car, hoping one of them might be a neighbour, but no luck.

'Gosh, Dad, you're soaking,' Simon chirped when he arrived home.

'Full marks for observation, son.'

'Why you all wet, Daddy?' Posy was out of her high chair finally and perched on a little booster seat, being a big girl. They had all been waiting for Trevor to have family dinner.

Trevor softened. 'Because, sweetheart, it's raining very hard and Daddy had no umbrella.'

He went upstairs to change, and came down to a roast vegetable and couscous stew. Saffron had opened a bottle of wine (non-organic).

'I thought I would have a little with water. I think it's safe enough in the third trimester and I knew you could use a little glass, Treasure, when I saw the weather.'

Trevor felt mollified; sure he was just an old grump. He had a lot to be thankful for. Saffron was beautiful – pregnancy suited her – and the kids were full of chat. He began to relax and enjoy his meal. He was a lucky man to have all this.

They had just finished pudding when Bill Nelson arrived at the back door looking a bit dejected. Trevor felt an instant pang of nervousness, but sprang up immediately and offered him a glass of wine.

'No thanks – you don't have a beer, do you?'

'No problem. What would you like?' Trevor named three kinds of fancy beers.

'Oh, anything, whatever's cold.'

They sat down, and Saffron cleared the table and spirited the kids out of the kitchen. She felt Bill wanted a man-to-man chat, possibly about his upcoming separation. Really, it was too awful for words. She fervently hoped Clare had somehow got the wrong end of the stick. Poor Bill – or maybe it was poor Laura. Whatever, no doubt Trevor would tell her all later on.

Bill almost drained the bottle in one gulp. Trevor opened the fridge door, took out a second and handed it to him.

'Cheers. I suppose you've heard the news, mate?'

Trevor shook his head. His legs had turned to lead, and he felt his throat constrict. He quickly poured another glass of wine for himself, sat down again and tried to look composed and concerned. Women were so much better at this, he thought.

'Laura is leaving me. I suppose you can guess why?'

Trevor gazed mutely at Bill. He was literally petrified. The words wouldn't form.

'I know, mate, nothing to say really. I should have appreciated her when I had her.' He shook his head slowly. 'Twelve years we've been married, twelve years. It's hard to believe.'

Trevor's fingers tightened on the table. The room was spinning. He took a deep breath and another large sip.

'Bill, I'm really sorry, these things can—'

'Listen, Trevor, you're right, we all do crazy things. I don't know what possessed me – insanity, male menopause, vanity, and of course she was willing . . . such a tease, and young and foreign and hot.' He looked intently at Trevor.

What was he talking about?

'Puri . . . I hate the name Purificacion. Ironic, eh?'

'Oh yes, the au pair . . . You mean you . . . ?' Trevor spilled the words out.

Bill stammered on, glad to confess, unburden himself. Trevor was almost jealous. There was no absolution for him.

'Anyway,' Bill continued, 'I'm sure you get my drift . . . I know it's not politically correct to say this,' he added hurriedly, 'but believe me, coming out of the bathroom and dropping her towel . . . things like that, you know. It drove me crazy. I was mad for her. She had me at her mercy.'

He bowed his head, as if to indicate the weight was too much. All that temptation had floored him. He had been blameless, like Trevor. For a minute neither man spoke, then Bill looked up, wanting only that Trevor understand. Trevor nodded furiously. Bill took the cue with gratitude.

'It's hard for men of our age – well, any age really – to resist someone like that.' He sighed. 'I should have, though. Laura came home last weekend . . . We were . . . you know . . . Seems she'd got an early flight. She . . . well, she fired her on the spot.'

Bill paused and drained the second bottle. He placed it on the table with a thump.

'Sorry to be drinking so much.' He gestured towards the fridge. 'May I?'

Trevor nodded wordlessly, concentrating on not passing out with relief.

'Anyway she's moved to stay with another Spanish girl, Puri has. I said I wouldn't see her again, but apparently Laura has decided our marriage was crap anyway. Can you believe it? Crap, that's the word she used.' He lowered his voice. 'Said I hadn't been any good in bed for years – I mean that hurt, that really hurt.'

Trevor reached across the table and patted Bill awkwardly on the hand.

'Women say things, Bill. I'm sure she didn't mean it. And are you sure it was just because of Puri?'

'Well, what else could it be?'

'And it was . . . just the once?'

'Yes, just the once . . . dreadful timing.'

'Yes, dreadful,' Trevor echoed.

Bill looked at him dolefully.

'I mean, I've been working too hard, and so has Laura. Puts a strain on things, but everything was fine. At least I thought so. Now she says she wants me out of the house by the time she and the kids come back from Devon.'

And to Trevor's utter horror, Bill put his head in his hands and began to sob.

35

Sally was hardly back to work when events in Marlborough Road suddenly speeded up. It was as if everything had been suspended until her return. Edith came home from hospital to a house that positively gleamed; even the searching rays of late summer sun could barely find specks of dust to float in them. On her first afternoon back, Otis announced he had bought a property nearby and would be moving into it at the end of the month. Edith didn't mind at all. In fact she found herself quite relieved at his announcement; though it was a great puzzle to her where on earth he had found the money to buy anything, let alone a house. She hoped he had done nothing illegal. Throughout his sojourn with her, he had constantly pleaded poverty. He had even missed the rent one month. Were it not for the fact that Marjorie, his mother, was so good to Ellen, she would have asked him to leave long ago.

Sally was especially delighted to be getting rid of him, hardly able to contain her glee. She had felt the house would never be clean with him in it. All that smoking in his room, and frying everything; he had even ruined the non-stick pan. But there was something else about him that unsettled her, though she couldn't quite put her finger on it. Still, good riddance, he was off soon. Meanwhile he was keeping a low profile, staying in his room on the rare occasions he was home.

Fintan had only a few days left until his departure, a real cause for sadness for both women. He was such an asset to Marlborough Road. What a pity Northern Ireland only staged operas a few times a year.

Fintan and Edith were having a cup of tea and a chat when he suddenly said to her, 'Edith, have you considered taking a break in the sun? A week somewhere before you begin the chemotherapy?'

'Why, Fintan, what a nice idea!' For a moment Edith thought he was asking her to accompany him, then quickly she understood that it was merely a suggestion.

'You know the holiday Sally won?'

'Yes, that was very lucky. She says you won it together.'

'Not really. Anyway, I don't think she will use it . . . Perhaps you could buy it from her? Would Isabelle go with you?'

'Oh, I don't wish to be unkind, Fintan, but Isabelle can be such a fussy old bore. I couldn't stand to be with her for a week. We went to Rome together once for a long weekend . . . she drove me crazy. More interested in the cats than the Colosseum.'

Edith didn't like cats; they peed on her plants and sprayed the tyres of her car.

Fintan smiled. An idea was forming.

'What about your going with Sally?'

Edith looked surprised.

'Going with Sally – me?'

'Yes, I expect Sally would be just the right person for you to go on holiday with. She's sensible and friendly . . .' He paused. He had to phrase this delicately. 'Years ago, Edith, someone of your class would have had a lady companion.'

227

'I couldn't suggest it to her; she'd think it strange . . .'

But Fintan was sure by the look on Edith's face that she was intrigued by the idea. And she hadn't said no. If Edith could get past the class thing, she would enjoy Crete with Sally. And it would be a good thing for Sally as well. It would give her a boost. They didn't have to stay welded together. Edith could take a few trips to museums and ruins; Sally could lie by the pool, maybe even take along a few of the books from her forthcoming English syllabus to read. He decided to leave Edith with the thought and changed the subject.

Edith was improving daily, though she was still weak. Clare drove her down to see Ellen twice, and then Edith's friend Isabelle volunteered for the job. She had known the Black sisters since childhood, so in a way it was more appropriate.

Ellen wouldn't be long for this world. Edith thanked her lucky stars she had heeded her own symptoms early. Mr Smedley had been most encouraging when he came round to discharge her, and even she knew doctors were reluctant to commit to anything these days, what with all the ghastly lawyers hounding them.

Even as she rationalised her own feelings about it, Edith knew that she was being terrifyingly unemotional about her illness, but she simply couldn't help herself. There was a guard, some kind of inner mechanism that made her do that. It stopped her giving way to the awful feeling of hopelessness and doom she knew was buried deep within her right now. At times she mentally compared it to a lid that pressed down and, as it did, snuffed out her true feelings about Ellen's imminent death and her own mortality. If she allowed the lid to open even a crack, she would find herself washed out in the tide.

At the end of her first week of recuperation, Edith was still feeling a little bit frail. Sally was coming today, so she sensibly decided to stay in bed. She had been to see Ellen the day before. She spent almost three hours at the hospice and it had taken a lot out of her. She didn't think her sister would last the week.

Sally brought her lunch on a tray, fixed beautifully. It held a plate with two triangular sandwiches filled with ham, cheese and thinly sliced tomato, a piece of shortcake, and a pot of tea (Earl Grey). Edith was most appreciative. The dynamic between the two women had shifted considerably since Edith's illness and Sally's return. It was now much more in the nature of friendship and mutual respect than a mistress/maid situation.

That was mainly down to Fintan, reflected Edith. He had made an immediate friend of Sally, and this had somehow permitted Edith to break through her class prejudices. Being ill, and counting her blessings and finding Sally at the top of the list, had put the seal on it. Certainly attitudes had shifted on both sides: previously Sally only cleaned Edith's bedroom when it was empty. This new-found intimacy also made Edith brave enough to heed Fintan's suggestion.

'That holiday you won a while back, Sally. Have you decided when you are going?'

'Ach, don't worry about that. I won't be taking any time off. I don't think I'll use it.'

'But what an awful pity. Could some of your family not avail themselves of it?'

'Well there's a chance Bronagh would go with a friend, but she's not that keen. I've offered it to my sisters as well but nobody's interested. Half of it belongs to Fintan, though. He might be able to use it when his next opera finishes.'

'Could you not find a friend to go with?'

'Well to be honest, not really. Anyhow, it only covers flights and hotel. I wouldn't be much use at finding places to eat somewhere like that, not knowing the language or anything.'

'Well, Sally, I have a suggestion to make. I wonder if you would consider my coming with you? I could go to look at the museums and ruins and you could rest by the pool. I think a break in the sun might be the very ticket for me.'

Sally was speechless. Six months ago she would have thought the suggestion outrageous – in fact Edith would never have made it – but improbably, it now sounded a perfectly reasonable idea.

'Don't answer now, think about it overnight. I expect we'd have to go in late September. The sun is more bearable then.'

Sally finished cleaning and took the tray down, leaving Edith to have a nap. Funny the way things turn out, she thought.

Ellen died the following weekend. Edith went to Portadown for the funeral and stayed a few days to sort things out. It was wretchedly sad, even if it had been expected. Edith allowed herself the luxury of tears, but those few outward drops only kept the pain in check. She would do most of her grieving in private, alone in bed, where she fought against a dull ache of loss and a deep sense of regret that she had always rationed or curtailed her hugs for Ellen. She vowed that she would change; she would start to show more affection. Perhaps like the child in the story of the Snow Queen, she too could thaw. Her neighbours – whom she also counted as friends – could and would be her role models. Previously she had lamented their lack of control, tutted inwardly over the abundance of affection and indulgence they displayed to their children. Perhaps from now on she would strive to become more like them. And Sally, who was being so solicitous of her; she would try to be more affectionate to Sally. Edith knew that if her attitude relaxed, Sally would respond. That was logical. And there was something else she could do for Sally. The thought of it made her positively gleeful. Perhaps she would get a chance to be Fairy Godmother sooner than she had thought. Ellen had been very thorough; most of her worldly goods were left to Age Concern, with a few of the family things set aside for Edith and some nieces and nephews on her late husband's side to choose from. Ellen had been very well off. She had left the bulk of her money to the hospice, but even so there was a sizeable legacy for her sister. Edith, who was not short of money thanks to an adequate pension and careful management over the years, suddenly went from comfortably off to rich.

Sally arrived for work promptly at nine o'clock on Tuesday morning. Edith was in the kitchen reading the paper. Emboldened by her new approach to life, she looked up.

'You have yet to give me an answer about Crete, Sally.'

Sally looked slightly disconcerted.

'I'm sorry, Miss Black.'

'Edith, Sally, please call me Edith.'

'Edith then. I suppose I put it out of my head.'

The opposite was true. Sally had thought of nothing else since Edith had made the suggestion, but she felt overwhelmed by the idea. Imagine Sally O'Neill going off to Crete with Edith Black. She was sure she couldn't cope. Suppose she hated the odd food? She had never tasted Greek food before. Goodness, she hardly even liked Chinese. She preferred to be able to make out what she was eating, and all that jumbled-up stuff confused her. What if Edith wanted to go to fancy restaurants? And there was another, even bigger reason, and that was the money issue. Sally managed her money well, but by the time she had paid the bills, there wasn't a lot left. Even if Edith paid her for the other ticket, it wasn't rightly Sally's; it was Fintan's, so she couldn't accept any money.

She said that to Edith.

'Oh, nonsense, it was Fintan who suggested I use it. I must admit it hadn't occurred to me. But I think it's an awfully good idea.'

Sally couldn't think of anything to say. She didn't want to

harp on about the money. Maybe she could manage it. She had some savings. But Edith had obviously read her mind.

'Sally, I know you might be worried about the financial side of things, but Greece is awfully cheap compared to here, and eating out is very reasonable.'

Sally hesitated. Here was an opportunity she might never get again. Maybe she could bring a couple of the novels Clare had given her to read. She could always talk to Edith about them. Bronagh was old enough to stay on her own, and if she put her mind to it, she could manage the financial side all right. Sure wouldn't she be buying groceries anyway if she was at home?

'Maybe I should drop into the travel agent's tomorrow on my way over. We'd need to check they have vacancies for whatever week we choose.'

'That would be wonderful, Sally. Oh, isn't it fun to have something to look forward to?'

And Edith sat back contentedly. Yes, this was the first step on the road to the new Edith.

On her way out, Sally met Fintan walking down the lane.

'I see you put Edith up to going on holiday with me.'

Fintan laughed. 'Well, there was no point in letting the trip go to waste, now was there? Never look a gift horse in the mouth.'

'Do you think it will be okay – me going off with her? I mean, we're so different.'

'Yes, you are, but you respect each other, and I think you both need the break. I wish I was coming along.'

Sally smiled, and thought how nice it would be if Fintan did accompany them on holiday. But of course she said nothing.

'I'm calling into the travel agent's tomorrow to see what dates are available.'

'Good. That's great news. Let me know how you get on.'

★

Sally arrived at the McNamaras' in a cloud of emotion, and even the presence of Iggy in the kitchen couldn't dampen her good spirits. Saffron, though, was not to know this. She hauled herself out of the chair when she saw Sally arrive.

'Oh Sally, please don't worry about Iggy, he's just here for a minute to say goodbye.'

Iggy sat immobile on top of the plate rack over the Aga, his heavy-lidded eyes fixed on Saffron and Sally.

'What do you mean, goodbye?'

'He's going. Simon and I have had a long chat about this, and since Simon will be going to school, and the twins will be arriving soon, there'll be no one to look after the poor old thing. So we've agreed that Iggy needs to go to a new home. We advertised at the reptile shop and we've found him a new owner, someone highly recommended. He phoned last night. He sounded a very friendly person, and he already has two other iguanas. He'll be here to pick him up at two. Isn't that great?' Saffron looked at her for approval.

'I hope it isn't on my account you're getting rid of him. I have put up with him for three years now.'

'Of course not, Sally, I promise.'

She lowered her voice, as if Iggy could hear what she was saying.

'To be honest, Trevor can't stand him either, and I don't feel as inclined to clean up after him, what with the pregnancy and that. Besides, Simon is so looking forward to going to school, and feels Iggy would miss him dreadfully if he left him alone all day.'

'Well I can't say I won't be glad, as long as Simon doesn't grieve for him. I remember Bronagh took it badly when the cat died.'

But as Iggy surveyed her from the top of the Aga while she cleaned the kitchen, Sally couldn't help feeling triumphant. She wouldn't have to gaze at that baggy oul' face again, and she was sure he'd be happy in his new home; sure weren't there two wee friends there for him to pal around with? Yes, life was on the up.

After dinner that evening, Sally called Edith and said she would definitely go to Crete.

'Oh Sally, I'm so glad. We'll have a wonderful time. Fintan assures me it's his favourite part of Greece.'

The following morning she was at the door of the travel agent's as soon as it opened. She handed over the voucher Evie had given her, and got all the details and a list of available dates. The last week of September was their preference. The girl looked up the predicted weather on the internet and told her it would be about seventy-five degrees during the day and a bit cooler in the evening. They could have two single rooms for a supplement of thirty pounds each, although Edith had told her she fancied an upgrade, which she would pay for. Sally felt that arrangement was essential; there was no question of sharing a room. She would be too embarrassed, and she felt sure Edith would want her privacy. The hotel looked lovely. It had a large swimming pool, and was very modern; probably not to Edith's taste, but it was near some Minoan ruins, which definitely were. The girl put that particular week on hold, and printed all the details out. She gave Sally a card with her direct line and told her to call when they had decided for sure. She would need passport numbers and the room supplements.

Sally drove to Marlborough Road feeling excited. She'd nip in to see Edith after she'd finished at the McNamaras' and they could sort it all out then.

There was just one more thing she needed to do to make the week perfect. She had heard from Eileen that Charlie was going off to Coventry in a week's time. He had two brothers there and one of them had offered him a job. She couldn't wait. She needed to talk to him before he left, though. She waited till Bronagh and Tiffany were settled watching a film and went upstairs. She found the piece of paper Eileen had given her and dialled the number on it.

'Hello, Charlie? It's Sally.'

'Ach, Sally, it's great to hear from you. What can I do for you, love?'

'You can come to the solicitor with me on Monday morning. I want a divorce.'

36

Sally and Edith saw Fintan off on Friday. The taxi that took him to George Best City Airport left behind two women with heavy hearts. The truth was, both of them were more than a bit in love with him. He had brought a lot of pleasure and a new focus to their lives. He left in a flurry of hugs and promises to stay in touch, and talked of getting back to visit at the beginning of October, when he finished in *Don Giovanni*.

Clare and Tony were going away too, finally getting off for their weekend break. Tony had booked a five-star country house in Donegal. The food was highly recommended and it was supposed to be luxurious. There was a spa as well. Clare had reckoned she was seriously in need of pampering. The snag was that it was a long drive.

Rory and Evie had promised to look after Anna and Lola the dog. Anna would spend a lot of the time at the McNamaras' anyway, though she had made Clare promise she could eat her meals at home. Poor Anna, she wanted to be a vegetarian really. How could she not, with Simon's constant proselytising? However, the truth was, she didn't like vegetables much. To calm Clare's nerves, Sally agreed to come in on Friday as well as Monday morning. If there was one thing Clare needed to do, it was relax.

It was Rory's idea to have the party. He had a barbecue in mind. That way, everyone could bring their own food and drink. He thought he would invite all of his mates, who, now term had finished, had descended on their parents to live off them during the summer months. But Evie was not going to let him get away with that. No way. If Rory was having a party, then she was inviting her friends as well.

'*Your* friends? Like Mikey and all his druggie buddies? I don't think so.'

'Well you're not having a party then. Mum will kill you if she finds out, and how on earth will you keep the house tidy?'

'It's a barbecue, stupid! Everyone will be outside.'

'Yes, but they need to be indoors to use the bathroom.'

'They can go in the bushes.'

'Get real! That is the most ridiculous thing I've ever heard. Just say the kids are around. Anna. Simon. Posy.'

'Well I'll tell them to use the downstairs cloakroom.'

'Aye, right, and pee all over the floor.'

'I don't pee all over the floor.'

'Yes you do. Mum is always giving off about it.'

'Sally's coming on the Monday morning.'

'So? You would expect Sally to mop up a smelly toilet? And what if Mum and Dad come home early? You'll never get away with it. You'll have to tell them.'

'I'll have the party on the Friday night; that way I have all weekend to clean up.'

'Rory, are you listening to me? You had better tell Mum and Dad. You can't expect people in the lane not to notice you all outside.'

So Rory was on his best behaviour for a few days, and then over dinner the night before Tony and Clare were due to go, he told them that he had asked a few friends round tomorrow night. Would that be all right?

'Please? Mum, Dad, honestly – you know them all. Sam, Ali, Smithy, Jules? Please? Look, it'll be okay, we'll mainly be outside.'

Clare and Tony exchanged looks.

'Listen, mate, this break is so that your mother can unwind. She can't be worrying about the house, and I don't want to be coming back to Armageddon.'

'Dad, I promise . . . Look, I've been working all summer, and I passed all my exams with no re-sits and you promised me something for that. Please? I swear we'll behave.'

'Well maybe this once, but definitely outside. And don't let it go on too late, and make sure you keep the noise down.'

'And Rory darling, don't forget poor Edith's not long out of hospital and Saffron's pregnant. She needs to rest. You won't let things get out of control, will you?'

'No, honestly. I promise, Mum.'

'Well okay then. But make sure Anna isn't up too late, and remember to feed Lola.'

Clare tended to give in easily to her only son.

So it was agreed. Of course Evie, after a mixture of threats and persuasion, got Rory to allow her to invite a few of her girlfriends. Mikey could come along later. He worked on Friday nights. She thought she might invite Bronagh as well, although she was aware that Bronagh might feel a bit out of place. Rory's friends were real rugby types, and had no idea how to behave with girls when they were drinking. They were so immature. She phoned Bronagh to ask her. Bronagh seemed pleased to hear from her, but was doubtful about the party.

'My mum would wonder how we even knew each other.'

'Don't be silly, we've always known each other.'

'Yes, but . . . you know what I mean.'

'She knows I go to the salon for my streaks.'

'You've never said anything about . . . you know?'

'No, of course not. I promised you.'

'Thanks . . . Mum says he's moving out.'

'I know. They are all delighted round here to get rid of him. My mum says even Miss Black will be glad to see the back of him.'

Bronagh said tentatively that she would consider coming. 'I'll phone you and let you know for sure.'

'You can bring a friend if you like.'

'No, I don't know anyone who would fit in.'

'Thanks!'

'You know what I mean, Evie.'

'I know. Rory has already called Mikey and his mates freaks. If you do come, just come by yourself, and come early. I'll be on my own; Mikey won't be here till the bar closes.'

Sally was pleased to hear Evie had invited Bronagh.

'Ach, that was nice of her. I'm glad you've made friends with Evie. I told you they're not bad kids; just a wee bit spoiled. Rory's a lovely boy, so he is.'

Bronagh said nothing. She was tempted by the invite, but surely Sally of all people knew it wouldn't be easy for her.

'You should go, you might meet somebody nice. You have to aim high, Bronagh pet. Do better than me, and find a man who can keep you.'

'For starters, I'm never, ever getting married, and I'll be able to keep myself. I'm going to open my own salon, and drive a Porsche like Alan.'

'Would you not go along even for an hour?'

'I'll see how I feel on Friday.'

They left it at that. Sally hoped Bronagh wasn't ashamed of her being a cleaner. She had never said anything to that effect to Sally, or acted as if she minded, but the young ones were so self-conscious about status, and more aware of what was available in life than she had ever been as a child. When Sally was

239

growing up, no one round where she lived had anything. Posh people were rarely encountered, and the only time she had felt inadequate was when she went to the grammar school. Bronagh had been to Belfast's only girls' comprehensive, but had chosen to leave at sixteen to do hairdressing. No role models, as Clare would say. It was just taken for granted that Evie and Rory and their friends would go to 'uni', as they called it, whether they were clever or not. It was indeed a different world.

On Friday morning before setting off for Donegal, Tony popped into the office to sign a few urgent letters. It was now almost noon and he hadn't come back. Clare had got herself into a state.

'Mum, you need to take a chill pill. You know Dad is always late,' said Evie helpfully.

'Yes,' snapped Clare, 'I do, unfortunately, but we have a long drive ahead of us, and I will be furious if we don't arrive in time for dinner; it's included in the price. The last thing we need is to be caught in the rush-hour traffic.'

Eventually Tony pulled up in front of a small crowd of onlookers who were trying to pacify Clare. As usual she had flitted from rage, to panic that something might have happened to him, and then back to rage as soon as she saw the car approach.

Tony went into the kitchen, muttering apologetically and started to gather up the bags. He was about to remark on the amount of luggage but thought better of it. Watched by Sally, Evie, Simon and Anna, he carefully loaded the bags into the boot and kissed Anna and Evie goodbye whilst dutifully listening to a tirade from Clare about her having to do his packing yet again. Clare twittered about the kitchen. Now that they were actually ready to go, she couldn't leave.

'Calm down,' said Sally. 'You'll not enjoy the drive. Here, don't forget your handbag.'

'You're right, Sally, we'd better go. Anna, be a good girl for Saffron, won't you? And Evie, please tell Rory not to overdo it tonight. I've asked Trevor to pop down to check on things.'

'Thanks a lot, Mum! It's for young people, not OAPs or randoms like Trevor.'

Tony started the engine. This was so bloody typical. He'd almost broken the sound barrier on the way home, and now Clare was doing her usual fussing.

'Right, we're leaving!' he yelled.

Finally the Saab wound its way back up the lane with Clare slumped in the passenger seat, and Sally, the children and the stray neighbours peeled off to their various tasks with a collective sigh of relief.

Sally hoped Clare would really unwind; she had been on wires all summer. She had to concede that at times Clare had a right to be infuriated with Tony. Sally hadn't laid eyes on him since she had come back. He rarely left that office of his, though what on earth he found to do there day and night she didn't know. Any dealings she had had with the Civil Service had given her the impression that they just spent the time thinking up ways to annoy people by inventing complicated forms to fill in. As she took the satisfyingly dry washing in from the line, she glanced up at the sky. It looked a bit iffy. She hoped the weather was going to hold, so at least the kids would have a dry night for their barbecue.

37

The layout of the Marlborough Road back lane prevented total privacy for any of the gardens, as they were situated on the other side of the lane from the houses. Some people had created their own space by constructing conservatories that shielded the garden from the general view – as in Miss Black's case – but others, like the McDonalds, had simply gone for the open-plan garden.

Rory and Evie's guests mostly knew to come down the back through the gates at the top. That evening, as they passed Saffron's kitchen window, she saw that they all carried large parcels of drink from the off-licence. She hoped that they wouldn't be too rowdy a bunch, for there seemed to be an awful lot of them, and she hoped too that it wouldn't go on all night. Her bedroom was at the back of the house, and sound carried.

It was early evening, summer was waning, and dusk was earlier. Simon and Anna were out roaming round like the free-range children they were. It was a safe environment, and the older ones were good to them. Saffron thought she'd give them till nine o'clock then get them in for bed. Anna was spending the night at the McNamaras', as were the extended hamster family.

Evie and Rory had borrowed garden furniture from a few of the houses to add to their own. Evie had also bought plastic cups, though most of the guests were drinking beer out of bottles. Earlier, on his way to work, Mikey had dropped in and, winking heavily at Evie, handed her a bag of 'brownies'.

'No, Mikey, don't be ridiculous. None of Rory's friends take drugs.'

'They're hardly drugs – there's only a wee bit of pot in them.'

'Well just take them away. Dad would go crazy if we did that in the house.'

'But I'm already late for work; I can't bring them into the bar.'

'Right!' Evie took them and shoved them into a cupboard. 'You can get them when you come back.'

By eight o'clock Rory had the barbecue ready and was cooking sausages, chops and steak; anything his mates had managed to purloin from home. This was Rory at his best, wise-cracking with all his old school friends. Most were off at different universities now, but when they met up in the holidays they reverted to schoolboy behaviour. They were still at that stage boys go through when affection is expressed with a mock punch. Evie thought them all too immature for words, and they were two years older than she was as well. Mikey and his gang didn't behave like that, but then they were different, they weren't students. Mikey was the only one in his flat in full-time employment.

Evie had invited three of her girlfriends, but was still hoping Bronagh would come too. She saw Bronagh as a sort of project. Even a week or so since the incident, she couldn't for the life of her work out why Bronagh had even gone near the dreaded Otis. She must have no self-confidence. Evie thought her very pretty – even if she wore too much make-up, and her earrings were too big. She did have a slightly pronounced Belfast accent, but she was a warm, friendly girl, and after all, her mother was almost part of Evie's family. She'd give Bronagh till nine, and then she'd call her to check if she was coming.

The barbecue was in full swing when the heavens opened. Chaos ensued, as the by now large crowd decanted themselves into the McDonalds' freshly cleaned kitchen. Evie and Rory exchanged a look of anguish. They knew they would be unable to relax for the rest of the evening – a fairly accurate guess as things turned out.

The din was deafening; the kitchen had the lowest ceiling in the house and was already starting to look trashed. Rory hoped fervently the rain would cease. He had been in and out to the barbecue in the downpour, and was getting fed up.

The girls, at least those who were Evie's friends, had made their way into the living room, and settled down for a running commentary on Rory's mates: who was fit and who wasn't. Evie just thought that all Rory's friends were morons, since they still roamed in a pack and acted like eejits when confronted with a bunch of girls.

The doorbell rang, and Evie went to get it. Bronagh stood on the doorstep looking apprehensive.

'Brilliant,' Evie exclaimed. 'I'm really glad you came. I hope there's some food left.'

'Well I've eaten already. I wasn't going to come, and then Mum said she'd pay for a taxi over.'

'Great. C'mon, I'll introduce you to my friends.'

Bronagh followed Evie into the room and was introduced to the gang. Her hair was pale blonde with a pink fringe, which drew admiring comments. The other girls were still at school and the rules did not permit multicoloured hair.

While the girls chatted and drank their alcopops and vodkas in the living room, the boys gradually loosened their inhibitions in the kitchen. Mikey drifted in after midnight. The decibels had climbed, and even Rory was starting to relax. As yet, no one had made the connection between the heightened euphoria they were all starting to feel, and the bag of brownies Rory's friend Robbie had found earlier in a cupboard and handed out. Mikey had a bottle of vodka with him, and this too was liberally distributed.

Bronagh alone remained sober. She was on her way to the bathroom when she noticed a bedroom door wide open and one of the boys passed out on the bed.

'Evie,' she called downstairs, 'there's someone lying on your mum's bed, looks in a pretty bad way.'

Evie disentangled herself from Mikey and ran upstairs. She was drunk, but not as much as some. She took one look at the prostrate body and ran down in a fury to get Rory.

'Rory, that moron of a friend of yours is upstairs lying on Mum's bed and groaning!'

'Which moron?'

'Robbie.'

'Is Orla not with him?'

'No, she's pulled Johnny and they're outside.'

'In the rain?'

'It's stopped raining.'

'Evie, just leave him. He'll be fine.'

'He won't be fine. We'd better call him a taxi.'

Rory went upstairs to check things out for himself, wondering why his head was spinning so much; he'd only been drinking beer. Besides, with policing his friends all night, he thought he had remained reasonably sober. Robbie was sprawled unconscious across the newly laundered bedclothes. His shoes had left large mud stains on the duvet cover. Rory gave him a shake and was rewarded by a low moan.

'Evie, he's passed out. We'd better leave him till he wakes up. A taxi wouldn't take him.'

'Well he can't stay there.'

Evie summoned help, and several rather drunken young revellers attempted to move Robbie off the bed. Suddenly he lifted his head upright, fixed his mouth into a wide O shape, and threw up all over the bed, the carpet and the magazine rack, Rory's jeans and shoes and anyone within three feet of him.

'Why did you invite this stupid eejit? I knew this would happen. He always gets wasted. Mum and Dad will be furious. We promised them there'd be no bother.'

'I'll clean it up in the morning, we can wash the sheets.'

'Right, well that's it! I'm telling everyone to leave now. The party is over.'

While Rory went and got a cloth and the vacuum cleaner, Evie flounced out of the room and stormed down the stairs.

'Out! Out! Now!' she screamed. 'Everybody leave!'

She seemed hysterical. A few people shrugged and started to move.

Bronagh had been sitting in the living room feeling some-what overwhelmed. This was the first party of this kind she had ever been to; in a private house, that is. None of her mates lived in anything big enough to throw a party. She had been at drunken gatherings before, in clubs and that, but even she had been kind of surprised to see how out of it most of the boys here were. She wondered had they been taking anything else. When Evie finally stopped shrieking and attempting to push people out the door, she went over to her, touched her on the arm and tentatively suggested this, and then wondered immediately if she had put her foot in it. But Evie didn't seem upset by the question. She shook her head.

'No way, Rory's friends are totally straight; they don't even smoke dope . . . Oh my God.'

She shot out of the room like an arrow and into the kitchen. Bronagh followed. Evie pulled open a cupboard door beside the Aga.

'Shit, shit, shit!' She glared at the already dwindling group of boys who remained in the kitchen. Some had already left after hearing the fracas upstairs. 'Did anyone here eat the brownies?'

Blank stares all round.

'They were in this cupboard.'

'Do you mean those wee chocolate buns?' Sam, Rory's best pal, asked her, words slurring, eyes rolling round in his head. 'Aye, we had those hours ago. They were class.'

'Aaaah! No wonder everyone's wasted! Why didn't I just throw them in the bin? Oh Bronagh, just say someone has taken an overdose? What'll I do?'

'I'm not exactly sure, but I don't think you can overdose on pot, though it would probably be better not to drink. No one is driving, are they?'

'No, absolutely not.'

'Well then, they'll just sleep it off probably.'

Mikey sauntered in then, vodka bottle in one hand, a lump of hash in the other. With a smirk he asked the group casually, 'Does anyone want to skin up?'

He was totally unprepared for Evie's reaction. She let out a loud roar, and despite her slight frame managed to push him bodily towards the front door and out on to the street before anyone could reply. He was too stunned – or stoned – to protest.

'Don't come back here!' she screamed after him. 'You've ruined everything!'

'Listen, I'd better call a taxi,' Bronagh suggested.

'No, it takes ages on a Friday night. Why don't you stay with me? Jennie's dad is picking all the others up at one. Please, Bronagh?'

Bronagh looked at Evie and immediately felt sorry for her. She was just a kid really. It had all been too much.

'Right, I'll text Mum and say I'm staying. She checks her

phone if she wakes up and I'm not in. Now, Rory, you collect up the bottles and Evie and myself will load the dishwasher. Then we'll all go to bed.'

Rory and Evie looked at each other in utter relief, thankful that someone was taking charge. The party had not worked out remotely as planned and they both felt somewhat defeated by events. Evie was so glad she had invited Bronagh. Eighteen-year-old girls were so much more sensible than boys of that age.

38

Sally listened carefully, trying to keep a straight face, as Evie explained how Rory had managed to break the vacuum cleaner. She had arrived first thing Monday morning to a surprisingly clean house; albeit with a rather unpleasant smell of sick mingling with Clare's best Jo Malone candles. Clare and Tony were due back at lunchtime.

'Hmm,' she had remarked, 'funny smell round here.'

'Oh Sally, it was awful. Someone threw up all over Mum and Dad's room and Rory tried to vacuum it up, and then he vacuumed a sock to clean out the hose, and then the sock got stuck in the hose and he tried to get it out with a wire coat hanger. And then the coat hanger got stuck—'

'And don't tell me – he's punctured the hose?'

'Yes, in six places.'

'Your mammy's lovely purple cleaner; and she only bought that new last year.'

'Did Bronagh tell you what happened?'

'She mentioned yiz had had a wee bit of bother.'

Bronagh had been surprisingly unforthcoming about the party, except to say she had enjoyed herself. Sally hadn't pressed her. She was quietly pleased that Bronagh and Evie seemed to be making friends. It would be good for Bronagh to widen her social circle, and good for Evie to know people who weren't indulged and middle class.

They were on the landing outside Clare and Tony's bedroom. It looked like a votive shrine. Evie had lined up every candle in the house and placed them around the room.

'Oh Sally, it really stinks. Do you think Mum will notice?'

They both knew that Clare had a nose like a bloodhound. There was no way she wouldn't register the smell.

'I would say so; sure it would knock you out of the house. I'll have a go at it with baking soda, and if you explain nicely, she won't be too hard on you. She'll need to know about her Dyson, though.'

'Oh Sally, I hope you're right.'

Sally did her best with the carpet, and with wide-open windows the smell faded. The vacuum cleaner was beyond repair. When she turned it on, it had the effect of wafting the smell of sick all over the house. She gave up and borrowed Saffron's. As she was leaving it back, she saw Tony drive in and park. Clare got out of the car. They both looked relaxed.

'Oh Sally, we had a lovely time. The place is gorgeous, and the food was lovely. I only wish we could have stayed for the rest of the week, though I did miss my baby,' she said, suddenly seeing Anna, who had raced out when she heard the car. Anna threw her arms round her mother. Tony unloaded the bags. Sally followed the small procession into the kitchen, which was as neat as a pin.

'Did you bring me anything, Mum?' said Anna.

'I might have. Just give us time to get in the door. I have to have a cup of tea.'

Evie was in the kitchen alone, Rory having gone off to work.

'I'll put the kettle on,' she said, and rushed to do it. 'Did you have a good time?'

'Yes, darling, absolutely lovely. Gosh, we should go away more often,' said Clare, amused by Evie's sudden helpfulness. 'Oh, how did your barbecue go, sweetie?'

'It rained, I mean really poured, and we had to come in, and . . .'

Evie looked at Sally expectantly.

'Well, Clare, there was a wee bit of a problem with the vacuum cleaner.'

'The vacuum cleaner? But it's hardly a year old.'

'Well, some wee lad who was at the party was sick, and Rory tried to vacuum it.'

'Vacuum sick? You're not serious?'

Tony walked back into the kitchen just then, having taken the bags upstairs.

'Has someone been sick in our bedroom? Unless, Clare, those expensive candles of yours are rancid. The smell is fairly overpowering.'

'Oh Dad, I'm really sorry!' Evie burst into tears.

'It doesn't matter, love,' said Clare, giving her a hug. 'These things happen at parties.'

Sally looked at Tony in surprise. 'You should take that woman away a bit more often.'

It was not just the relief of her mother's being so understanding that prompted Evie's tears. Bronagh had stayed in her room on Friday night and they had chatted well into the early hours of Saturday morning. Slowly she had come to the conclusion that Mikey was the wrong boy for her. She had known that all along, but somehow having someone her own age disapprove of his liking for drugs clarified things.

The following night she had met up with him and broken off the relationship. She could have dumped him by phone, so his reaction, which was bitter and included calling her a spoilt middle-class bitch, threw her. It also had the effect of making her even more determined to stick to her guns. She assessed her situation. She had been dossing all year and her marks were down. She determined to work harder next year and pass all her A levels. She suddenly saw with great clarity that she wanted to go to university and make something of her life. Perhaps if she did well in her exams she would take a gap year first, as Rory had done, but that was a long way away. She didn't say any of this to her parents; even she realised that it was time for action, not words.

39

The last few months had been a whirlwind for Sally: Charlie getting out of jail, her starting and finishing at Maids to Order, leaving and going back to Marlborough Road. At times she had thought her life was rushing wildly out of control, but now suddenly the storm had passed and she had a focus again.

She was looking forward to her holiday, and afterwards to going to college. She had taken Clare's advice and bought a few classic books. They were only a pound each – imagine! When she had been at school, books were expensive. She was forever making excuses when she came in without the money for a new textbook. Comparatively, these paperbacks were so cheap. She got the titles Clare had suggested, and then added *Wuthering Heights*, *Emma* and *Oliver Twist*; all books she had read while at school and loved. She wasn't that struck on TV anyway; she had always enjoyed reading and never given up on it. But like many others, she was fond of the new chick lit and crime. Not any more; she was on the road to self-improvement.

She persuaded Bronagh to do Edith's hair. Otis had snaffled the original free voucher, but Bronagh said Miss Black could come to the salon on Wednesday evening. It would give her a boost. She was making a steady recovery, but she had been through a lot. First her operation, and then Ellen dying; and she had a week of chemotherapy ahead of her before the trip.

Fintan had been as good as his word and phoned both Edith and Sally to tell them he was settled in Glasgow. He had borrowed a friend's flat in the West End and was managing nicely, though he missed Marlborough Road. He was keen to hear all the details of the forthcoming trip to Crete, and his enthusiasm was adding to Sally's anticipation.

The others in the salon were giving Bronagh funny looks; Miss Edith Black was not by any stretch of the imagination their usual type of client. She had phoned for an appointment and arrived on the dot, announcing loudly that she was a client of Bronagh's. Then she had proceeded to tell all within earshot what a pretty girl Bronagh had turned out. Bronagh was glad she had dyed her hair back to her own natural brown this week. She smiled weakly as Edith filled Alan in on their connection.

'I have known Bronagh since she was a little girl, so I am prepared to put myself in her safe hands. Her mother and I are off to visit the Minoan ruins together in a matter of weeks.'

Alan nodded in a knowing way, though he hadn't an idea what she was gurning on about. Still, she sounded well-spoken, a potential regular, and he was impressed in spite of himself.

Edith explained carefully to Bronagh that she merely wanted a trim, though she was persuaded to have her hair shampooed first, a job Bronagh did not trust to Jimmy, but did herself. She then conditioned Miss Black's surprisingly long, thick white hair and was now carefully trimming the ends. Edith chatted away at the top of her voice as if she thought Bronagh was a bit hard of hearing. She seemed oblivious to the fact that the entire salon was listening, even above the hairdryers.

'Oh yes, Bronagh, your mother is a national treasure, so competent. I can't think how we would manage our lives without her.'

Bronagh put Miss Black's hair into a French pleat. She thought it looked great, very elegant. She had used a tinted shampoo, which had taken the yellowish tinge out of it. She held the mirror so Miss Black could see the back.

'Oh, that looks wonderful, Bronagh. Aren't you very clever?' She fumbled for her purse and produced a few pound coins, pressing them into Bronagh's hand as if it was a fortune. 'Thank you so much, and please do give Sally any more free vouchers if you get them. I'm very pleased with this.'

And she patted her head approvingly, had a final glance in the mirror and swished out of the door of the salon.

Sally and Charlie met in the solicitor's office. Sally was delighted her solicitor was a woman; Charlie was indignant and demanded to see 'the boss'. It was embarrassing. Their decree nisi was a formality anyway. In Northern Ireland you had to prove you had been apart for five years to get a divorce; well, since Charlie had been locked up for more than that, it wasn't much of a problem. Sally had got a legal separation about six years ago; it was necessary in order for her to get housing benefit. Her wages weren't enough to cover her rent.

In the days following her phone call to Charlie, the more Sally thought about it, the more convinced she became that now was the right time to get a divorce. She was, in a sense, beginning a new life, and perhaps it was better to start it as a single woman. Besides, it would in a way be a deterrent to Charlie. At least he could be sure that she meant it when she said she would never have him back. It also might speed his journey across the water.

Yesterday, when she had spoken to him to remind him that they were meeting the solicitor, he had seemed reluctant.

'I thought maybe you were ringing me up to say you wanted me back.'

'Charlie, that's not going to happen.'

'I've paid my dues, Sally.'

'I know, but sure we weren't even living together when you were put away.'

'Put away! You make it sound like I was a dog or something.'

'You know rightly what I mean.'

'Did Bronagh tell you I had a wee chat with her?'

Sally's heart sank. So she had been right about Bronagh seeing him. She wished her daughter had felt able to confide in her. But she didn't want Charlie knowing that.

'Yes, I think she mentioned it.'

'She'd like us back together.'

'Well Bronagh of all people should know that's just a fantasy. I need to move on, Charlie, and so do you.'

'We're getting on, Sally; neither of us is a spring chicken.'

'You speak for yourself!' Sally was forty-two, young enough to start again. Sure she was younger than Madonna, for God's sake. 'I want a divorce, Charlie, and I can get it with or without your permission.'

He had agreed to the meeting then.

The solicitor said they would get legal aid and it was just a matter of signing a few forms; there wasn't much in the way of worldly goods. The contents of Sally's house had all been bought and paid for by her, and the house, until she could get the money to buy it, remained the property of the housing executive. So Charlie was due half of nothing.

They filled in several forms. The woman told them the divorce papers would be mailed out to them.

Despite everything, Sally was sad as she left the office. Charlie lingered. He seemed unwilling to walk away. He touched her awkwardly on the sleeve.

'I'm dead sorry it all had to end, Sally. We were a great wee couple at first.'

'I know, but that was a long time ago, Charlie. It's all water under the bridge.'

She was sounding a lot harder than she felt, because she was gutted by it all really. It had been a while since she'd had any illusions, but they had started their marriage with so much hope. She had really meant it to be 'till death us do part'. For all his flaws, she was sure he had too. Still, it hadn't been all bad: they had produced Bronagh.

'I'm sure Bronagh will stay in touch with you.'

'I'd like that, but she seems to think it would upset you.'

'Charlie, I would be more than happy if she kept in touch. She's eighteen now, and whatever has happened between us, you're still her father. Sure isn't she the image of you?'

Charlie's expression softened, and he smiled for the first time that morning.

'D'ye think so?'

Sally took a look into his lovely blue eyes, ignoring the beer belly and the receding hairline.

'Yes, of course I do, I'll tell her to give you a ring.'

When they parted, Sally got on her bike and drove in the direction of Marlborough Road. Her face was wet with tears.

Bronagh got up to clear the plates. Sally had been sitting throughout dinner wondering how to broach the subject of Charlie and the divorce. The last thing she wanted to do was to make Bronagh feel guilty. It wasn't as if she wanted to wring a confession out of her. Who could blame her for wanting to see her own father?

'I saw your daddy today, this morning actually.'

'Oh?'

'We're getting divorced; we had to sign the papers.'

'Well, Mammy, it'll not make the *Irish News*, will it?'

'No, I just thought you'd like to know that it's official, legal, whatever. That's all.'

'Okay. I hardly thought you'd be getting back together.'

'Bronagh love, I just want to tell you that I don't mind if you go out with your daddy now and again. I know he's off to work in Coventry with Tommy any day now.'

'Why would I go out with him?'

'I just thought . . .' Sally trailed off uncomfortably.

'He came round here once; you were at my granny's. I didn't let him stay. That's the only time I've talked to him.'

'Oh . . . ?'

'You needn't believe me if you don't want to.'

And Bronagh rushed from the kitchen and upstairs. Sally waited a second and then followed. Bronagh was lying on her bed sobbing her heart out. Sally hugged her.

'There, love, there, I didn't mean to hurt your feelings. It's just that one of those nights you said you were out with Tiffany, well, she called looking for you.'

Bronagh sat up and stopped crying. She really didn't want to tell Sally about Otis. There was no point now, and in truth she was a bit ashamed of it all. Viewed from this distance, it had been a big mistake. She wasn't sure what she had been hoping for in going out with him; certainly not romance; maybe the chance to make her way a bit in the realms of culture. Even though the relationship, such as it was, had been a disaster in the end, she'd enjoyed going to different places and wouldn't be afraid to try new things next time, and in a way it had helped strengthen her friendship with Evie too.

Sally was waiting for her to say something, but she decided there was little point in explaining. It would be better for her mother not to know. She trusted Evie and Tiffany not to say anything.

'I was going out with a boy and Tiffany didn't like him,

that's all. I didn't really think you would like him either. Anyway, it's over now and I'm okay.'

'Are you sure?'

'Yes, Mammy, I'm sure.'

Sally decided not to quiz her any further. Whatever had happened was done with anyway.

40

Marlborough Road was calming down, in a manner of speaking. The birds still sang, Lola still barked, but summer was definitely drawing to a close. The trees were slightly less lush. The conkers were hardening on the chestnut trees. There were a few late-blooming roses, but the apples were on the trees, and since it had been such a hot summer, the blackberries were ripening early on the brambles in Saffron's garden. Sally hoped fervently that she wouldn't take one of her mad notions for jam. The thought of all those big messy pans made her shudder. It hardly seemed possible that the kids would all be going back to school next week.

The first week of September, Edith was going back into hospital for her chemotherapy treatment. She was being very positive about it, although naturally enough this was all on the surface. She had discussed it with Clare and Saffron and with her friend Isabelle, and of course she had talked things over with Sally. Sally planned to call in on her every day on the way home from Marlborough Road, and assured her that she would have the house shipshape for her return. Not that there was anyone there to blight the perfection of number

29; without any lodgers, the place was astonishingly quiet.

Sally wasn't sure if the quiet suited the house any more. In her mind, Fintan had changed the dynamic of the place for good. He had added pizzazz to the quiet Victorian house, and it didn't seem to want to settle back down. Another lodger had been due to arrive mid-September, but Edith had cried off because of her illness. She would participate in the programme again come spring.

Sally herself was focusing on the fact that, like the children, she too was going back to school. After all these years she would be a student again. Her heart was in her mouth at the thought of it, but she was also looking forward to it. She had bought some pens and notepads and couldn't contain her excitement at the idea of having lectures. She would miss two nights because of the holiday. Her tutor, May, had been very understanding when she explained she was going off for the week with a friend who would be recuperating from chemo. She told her she would catch up easily.

Bronagh was impressed by the fact that her mother had actually got around to enrolling in the classes. Sally's sister Eileen, however, seemed to find the idea odd, and said so to Bronagh.

'Your mother's getting some rare ideas, doing her GCSEs at her age. She always said she couldn't wait to leave school. I don't know how she can be bothered going back.'

'She had to leave school early. Granny and Granda needed the money. She was the oldest.'

'I know she's the oldest, but why on earth would she want to go back and learn now?'

'Maybe because she wants to make something of herself, Eileen. I mean, there's more to life than drinking in bars, you know.'

Eileen, affronted at Bronagh's cheek, was for once lost for words. Bronagh was grimly satisfied at having snapped at her aunt; she was glad Sally was nothing like Eileen. She was beginning to appreciate her mother more than ever, realising how solid a support she had been all her life. It couldn't have been easy for her to get herself over to south Belfast every working day for the past ten years and clean houses. She deserved a chance now to do something for herself. It would be brilliant that Sally had somewhere interesting to go two nights a week; maybe she'd even make a few new friends, or meet someone else. And having reacquainted herself with Charlie, Bronagh was even more convinced that her mother was doing the right thing. If they had ever had anything in common, those two, Charlie's behaviour had put paid to it. Bronagh would keep in touch with him, though. He was still her da after all. Maybe if she ever got married he could give her away, she thought wryly.

Saffron was impossibly large, and could hardly get about. Sally noted that Trevor seemed back to his old adoring self. He was living on his nerves, though, winging it on a daily basis. Each day that passed uneventfully, without the prospect of Laura looming in front of him, he took as a blessing. He arrived home from work on time each day, and thanked the gods that Saffron was having an uneventful if taxing pregnancy.

Since his emotional evening at the McNamaras', Bill Nelson had rarely been seen around, though his car went up the lane each morning at eight on the dot. Neither Laura nor the children had reappeared. A For Sale sign had gone up on the house, and there was much speculation about what it would fetch; property prices in the area had soared. The break-up was a considerable source of speculation. Patricia Thompson, who was closer to Laura than either Clare or Saffron, told Clare that things hadn't been good between the couple for quite a few years. It appeared that having the twins had done for them. Laura had tried her best to combine motherhood and her job with only a series of au pairs for support. But the twins, as Sally had always observed, were not the easiest, and Bill had rarely been at home while they were small. Laura had been nagging at him for ages to move to England to be near her parents, and getting nowhere. Clare repeated all this to Sally and Edith, but both agreed not to pass on to Saffron the bit about the twins – it was better she was kept in the dark about that particular detail.

On Monday morning, Clare and Sally took Edith to the hospital for her treatment. She would be there for a few days. In line with her new attitude, she allowed them to fuss over her and agreed readily to any proposed visits. Sally had insisted she buy herself some new nighties, a pair of slippers, and a lovely pink silk dressing gown, which Edith thought was positively frivolous. She had been about to complain at the expense when Sally silenced her by assuring her that she would get many years' wear out of it. This thought in itself cheered her up.

'You're right, Sally,' she said. 'I'll just have to live long enough to wear it out!'

Edith was really enjoying the relief of dispensing with the stiff upper lip. If people wanted to make a fuss of her, well then, she would let them. It was only a matter of learning not to say no at once. She would obey her instincts of course; at this stage in her life she didn't want to turn into some maudlin old cow. She had had an aunt, a sister of her mother's, who went that way in later years. It was most embarrassing for her parents. However, the other side of Aunt Maud's 'condition' was that she became very affectionate towards Edith and Ellen. The two girls had liked that part.

Edith thought that she and Sally might even have some fun on this forthcoming holiday. She was looking forward it. Clare had given her an up-to-date book on Crete to take into hospital. She would concentrate on that and just find a way to cope with the ghastly chemotherapy. She'd be at home for two full weeks after her treatment, and with luck would be back to normal before they left for Crete. After all, as Mr Smedley said, this was a 'belt and braces' approach; he was just being extra sure. At any rate, she felt extremely optimistic.

There was little anyone could do to make chemotherapy a pleasant experience, but Sally was determined Edith would get through it with the minimum of unpleasantness. She had worked out a game plan. She would make sure Edith ate no hospital food, so each day she dutifully picked up a little package lovingly prepared by Clare and brought it up to the hospital. Clare was such a good cook, and made delicate little sandwiches and sent small jars of French yoghurt and flasks of beautiful homemade soup. Edith was ecstatic in her appreciation. She looked forward to Sally's visits, and despite the unpleasantness of the drip, she was holding out bravely. Saffron had loaded her up with herbal remedies as a protection against hair loss, but she had further treatment to come on her return from holiday, and was aware her lovely thick hair might be affected. She had chosen a rather elegant wig just in case. But she might be lucky. She was taking each day at a time, the thought of the Greek sunshine determinedly in her thoughts.

41

Sally brought Edith's suitcase down from the cupboard at the top of the house. She and Clare were helping her pack for the holiday. Sally had ironed every item carefully and was folding them into the suitcase. She had Edith's shoes all polished and in lovely cloth drawstring bags, her underwear packed in silk envelopes with zips. The two of them were off tomorrow, and there was an air of excitement in the gathering.

'I'm so jealous. I wish I was going with you,' Clare said.

'Oh Clare, you're hardly back from France and you told me you had a wonderful time.' Saffron looked a bit rueful. 'Trevor says we're following your example next year; no more wilds of Donegal for him. He has visions of pastis before supper, and divine Provençal wine to drink, sitting on our terrace overlooking the lavender fields, or endless rows of strong, erect sunflowers.'

'Good, you'll love it. Perhaps we could have a magical mystery tour from the lane to Provence.' Clare shuddered inwardly at the thought of spending a summer holiday with four extra children and two vegetarians, but she knew it was just chat. It would never come to pass; Tony would put his foot down.

Saffron smiled benignly, now and then readjusting her bulk. Her belly was huge, and any excitement caused the twins to somersault and twist around inside her. Their movements were visible to all. Posy spent a lot of her time these days addressing her mother's bump, telling the two wee babies in there that they could play with her dolly and watch Pingu if they would just hurry up and come out. Even Edith, who had never been involved in the pregnancies of any of the women in the lane, was fascinated by the whole process, so the packing was quite a long-drawn-out affair. Eventually the case was ready and Clare and Saffron left.

Sally busied about, setting things right. The flight tomorrow was at a respectable time. The plan was that Sally would come over to Edith's and Trevor would drive them to the airport. She herself would finish packing tonight. It was all done really; she had been putting things in her suitcase for a week now. She had only to close it.

She was on her way out the back door when Edith called her back.

'Sally, there's something I want to say to you before we leave. Please sit down.'

Sally put her crash helmet on the kitchen table and pulled out a chair. She felt apprehensive; for a brief instant it flashed across her mind that Edith was going to say she had changed her mind about the holiday. It was all a bit unreal anyway, too good to be true.

'Sally, I have been doing a lot of thinking whilst in hospital, and I have decided to let you know that I had intended leaving you quite a large sum of money when I die.'

'Ach, Miss Black . . . I mean Edith, sure didn't the surgeon say you were great? It'll be a long time till you go.'

'Precisely. I aim to be around for quite some time. So I have been having a rethink. Ellen has unexpectedly left me an extremely large amount in her will. I have no immediate need

266

of it, so you may as well have your legacy now. It's possible that I could live to be a hundred – a lot of women do these days.'

Sally was dumbfounded. Had she heard correctly? Edith Black was going to give her a large sum of money?

Edith sat across from her with a smile on her face, waiting for her to speak.

'Well, what do you think?'

'Edith, I couldn't . . .'

'Yes you most certainly could, but assuming you accept, there are two conditions that I will expect you to adhere to. We'll have my solicitor draw us up a proper contract.'

'Two conditions?'

'Yes. Firstly, I want you to use the money to buy your house.'

Here she paused and took a deep breath.

'And the second is this, and I am very aware that this is a selfish stipulation: I want you to continue working for me as long as you are physically able. Now what do you think?'

Sally wasn't sure what she was thinking. She was dumb-struck.

'I know it's rather sudden, announcing it like this. I was going to tell you while we were away, and then I thought it better to let you know now. That way you could perhaps enjoy the holiday more, not having money worries, and perhaps you and I could treat ourselves a bit as well.'

'Edith, it's really kind of you, but I'm not sure if I can accept it.'

'Nonsense, of course you can. As I said, I have had lots of time to think whilst in hospital, and there's an old saying – I'm almost certain I heard it from you – "There are no pockets in a shroud."'

'You probably did. My mammy says that a lot.'

'And your mother is right. You know, my sister Ellen enjoyed her life and still managed to leave a considerable estate. I feel

267

I should follow her example. I have more than enough money to enjoy whatever is left of my time. I don't have expensive tastes, so it seems entirely logical to share some of my good fortune with you. Now what do you say? If all goes well in Crete, this need not be the last of our trips.'

Sally felt her emotions surge up, and before she could think about it, she went over to Edith, threw her arms around her and gave her a big hug. Edith, although slightly taken aback, found she liked the hug very much. She patted Sally on the back, and realised that the younger woman was on the verge of tears.

'Oh Edith, I just don't know what to say.'

'Well how about "thank you" and "I agree"?'

'Thank you very much . . . and yes, I agree.'

42

Later that evening, just as Sally was putting the final touches to her packing, separating the things that could go as hand luggage from those that had to be checked in, the phone rang. It was Fintan. He often phoned to find out how Edith was and to see what was happening on Marlborough Road. His voice sounded warm and friendly.

'I hope I'm not calling too late. I just wanted to say *au revoir.*'

Sally felt a warm glow. His voice really affected her. As far as she was concerned, it would never be too late for him to call.

'No, Fintan, not at all. I never go to bed early. It's lovely to hear from you. I'm finishing off my packing.'

'Good. I hope you and Edith will have a fantastic holiday in Agios Nikolaos. You'll love it. I've given Edith the names of a few good restaurants.'

Agios Nikolaos was the name of the town in Crete where Sally and Edith would be staying. Sally wasn't sure of the correct pronunciation; even Edith pronounced it differently each time, and made a joke of it by saying: 'It's all Greek to me.' Over the last few weeks Sally had taken to looking at the pictures of the town in the book Clare had given Edith, and of course in the holiday brochure too. It was a harbour town, and their hotel was one of the prettier ones, overlooking a lake. In the pictures it looked lovely.

'I spoke to Edith earlier, and she told me you had everything packed for her. You're very good to her.'

'Well she's very good to me. I enjoy doing it anyway.'

She was tempted to tell Fintan about Edith planning to give her the money for her house, but decided not to. It hadn't happened yet. She wondered if Edith had told him, but he didn't mention it, so Sally supposed she hadn't.

They talked about Edith's health, and Fintan said he'd try to get to Belfast soon for a long weekend. He'd been offered a job in Dublin in October and could just take the train up. He was off work all this week and was sorting out his flat in London. It had been months since he'd been in permanent residence.

'You wouldn't approve of the mess, Sally,' he laughed. 'You'd have all the rubbish in a bag ready to go out.'

After a few more minutes of chat about the lane and how Clare and Saffron and the others were keeping, he wished her a safe flight and said he'd talk to her very soon.

Sally put down the phone feeling unsettled. She knew she was being ridiculous, but Fintan's remark about her clearing out his rubbish had upset her. That was all he saw her as really, a cleaning lady. She quickly dismissed the thought. Sure he was just teasing, and hadn't she told him often enough about her desire to throw all the rubbish out of Saffron's or Clare's? That was all he meant. She had been up to high doh all evening anyway. She could think of little else but Edith's intention to buy her home for her. She walked around the house thinking how lovely it would be not to have to pay rent any more. This would all belong to her.

Bronagh came in shortly after Fintan's call, and assured her mother for the hundredth time that she would be able to manage fine on her own.

'Mum, I'll be grand. You just go off and enjoy yourself. I bet you'll have a fantastic time.'

'I hope so. Miss Black is going to hire a car. We're going to see some important ruins, and she says there's lovely wee fishing villages we can drive to. She doesn't like the sun. I hope she won't mind if I lie by the pool a wee bit; I'm so pasty-looking these days.'

'Mum, will you stop obsessing? You told me she said she didn't mind if you spent the entire holiday by the pool.'

'I know, but she's maybe just being polite. I'm sure she'll want somebody to go with her to look at the ruins. I don't know a thing about Greek ruins, but I suppose they'll tell you everything when you get there. Clare says it's just a lot of interesting stories about Greek heroes and that. It's called Knossos.'

She pronounced it *Konossos*. They both started laughing.

'I think that's how you say it.'

'I hope you get good weather, that's the main thing.'

'Oh, Clare has checked the forecast. It's supposed to be sunny all week.'

'Well then, what are you yacking on about? Just go and enjoy yourself.'

Next morning Sally arrived over at Edith's with her case. There was virtually a crowd there to see them off. Clare and Saffron fussed round making sure they had passports and tickets and that toothpaste and the various cosmetics were in see-through bags. Sally hoped Saffron wouldn't unexpectedly have the twins while they were gone; she appeared to have got bigger overnight. Posy had made Edith a 'Have a Lovely Holiday' card; at least that was what she said it was. Sally thought it looked like a drawing of Iggy the iguana.

Trevor was as prompt as any taxi and very chatty on the drive to the airport. He got them there with hours to spare. Sally was a bit apprehensive about the flight; she wondered what on earth she would find to talk about to Edith for almost five hours, but she needn't have worried. Edith seemed to want to talk about growing up in Belfast, and how things had changed so much since her youth, and Sally wasn't bored at all. Edith had lived in the terrace all her life, and she chatted about the various families who had come and gone over the years. The current residents had mostly been there for the last twenty years. There would be some competition for the Nelsons' place, since houses in Marlborough Road didn't make it on to the market very often.

She asked Sally about where she lived, and Sally told her. It seemed like a different world.

'You know, once you own the house, you can always sell it and move. You don't seem to like living over that part of town.'

That was true: Sally didn't, although things had been a lot better since the Troubles had ended. Most of the people who lived in her area had been there all their lives. And her parents were nearby. That had been a godsend when Bronagh was young; it meant that the child had somewhere to go after school when Sally was working.

She was glad Edith had brought up the subject of the house again. It reassured her that she hadn't just dreamt it all. They chatted happily about the holiday. Edith seemed to take flying in her stride, but then she had travelled quite a bit. Sally hadn't flown much in her life; about six times, she worked out. It was a bit bumpy going over the Alps, and Sally had to suppress her fear. She was glad when they landed safely and she could relax. Edith had dozed off during the last part of the flight. It was tiring for her, but at least they would be in their hotel in about an hour, and they could go to bed early. There was a coach organised, but Edith had decided they would take a taxi.

'By the time they have everyone rounded up, we could be in our beds,' she declared.

They had been served dinner on the plane; it wasn't great, but it would do them for tonight. It was ten o'clock local time when they stepped out on to the tarmac. Darkness had fallen, but even so the air was balmy. Sally felt bleary-eyed and concerned about Edith, who looked exhausted. They made their way in a straggle through passport control and to the baggage reclaim. With luck they would get a taxi quickly. At least they had the euros and no worries about currency. The first time Sally had been abroad was to Spain, and she had spent the entire time trying to work out prices in pesetas. She thought the euro a great idea.

She found a trolley and loaded the bags on to it, and pushed it through into the arrivals lounge. The signs for taxis were in English and Greek, and they were just about to head in that direction when Edith's phone rang.

The mobile phone was a recent acquisition of Edith's. She had bought it when Ellen was dying, so she could be contacted at any time. Sally thought it was hilarious watching her use it. She didn't seem to realise that it wasn't connected to anything, and appeared to have the idea that it was necessary to speak up and enunciate very loudly while on it.

Sally hoped nothing was wrong. She had planned to text Bronagh when she got to the hotel, so she couldn't even understand why Edith had switched her phone on. Unless she had forgotten to turn it off in the first place, though that seemed most unlike her.

Sally stopped beside her and made a show of fixing the luggage in case Edith thought she was eavesdropping.

'There's no one there,' Edith said with some annoyance. 'It's just a text saying I can use my phone here. Honestly, as if I didn't already check that.'

Suddenly Sally felt a tap on her shoulder. She turned round

abruptly and almost fainted when she saw Fintan standing in front of them with a wide grin on his face.

'Oh my God, Fintan, what are you doing here?'

She turned to Edith, thinking that she must have known, but Edith was also looking at Fintan as if she had seen a ghost.

'Heavens, Fintan . . . you're here?'

'Yes, sorry it had to be such a surprise, but I wasn't sure of my timetable until yesterday.'

'But I talked to you last night!' Sally exclaimed.

'I know, I know. I booked the flight two days ago on impulse. It's easy to get one at this time of year . . . I got in two hours ago from London. I had intended to tell you when I called last night, then decided it would be better to surprise you both . . . I mean, you might have dissuaded me from coming.'

'As if we would,' Edith replied. 'It's just delightful to see you here.'

The two women looked at each other with a mixture of pleasure and confusion, both obviously thrilled that he had appeared. Sally relinquished the trolley to him and Edith took his arm, and the three of them walked towards the exit.

'I know we're going to have a really perfect week.' And Edith smiled blissfully at Sally, who nodded mutely, feeling absurdly happy, as if she was in a dream.

'Good, that's settled then,' Fintan said happily. 'Now, ladies, I've already hired a car, and it's waiting outside. I have been thinking for the last week – ever since I found out I was free – that I couldn't leave two lovely ladies like you for an entire week without an escort. So here I am to offer my services as a guide. After all, I know my way around here, and you both need to be handled with care.'

The two women smiled in agreement and allowed him to manoeuvre the laden trolley expertly towards the exit. It looked like the holiday had got off to a flying start.

When Fintan had loaded the car and was heading out of

the airport towards Agios Nikolaos, Sally and Edith began to relax. The windows were down and the balmy night air with the fragrant whiff of wild oregano drifted around them.

'You know, ladies,' Fintan said with a smile in his voice, 'I've never missed anywhere as much as I have Marlborough Road.'

Sally immediately thought of the For Sale sign that had gone up on the Nelsons' house just yesterday. She could hardly mention that, could she? But Edith didn't miss a beat.

'Well, Fintan,' she said quickly, 'I think we have a house coming on the market very soon. I could always mention your name to the residents' committee . . .'

Your Cheatin' Heart

For Iain, Katy and Duncan

1979

'Honey, you should have killed him, fat ole' Beefcake Buford, not this pathetic piece of white trash,' Sharla says calmly.

I say nothing. We both stare at the prostrate figure of Buford's 'baybay' doll – slut, mistress, former Miss Oogamooga County, Sue Lynne Crutchley.

'Well, am I right or am I right?'

'Sharla, you are right,' I mumble. For some reason my voice doesn't seem to be working properly. 'It's just when I saw her looking at me like that, her smug face all pink and shiny with triumph, and her pouting "Bee-stung" lips glistening at me, I couldn't stop myself, I pulled the trigger.'

That was true, I think, and for a minute after the gun went off, I felt my arm had jerked right out of its socket. The explosion knocked me clean across the room; I thought the gun had backfired and I'd shot myself. Even now, ten minutes later, my body is tingling unpleasantly, and my ears are ringing. But I guess I'm still in one piece and she's lying here dead as can be, and I'm wondering how long it'll take for the police to arrive. It seems like an hour since Sharla called them.

Sharla and I look at Buford: he's in a state right enough.

He doesn't know what to be at. One minute he's lying over Sue Lynne's body, dragging her up and hugging her, giving her the kiss of life. Then he's flinging her back down on the floor with screams and wails that would put you in mind of a mad banshee. Next he starts pacing the room, getting redder and redder by the minute, his big wobbly gut swaying and bouncing, sweat flying off in droplets, calling me every low down name he can think of – and that's saying something. The foul language is pouring out of his mouth like effluent.

'You goddamm murderin' Aarish bitch. Yew've gone and kilt the lurve ah ma laafe.'

I'm starting to panic in case he has a heart attack and dies as well. One dead body is going to take enough explaining.

He makes me want to spit – Buford aka 'Big Boy' McConnell, *Mr Maple Syrup* himself. He, and his soon-to-be *fifth* wife, Sue Lynne, who is at present lying on my pale blue 'winter frost' shag pile carpet – one of Zollie's more useful trade-outs. I have to say it is a good backdrop for her body, and thankfully there's no blood to be seen, so I won't need to have it cleaned at least. She looks like a dead Barbie doll. She's even conveniently dressed from head to toe in Barbie pink. She looks as if she's faking death. Her make-up doesn't even look mussed, her long false eyelashes are lying like two little frills on her cheeks, her pink lips still forming a perfect shiny O – or maybe Buford was holding them open like that to get the air in better. God knows why. Her head is full of it.

Bloody Buford, I think despairingly as I look at him, what a waste of space, what a blight on my life. Sharla and I look at him, our heads moving in tandem. He is, as my mammy would say, 'A sight for sore eyes'. His fat thighs are bulging in his blue jeans. His belly, seemingly with a life of its own, looks like it's straining to break free of his thick leather cowboy belt, explode and smother everyone in the room. He keeps lifting his cowboy hat to let the steam escape and to fan himself. I

2

notice his remaining strands of hair clinging damply to his clammy head. I am utterly repulsed by him, but I am also scared – really scared. This is a waiting situation now. I fired the gun. Sue Lynne fell down. Sharla called the police.

It's been fifteen minutes now and I have stopped shaking but I'm numb, frozen. Even the words I speak are coming out of my mouth and bypassing my head; I am listening to them as if I am hearing for the first time. It's not every day you kill someone with the first shot you ever fired, let alone the first gun you ever held. I'm so glad Sharla is here.

Sharla is my best friend. She has always had impeccable timing. She's a girl who knows how and when to make an entrance. She arrived just after the shot had been fired, took one look at the situation and then went right into the kitchen; picked up some limes, avocados, picante sauce (Hot), fixed us a large bowl of guacamole, and opened a jumbo packet of tacos. Sharla loves Mexican food. Then she dialed 911. I didn't hear what she told them. I was, and still am, almost deaf from the explosion.

'Yep honey,' she says now, as she sashays out and places the tacos on the table. 'It's gonna be real awkward, on account of him having been here and seen it all.'

We both look again at Buford, but he is still sobbing and ignoring us both. We can't ignore him; he's making a noise like a whistling kettle and blubbering over Sue Lynne's body. I notice a glob of snot hanging on his moustache. I really did shoot the wrong person. The police and paramedics are on the way, but they are certainly taking their time. I think Sharla must have sounded too calm.

I'm feeling a bit queasy now; the fact I'm a murderer is starting to reveal itself to me. I hear the sob in my voice beginning. Sharla gazes at me reassuringly, fluffing her mane of blonde hair with her long, perfectly manicured nails.

'Oh Sharla, why did I do that? I don't know what possessed

me, it's like someone else was inhabiting my body,' I blurt out at her, wanting her to forgive me. I know sure as hell the police won't. I'm a registered alien, and Tennessee still has the death penalty. I wonder briefly, would that apply to me? It's a chilling thought. I see the headline in my brain, engraved *National Enquirer* typeface:

REGISTERED ALIEN TO FRY AT DAWN
WILL HER LAST MEAL BE IRISH STEW?

People will assume it is something to do with UFOs. Anyhow, there is little point in speculation. Sharla absentmindedly hands me a taco. I notice she has almost finished the bowl.

'Can you believe I shot her, Sharla? What made me do that?'

'I guess you had a reason, honey.'

'Yes, I must have. Mustn't I?'

'What did she say to you this time?'

'Nothing,' I sobbed. I try to remember precisely why I had pulled the trigger, though I hadn't known the gun was loaded. What was going through my head other than sheer distaste? Contempt? Rage? Loathing? Revulsion? I can't remember. My brain feels cloudy.

Sharla gives me one of her searching looks – her green eyes fixed and glittering. 'Well, honey?'

'It was the way she looked at me,' I say haltingly. 'So tri-umphant when she said she and Buford were going to have a baby, it was so unexpected her being pregnant. Her mouth was fixed in that pout she does, it sent some signal to my crazed brain, you understand, don't you?'

Sharla nods sagely in between mouthfuls of tacos. 'Don't worry, baby, I know you were provoked.' (Sharla pronounces it preevoked.) 'I mean, I know that pouty look of hers, it's sick-ening, jest sickening, looks like they've just pulled her off a dick. I'd a killed her maself.' Sharla pauses as if something has

4

just struck her. 'Pregnant? Are you shittin' me? I thought he had been fixed?'

'No, that's what she said. They're going to have a baby.'

'Hell, honey! Forgit Sue Lynne, baby, that means those ole' raaght to laafhers are gonna kill your ass – we need us a lawyer. We oughta call Big Billy Buchanan the third. He specialises in Murder One.'

My heart sinks. Big Billy Three, no less. This is gonna be some murder trial.

I'm not going to bother to quote Sharla phonetically from now on; it would be hard to get her down on paper anyway. You just have to hear her. She has one of those twangy east Tennessee accents that most people, even other Americans, don't quite believe. I can translate no problem now, but then it's been a long time, and we've been through a lot together. Besides, she couldn't understand me at first either, me being from Belfast.

1

Daytona Beach, Florida, summer of seventy-seven. It is sunny, glamorous, and full of college students, Vietnam vets, and crazed loons of surfers looking for waves. It's so different, so teeming with vitality, so tropical and exotic, so tacky and exciting, so unbearably hot and here we are, three milk-bottle white Irish girls traipsing the main drag looking for summer jobs. It's a far cry from war-torn Belfast, I can tell you, and *nothing* but *nothing* will make me go back there, at least not for a while. I have finished my finals and at present am awaiting the results of my degree. I have absolutely not a clue what I want to do with my life, despite my mother's fervent hope that the nuns will turn up a *wee teaching job* for me, even though, against their 'wishes', I did Social Anthropology. Well, this is as good a place to study another tribe as the next. I won't even allow my friend Patricia's endless whinging to dent my optimism. She's at it now.

'This is all your fault, Maggie Lennon. You told us it'd be far easier to get jobs here, so you did.' Patricia sniffs loudly, self pity bubbling up in her throat. 'And I can't stick this heat; it's not natural for people from Ireland to live here—'

She pauses in the middle of her tirade to adjust her cork-heeled platform sandals. I bite my tongue. Maureen, my other friend, says nothing. She has learned not to interrupt Patricia's rants; it only winds her up more. I adjust the cheap sunglasses I bought yesterday for a dollar and squint back at my two friends. Their white legs look almost luminous. I feel so alien, yet I am deliriously happy to be here and feel the hot sun beating down on me. It is so bright and blinding, but Patricia has a point; we are in a bit of a fix right enough. We've been here almost three days now and not the slightest sniff of a job. I alone of the three of us am hopeful we'll get jobs soon. We had better. We have only about fifty dollars left. We are staying in a tacky motel well away from the seafront; three of us in one double bed. Not pleasant.

'Do you need another sticking plaster?' Maureen offers one to Patricia in an effort to placate her. Patricia sits on a low wall and attempts to get it to stick to her squelchy feet.

'And another thing – that fella in the chemist – you'd have thought I was speaking Greek. Imagine! *band aids.*' Patricia spits the word out. 'Why in the name of God would you call a plaster a *band aid*?' She steps down from her shoes and surveys her ruined feet. I don't point out that if she'd brought proper sandals this wouldn't have happened. We are outside a restaurant that overlooks the beach.

'Let's go in here and get a Coke,' I say. 'Look, it says it's air conditioned.'

Grumbling, they both follow me into Paesano's Perfect Pasta and Pizzeria. I order three Cokes and a waitress brings them to our table. They are massive and seem to be composed entirely of ice with a dribble of Coke. We sip them gratefully. It is so cool inside, cool and dark; the temperature is practically freezing. I'm getting used to this. Burning up one minute, teeth chattering the next; it's interesting.

'Maybe we should have taken those jobs in Asbury Park after all,' Maureen ventures.

'Hmmm!' Patricia snorts with derision. She stares accusingly at me.

'Well, everybody else from Ireland was going to New Jersey; it seemed a good idea to come here. Anyway, we haven't met any other Irish people. I'm sure we'll be a rarity and get more tips.'

'A rarity, a rarity! Maybe we could get jobs in the zoo.'

'Do you think we *will* get jobs, Maggie?' Maureen sounds worried.

'Sure, maybe they need people here.' I hope I sound more confident than I feel. I get up and walk over to the waitress and ask her if there is a manager I can speak to. She tells me the owner will be back in half an hour. I go back to the table. 'The owner will be here in half an hour. I'm going to wait.'

'The place is half empty, I doubt if you'd make much working here.' Maureen sounds dubious.

'Wait if you want,' Patricia announces. 'I'm going to try the hotels.'

Two Cokes later, the owner arrives. He is a squat little peasant with a tanned, gnome-like face. He is solid, rather than fat, with very white teeth and the palest blue eyes. I go over to him. I am officially freezing now, my teeth are chattering.

'I'm looking for a job as a waitress.'

'No vacancies for waitresses.' The blue eyes stare unflinchingly at me – not offensively though. 'Where are you from?' he asks eventually, adding: 'It's too late in the season to get jobs.'

'I'm from Belfast, Northern Ireland. How is it too late? It's only June.'

He shrugs. 'Season starts in May.'

'Where are you from?' I ask. 'You aren't American.'

For a moment I think he isn't going to answer. 'Everyone's an American – eventually.' He smiles finally. 'Greece via New Jersey.'

'I've been to Greece every summer until now,' I tell him. 'I love Greece.'

'What's your name?'

'Maggie Lennon.'

He indicates for me to sit down, and pours us both a coffee. It is bitter. It burns my mouth. 'Tell me about Greece.'

An hour later I have a job, and he agrees to see Maureen and Patricia. He says he'll fire some people. That's the way it works in America. You see something or someone you like better, you swap. Paesano has a friend who owns apartments. He rents them cheap to Paesano's staff.

Maureen is thrilled, Patricia less so. She has got her own job, thank you, working at the Ramada on the beach, but it doesn't have accommodation and it is waitressing during the daytime. Hence the chance of returning to Belfast bronzed and Goddess-like (as if) is slight. The summer is to resound to her whinging about how much better off she'd have been if she had stuck to her guns and taken the job at the Ramada.

I don't care; I am thrilled silly just being here. Belfast was never like this. Just the warmth of the sun alone is enough to make me feel exhilarated. Every morning it is still shining. I check first thing when I wake up. I feel as if all my muscles, which had been tense and cramped from hunching under grey, weighty Irish skies, have suddenly relaxed and allowed my bones to move more freely, and consequently allowed me to free myself too. It is intoxicating. Every day the sea is still blue. Blue and warm with the palest, whitest sand imaginable, and crazy rolling waves that fringe the entire Atlantic side of Florida. The clouds are white and wispy when they appear at all, and they never hide the sun, they float past it high in the sky like cheeky little frills to set it off. If you look out to the horizon, Daytona seems like paradise. Looking inward is tawdrier and trashed; lots of neon and endless tacky souvenir shops. So all summer long I look out when I can. Ireland is the nearest land to here. The same ocean touches both shores. It is impressive and it makes my heart surge. I am happy. The people are different from people at home, more assured, confident, they are larger than life. They demand more too, of course, but tipping comes easily as they appreciate good service. I learn fast. I make good tips.

Paesano's Pizza Parlor is open twenty-four hours and we work the afternoon shift. It would be better to work nights because of the tips, but we are on afternoons till we are 'trained'. The apartments are okay. Better than the motel, and at least we are earning now. We will get one dollar fifty an hour and we can keep all our tips. Last week I called my parents and told them I have a job. I made it sound brilliant because they feel concerned and are worried sick about me; although not as much as when I'm at home. The first two weeks fly by, waitressing is hard work but fun. I can't wait to move to the evening shift. That's where all the money is, and Paesano has promised me first vacancy on one. Then I'll get to work on my tan.

Maureen and I are walking home to the apartment. We have had a good day; there was a big crowd in for lunch and they were generous. We are comparing tips. Maureen has made over twenty dollars. She is an open-hearted, friendly Irish girl and the customers love her. The red hair helps. We arrive at the apartment to find that a virtual river is running freely out the door and down the steps. Even at six o'clock it's still hot and steam is rising from the torrent. Maureen rushes to open the door and we view the devastation with horror. The floor is awash and there are clothes everywhere, wet, soggy ones. Even as we look, my purple and red tie-dye shirt is bleeding profusely into my new white jeans. There are no wardrobes, no chests of drawers in the apartment, so we have been living out of suitcases and these suitcases are completely flooded. The water is pouring through a large gash in the

10

ceiling and Maureen's bed is directly under the torrent. It is saturated.

Maureen takes one look at it and her screams resound through the building. A girl of about our age hears them, and comes rushing down from the floor above to explain. I recognise her at once; it would be hard not to. She is barefoot and wearing an extremely small, shocking pink bikini. Her stomach is completely flat. I want to touch it. Her fingernails and toenails are painted the exact same shade of bright pink. She smiles at us, and introduces herself as our upstairs neighbour.

'Hey, ah'm Sharla – ah live upstairs. Ah sure am sorry,' she says in a languid southern drawl, pointing at the river running down the wall and the torrent under our feet, 'but ah've had a little ole mishap. Ma waterbed just burst – well, maybe an hour or so ago.'

Little old mishap? Are we hearing her right? A virtual Niagara Falls roaring down our walls a mishap? Her waterbed has burst? I have heard ads for waterbeds on the radio but have never actually seen one. She repeats the apology.

'It's okay, isn't it?' I say to Maureen.

'It's okay? *Little* mishap? Excuse me but I don't think so! This is a bloody catastrophe. Everything is ruined,' Maureen snaps at her.

Sharla smiles back. She is slim, tanned and gorgeous, twenty-one or two, and a natural blonde with big hair and a dazzling smile. Easy, since she has at least four dozen sparkling white teeth. Her eyes are an unusual shade of green and she has the slightest hint of a squint, or a turn in her eye as my mother would have said. This has the effect of making you feel she is gazing intently at you. In fact, I find out later she is short-sighted and just trying to see better. She has smooth olive skin, the type that turns brown easily. It had taken all three of us barely two weeks to discover that we turn red, peel, and then turn white again. This is obviously not one of Sharla's problems.

11

I try not to loathe her. I want to look like that. I can't take my eyes off her.

Sharla squints at me, possibly sensing I am more sympathetically inclined. I notice then that her eyes are extremely bloodshot and assume she's been crying. But, as I am to learn later, she is simply stoned out of her brain. She speaks slowly, very slowly, like she is just getting used to having a mouth.

'Ah sure am mighty sorry about the bed. I was trying to figure why we were just soakin' wet, and why we were just skidding on the bed like crazy.' She pauses and looks at us. We wait. Finally she continues, with a sort of 'silly me' expression on her face. 'I guess I thought Buddy was sweating a lot. He puts so much effort into satisfying me.' She stops as if some amazing thought has hit her. We both look at her expectantly. 'Though it occurs to me right now that the air conditioning works real well,' she adds.

It suddenly dawns on Maureen and me that this is the explanation for the swishy, thumping water sound from upstairs that usually stops about five-thirty each day. They had been at it. And we had spent the first week in the Beachcomber Apartment Building thinking it was related to the plumbing.

Sharla extends a languid hand and smiles again, dazzling us. 'Well never mind the waterbed, ah sure am finally glad to meet y'all. Ah've been meaning to say hi to y'all before this here mess. Ah'm Charlotte Emily Anne Williams and ah'm from Bristol Tennessee. Ah'm a Cosmetics and Psychology of Selling major at ETSU.'

'Oh,' I say brightly. 'Your parents must be Brontë fans.'

She looks puzzled at this.

'You know, the Brontës, *Jane Eyre*?' No response. '*Wuthering Heights*?' I venture. She smiles hopefully. Perhaps she thinks I'm speaking Gaelic.

'Come again?'

I realise quickly that an explanation would confuse her further. So I don't bother. After a lot of unravelling we find out that her name is Sharla Emma-Lea Ayn. Names are like that in America.

Our immediate problem is what to do with a soggy apartment. The water has slowed somewhat but is still cascading down. Maureen is sniffling and picking up her bits and pieces. We arrange them on the grass outside. The grass is thick here, tough and rubbery; it doesn't feel real.

Sharla helps in a sort of distracted fashion. She does reassure us that the landlord, another gnome-like little Greek called Mr Stanisopoulos, has been told, and he will be fixing up for us to move to another apartment later on. This is fine. The clothes will dry and Patricia doesn't like the apartment anyway. The shape of the toilet seat has made her constipated. It is very tall and narrow and she has short legs and is a bit tubby, so she has to clench her buttocks too hard to balance on it – hence constipation. For the last two weeks she hasn't had a crap. Not as much as a rabbit pellet since the day we arrived. Her tummy has become hard as a rock, and in between serving customers she has been groaning in pain and drinking senna pod concoctions. Not even a fart has resulted. Just as well, the atmosphere in the apartment is poisonous enough.

I am really glad Patricia has gone to the drugstore for an enema on the way home from work; she would have ruined Sharla's sweet explanation by screaming abuse at her. Patricia has been locked in an ongoing row with our landlord about the cockroaches, the badly functioning air conditioning or lack of it, the fact that there are only two cups, and various other things. She hates him and thinks him a fat, greedy, Greek peasant, but Sharla has obviously seen qualities in Mr Stanisopoulos that have passed Patricia by. They've passed me by too, for that matter.

Sharla fixes us again with her crooked gaze. 'Lil' ole' Mr Staniswhateverpolos, ain't he such a honey?'

We say nothing, Sharla continues. 'He wanted to take me out to dinner 'cos he could see I was real upset. But I told him I wouldn't feel like eating till I was safely moved into ma new place. I think he understood that. He was real, *real* understanding.' She nods her head as if she is agreeing with herself and moves closer. She grabs Maureen by the arm and talks straight to her. Maureen freezes. 'I called him in considerable distress and why honey he dropped by at once. Held my hand and comforted me, and now he's gone to get him a plumber, I believe.'

She smiles serenely, confident of her charms. She reaches out and clasps my arm this time. I think Maureen's rigid stance has unnerved her slightly. 'But hell, right now why don't you guys come upstairs to the porch and meet Buddy? We can smoke a jay and forgit this here mess.'

Maureen refuses on the spot, and had she known the number of the narcotics bureau would no doubt be on the phone to them now.

'I'll come,' I say. I am curious. I follow her upstairs and leave Maureen in the flood.

Sharla's apartment makes ours look sparse and unlived-in. It is draped with silk scarves and smells heavily of incense. The walls are covered in Day-Glo posters. The largest of these features a sort of Hell's Angel type of guy with a machine gun. It says: Yeah, though I should walk through the valley of death, I will fear no evil for I am the meanest motherfucker in the Valley.

Sharla catches me looking at it. 'Don't that just crack you up?' she says.

I agree, glad that Maureen passed on the invite. I look around. A lava lamp bubbles quietly in a corner. There is a guy sitting beside it looking at it fixedly. He says nothing. The floor is awash and a large deflated waterbed is quietly seeping onto it; oh, so that's what they look like. I wonder briefly why Mr Stanisopoulos has gone for a plumber. A mop seems more appropriate. I offer to clean up but Sharla shakes her head.

'Forgit it, honey, it'll soon dry out. Anyways, we don't have a mop.' She goes to a drawer, takes out a joint, lights it and offers me some. I decline graciously. But we sit on the swinging chair on the upstairs porch and chat. I've never encountered anyone like this. Her accent and crazy logic are mesmerising. I am hooked.

Buddy, the boyfriend, isn't exactly a contributor. He spends all of the time staring at the lava lamp, listening to Lynyrd Skynyrd, laughing to himself and playing the air guitar. It is weird and somewhat unnerving. I look at him quizzically a few times but he doesn't respond; Sharla notices my gaze.

'He's real mellow right now. Sex and drugs always does it for him,' she informs me. I nod, knowingly I hope.

A lot later that evening, Stani, as Sharla has nicknamed him, arrives to move us to our new apartments. He only has two available at short notice. Each apartment is for two people. If we want one to suit three people, we'll have to wait another week. It is a dilemma. They are much nicer apartments though, and a lot nearer the beach. But there are three of us.

Sharla has the answer. 'Why don't you move in with me, Maggie? I'd love a roommate and you'll be right next door to your friends here.'

It seems a really daring thing to do, but what option do I have? Patricia isn't speaking to me anyway at this stage, you'd think I'd burst the bloody waterbed myself. And although I have come to the USA with Maureen and Patricia, they are the best friends – I am always the gooseberry. I feel I need a shot of adventure; I want to do something a bit different, so I might as well move in with Sharla. I can always move out if it doesn't work. So I agree. It does seem a much better arrangement all round.

And that is it. My life has changed – forever.

★

There are three things that Sharla converts me to within weeks of our meeting. One, I start to shave my legs; Americans have a horror of women with body hair. They simply can't cope with it. I had already started to remove the hair under my armpits (in the summer anyway). But up until now, I had seen no real need to shave my legs. The hair was blonde anyway and hard to see. But Sharla can see it glinting in the sun as we sit on the beach a few days later.

'Y'all need to shave your legs, honey,' she says. 'You look like a lil' ole' fuzzy peach from where ah am.'

Later that day, in the shower, I do, and quite enjoy the new sleek feel of my tanned (well, pink) legs.

The second and even more important thing (though only just about by Sharla's reckoning), I lose my virginity, quickly and enthusiastically, with a large, blond, stoned surfer friend of Buddy's. The third thing is that I am stoned too – for the first time.

I meet Jay at the restaurant where Sharla works when he and Buddy – Sharla's boyfriend – arrive to pick up some left-over pizza. Jay is from Gary, Indiana. He is tall with sun-streaked hair and an easygoing personality. I like the look of him. He seems the sort of all-American type I had envisioned spending time with when I was planning my trip to the States. The reality is that up until now I have only been asked out by one or two obese rednecks who come into the restaurant regularly, and Calvin, the buss-boy, who has no teeth.

Jay is more like my idea of a boyfriend. So when Buddy brings him in I chat him up a bit. He starts dropping in regularly after that. He is funny. He likes to hear about Ireland. His ambition is to hitchhike round Europe. I suppose I flirt with him a lot. At first I think it isn't getting me anywhere, and then about a week after we first meet he arrives round at the apartment without Buddy. He asks me if I want to go and watch him shoot basketball on the Boardwalk. He plays basketball for one of the big college teams, despite being only

16

5'11" and white. I don't know whether this is a big deal or not, but I take him at his word that it is. It is my night off and I am happy to go out with him. He has teeth and looks normal; well, good-looking actually. He is amiable and undemanding. He smiles a lot, probably due to the number of joints he smokes, but I don't care. His sunniness is infectious and he cheers me up. And besides, Sharla spends a lot of time with Buddy, heaving away on the waterbed – they have mended the hole, turns out you can fix it like a bicycle puncture – and I am beginning to feel a wee bit left out. I have actually phoned home twice in the last two weeks. My sister Sinead thinks I need an American boyfriend and here I am going out with a surfer – how much more American can I get?

The Boardwalk (I have never been until now) is a sort of permanent funfair. There are lots of stalls full of tacky little prizes, the usual old rubbish. Three of them give you three shots at a basketball hoop for a dollar. The star prize is a teddy bear. The teddies are awful-looking things: the body is plaid, or check as we call it back in Ireland, and they have big googly eyes. Jay wins three at the first stall, and then the guy says he can't play any more. He gives them to me. I am touched by these awkward, tawdry gifts. I am living the American life, with my boyfriend shooting basketball on the Boardwalk. It is exhilarating. I want people to look at me, see my happiness, my sudden sense of belonging. We repeat this at two other stalls, until we are staggering about laughing our heads off and clutching nine check teddies. No one else on the Boardwalk will let Jay near a stall. We bring them home to the apartment. I feel very warm towards Jay. It's not every day a girl gets a present of nine ugly check teddies.

'Maybe I could sort of spend the night here and we could make out?'

'Well, you could have a beer,' I say, having the idea of a cuddle in my head. This is a first date, after all.

17

Jay takes out his little box and starts to roll a joint. I don't mind. I quite like the smell of it.

'Here,' Jay says, holding out the joint. 'You have some.'

'I can't do it, I don't smoke.'

'Whaddya mean, you don't smoke?'

'I don't like tobacco,' I say.

'But this is grass. It's different.'

I shake my head. 'I don't think I'll like it.'

'You'll love it, babe; look, hold on a minute. Open your mouth and suck this in, and swallow it.' He takes a long draw from the joint and then blows a large jet of smoke into my mouth. I do what he says. I suck like crazy. I love the proximity of his mouth.

'You call this a blowback,' he tells me. 'Just tell people you can't smoke and they'll do this for you. It works just as good.'

It feels glorious; sensual and sexy. Suddenly I love him. He is my real live check teddy, and so talented, a sharpshooter no less. He begins to kiss me. He has a soft, warm, melty mouth. Five minutes later we are totally naked on Sharla's waterbed (not hard since we are in Florida and had been wearing very little to start with), rolling about in ecstasy, making love till I am seasick. I am deflowered at once. All the nine check teddies look solemnly on. It is the seventh of the seventh seventy-seven. It has been ordained.

Sharla comes home early next morning. Jay and I are fast asleep on the waterbed. I tell her what has happened and she almost passes out with enthusiasm. She is busy cracking vitamin E capsules on to her nipples at the time to keep them supple.

'Maggie, honey, that was real smart. I am so proud of you. You really needed to unload that baggage. I'm sure you feel normal now.' She studies me critically. 'Why I believe you look better already, and to do it yesterday especially. The magic date. It's apocrital.'

I think she means apocryphal, but I'm not sure.

18

I'd almost given up the virginal state earlier that year. I went on holiday to Southport for Easter with an English boy from university. Myles was his name. His mother ran a B&B there. We'd been going out all term. Despite the earnestness of his passion, I had refused to give up my virginity on Irish soil. But I had agreed in advance that we would do it that holiday. I had decided it wouldn't be a sin if I did it away from home.

One morning, before breakfast, Myles came to my room looking for action. We fumbled around a lot; even though I had already decided to surrender, I wasn't going to hand it to him without a fight. However, just at the height of our passion, when I was finally swooning into agreement, his mother shouted up to ask if he would put the fish fingers out to defrost for lunch. It was all downhill from there. In the end, he seemed to get his willie mixed up with his pyjama cord, and I left Southport a virgin.

The surfer, fortunately, is not a great man for pyjamas. Being naked suits him. He spends a lot of time that way, or trying to *get nekit* as he calls it. I fancy him rotten. His life consists of surfing, eating and fucking in that order. He isn't much of a conversationalist, probably on account of the pot. But I am comfortable with him. He is undemanding.

Sharla unfortunately shares my good news with Maureen and Patricia. She thinks they'll be pleased. They aren't. They corner me in the toilet at work.

'Sharla told us what you've been up to. God forgive you, Maggie Lennon. No self-respecting boy back home will ever look at you again. Soiled goods, that's what you are,' Maureen tells me piously.

You could say neither Maureen nor Patricia had heard of Germaine Greer. They are appalled when, under questioning, I admit that I have thoroughly enjoyed losing my virginity.

'You're not supposed to enjoy it,' Patricia snarls at me. Part of me hopes they don't go home and tell everyone I am a fallen woman, but the weirder thing is that I feel I am actually doing what I want to do for the first time in my life.

So now I have experienced the sex and drugs, and with Sharla's prompting I stumble into rock and roll.

My accent already goes down a treat with everyone. I had figured out after a mere week working in Paesano's that the fact that I talk *funny* is a great tip-booster. Maureen and Patricia do this too, though not so flamboyantly. Bob, the manager at Paesano's, cashes in on his Irish waitresses too. He encourages the customers in the belief that we are political refugees from the conflict in Northern Ireland.

Sharla, however, has bigger and better ideas for me. My accent is a vital commodity waiting to be exploited. Not squandered on mere waitressing. She has plans; she thinks I should be on the radio. There is a great rock 'n' roll station called WA1A that we all listen to.

'You should be on the air, honey. Your accent is so cute, and WA1A has no female DJs. They need them one.'

Sharla encourages me to phone and ask for an interview. She has a car; we drive out on my day off. WA1A's DJs talk eloquently about the station being on the beach with the Atlantic waves lapping outside its door. Such a romantic image, I am really looking forward to seeing it.

The reality is anything but. When we finally locate it we find it's a converted lock-up garage in the sticks. The closest water is a mosquito-infested swamp, and the place is about as far as you can get from the ocean. Once you have this inside knowledge and listen carefully, you can hear the frogs croaking during the quiet parts of 'Us and Them'. WA1A plays good music though. And I am getting used to things not being as they seem. After all, we aren't too far from Disneyworld.

Zollie V Follie IV, the station owner, is sitting behind a humongous desk in one of the small rooms. He is wearing a large cowboy hat and matching boots, a check shirt and denims. He looks about thirty something and he stands up to shake my hand, grinning broadly (more teeth). He is tall, and reasonably handsome in a louche sort of way. I am not sure what to expect. He speaks with a lazy drawl.

'Ah'm real pleased to meet you, Maggie. I'm Zollie V – for Virgil – Follie the fourth, and I'm from Tennessee, the Volunteer State. In other words' – he thumps the desk loudly – 'I'll volunteer for most things.' He follows this statement with the laugh of a crazy person, but I take an instant liking to him anyway.

'I'm Maggie Lennon,' I say, 'from Ireland, and I wondered if you need any more DJs?'

For a minute he says nothing. Just looks at me with a bemused look on his face. I blab on.

'I mean, I'd like a job as a DJ if there is one. Anyway you need a lady DJ, it's an oversight not to have one.'

Zollie fixes me with his large grin. 'An oversight, huh? A lil' ole' ladee DJ, huh?'

'Yes, I think I'd be good.'

'Well, ma'am, you're British? Right?'

'Yes, well, Irish, but from the North. I suppose British. Ish.'

'Irish? How come you speak English so good? You talk like the BBC.'

'Thank you.' Immediately I reappraise my Belfast nasal.

'Have you met Pink Floyd?'

'No.'

'How 'bout Led Zeppelin?'

'No.'

'You related to *John* Lennon?'

'No, I'm afraid not.' I feel fairly useless being related to no one. Then I hit inspiration. 'I might be a cousin of his,' I say. 'I've got fifty-two first cousins and some of them live in Liverpool.' This is true and I add for good value: 'My cousin saw The Beatles in Belfast in 1964 and got me their autographs.'

'You did? Hellfire, sheeeit! I'm impressed! You have them with you?'

'No, but I can copy them from memory.' (I really can.)

'You got a social security number?'

'Yes.'

'Hell, you're hired. I just lost me a DJ 'bout five minutes ago.'

He had just fired the all-night man for getting too stoned and breaking FCC regulations by saying 'Mother fuckin' sonofa-bitch' on the air. So it is fate. I have come at the right time. To quote Sharla it is apocrital.

Zollie gives me a tour of the station. We start with the studio, where I will work my shift and play the records. He intro-duces me to Bilbo, the engineer, who is small, dark-haired and sort of tubby. He seems a sweet and shy guy, and says he will give me a crash course on how to turn a turntable.

Zollie calls it the studio but it is a joke of a place. A small, poky room, three walls of which are covered with lots of egg-box-shaped soundproofing which is made from fibreglass. I find this out to my cost; I touch it and get a splinter in my hand. The other wall is covered in shelves for the carts. A cart, I learn, is a sort of tape thing, and these are all loaded with the individual songs which saves playing vinyl. All the vinyl is kept in Zollie's office; Bilbo explains it is locked away from the Kleptos, so called for their ability to rip off any LP left lying around. Only Bilbo and Zollie have keys. If I need a cer-tain album I am to ask Bilbo, and he will get it out and give it to me. The entire current playlist is already carted up. Mainly Bob Seger and Fleetwood Mac, I notice. *Rumours* is a hot album this summer, along with Steely Dan's *Aja*.

The studio seems a bit claustrophobic, but I guess that is usual enough for radio stations. WA1A has no windows at all. It consists of three rooms – the studio, the office and the back room where the station Kleptos/groupies hang out. I think the building is only a thousand feet square – Bilbo tells me it was once a mushroom farm. It does smell odd, but then so does he.

I agree to start the following evening, and go back to work my last night at Paesano's. Zollie assures me he will spend the next day advertising my arrival to listeners. He will give me a big build-up. I am in bits with excitement. I float out of the station on a high – a natural one. Sharla is waiting outside for me.

'Well? How'd it go, babe?'

'They've offered me a job! I'm starting tomorrow night.'

'Didn't I tell you your accent would make you famous, honey?'

I hope they don't find out in the foreseeable future that there are at least half a million more people with exactly the same accent in Belfast.

We drive back to the restaurant delighted with the whole adventure. Paesano is just as excited as we are at my big break. It is slowing down anyway and he will be laying off staff. He gives me an extra day's wages and says I can have as many of the leftover or uncollected pizzas I want tonight. We usually have about six of these a night, from the people who call in and order and then get too stoned to remember where to pick them up. It is balanced some nights by those who have been too stoned to order, or who think they have, and come to pick up pizzas someone else has ordered. Jay lives on them.

I can't wait to start. I go through the evening in a haze. Funnily enough, I make more tips than ever. I will be taking a dip in wages but I don't mind. My head is already turned by the prospect of becoming a DJ.

We play Radio WA1A in the restaurant. We turn it up loud. The customers like it like that anyway. It is such a thrill to hear Zollie keep his word and give me the build-up he promised. We all listen, Maureen and Patricia with their mouths open in disbelief. It's obvious they both think I'm insane. But I bet they're impressed really.

'WA1A is real, real proud to introduce to all of y'all the one and only real authentic British person on the aayer in Florida – Maggie Lennon, a close personal relation of Beatle John. She'll be playing for y'all night-time listeners the records of many of her close personal friends – all of which speak funny like her. You know whom I'm referring to folks! Yes, y'all do! Here's just a few names for starters: The Beatles, the Stones, Pink Floyd, Yes, Genesis, The Moody Blues, Led Zeppelin and many, many more! Yessir, remember only here on Dubya Ay One Ay, the station with the Atlantic waves breaking outside our door, can you hear the close personal friend of British groups play non-stop ass-kicking British music from midnight till dawn. Be sure to tune in.' This is screamed loudly in Zollie's Tennessee sharecropper drawl to backing music of '19th Nervous Breakdown', Zollie's all-time favourite British hit.

'And you'll be up all night?' Patricia asks me. She hasn't stopped gurning at me since I told her.

'From eleven to five in the morning?' Maureen echoes.

'Yes, I don't mind the hours.'

I reason that I can sleep all day on the beach. I will buy a little fold-up sunbed and lie just exactly where the waves hit the shore, and the breeze takes the pain out of the sun. I will cover myself in Hawaiian tropic coconut oil and hopefully get a tan just like Sharla's.

2

So here I am, twenty-one, Queen of the Airwaves in Daytona Beach, Florida. WA1A is an AOR station. That means Album Oriented Rock, and its audience is mainly college students. Daytona is full of them in the summer: just about everyone you meet, regardless of ability, seems to be at college. You can study anything in the States. A degree in beauty skills is perfectly acceptable, no intellectual snobbery here. I don't know what they'd make of Punk though. That's what's happening musically at home. But I soon take to the AOR sound; it fits in with the good weather and easy lifestyle.

It is surprising how fast you get used to a totally new way of life, 'cos let me tell you, working for Zollie, I soon find, takes some mind adjusting. He is crazy – in the truest sense of the word. Everyone he surrounds himself with is crazy too, a cast of fools and lunatics, all except Bilbo. Bilbo is the first workaholic I have ever encountered. He doesn't appear to have a life outside the radio station and he almost lives there. Trouble is, it is hot and stuffy in that place and, delightful as Bilbo is, he has what I quickly learn to call a hygiene problem. I guess his weight doesn't help. He is a little tublet. Nor does the fact that everything he wears is man-made. He crackles with static, like those old nylon sheets that were so fashionable years ago. We all pretend not to notice – all except Zollie. He isn't what you would call the soul of tact about it.

Zollie comes in early on my first day here (I am in getting a turntable lesson from Bilbo), sniffs a bit and then hollers at the top of his voice: 'Goddamm, Bilbo! Has something died inside your armpits? You got two skunks up there? Hell fire! I need to get me some kind of deodorant trade-out.'

Poor Bilbo moves as far away from Zollie as possible. He remains impassive.

Zollie begins again. This time his voice is quieter, almost pleading. 'Have you heard about plastic surgery where they remove your armpits? You need to read up on that, buddy.'

No response. Then finally: 'Godammit, Bilbo, baby! How can I eat my donuts with that aroma round me? Call Eckerd's now! I need to get me a trade-out for Sure.'

I am almost dying of embarrassment, but poor old Bilbo had obviously heard it all before. He slinks into the loo and sprays something that smells like air freshener on top of his already humming armpits. We spend the entire day with the air conditioner on so low that our teeth are chattering.

Yes, you could say it is an unusual environment.

Over the following weeks I get to meet the cast of weird-oes who hang around the station. The most mind-bendingly insane of the lot have to be Chance and Vance Prince, or Vance and Chance Prince. Twin brothers, who look like famine, and the cause of it.

Vance is 5'6", easily 350 pounds. His skin and hair and eyes are pinky red (though that might be directly attributable to the dope). There isn't a lot of his hair either, just a few seaweed-like strands clinging vainly to his round, pink head. He has sort of smooth, girlie skin which is always covered in a thin, shiny film, though he smells okay, which is a relief.

26

His brother Chance – his twin – is so different. Chance weighs about 130 pounds and is over six feet tall. He has long, jet-black hair which he wears in a braid down his back, black beady eyes, and a long, untrimmed beard. He looks like a roadie for ZZ Top. They have opposite voices too. Chance has a deep, growly voice, and when it emerges people always look at the wrong guy. Vance has a thin, effeminate voice.

Zollie knows the family. They hail from Possum Creek, Tennessee. Zollie has a theory, not as preposterous as it sounds, that their Mama, who goes by the name of Evangeline Oreya Prince, had been fertilised by two different sperm the same day – possibly by two of her own brothers. She was fond of the drink, apparently, and to this day their Daddy isn't in evidence, so he could have been any shape at all.

Not having made it to Vietnam is a constant source of anguish to Vance. He spends hours telling us what he 'Woondo to them Gooks over thar'. That is, had he only been given the chance. He'd applied twice to go to Vietnam (or *Can*bodya) which just about convinced the military he was crazy. I mean, every sane American male of draft age was in Canada during the Vietnam War. Here it is 1977, the ghastly war is over, and he is still calling the draft board volunteering like crazy. He certainly was taking the fact he came from Tennessee seriously. I don't think he knows the war is over yet, though he's been told often enough. Hell, he thinks Nixon is still president.

The Prince Twins are regular visitors to the station. I meet them the first day on the job. I wonder why they hang round there so much; they don't appear to do anything but get in the way. It is several weeks before I realise that they are Zollie's drug dealers. They also supply stuff to Big Al, the morning drive jock, and Art, the afternoon DJ. At this point, the trade is mainly pot and Quaaludes. Later, with dire consequences, they progress to cocaine.

Vance has a sort of notion of me. After the first week or so

I get used to it and learn not to find it offensive. We have the same chat about every third night. He waits till I put on a long track, or three in a row (which is one of our 'features') and sit down with my coffee. I wait for him to sidle over.

'Whur you from Maggie?' he asks.

'Ireland, Vance. I'm from Ireland.'

'Yep, that's raaght, I believe you already tol' me that.' He pushes his strands of hair back and his pink cheeks flush with the effort of remembering. Then he gives up. 'Where d'you say Ireland was at?'

'It's in Europe, actually.'

'Is Europe y'all's hometown?'

'Sort of.' (I mean what's the point?)

'Shit, Maggie, how come you speak American so good?'

'Picked it up, Vance. I'm a fast learner.'

'Damn raaght!' He pauses. You can see the wheels go round. 'They all talk like you thur?'

'Yes they do, Vance.'

'Well, ain't that cute. Can they all understand each other?'

'Yes, no problem.'

'Well, hell, you know I'd like to go thur sometime, meet your folks. Maybe me an' Chance'll drive back with you at Thanksgiving. Or maybe Chance and me'll go thur some weekend, go fishing or something. Good fishing there, raaght?' (I have told him that the first ten times we had the Ireland conversation.) 'Whaddya think Maggie?' He then beams at me, showing his bottom row of decaying teeth, and two ill-fitting, yellowish crowns on the top row, which seem to belong to someone else's mouth. I wouldn't be surprised if he had robbed them from a dead body. I fix a smile. He has to be tolerated. I like this job. In the background Bilbo rolls his eyes. 'You like a ride home t'see yur folks?'

'Sure I would,' I reply, 'sounds great.' I found that this was the least painful reply. When we first had this conversation, I

28

had vainly attempted to explain to him where Ireland was geographically, but I realised he is completely a moronic git. So now I humour him.

'Well, howja say we give you a ride home some of these here weekends?'

'Soon as we can organise it, Vance,' I reply.

'Fantastic, thet gives me a reason to live, baby.'

'Great, Vance. Me too,' I lie.

'Want me to eat your pussy?'

'No thanks, Vance. It's not an Irish custom.'

'Raaght, well it sure is here.'

I wasn't familiar with this custom, and not being local I hadn't heard the term. I thought at first they were going to eat cats, but Zollie was quick to apprise me of the fact that they were referring to the male prowess in performing cunnilingus. Americans have oral fixations I think. I take a decision fairly early on in the job not to be shocked about all this tacky talk, because as I quickly learn it is purely talk. They are so courteous to me otherwise. Zollie has begun to introduce me to his friends with the line: 'This here's Maggie Lennon, she's Irish, and she thinks that oral sex is talking about it,' and then we all laugh and that is it. Zollie is very proprietorial: if he sees any guy getting too chatty he intervenes, and he manages to keep a lot of unsavoury types at bay. He needs to; this station attracts loonies and misfits. Not all are as hard to take as the Prince Brothers. Some are a delight. Maybellyne is, for sure. She is the secretary cum accountant cum sales person cum everything. I meet her on my second night on the job. She is about twenty-five, has a very pretty face, a sunny smile and nice, wide-open grey eyes, but she is extremely fat. No, that's wrong. She is actually outrageously fat. I try to look as if this is normal, but a small gasp must have sneaked out of my mouth, for she is easily three times fatter than I am, and she is about my height. I weigh 105 pounds, that's about 7½ stone. I have

29

learned to say pounds 'cos stones confuse people here. Zollie introduces us.

'Maybellyne baby, this here is Maggie. She's Irish and John Lennon is a real close relative of hers. She talks funny but she's gonna be working for us on the midnight till five a.m. slot.'

Maybellyne looks at my mouth, which is hanging open in a sort of rictus. 'Yes, I know hon, I am gargantuan. I expect I'm the fattest person y'all ever met.'

'No,' I say hastily, choking at the same time. 'No, not at all, I've met loads of fat people.'

'But no one as fat as me, raaght?'

I smile weakly. 'Well, no actually.'

'Dead right, Maggie, ole Maybellyne here could git her a job in "Ripley's Believe it or not" museum couldn't she?' Zollie grins from ear to ear at my discomfort. Maybellyne doesn't stop smiling. Zollie keeps on. 'Boy, she can cook the best cheese grits I ever did taste though, and her ham is to die for.'

As it happens, Maybellyne and I become firm friends. She has so little sense of her own worth, and yet she is such a kind person. She quietly shows me how everything works. Nothing is too much trouble for her, unless it involves moving fast. She is too fat to drive, so a cousin/brother type (I never do work out what he is), rolls her out of a large van every night at eight, and picks her up and hoists her back in at about six a.m. I get accustomed to the loud honk and the shout from the relative: 'Maybellyne babe, your haulage truck has arrived'.

I spend a lot of time trying to improve her self-respect and helping her stick to her numerous diets. She wears a sort of rubber wet suit garment under her clothes and I even guard the loo for twenty minutes every hour for a week while she finds the opening to pee. Whoever sold it to her had guaranteed it would *Sweat off all that ugly flesh in just one week!* All she has to do to double its potential weight-losing power is perform strange crab-like movements four times an hour. These

30

exercises have the effect of wafting a rubbery smell throughout the station.

'Goddammit! Maybellyne baby!' Zollie yells at her with his usual tact. 'You smell like a used rubber.'

Through the week she perseveres, the sweat lashing off her as she gets on with the job of answering the phone and doing the books. She looks like a bouncy ball climbing out and into the van in the nights and mornings. She must have emptied a ton of talcum powder down her neck in a vain attempt to stop the constant itching and combat the build-up of body odour. After ten days she has to be cut out of the rubber suit, and unfortunately the poor thing has developed an allergic rash from wearing it next to her skin. So now she is red and itchy as well as hopelessly fat, and she has only lost two pounds. It doesn't seem fair.

3

As soon as I begin working at WA1A my life takes on a new dimension. Well, actually that's an understatement. I begin to live in some sort of new dimension, as almost everyone at the station seems to – most of it drug-induced. The station has been in operation for one year and is, I suppose, a fairly successful commercial venture. But maybe it isn't. I really don't know if Zollie makes a lot of money out of it. Very little money changes hands as the whole set-up appears to be run on a kind of barter system where everything is freebies or trade-outs. Zollie is out there every day of the week bullshitting from dawn till dusk, getting every little business within a twenty-mile radius to advertise with us. He promises results within days, and many of them buy into the hype. I quickly gather the truth doesn't play too big a part in his selling, and boy can Zollie V Follie IV sell airtime. That's where the money is *supposed* to come from – advertising time. The whole station runs completely on the amount of ads sold. It is hard for me, used only to listening to the BBC, to take this in. This is my first brush with commercial radio, and boy, are we commercial!

We advertise anything and everything. The commercials bear

no resemblance to reality, since our chief copywriter, Merlyn, is always on acid, so I learn to write copy fast. One of our accounts is a dry-cleaning shop, Sanitary Cleaners. Their ad goes something like this: *What does Sanitary mean to you? Let us tell you what it should mean. It should mean fresh, soft and good-smelling. Well folks, here in Daytona we have finally found a haven for your clothes. Right here at Sanitary Cleaners your special garments are pressed and ready to go before you get back to the car park, and for an extra fifty cents Sanitary Cleaners make them smell like they'd been tumbled in a mountain stream. Gaze into a sunset full of peace and love, wearing clean clothes fresh from Sanitary Cleaners. Yes. Yes, I know.* Reading it, it's hard to justify. Why don't we abort the ad or napalm the copywriter? Hey, it's business!

Zollie has persuaded the owners of this particular business that their trade will boom once this ad hits the airwaves. They are a small concern and haven't got a big advertising budget, so they have traded the advertising out with us – $250 a week's worth. That means that all three DJs, Bilbo and Zollie can have up to $50-worth of clothes dry-cleaned every week. I don't own that many clothes so send everything, even my knickers, to the laundry section. Our jeans have knife-edge pleats, and there is so much starch in my underwear that it hurts to walk. Bilbo's man-made fibres, which still smell bad, are turning to plastic, and my bras have stiff points.

Zollie has also arranged a trade-out with the local funeral parlour, Green Glades. No one seems sure why. He met the owner on some drunken night out in a bar on Atlantic Drive and I guess he just can't say no to any chance of airtime. We use the trade-out just twice. Big Bubba, a beer-drinking friend of Zollie who doesn't even work for the station, has a pet monkey called Marmaduke who is shot by the police for biting a tourist on the nose. We give Marmaduke the equivalent of a state funeral, right down to the solid brass coffin in order to use up as much of the trade-out as possible. The music Bubba chooses as Marmaduke is being cremated is 'Heaven's Just Sin Away' by the Kendalls – some old country song. Chance begins laughing hysterically at that point and we watch in stitches as he is hauled out of the crematorium by two sour-looking attendants for showing disrespect. Zollie promises to cut them a new commercial to calm them down. It's me that has to do it.

Cutting commercials is the down side of the job. I already loathe it. Every day I come in to a tray full of bad copy, littered with spelling mistakes, bad grammar and clichés. I always have at least two to cut – my voice is popular because it is different, distinctive. 'Give it to the gurl who tawks funny to make,' they say, and despite my protestations about being over-exposed, Zollie obliges. It pisses me off. But I can't object too much, it comes with the territory and besides, I just love being a DJ.

My show, I think, is distinctive. No disco for starters, and it consists mainly of British acts. For variety I also have a little call-in quiz where I pitch my wits against the listener. If I fail to answer their rock 'n' roll trivia question they get a free album. Usually it's something like, 'What group was Rod Stewart with before he went solo?' Yes, there are people out there who really give a shit. Mostly people lose, so the staff get the free LPs that we have bummed from the record companies. The callers don't have a hope really, because we also have a massive rock encyclopaedia on the desk and Maybellyne looks it up, then Bilbo vets the questions. We have to; there are lots of crazy types out there listening during the night.

There is a problem though. It is now August and my return flight is for September 5th. As it approaches I am apprehensive. I really don't feel like going home just yet. I have passed my degree – a third, a shit degree – and I have been accepted to do a DipEd which will enable me to get a teaching job in a Catholic school, if I am lucky. Anyway, things are bad politically

34

right now. Even my parents like the idea of one less child to worry about. Belfast is scary these days. Every letter my mother writes is full of woe and death and stories of someone else we know who has been shot or bombed, and of course the weather's crap. It is a major dilemma. Chance has fake phone credit card numbers which mean we can call anywhere in the world for free, so I have taken to calling home about once a week. I lie to my mother that the job pays for the call, but they still get all panicky at the cost. I am gradually convincing them I should stay on. They have no concept of the radio station anyway – I expect they sort of think I'm famous. My sisters enthusiastically send me punk singles but I haven't the heart to tell them that people here are still swooning to the Steve Millar Band.

Maureen and Patricia have given up on me too. They both graduated last year and have just passed their teaching diplomas, and are going back to teaching jobs. To be fair to them we have sort of patched things up, I mean they were best friends and I was sort of an interloper who needed chums to go to America with. They do earnestly try to point out the folly of my staying on, not least the fact that my return ticket is non-refundable. But I can't face returning. I have got some crazy urge to stay and I know that going home to Belfast now will finish me off. I guess I have seen something else of life. For all its flaws, America has given me the chance to reinvent myself, forge another Maggie, give in to the side of my personality that I have been repressing for years. Eventually they accept that I'm staying on and shut up about it – I'm a lost cause. Zollie throws a party for them the night before they leave and Patricia gets drunk and tells me she admires my nerve in staying. I promise to write, and phone with the 'funny' cards.

For quite a few days after they've gone I am seriously scared, and Sharla is going next. I am to take over the rental lease on the apartment then. It is a daunting prospect. As soon as Labor Day is over Sharla leaves, tearfully, but with a firm promise that she will be back for a weekend very soon, and if not, then I am to visit her in Tennessee at Thanksgiving. It is really hard to see her go. I am all alone. But I wave her off brightly. I have a new family now, all the crazies at the station.

Almost instantly, things in Daytona slow right down. It's a summer town where the students and tourists account for most of the population. We are into old people now, lots of them. Florida isn't called 'God's Waiting Room' for nothing, and you know what? These guys don't care much for rock 'n' roll. Even Andy Williams would make them agitated. By the beginning of October, Zollie is getting restless, very restless. He can't concentrate on anything, and I notice we aren't doing as much business either, which bothers him. But leaving that aside, he isn't his usual self. I mention this to Bilbo.

'Hell, pay no attention to him, he gets antsy in winter. He'll settle down eventually. He got that way last winter too. Apart from mid-term break, he doesn't really pick up again till spring.'

The commercials are starting to change too, from disco bars to rest homes. 'Happy Haven – the only place to spend your twilight years', was one of our big advertisers (no trade-out). It was a far cry from The Pink Pussycat, and Dewayne's Drink-Till-You-Burst Beer Hut! Things are about to change more drastically than that though.

4

Vance and Chance are directly responsible for the demise of WA1A. They had started out as two amiable potheads long before I joined the scene, but by the time I meet them, Vance and Chance are beginning to get heavily into other drugs. Not hard drugs at first, no needles, nothing too serious. It doesn't really bother me. They smoke a lot of dope, but then a lot of people do, and they drop Quaaludes, or lewds as they call them. Quaaludes are sleeping pills, famous for making you horny – which is American for sexy – or at least that's the claim. Vance and Chance claim they give them to all of the women they date. A wise move on both their parts because, let's face it, anyone would have to be on some kind of drug to even talk to Vance and Chance for longer than ten minutes. And as for sex with either of them, well, no one in their right minds would touch them with a barge pole. So they figure it is a good idea to make the woman as unconscious as possible, otherwise they will wise up and leave. I guess it has a certain kind of crazy logic.

The Prince Bros, I believe, drop acid as well. But essentially they are so messed up to start with that life must be like a bad trip for them most of the time. But all this drug stuff is pretty minor league till they start experimenting with cocaine. That's when it gets dangerous.

According to Bilbo, Zollie had been trucking right along smoking the odd joint, but more or less clean of any other drugs. Then about a month before I started, Vance laid him out a line of coke. He became an instant fan. It helps him sell, keeps him bright and breezy and full of meaningless chat. At first Zollie is shrewd, he just uses it for special occasions and he never uses too much of it. He keeps a little vial of it in the pocket of his suit. He doesn't exactly flaunt it – I am completely unaware of it.

The first time he offers me some is the night after Sharla's going away party when I come into work with a hangover. I didn't have too much to drink, but the party had started at three p.m. because I had to be in work for midnight. It was some party, and they were still going when I arrived home the next morning. I joined in again, so by the time I arrive at work that evening I am away with the fairies. Zollie comes into the station to see why I sound so goddamm depressing. He always checks out my show.

'Goddamm, Maggie, you sound like you are about to die! You may as well put Leonard Cohen on, do a giveaway for razor blades, and go home.'

'I'm really sorry, I haven't been to bed for twenty-four hours. I'm just sleepy.'

He breaks into song – Rod Stewart's 'Maggie May' which he thinks is hilariously funny. I don't laugh, mainly because this is about the fiftieth time he has sung it since I've met him. He thinks for a minute, then says. 'Have some coke, Maggie, that should keep you going all night, baby.'

'No thanks,' I say, 'Coke doesn't work for me, and besides we could get it free in Paesano's. I got sick of it.'

'Sheeeit Maggie, y'all got free toot at Paesano's? Why'd you leave?'

'Yes, as much as we could drink in fact. I think my teeth are rotten at the front from too much of it.'

'It rots your teeth? How does it do that if it goes up your nose?'

'Oh that coke!' It suddenly hits me.

'Hell yes, Maggie, are you acting the dumbass or what? Are you in rock 'n' roll or ain't you? I'm talking about cocaine, honey, ye oldie Colombian marching powder.'

I am genuinely shocked. 'Zollie, it's a dangerous drug.'

'Yep baby, you got it! It sure as hell is, it's a class A *narr-cotic*, but it's nice, real nice, and it'll wake you baby, so you don't sound dull on the air. Try some, just a lil' ole tootski, a liddle pop.'

I don't want to, it's too scary. I'd made one leap, thanks to Jay, and was by now pretty relaxed about smoking pot. But cocaine? I don't know. Jackson Browne had a song out about it, so did Eric Clapton. It was one of Zollie's favourites, naturally. Coke, or toot, was the hip thing to do.

Zollie pulls a small brown bottle out of his pocket. It has a teeny little spoon attached to it. He swings it like a pendulum before me. 'Well? You gonna fall asleep on me baby, lose me all ma listeners are you, Maggie? Or you gonna try some? Well?'

I get a surge of recklessness. 'Well hell, why not?'

He gets out the gear and I am fascinated by it. I have become blasé; I have already decided pot doesn't count. But this is my first close-up of real drugs. His little kit is made of brown suede and looks like a small diary. It contains a mirror, a small silver straw, a spoon and a razor blade. I watch open mouthed as he does a bit of chopping, and lays out two even white lines, then he rolls up a twenty-dollar bill, clamps an index finger first to one nostril, then the other and has two noisy snorts.

'Goddammit Maggie! This is good snow. Peruvian flake no less!'

None of this means anything to me. I am a coke virgin. It is my turn now. He chops again with a flourish, lays me out two lines. I look at them and hesitate. Am I really going to do this? 'I don't think I will after all, I might get addicted.'

'Maggie, honey, you won't. Not with one lil' toot.'

You could say I should refuse, but I am curious. I sniff each line cautiously and wait. I look at the mirror and it is all gone. It must be up my nose. At first nothing happens, then suddenly I am alert, jittery but alert, and just a bit scared. 'Yes, you're right, I do feel more awake,' I say to Zollie after a few minutes and a greatly increased pulse. This is an understatement: my pulse is about two hundred and fifty.

'You betcha you are a *lert* Maggie. Be a *lert* what exactly is a *lert*?' Zollie cackles insanely, slapping his leg.

I guess we had lots of lerts at WA1A, and Zollie was lert Number One. Thank God Maureen and Patricia have gone home to Ireland. They'd die on the spot at this step too far, me snorting coke instead of drinking it. Doubtless the fires of Hell will intensify for this. Coke is, as Zollie says, a class A narcotic, a felony of high proportion. I am doomed. Somehow I don't think Zollie can trade this one out – it's expensive, $75 a gram. But that's where I am wrong. He does. Yes, he certainly does. Some bloody trade-out it turns out to be.

About mid-July, a few weeks before I had started to work at WA1A, certain South American friends of Vance and Chance had opened a new restaurant-cum-Laundromat. No, I haven't got that wrong. You can watch your clothes wash while you drink a beer, play pool, or have a barbecue sandwich. It is called Sudsy's. They needed to advertise and Zollie was keen to sign them up. So now we have a huge trade-out at Sudsy's. We, that is all the DJs plus Bilbo and Maybellyne, can eat there, wash our clothes there, and generally hang out. They must have a commercial on WA1A at every break. It is overkill. You literally can't hear anything but the Sudsy's ad between songs. Zollie cuts the commercial himself, in his usual over-the-top, hard-sell voice. It goes like this:

'*You wanna party? I guess you do.*

You wanna smell bad? I guess you don't!

Got that established folks?

Well, why not have a beer and munch along to one of the best barbecue sandwiches in town, while . . .

Sudsy's washes your clothes and folds them in a real nice pile.

Hell Folks! Sudsy's will even iron your undies while you wait.

So if you wanna have good clean fun, don't hesitate.'

At this point he cranks up the backing track and yells in his most deranged voice:

'*Why not be mean, and stay clean. Eat and drink the night away. At Sudsy's on the Beach! Only ten dollars for all you can eat and drink plus laundry.*'

I think Sudsy's accountants have taken the meaning of laundering too literally, but anyway, the place was a smash. Easily the most popular place on Atlantic Drive. Full of students all night long until Labor Day, and now – not a soul. I guess the ordinary residents of Daytona Beach have either got washing machines or they don't fancy swilling beer and having their ears blasted by Lynyrd Skynyrd while they do their weekly wash. We are still running the ads though, six an hour.

Maybellyne is troubled. There's no money coming in and she is starting to get the books together for the taxman. She takes her job seriously and wants it all in order by Christmas. Ostensibly, we are letting Sudsy's have $1000 worth a week of airtime, and what are we getting in return? Not a penny in real money, just the trade-out, and even though Vance and Chance had said the deal would be half-and-half, Sudsy's wasn't paying up. We can't fit that many visits to Sudsy's in if we tried, and Bilbo and Maybellyne have washing machines and are both dieting all the time anyway.

So it isn't one of our more successful deals. We'd got more

41

use out of Green Glades Funeral Home. First Marmaduke's funeral, and then about two weeks ago Art, the afternoon DJ, his grandma died and Art is able to use up practically all the rest of the trade-out on a coffin. He swaps it for two weeks' wages. Zollie is delighted since Art is one of the highest paid members of the team, and Green Glades are more than happy to oblige. Art picks the grade A coffin, the one people are 'Dyin' to lie in'. He wants it delivered to Alabama for the funeral, but Green Glades don't do out-of-state deliveries. That doesn't deter Art. He picks up the coffin himself and comes by the station to show it to us all. It is most impressive, like something out of *The Godfather*. It is solid brass and lined with purple silk, and absolutely massive. You could fit a gorilla in it – his grandma had been a large lady. She had lived in a trailer but had become so fat that she hadn't been out of it for almost ten years. She died from diabetic complications. Art tells us they had to chainsaw the front of the trailer off to get the body out. Big Al, Bilbo, Vance and Chance help him tie it more securely on to the back of his pick-up. We all wave him off. He intends driving all the way to Selma, Alabama, with it. About three hours after Art leaves, we get a call from a highway patrol station on I-95 just outside St Augustine. I take the call. It's Art. He is in hysterics.

'What's up, Art?'

'Oh hell! Maggie, I'm in a state patrol station, and they are ripping ma grandma's beautiful coffin apart.' A large sob escapes him. 'What am I gonna do, Maggie? I think they're searching it for drugs.'

'Is it clean?' I ask hastily.

'Yes ma'am!'

'Did they tell you why they are searching it?'

'Well Maggie,' the words come out of Art with difficulty, 'seems like some asshole has gone and stole him a big ole alligator from Gator World. They think I might have done had it in ma grandma's coffin.' He sobs again pitifully. 'Imagine what ma pore ole Grammy would think.' My heart goes out to him. 'It's all plain disrespectful, Maggie. Her funeral cain't take place till I arrive with the coffin and I jest cain't convince them to let me go.'

He sounds an emotional wreck. Zollie and I agree there and then to drive up. What else can we do? It takes us two full hours, Zollie drives like crazy. I don't know how we don't get a speeding ticket. We arrive at the highway patrol station, and are led into a room where we behold a sobbing bundle of emotion formerly known as 'Art the Coolest DJ in Daytona – cool as the waves that crash on the shore'. Well, he is anything but cool now. He falls into my arms and points out the window with a shaky finger. Exhibit A, the big brass coffin, is lying outside on the lawn. It is wide open with the lid lying beside it. They have established that there is no alligator in it, and although Art has explained that he is taking it to Alabama to bury his grandma they are still refusing to let him go. They have searched it for drugs, but not just a straight search. This is the bit that broke Art's heart. He points to the beautiful purple silk lining. It has several large slits in it. Zollie and I look at it in horror. Is this the 'Top Brass', the pride of Green Glades, the coffin people are dyin' to lie in? Surely not?

'What happened?' I ask.

'Well,' Art says. You can tell from his expression that it is causing him pain to relate the story. 'They got a kinda knife thang and this here guy . . .' He indicates a fat red-faced cop with a hat who is watching us from the door of the station. 'Well, he made these slits and felt inside. I told them there weren't any drugs, but he still did not believe me, they didn't even apologise for ripping a hole in the lining.'

Zollie tells us to wait, and he goes off to talk to the officer in charge. Art and I go out to the lawn. The coffin lining is

43

not only slit open and torn. It is covered in stains as well and has a large wet patch.

'What's that?' I ask him. 'How did it get all stained?' My question provokes a further bout of sobbing. I hadn't realised Art was so emotional.

'Well, Maggie, after they finished searching it by hand, they came back with a big ole German shepherd dog, a real nasty type of critter who jest crawled all over it, sniffing, showing jest no respect.' Art pauses, his voice choked with emotion. 'And Maggie, I think I done saw him pee on the lid.'

I look closer. I think Art done saw right. The smell assaults my nostrils, and I notice the dog has left drool stains on the purple silk lining as well. I hold his hand and mutter words of comfort. It is hard to know what to say under the circumstances. Finally Zollie emerges from the station, followed by two police officers. Zollie is smiling broadly.

'Looks like you can be on your way, buddy.'

They have contacted Art's local police station to check his story out. They now believe him. They are profuse in their apologies. They help him close the coffin and offer him a police escort to the state line. They say they will also radio to both Georgia and Alabama state police not to stop him.

Poor old Art, he had been getting more and more frantic that his ma would panic and buy another coffin, ruin his big gesture. We say goodbye, and Zollie and I head back. I wondered what Zollie had said to get things moving so quickly. It turns out he had just given them all a box of records from the trunk of his car, and a pile of WA1A T-shirts. It did the trick.

Art phones us from Alabama the next day. He sounds a bit more like himself. The funeral worked out fine in the end. Everyone loved the coffin, and once she was in it you couldn't notice the mess. It took six of his family to lift her into it and even then they had to bend her arms backwards. But it was worth it, Art said, she looked fantastic. Better than he'd ever seen her look in her whole life. He paid a professional beautician to do her make-up. She had long, false eyelashes and green shiny shadow to match her green sparkly dress, ''Cos of her Irish blood', he informs me proudly. Jesus, I think, that Irish blood sure travels. But I know he expects me to respond. 'That is really touching, Art,' I say dutifully, with no irony creeping into my voice I hope. 'I'm sure she would have loved that.'

'Yes, Maggie,' he continues, 'I knew you'd be impressed. I sorta did it for you.' He had polished the brass coffin till it shone. He said the family was reluctant to bury it, it looked so good. He felt he had given her the best send-off possible. The coffin had been worth more than her trailer, which was now irreparable.

Yes, every trade-out is working well except Sudsy's. Maybellyne is really troubled. By mid-October, Sudsy's owes us over $18,000 in food and laundry. The station isn't making that much money; we can't afford to keep running the trade-out. We can't make a dent in it either, unless we all move in to Sudsy's or have a party every night for a month, and we are crowding the airwaves with the bloody commercial. People are starting to complain.

Maybellyne decides she'll speak to Zollie. Unusually, he doesn't seem to want to sort it out, doesn't want to talk about it. It isn't his account. So she speaks to Vance and Chance; after all, they'd set it up. Maybellyne suggests they could maybe cut the ads down to five a day or something like that. The guys say they will check with Julio and Felipe that very evening.

I am on the air when they come back, well after midnight. I put 'Layla' on – it is the longest track to hand – and go in to see what has happened. They have obviously availed themselves of some of the free beer and are both somewhat the

45

worse for wear. They seem rattled, twitchy, like they are coked out of their heads.

'Well?' Maybellyne wants to know. 'Can we cut the ads?' They shrug. Vacant expressions all round; so no change there. 'Well?' Maybellyne insists, unusually firm for once. 'Can they stick to the deal? Trade out half and pay us the rest?'

Vance and Chance mutter in unison, the pitch of their voices clashing discordantly. Apparently not. Julio and Felipe say they need the ads more than ever now that the students have left. Business is bad, so advertise more.

'Raaght? You havta admit they do have a point, Maybellyne, honey,' Vance eventually manages. He smiles uneasily at us. 'We jus' left there. There wasn't one of the machines turning tonaaght. It was spooky in there, real, real quiet. No business worth a damn.'

'That's raaght, Maybellyne, honey,' Chance echoes, 'they done got them no business.'

'But we can't use the trade-out up!' Maybellyne tells them. 'So there's nothing in it for us. Right?'

Wrong. Julio wants to talk to Zollie. Seems he has a proposition to put to him. I don't like the sound of this, but Derek & the Dominoes are just coming to an end, so I have to leave. I have that old gut-wrenching feeling, as if something bad is about to happen. This whole business smells bad. I hope Zollie can sort it out. But even he couldn't sort this one out. By the time I realise that, we are on a night flit to Tennessee.

5

One of the things Zollie is most proud of is WA1A's van, The Crazy Wave Cruzer. It is a huge psychedelic thing that Tim has customised for the station. Tim is a really talented hippie guy who lives in a boathouse out on the North Halifax River. He is a gentle soul who spends his days painting and lacquering and doing a lot of work on Harley Davidsons.

I was out there with Vance once, after he had scratched the van and was getting a quick touch-up before Zollie found out. There were at least a dozen Harleys parked about the place. Each was more fantastically painted than the next, an assault of colour with swirling rainbows, fantastical dragonflies and every mythological creature one could conjure up. It was obvious that Tim had more work than he could handle, so when Zollie had wanted his van painted in exchange for some advertising, Tim had quietly refused him. But Zollie desperately wanted a sample of Tim's work. He has to have the best, and Tim is the best, so Zollie paid for it – cash, apparently. I guess even Zollie knows when the trade-out won't work.

The Crazy Wave Cruzer is one of the most distinctive vehicles I have ever seen, it is just unbelievable to look at! It looks like a big acid trip on wheels. It has every rock 'n' roll legend imaginable painted on the sides. Jimi Hendrix, Clapton, Robert Plant, The Beatles (the *Sergeant Pepper* cover), the Stones, and best of all as far as I am concerned Van the Man in a white, flowing kaftan, straight off the cover of *His Band and Street Choir*. It had been one of the first things I'd noticed when I first saw it drive past Paesano's long before I even worked at the station – Van on the Van. I was dead chuffed, him being from Belfast and that. The back doors are black, painted with a perfect prism, straight off the *Dark Side of the Moon* album. Everywhere it goes, The Crazy Wave Cruzer draws a crowd. I feel so important riding round in it.

Suddenly, the night after his meeting with Julio, Zollie wants it sprayed black. All of it. And the rainbow prism obliterated. Sprayed black? He can't be serious! Something is up, something strange. We are called in to a meeting in the office. It is Wednesday. Thursday is pay day. Zollie looks grim-faced and nervous. There is Maybellyne, Bilbo, Big Al, Art and me. Zollie asks us to sit down. There isn't enough room for all of us to sit, so we arrange ourselves haphazardly on the three available chairs, expectant, fearing the worst. He clears his throat.

'Well, folks, there's bin a major, and I mean *major*, fuck-up here, and I can't say what it is, but I am going back to my home state, Tennessee, real soon.'

'You're going when?' Big Al's famous growl could be heard for about a mile.

Zollie shifts uneasily. Al is over six feet, and volatile, very volatile. 'Well, Al, I'm goin' tomorrow as a matter of fact, well, tonight really, as soon as the paint on the Cruzer is dry. The van will be ready at four a.m. Art is going to follow me in my car. I'm going to record my shift now, and the station will be on automatic for the next forty-eight hours.'

No one says a word. We can't think of anything to say. Not even Big Al. This is surreal. Zollie continues as if on auto-pilot.

48

'Vance and Chance are gonna run things for a few days till the new owners settle in. I'd like y'all to record your intros and outs of all the records. I'll pay y'all one week's wages, and I'm real sorry, folks, but this is out of my control. I've sold the station as of Friday and none of y'all can work here anymore.'

We are stunned. I certainly am. Just when my career is flying and I am having the time of my life, I am out on the street.

'What about us?' I finally manage. 'Well, Zollie? What about us?'

'I'm sorry, Maggie, I guess it's hard for you, not having folks here and that, but I need to get my ass outa town soon.'

I am on the verge of tears. My mind is racing. First thought: Paesano would probably have me back, but what a comedown! Serves me right for thinking I was an amazing DJ. Second thought, which is nearer the truth, it is October, Paesano is down to skeleton staff for the winter, and maybe I can't get my job back. I have no return ticket. I have a Social Security number at least, but my J1 work visa is also technically expired. I pay the rent monthly and we are halfway through October, so I have two weeks left, one week's wages to come. Not much in my case, in anyone's case actually. Zollie being the trade-out king that he was, pays us in hair appointments, free meals (in at least five different restaurants), free dry-cleaning and free gas – if you have a car, which I don't. Oh, and free burials of course. I think Green Glades is the only trade-out we all feel like using right now. It is truly depressing.

I don't know what makes me do it, but I suddenly blurt out 'Can I hitch a ride with you to Tennessee?'

Zollie looks at me. 'What on earth would you do there, Maggie?'

'I can stay with Sharla,' I say. 'She's in Johnson City, are you going near there?'

'Maybe, maybe not, lemme think about it. Do your shift and record tomorrow's.'

49

Recording is easy. You just have to say things like: 'Hi, this is Maggie Lennon, and you're listening to WA1A, the much more music station. You've just heard "Josie", a track from the new Steely Dan album, *Aja*, before that you heard "Night Moves", Bob Seger, and we started the set with "Doctor My Eyes" by Jackson Browne from his album *Late for the Sky*. I'll be with you right through the night with your favourite rock 'n' roll tunes. And now this is Fleetwood Mac with "Rhiannon".' Then you press a tone button and that tone trips the next record. Then you rattle off some other spiel about the last three or four songs and that's it, on and on and on and on. It is possible to record a four-hour show in about thirty minutes, so it's a wonder there is any live radio around. A lot of stations are automatic since it's a lot cheaper. It means a DJ can do up to a six-hour, even an eight-hour shift, in a short time. You can run a station with only three voices, and the DJs can be out selling advertising slots while they are also on the air. The only thing you can't do is tell the time or, in Florida at any rate, mention the weather. It tends to rain in the afternoons, but not every day. Zollie has frequently pre-recorded his show and remarked on the bright sunshine during a particularly violent rainstorm.

Up until a month before I arrived in Daytona, WA1A had been an automated station and Zollie had been making money. Then he got ambitious. He had decided to go All-Live. He hired three extra DJs and gave himself the early evening slot so he could still sell advertising during the day. The station's popularity increased but so did his running costs. He is cash poor. I didn't know any of this at the time. I found it all out on the long, tiring, twelve-hour drive to Tennessee.

Black Thursday, I come off the air at five. I record my show for the next two days, feeling lousy, trying to sound chirpy and up, feeling anything but. I am finished by six. I usually love the dawn. The air is still and soft. The only sounds are the songs of birds, exotic, unfamiliar birds, and the thrum of the ceaseless ocean way in the background. The colours of the sky on my walk home after a night cooped up in the box of a station are uplifting. Long streaks of fiery red and gold, soaring through the azure. Clouds stretched out like dreams.

This time it is different. The dawn is as sombre as our mood. No uplift. Bits of the night linger. Zollie has left to collect the Cruzer. Big Al has followed me into the studio and is doing his show. I push open the door on to the morning. Even in October it is already warm at this time. Bilbo follows me outside. His mood isn't any livelier than mine.

'What's going on?' I ask. 'I know Zollie has told you!'

Bilbo looks on the verge of tears. 'Maggie, I cain't really say, but I've packed all my things and I'm off with Zollie. My folks live in Mentone, Alabama, anyways. He can give me a ride to Tennessee and my brother Lee is gonna come get me there. There's no point in me staying here.'

'What are you going to do there? Why don't you stay here and get another job?' I ask.

Bilbo shakes his head. 'I never go to the beach. Anyhow, I cain't swim and I hate water.'

I can't disagree with the last bit. 'But what about your apartment?'

'It's paid through October, that's all. I save any money I earn. Eat only trade-outs, as you know. I only got about one case of clothes. I got no friends here, 'cept at the station.'

That is all true. But it is true for me too. Maureen and Patricia are long back in Ireland and Sharla is in Tennessee. I am working all night, sleeping most of the day, and I haven't bothered to make any new friends. It hasn't seemed important. The station life is still too new and fresh for me to be bored yet. Jay, the surfer, left a few weeks earlier in search of fresh waves. Lynyrd Skynyrd has nothing on me. I am free as a bird. The words of the song 'all gone to look for America' float tantalisingly through my addled brain. If I had any money I could go and see the place, but I am broke – all those trade-outs, all those fucking trade-outs.

We sit miserably staring at the dawn. The red streaks spread like dreams, the day is going to be warm. A large van pulls up. It is matt black and smells strongly of paint. Our hearts break at the sight of it.

Zollie gets out carrying two bags of donuts. 'Any coffee, Bilbo?' Bilbo doesn't answer. We are both looking at the black van, mesmerised. All Tim's lovely work wiped out, annihilated, just like that. I have goose bumps. I rub my arms while Bilbo goes to get us some coffee. I try not to have it in the mornings usually as it tends to make it harder for me to get to sleep, but this is different. I drink it eagerly and wolf a few donuts. Bilbo eats six. So his appetite is unaffected, I think. We sit in silence. Eventually Zollie says:

'Well, Maggie, I've bin thinkin', and I guess y'all can come with me, since you're only a poor abandoned Irish girl. My momma will love you, and I'm gonna stay with her till I get me another station.'

And that was that really. Nothing else to say. No time to change my mind. Maybellyne isn't coming though. She will follow on to Tennessee when Zollie gets settled. She needs her special van to drive her, and her cousin/brother isn't available. She plans to lose weight in the meantime so she can catch the Greyhound. Some chance of that! I promise to call her as often as possible. We are both in tears. I'll miss her big, cuddly body, and her self-effacing, wry humour.

We go by my apartment – I am already saying go by, instead of call in to. It tickles me. I pack everything I have in ten minutes, only one suitcase full of clothes, but I also have a few bits and pieces I have got from various trade-outs. I have a good stereo system as we advertised Sound Blasters a lot and the guy there liked my accent, hence the extra good stereo. I have three lava lamps that the old hippie warehouse, Planet Zog, had traded for some ads about their flying yogi gatherings, and I now have my own bed linen, which I had to buy from Sears. I also have a pile of dry-cleaning at Sanitary Cleaners so we stop by there as well. Poor old Mister Skidelsky is distraught at the idea of us leaving. He had enjoyed the craziness of advertising on a rock 'n' roll station. I expect he got vicarious thrills from removing the little cocaine bottle from Zollie's suits and pinning it by the little spoon to the lapel every time Zollie forgot to go through his pockets before bringing in his clothes. And that is it. I decide to skip saying goodbye to Paesano. He doesn't come in this early anyhow. I'll send him a card.

So Zollie, Bilbo and I hit the road. I haven't quite got my thoughts together as I am totally exhausted from being up all night, and have so many emotions about leaving so quickly. It is barely nine o'clock. I should be tucked up in my bed now, the air-conditioning unit blasting away. But no, here I am, beetling up the I-95 towards Jacksonville with Zollie at the wheel, singing along with our radio station. Bilbo is slumped in one of the back seats, overcome by fumes from the brand new paint job no doubt.

Bob Seger's 'Night Moves' is blasting away. Every third or fourth track, the ads cut in and I hear myself extolling the virtues of Sudsy's On the Beach, Paesano's, Pancake Pete's, and then Zollie comes on, doing his quiet TV missionary voice about sending your loved ones to the Lord via Green Glades and so on. I feel heartsick. I will miss it desperately. Surely this isn't the end of my radio career so soon after it has begun?

'Maggie? You look too goddamm morose, honey! You need to lighten up! Here!' Zollie hands me a little bottle and a big bottle. 'Have a lil' pop, or if you want to crash, have a 'lude.'

That's it really, I have two choices: wake up, or pass out. I decline both.

'Okay,' he says, 'we need us a big ole joint to lighten your mood then. I wouldn't have brung you if I'd thought you were going to be this dismal! Bilbo buddy. Roll us a big one, y'hear?'

Bilbo, although he doesn't partake himself, does what he is told. It is amazing how much more relaxed the journey becomes through a haze of dope. I start to enjoy it. By mid-afternoon, we are on the ring road round Atlanta. Two hours later we still are. All Zollie's nonsense about being a better navigator on dope was bullshit. Automatic pilot my arse. We pull into a Cracker Barrel. We have the munchies now anyway. After a massive stack of pancakes and country ham we are off again, this time in the right direction.

By the time we hit the I-24 into Chattanooga I am starting to feel excited. We have driven up the interstate I-75 with all these signs *Visit Rock City*, *See Ruby Falls*, *Fireworks For Sale*, *Buy Pecans*. I'd discovered a pecan was a nut and not a bird as I had originally thought when I first read it. Closer to Chattanooga the billboards are urging us to visit the Choo Choo. I ask Zollie to stop. I want to see it.

'Hell, honey, it's only a Hilton Hotel now got all red brothel bedrooms. You'd hate it!'

Tennessee looks beautiful though. It is green and lush, all trees and mountains and much more like home than Florida. I haven't travelled down through America before, I'd flown with Maureen and Patricia from New York to Daytona on an Eastern Airlines special that had somehow worked out cheaper than the Greyhound, so this was my first journey through the States.

We decide that Bilbo and I will spend the night with Zollie's mama. I can call Sharla and take it from there. Zollie's mama, Annie Mae, lives in a clapboard house with an all-round porch near Nickajack Lake, which is between Chattanooga and Nashville. She is a big, comfortable woman with twinkly eyes and a huge smile who makes me feel at home from the minute

54

I meet her. She tells me her kin had been Irish, family name of Foley. Zollie changed his second name from Foley to Follie because he thinks it sounds good on the air. He also added the IV – he thinks that makes him sound like he is from an old family. I can't stop thinking about his choice of 'Follie'. It seems apocryphal somehow.

Annie Mae has been expecting us and accordingly she's been cooking all day. I have never seen so much food! She has made baked beans (not the canned variety but her own recipe), broiled spare ribs, baked potatoes, a huge salad, and warm corn muffins. It is my first meal in a real home since I arrived in America and it is exquisite. I think I am about to explode from overeating when she produces cherry pie and cream. Bilbo and Zollie are in heaven. Zollie sits there, despite all his troubles, beaming like the crazy person he is, and every now and again saying, 'Well Maggie, don't you just love my momma?' While he talks, he keeps patting her hand and giving her hugs and kisses. I have never seen a man display so much affection before. It is quite affecting. She just beams back at him with pure pleasure. I decide that no matter what he's done, I will always like him for that.

That night I sleep in a huge, soft bed under lots of sweet smelling linen and a beautiful patchwork quilt, which Annie Mae has made herself. It is bliss, and we stay a couple of days. I phone Sharla and she says she will drive down and get me at the weekend, assuring me that I can easily get a job working as a waitress in Johnson City, maybe even as a DJ at the College Station, but she'll sort something out.

On Saturday morning, Bilbo's brother, Lee, who looks just like him, comes up from Mentone to get him. He seems more driven than Bilbo, a lot thinner, ferret like. Not as nice either, a bit shifty, I think. His car is a flashy Trans Am. He is a businessman, he tells us, says he is thinking of opening a ski resort in Alabama in December and Bilbo – or Bill, as he prefers to call him – could work there in the meantime. Skiing in Alabama? It sounds fairly deranged to me, but hey, what do I know any more? Craziness works in America. Who am I to knock it?

I leave reluctantly with Sharla on the Saturday afternoon. I pile all my bits and pieces in to the trunk of her car with a large lump in my throat. I hate leaving Annie Mae. She has baked me three pies to go, and I have put on about a stone in the three days I have been here. She cooks non-stop and seems to constantly clear the table and reset it. We must have had six meals a day. Zollie is eating too. He is obviously off the cocaine. His mama would have thought it strange if he hadn't been eating a lot – she doesn't take no for an answer as far as food is concerned.

Zollie says he'll be in touch with me as soon as he gets another station, maybe in a month. I am not feeling too hopeful, I am desolate. I get in the car with Sharla trying hard not to cry, and when we drive off I am thinking I'll be lucky to see any of them again.

6

I'd been in Johnson City with Sharla for barely two weeks when the call comes. Zollie has bought another radio station. It is a former gospel station located in Suck Creek outside Chattanooga. The owners have skipped town after the listeners discovered their 'Hundred Dollars to Heaven Concert' turned out to be a scam. They had asked all the listeners to send in a one hundred dollar bill. In exchange, Brother and Sister Precious Love, the station owners, assured them that the Lord would personally guarantee them a straight entry to heaven on their death, and while they still trod this vale of woe they'd get a pair of tickets to a concert with Kenny Rogers, Dolly Parton and Crystal Gayle. Then, about two days before the concert was due to happen, the fans were told over the air that the concert had been cancelled and the ticket money was going straight into the Precious Love Fund to purchase them all double bonus certificates which guaranteed them and another family member direct entry to heaven.

Well, they sure had underestimated their listeners – it seems God hasn't the same pull as Kenny Rogers or Dolly. Two irate Christians showed up at the station with a sawn-off shotgun looking for their money back plus their guaranteed entry to heaven certificate. When neither was forthcoming they almost blew the brains out of the unfortunate engineer who was playing the reel to reel gospel songs. When word got out, Brother and Sister Precious Love disappeared fast. So, the station is up for grabs, and Zollie lucks out. He gets the license dirt cheap.

'We're gonna be automated for eighteen hours a day, Maggie, with two live shifts. I'm doing morning drive, and you're doing afternoon drive. Sound okay?'

It sounds fantastic. Nice as Sharla and everyone have been, I feel in the way. They are students and I am a working girl. Sharla's friends are delightful, but all they think about is men, well, boys really, and their lives are dedicated to preparing themselves for possible dates. They spend most of the time rolling their hair and rubbing their bodies with creams and exfoliating and debilitating, removing hair, or whatever it is called, and they douche with strawberry-smelling stuff. Douche with it! I am appalled. Why? I hadn't even known what a douche was before I came. French for shower, I thought. The bathroom smells like a candy store. It is so unIrish. They are driving me crazy with all this endless obsessing about their bodies, and are making me homesick for people with greasy hair and dirty jeans. But worse than that, I am so bored. I have a waitressing job four nights a week in a hamburger joint, but I am not making any money because the town is all students and they are lousy tippers. Sharla and her roommates, Angelina and Connie, won't take any rent, which is sweet, as their parents pay it for them, but I feel I have to cook more in return, and they are all slobs, so I do most of the housework as well, and I end up feeling like the Irish maid.

Zollie's call lifts my spirits. To be fair to Sharla, she is thrilled for me. She knows I haven't been happy, even though I have become a bit of a celebrity purely due to my accent and the fact that she has told everyone I am John Lennon's cousin. I mean, I can't let her down in front of her friends, can I? So, I play the part, even down to speaking fondly of my Great Aunt Mimi whenever appropriate. I quite enjoy that aspect of it. One night, after a few joints have been passed around, I find myself railing with indignation about the fact that Yoko has caused so much family stress by persuading John to pose in the nude. Even Sharla is convinced. She asks me if she can come with me next time I visit John. She has always wanted to meet him. I tell her she can, of course. He'll love her.

The radio station will be ready next week and it is getting new call letters, Zollie explains. 'W' something, I suppose. All stations east of the mighty Mississippi have 'W' and all stations west of the river have 'K' at the start of their call letters. Like KLOS in LA and WNEW in New York. Our station was to be WQQQ on the frequency ninety-two. Therefore we would call it Q92. There are probably loads of Q92s all over America, so you tag the name of the city afterwards, like Q102 Tampa. But this is the only station broadcasting from Suck Creek, you can be certain of that. We will pretend that we are broadcasting out of Chattanooga though. I mean, would you listen to a station based somewhere like Suck Creek?

I am to start in three days. Zollie has arranged an apartment for me in the same block as his and he tells me he'll pay the first two months' rent. I am to sell advertising as well as do a shift, which I hate the sound of, but at least it is better than waiting tables, and I'll get commission on everything I sell. It also means I have to get a car. The thing is, I have never learned to drive. Zollie doesn't seem to think this will be much of a problem.

'Hell, Maggie, they drive funny over there in Britain anyways, don't they?'

'No, they just drive on the other side of the road.'

'That's 'zactly what I said, funny, like they talk. Can you imagine what that would do to traffic here if they all decided to move to America? Goddamm Armageddon!' Warming to his theme he continues, 'Now if you had bin drivin' you would be at a *disadvantage*, but seein' as how you weren't, you have the *advantage*.' I must sound unconvinced. 'Let me tell you, Maggie, drivin' is real, real easy. It's like shootin'. Everybody in America can shoot a gun and everybody can drive a car. You can learn real quick.'

So once I arrive in Chattanooga I learn. No gears anyway, you just have to start the engine, press the accelerator and steer. Zollie trades me out some lessons from the AYBEECEE School of driving, and Bilbo and I spend every night for two weeks driving round a K-mart car park. (Bilbo has also been re-recruited by Zollie.) Round and round and round. It's good fun. Then Bilbo takes me along to the Highway Patrol and says I had had a British licence, which I had lost. They make me take a Highway Code test, a 'press the button' sort of thing, guess the answer. It works. It is all fairly obvious. Then I go outside with a pompous little twerp called Leon. I fix my face in a reverential smile and nod humbly at all he says. We get in the car, I drive around a fixed course and manage not to hit anything, and he signs a form, shakes my hand and I go back in and they give me a driver's licence. I am thrilled. I drive to the station with Bilbo sweating profusely beside me, and crash the car into the entrance door. It is broadcast all over Tennessee. Zollie is on the air at the time, and he announces to all the listeners that Maggie, the mad Irish DJ, has literally driven all the way to work, right into the studio. I wait for them to call up from the Highway Patrol place and demand the licence back, but they don't. I am a real American. I can drive.

7

The new station is the clean slate Zollie needs. Over dinner the first week back together, he more or less admits to Bilbo and me that Sudsy's owners, Felipe and Julio, were drug dealers, and in a *major*, major way. They had been supplying Vance, Chance and Zollie with loads of cocaine at inflated prices in exchange for the advertising. The food trade-out was a smokescreen. The trouble was that the Prince Brothers had noses like vacuums. They were going through a ton of the stuff, and Julio was getting more and more pissed that the advertising wasn't paying off. He needed customers, not to make money, but to keep up a front for his drug business. All very sordid. These were hard men and they had called in the chips. Zollie was lucky to get away when he did. He had a friend in the police who tipped him off that some really heavy stuff was about to happen, and if he stayed he could well find himself involved in a major drug scandal, or dead, so Zollie sold Julio and Pedro the station. They gave him a fair price apparently, although they had to buy it through a third party because they weren't US citizens.

Financially it wasn't all that successful a venture anyway, and Zollie had been hankering to return to Tennessee for a while.

He moved to Florida in the first place because he had been married to a girl from Tallahassee called Sherilee, known to us as Sherilee the witch because she'd upped and left him and gone back to her mama before I started working there.

Maybellyne and I chat on the phone a lot. She tells me she hasn't been out of the house since we all left, so she hasn't seen Vance and Chance, and there is no answer from their apartment. I miss Maybellyne, but she plans on joining us at the new station. She is sticking to her diet, she tells me, and should be here by New Year. I hope so. It all looks hopeful so far, and I think I prefer it here to Florida. Despite it being so far from the sea, the landscape is more interesting. I like the tree-covered mountains and the width and sweep of the Tennessee River as it meanders through town, and I like the clearly defined seasons.

This will be my first Christmas away from home ever. My parents want me to come back to Belfast, but I told them I honestly can't afford the fare, and neither can they, so we were just going to have to wait until I make it. This new station is really going to launch my career, I have high hopes for it.

'You know, Maggie,' Zollie says, 'I reckon the Lord has given me a second chance. No more chemicals will enter my body. I am going straight. No more toot, no more 'ludes.' I must look unconvinced. 'Well, maybe just a little ole toke of a joint now and again, because that baby is organic!'

I hope he means it. I expect he does. But he shouldn't have changed his second name to Follie.

There is to be a grand opening the week before Thanksgiving, which, incidentally, I am to spend with Sharla's parents and her brother, Brother. Yes, that is his name. At least that is what they all call him, though his real name is James. All the years I live in Tennessee I never get used to the way people are known as Brother or Sister. A regular exchange would go something like this:

'I'd like you to meet ma husband, Brother Walls, Maggie.'

'Sorry? Your brother?'

'No, my husband, Brother.'

'Your husband's brother?'

'No, ma husband, he's called Brother.'

'Your husband is called Brother? Why?'

'Well, honey, Brother is his name, well that's what his family call him. His name is really Arnold. You see, he was the second child so his sister called him Brother, then his baby brother called him Brother, then his momma and poppa joined in. It happens a lot.'

Of course, it's obvious really! Why did I take so long to catch on? But I think it's a stupid old tradition. Even Bubba or Buddy is a step up from it. Every other man appears to be called that. But silly things like that apart, I love Tennessee, and I am excited about the new station.

Zollie plans to make an instant impact, grab as many listeners as possible. We are on FM, which means that the mountains sort of get in the way of our signal, so people will have to know we are there to tune in and pick us up. I am dispatched to the local paper to give a lifestyle interview. It is all pure bullshit. Zollie's old buddy, Ed, works on the features section and he sets it up for us. Zollie has told him I am a direct import from the BBC and Zollie had heard me on the air on a European tour and 'headhunted' me. That is the word for stealing an employee from somewhere else. Ed reproduces this bullshit word for word. They take cutesy photos, and talk a lot about my 'lilting Irish brogue'. I am glad no one from home will read it, it is monstrously embarrassing. But I tell myself it is all in a good cause. We have to attract listeners. I just hope I won't be too big a disappointment to them. Zollie has also called in favours from a friend who owns the local TV station. I can't quite grasp the concept of someone owning a TV station, but they run wall to wall ads about the new non-stop Music FM Q92 all week.

We kick off at noon on November 17th, 1977 with Springsteen's 'Born to Run'. We are, as they say, 'happening'. The phone lines open and we invite listeners to call in. Our first call is from a woman of seventy-six from Possum Creek who had been getting into a worshipful mood for church on Sunday and had tuned in to her old faithful station to relax in the arms of Jesus. She was unaware how high she had left on the sound and had been knocked out of her armchair by Robert Plant singing 'Whole Lotta Love' at mega decibels. Bilbo talks her down and offers her one of our fifty star prizes: a weekend's skiing for two in Alabama at Christmas. She accepts with alacrity, and praises the Lord, of course.

I am slowly getting my bits and pieces together. My rented apartment is already furnished, albeit in 'Early Motel' style, but I feel a good bit lonelier than I ever was in Daytona. I call home a lot, even though I have to pay for it now. My sister Sinead promises she will visit soon. Also, another thing that isn't helping my frame of mind is that it is winter and my clothes are all wrong. I have nothing warm to wear. Zollie is sympathetic to my plight. He comes in halfway through my shift just a week after the launch, waving a contract triumphantly. 'Maggie, honey, you're gonna be the best-dressed gal in Tennessee.' He has just traded out $500 of women's clothing from a store in town, and I have to cut the commercial. They are going to run $1000 worth of ads, half cash, half trade. We are on our way, back to business! I can't wait for my new wardrobe so I go there first thing next morning.

Unfortunately, Mamie's Modes isn't exactly my scene. It specialises in clothing for the 'smart woman about town', in other words Crap Clothes Inc. Had I wanted to wrap my body in silver lurex dinner dresses or one hundred per cent polyester suits I would be in seventh heaven. But I don't. All the assis-

64

tants look like Dolly Parton and I want to look more like Stevie Nicks. They are so wonderful to me though, and I spend the entire morning there rejecting all their attempts to dress me. I drink their coffee, eat their proffered chocolate chip cookies, confident for once that they aren't laced with hash oil.

This is a recent paranoia of mine, suspecting that all chocolate chip cookies contain hash oil, and understandable given my experience of the previous week.

The third day we were on the air, Zollie had a packet of chocolate cookies on his desk and I took one to eat with my coffee. I was unaware at the time that they contained hash oil. Midway through my shift I developed a co-ordination problem, both with my speech and movements. I talked incessantly right through the intros of all the songs, played 'The Pretender' six times in a row and confessed to the listeners that I want to snog the face off Jackson Browne. My tirade went down surprisingly well, actually, and it made me think that maybe just a bunch of stoned hippies are listening to us. Zollie phoned the station to ask why I was running my goddamm mouth off so much, and after a bit of detective work traced my garrulous behaviour back to the cookies.

But back to Mamie's Modes and my winter wardrobe. There is definitely no hash oil in Mamie's cookies. No sirree! She has baked them herself, from her momma's recipe. A pity really. You would need to be on drugs to buy the clothes. At lunchtime, after trying on virtually every stitch in the place, I leave with the only item in the store made of natural fibres, a bright, cobalt blue cashmere sweater costing $90. It is the most expensive piece of clothing I've ever owned. I promise 'the girls' I'll be back for the other $410 worth soon, and that I will have a good look for 'Rhinestone Cowboy', the Glen Campbell record they want me to play. But there is no way in hell we have a copy of any country song. No chance. Zollie plays frisbee with anything that isn't 'balls to the wall rock 'n' roll'. Later I call them to explain we don't have it, and I play Andrew Gold's 'Thank You for Being a Friend' instead. They are touched since they had spent the whole morning telling me how cute my accent was.

Zollie is mad at me when he hears I've only got a sweater 'Goddamm Maggie! How in the hell is anyone going to take us seriously if you look like you do? You need to get you a new hairstyle. People expect the stars of Q92 to look the part. You look like shit. You need to wear make-up and braaght colours – not that goddamm hippie look.'

I wear a lot of denim. I like to dress casually. Power suits aren't quite my image, in my own head that is. I understand his concern but I need a store which caters for the under fifties. Mamie's Modes just doesn't fit the bill. He eventually sees reason, and agrees to give the rest to Annie Mae for Christmas and find me somewhere suitable.

He is working hard to get the station off the ground, out all day selling airtime, chatting up the proprietor of every little store for miles around Chattanooga. He won't let up on the way I look though. He has a real thing about my appearance. If I am going to be the star female DJ, I have to look the part.

I think I look okay. I am slim, my hair is long and straight, and a lot blonder than usual after a summer in Florida. My teeth are white, and I have large eyes. Attractive enough, not knockout, not a raving beauty, but it has got me thus far. Zollie's idea of female beauty is way on the trashy side. He has fixed himself up with some kind of a secretary cum salesperson that I think he is paying in drugs and sex. Sue Lynne is her name. She seems to think he is the stairway to her future. I am not too struck by her. I am prepared to swallow my distaste and like her at first, but when I hear her tell a friend over the phone that all she had to do with Zollie was 'wave ma pinky and it was real easy to git thangs from him,' I decide to loathe her instead.

She looks like a Barbie doll but Zollie thinks she looks classy. Shows you what he knows. She has an IQ roughly the same as the size of her waist, but she does all the typing and filing and, more importantly, she keeps Zollie out from under our feet. I console myself with the fact she'll be leaving when Maybellyne arrives. Sue Lynne has one of those breathy baby voices, like a girl rabbit from Looney Tunes. She wears a ton of make-up and dresses in bright, tight, polyester suits. She has that big hair that is currently in fashion, and somehow the comparison with my long, straight hair drives Zollie crazy. Eventually, fed up with him droning on about my hair-do, or lack of it, I let him fix me up with a hairdressing trade-out. It changes my life. I get to meet Herman.

There is a salon on Racoon Mountain called Herman's Heavenly Hair Haven, and Zollie tells me I can get my hair done for free there. The owner is going to advertise with us, so off I go to be transformed. Within minutes of meeting him I can see why Zollie thinks he is a soul mate. Put quite simply, Herman is barking mad, but adorable. He is a talented hair-cutter and he looks after my hair like it was his pet rabbit. His philosophy is total hair care. I don't know what this means but this is the first thing he tells me when I have my one hour full consultation. You have to do that before he will allow you to make an appointment.

He tells me he is violently into health products, vitamins and drugs. He just loves drugs. That's an understatement. I don't think he could function without them. He rarely cuts hair until he's smoked about two joints and snorted a few lines. Then he expounds with enthusiasm about his ancestry. Like all Americans, Herman knows by heart all the various mixtures that have gone into the delicate gene pool that has produced him. I am getting used to hearing the phrase, 'Oh

I'm part Irish!', and learning not to say, 'Which part?', which only confuses them.

Herman is part Austrian, part Cherokee, part English, part Dutch, and hails from Kentucky. He is tall, thin, and has dark black, glittery eyes, and long, dark hair that he keeps tied back in a braid. His facial features are pointed and he looks more Middle Eastern than Cherokee, but he certainly looks exotic. His manner is rather effete, and he speaks with a pronounced Southern drawl. He talks incessantly, and most of what he says doesn't make any sense, but it sounds good. It seems to be mainly about our hair being made up of various proteins and vitamins and chemical elements, and how we are composed of water and the same elements as the ocean. When he finishes this speech, he puts on 'Quiet sounds of womb and shore', a piece composed especially for him by a musical friend, and talks about trace elements in hair, or some other monologue about drugs. I never quite figure it out. It doesn't seem to matter as it is the ambience of the place that counts. Going there is an experience unlike any other.

He has a little machine in which he places a single hair that he then winds round two pins, stretches it out, and turns a handle. If it breaks, which in my case it always does, then that means your hair is 'fucked, baby'. He says the whole nation of America's hair is a cause for concern and he is dreaming of the day when a single hair will remain unbroken. I watch him break down almost in tears when he tells me this, so I venture ideas as to how this day will come about, but he is inconsolable. So I suggest how he can avoid breaking all the hairs he tests. I tell him not to wind it so tight, but he says that would be cheating. He prefers to practise preventative haircare to treat the atmosphere. Saturate us with vitamins. Strengthen our living protein. Revitalise us all.

He is a great hairdresser, though, and gives me a brilliant Stevie Nicks cut. He perms my hair, streaks it, and cuts it all shaggy. It looks great, and everyone at the station is really complimentary, except Sue Lynne who grimaces and says nothing. Bitch.

A few days after my first visit to Herman, we are doing a live broadcast from a local mall. I drive there in the Cruzer and I must admit I am scared. I have only had a licence for a few weeks, and driving my new, pale mint green VW Rabbit, which I had bought on some hire-purchase scheme, was one thing. Driving something that feels like a jumbo jet is another. The van badly needs a new paint job, or for the underneath to be re-exposed. This is out of the question, although Zollie lives in hope. He hasn't quite got the money or, for that matter, someone as talented with a paintbrush as Tim, so in the meantime it's known as The Big Black Box. It has Q92 in large stick-on silver letters on each side but it doesn't quite have the same effect on the crowds as The Crazy Wave Cruzer did.

I reach Northside Mall where the broadcast is to happen, and drive with extreme care into the parking lot. I circle for a while, looking for somewhere to park. I need a real big space but there isn't one. Finally, after driving round for ten minutes, I spot what I think might be a big enough space and start to reverse in. After about six attempts I am in tears and the bloody thing is still parked crooked and just about inches, no *centimetres*, away from a very shiny new, silver Porsche. It looks like a Tonka Toy beside the van. I just about manage not to mow it down, but I have effectively trapped it against a wall. I am afraid to back out and straighten the van in case I bang against the Porsche. I turn off the engine, still sweating from the exertion. There is no way the owner will be able to get out. I am completely frustrated and raging at my own inadequacy, and though I hate admitting defeat, I know I haven't the skills to park the thing.

I decide to go into the mall to find Zollie, Bilbo and Rick, our new DJ. I have arranged to meet them at Hits for Less

Records where the show is being broadcast. I have all the equipment in the van though, so they come out with a trolley to fetch it. I mention to Zollie that it isn't particularly well parked, an understatement, and he is tickled. He just loves seeing me so flummoxed over a simple matter of parking. We arrive back at the van just as the Porsche owner realises he can't get out. He is just sitting there and he doesn't seem particularly fussed by being trapped, but I go over to him to apologise.

He is gorgeous. Simply put, he is a large hunk of prime US male. He has floppy light brown hair, piercing blue eyes fringed with dark lashes, a long, straight nose and of course he has white teeth, dozens of them. It looks like someone has drawn him and he's jumped off the page. He is almost too good-looking, and he obviously knows it. He has that easy way that good-looking people have, of just being. He is wearing a short-sleeved blue shirt, in December, though in fact it is dry and sunny, and his arms are brown and muscly. He probably has a shite personality, I reason, but I don't know that yet and hell, maybe he hasn't.

I fall madly in lust at once. Suddenly, I realise that since the exit of Jay the Surfer I have not been practising my new-found sexual technique. I have been celibate, and for what? All those little white pills I pop with such efficiency each evening are lying inside me, altering my hormones, not being put to use. I am polluting my body for no just cause. I stand there, all this flashing through my mind and I can't think of a thing to say, for a minute at least.

Zollie knows him, of course. I am beginning to think Zollie knows everyone in the entire State of Tennessee. 'Well if it ain't Nate Gilmore! How're you doin', buddy?'

Nate stops appraising me and turns to Zollie. 'Fine, Zollie, I'm doin' just fine. Nice to have you back in town. Bin listening to the station. Sounds real good.' He raises an eyebrow. 'This nicely parked object here your van?'

'Sure is, and this here's Maggie Lennon who parked it. Or tried to park it!' Zollie turns to me grinning broadly. 'Maggie, honey, looks like you flew in from above, how'd you get it at that angle? Maggie here is Irish, Nate, and she cain't drive for shit.'

Zollie roars with laughter at his own wit. Nate looks at the four of us and I smile at him. He obviously expects me to say something.

'I'm sorry,' I say. 'I'm afraid I've only been driving for two weeks and that bloody thing is as big as a Chieftain tank.'

Nate smiles back. 'That bloody thing,' he repeats, smiling that dazzling smile at me. I try not to melt and roll under the van in ecstasy. 'I'm sure you're right, ma'am.'

He climbs out of the car, leaping over the door without opening it, and holds out his hand to me. He is tall, I notice, about six feet, maybe more. His hand feels dry and warm, his handshake firm. 'Nate Gilmore, Maggie, I'm pleased to meet you. I've heard your show. I love to listen to your voice, makes a change from all the good ole boys on the air here. I think we like the same music,' he adds.

I'm sure we do, I think. We must.

Zollie grins at him. 'Well, Nate, that's real nice of you, I'm real pleased to hear you say that. Maggie here is going to do a show for us from Hits for Less Records, and we need us some help here, so since you're on your feet why not give us a hand with all this? Get yourself a free Q92 T-shirt.'

He points to the stack of equipment, which has been left beside the van. While we've been chatting, Bilbo and Rick have loaded the sound system on to the trolley and are heading towards the record store.

Nate smiles, shrugs, and says, 'Hell, why not?' He lifts a box of giveaway albums and I take the coloured lights and Q92 sign and walk beside him into the mall. He has long, easy strides. I make quick little running movements to keep up, and

I rattle away, turning on the charm full-blast, showing off I suppose.

Zollie comes up behind me, and whispers loudly, 'You got the hots for him, Maggie?'

I ignore Zollie and continue chatting to Nate, hoping he hasn't heard, while he helps us set up the equipment. He can't have had anything else on, at least he doesn't seem to be in a hurry to leave. With an exaggerated wink at me, Zollie suggests he stay while I do the show.

I am really nervous. I have only done one other outside broadcast in my life, in Daytona, but lack of experience doesn't seem to be a factor in anything to do with my new life. I am learning fast to busk things. Zollie and the guys help, so I just have to intro and outro records, read a few requests (mostly from the crowd in the store), and give away the latest Warren Zevon record, 'Excitable Boy'. During tracks I feast on Nate. He sure is easy on the eye. I am on a high, and even better, a completely natural one. I flirt with him, the people in the store and, of course, the listeners. I am flying.

The only thing that is really pissing me off is Rick, our new DJ. He is hanging out of me as if we are an item. I catch Nate looking at him a couple of times and I feel like screaming. I just know Nate is clocking Rick's pathetic attitude to me – he's fixated on me purely on account of my accent.

Rick is a weedy guy from Cleveland, Ohio. He's had a complete charisma bypass as far I as can see, and his personality on and off the air is exactly the same: shallow, loud and full of clichés. He is a nerd with a head that is a mine of Rock information. He knows everything from the fact that 'Dear Prudence' was written in India about Mia Farrow's sister, Prudence, to how many guitar strings Jimmy Page breaks in a year. He needs to get a life and obviously thinks Q92 is it. He is working for peanuts too. Zollie has convinced him that Q92 will be the start of an amazing career. He is a sad git! I should feel sorry for him. But no! Anyway here he is, smiling away at me like his big, ugly face had got stuck at 'beam' and handing me the music carts, laughing at every stupid thing I say, and calling me babe. I am not his babe! I have just spotted someone whose babe I really want to be, and here is ole shit features queering my pitch. I fervently hope Nate will stay till I come off the air so I can put him right, but of course he doesn't. Just about ten minutes before I play the last track he catches my eye, gives me a friendly wave, and leaves. Just like that. Gone, the most beautiful man I've ever seen. I am incandescent with rage at Rick. Nate didn't even wait to get his free Q92 T-shirt!

'Well,' Zollie pats me on the back after I come off the air. 'You were good, Maggie. Real good, you'll make you a DJ yet!'

Rick sidles up to me. 'Great show, honey! Great show, classy! Whoa yeah, real classy honey!'

'I'm not your honey!' I snap. His face falls.

'It's just a manner of speaking, Maggie.'

'I don't give a shit. Don't call me honey, okay?'

'Fine, fine. I didn't mean nothing by it.'

He starts to pick up the bits and pieces and slumps off looking dejected. I don't even feel guilty. What a stupid bastard. He has just about convinced Nate I was his, I can tell. Boy am I sore. I suddenly feel like bursting into tears. I am lonely. Underneath all the fluff and jollity, I am lonely. I am homesick, I miss my mammy, my daddy and my four sisters, and I have no friends here. No female friends. Maybellyne is maybe coming after Christmas, maybe not. I decide to go back to my apartment and call home and talk to my sister Sinead. It's bedtime in Belfast so she'll be home. I need a comforting chat, and we always tell each other everything. I walk towards the bloody Cruzer. The Porsche has gone. I am about to leave but Zollie has other ideas. He calls me back with a wide grin on his face.

'Maggie, we're all going over to this real nice Chinese restaurant on Hixson Pike for dinner, you fancy joining us?'

'Is that asshole going?' I point in Rick's general direction.

'I expect so.'

'Then I'm not. I can't stand him. He paws all over me. It makes me sick.'

Zollie eyes me up and down. 'You wouldn't be feeling sore about ole Nate leaving early, would you?'

'Don't be ridiculous! What gave you that idea? I don't know the guy from Adam. Anyway, he's probably married or has a girlfriend.'

'Nope, he ain't married. I know that for sure. His rich ole daddy would love that. The Gilmores own half the county. Somebody has to inherit it. Ole Nathan Gilmore the fourth would love for lil' Nate to settle down. And I know he don't have a girlfriend either, leastwise not at the moment. I believe there was someone, just before I moved to Florida. A girl he met at Ole Miss. She was a real good looker, I believe, a runner-up in the Miss America Contest. Everyone thought they'd marry.'

My heart sinks. Miss America. Obviously he prefers looks to brains.

Zollie laughs. 'What's up, Maggie? Cupid hit you raaght between the eyes?'

'No, I just thought he was good-looking and polite, which seems to be rare. I'm going home. I'll see you tomorrow.' I turn to go and Zollie calls after me.

'Well, Maggie, that's a real pity, 'cos I thought maybe you were in the mood for a little bit of lovin' and I've asked him to join us for dinner. He went on home to purdy himself up.'

I could hug Zollie then. Suddenly I am in brilliant form. 'In that case,' I say, trying to sound casual, 'I'll go home and change and I'll meet you there.'

'It's a deal! Now maybe you'd better have my car, and I'll take the Cruzer.'

I certainly agree to that. I don't want to arrive at the restaurant in a sweaty heap.

We go to Ho Lo's Chinese restaurant. I am in a state of high anticipation. I have spent the previous hour deciding which items in my paltry wardrobe look the best. Zollie tells me I look 'Like a fox', so it must have been worth it. Nate arrives looking like a movie star, and throughout the meal he chats mostly to me. I ignore Rick, which isn't hard. He is still wounded by the remarks I made to him earlier. The food is lovely and the beer is cold. At least I think it is. I waft through the whole evening delirious with happiness. Love is the drug, no doubt about it. Finally it's time to go. I stand up to say goodbye and Nate helps me on with my coat. I can barely get my arms in the sleeves I am so thrilled. He offers to walk me to Zollie's car. I try not to catch Zollie's eye but I can see he is watching everything with a large grin on his face.

When we part in the car park, Nate kisses my hand with an exaggerated flourish and tells me how much he's enjoyed the evening. He doesn't suggest taking me home, but I figure it is because we each have a car, and when I am tucked inside the car he asks for my phone number and suggests we might meet for lunch the next day. I tell him I will see him tomorrow and drive home in a state of undiluted bliss.

8

When I get home I immediately phone Sharla, then Maybellyne for intensive post mortems. They are thrilled for me and say they can't wait to meet him. In the morning I finally phone home and talk to my mammy – all the girls are out. She tells me to be careful, especially when I tell her he is rich.

Later Nate arrives to pick me up in his Porsche (his Porsche!) and drives me out to his house on Chickamauga Lake for lunch. I try my best to act blasé about being in a Porsche but I am giddy with delight. Nate's house is one of the most amazing I've ever been in. It is very modern and has wooden floors throughout, all covered in exquisite Turkish carpets. The living room has a high ceiling and is made of wood and stone. We sit on one of two huge settees with a glass coffee table as large as a double bed, scattered with coasters, in front of us. Nate vanishes momentarily and comes back with two ice-cold beers in frosted mugs. He eases himself on to the sofa beside me and starts to nuzzle my neck. Every hair on my body stands to attention. I think I am about to swoon.

'Where are your parents?' I ask.

He looks at me, a smile hovers about his lips. 'Why? Don't you want to be alone with me?'

'No,' I stutter, 'eh, I mean yes, of course, but what if they come in?'

'Well, I guess I would just say that they hadn't been invited to dinner. This is my house,' he continues. 'My parents have a big old family home on Lookout.'

'You mean *you* own this?'

He nods, smiling. 'Yep, I sure do.'

'All by yourself?'

'Yes ma'am. All by maself.' He lapses into the Nilsson tune on the last few words. I have to laugh.

'Wasn't it expensive?'

'Yep, but my Granddaddy died two years ago and left me some money, so I decided to invest in a place of my own.'

I am thunderstruck. No one at home would believe this, a man of twenty-four owning a real grown-up house. We finish our beers and he leads me into the kitchen. It is incredible, all ceramic tiles and old pine. I feel like I am in a Hollywood movie. This is a feeling I will get repeatedly during the day. He has a long piece of meat marinating: he has decided to barbecue a filet mignon, a *whole* one.

'I can use it for sandwiches next few days,' he explains.

There is a gas barbecue on his outside deck which overlooks the lake, and there is also a hot tub. I sit contentedly enjoying the view while he 'fixes' Sunday lunch. He serves the steak with baked potatoes, a green salad and an absolutely gorgeous Californian wine. It is the first time I have tasted good Californian wine, mostly we buy the jug stuff.

We smoke a joint before we eat. I am flying, and horny as hell. Horny is my new word. Sharla has introduced me to it. In Ireland we say randy, but that is a boy's name here. After lunch, we snuggle up on one of the big sofas, and listen to James Taylor's *Sweet Baby James*. I realise I am behaving like something out of a *Playboy* spread. I pose and pout and rearrange myself provocatively. I do everything but rip my clothes off and jump him. Nothing! He cuddles me a bit, nibbles my ear, and strokes my hair a bit and we talk, and talk, and talk! We swap life stories. Then about eight o'clock, he says, 'Well, Miz Maggie Lennon, I guess you need your beauty sleep.' I look expectantly at the bedroom door. Not too obviously though. But he misses the cue. 'I better drive you home.'

My jaw drops but I try to act normal. It is too soon anyway. What has gotten into me? I am behaving like a slut. At home I would have died if a guy had expected me to sleep with him on a first date. We part with an arrangement to go to a movie during the week. I tell myself to calm down, take things slowly, stop smoking pot, my God! The things I want to do when I am stoned.

Maybellyne and Sharla are both reassuring on the phone once again. I call Sharla first. After all, she is a girl with experience. She takes me step by step through the day.

'Had you shaved under your arms, Maggie?'

'He didn't see under my bloody arms!'

'Never mind, honey, all it is, he doesn't want a quick screw, Maggie. He would only do that to a girl he didn't respect. He must be in love with you. He must be regarding you as a potential wife.' Sharla is adamant.

An hour later as I obsess to Maybellyne, she agrees with this pronouncement. 'If he looks like you say he does and he's rich as well, *and* kind, don't you be rushing things. You know, honey, you've been away from home a while now, and you don't know too many people yet. You go easy. You just want someone to love. Take it slowly.'

She is right actually. They both are. Nate is the first guy I've fallen for. Jay had just kind of slid into touch, rescuing me from the dreaded curse of virginity. I am quite sure Maureen and Patricia have gone home to tell everyone I was leading a life

78

of sin. I have had a card from my mother to say she has enrolled me in some kind of perpetual novena to the Blessed Virgin. Perhaps she is trying to tell me something. I have always felt a certain affinity with the Blessed Virgin Mary, or 'Our Lady' as we all call her in Ireland. We have the same initials – BVM. My full name is Brigid Veronica Margaret Lennon. That drove me mad when I was at school. My mother has always sworn that it wasn't deliberate. She had wanted Brigid, and then added the Margaret on the insistence of her mother, Veronica, who felt my Daddy's mother, Margaret, would feel annoyed that she wasn't featuring. Daddy hates the name Brigid and began to call me Maggie, thank God. Mammy needn't have bothered calling me after the two grannies, but she didn't dream she would have three more girls. She could have gone back several generations of grannies and still not run out of names.

I float into work the next day. I need to collect my car from the body shop. Rick offers to take me.

'Well,' he says, leering at me, 'did you have a nice weekend with Pretty Boy?'

I ignore the jibe. I can be magnanimous to him now, though he still makes my toes curl. Zollie has made him Music Director, which really pisses me off. Up to this point it was a non-job. But it sounds good. Unless I move fast he will get to go to all the record conventions, talk to the trades every week, and when the record promotion men come to town they will take *him* out to lunch. What a bummer! I like that expression.

Al had done the job in Daytona, and I had watched him. Al had the whole thing sewn up. He was a real lurker. Always on the make. He landed a huge job in Tampa after WA1A folded and is down there now making a packet. That's why he hasn't joined us in Tennessee. Al had really intrigued me in Florida. He did a morning shift and then spent the rest of the day on the phone. He seemed to be able to get all the free albums he wanted. He spent large parts of his day being chatted up by the record companies and they sent all the freebies to him, along with all the promotional stuff, T-shirts, baseball caps, and other goodies.

I want to be the Music Director. It is the only bloody job at the station worth having. Normally the Program Director gets all the kudos, but Zollie already calls himself Program Director. That is the main job. He is supposed to consider what the new releases are each week, listen to them, then add the ones he thinks are good. Call the stores, find out what people are buying, and report all this to the trade magazines. This is all too much bother for Zollie. He needs a slave to do all the shit work. Calling the trades alone takes up an entire morning, mostly on 'terminal hold'. Trouble is, not all the trades want to hear from you, unless you show up in the Arbitron. That is my first real brush with ratings. Ratings are everything. No ratings no nothing, and if you report to all the top trades, then you get lots of goodies. Since Q92 is a new station we don't report to anyone. Not yet.

Yes, I definitely have my eye on Rick's job. I am working my way up to it. I have been working for Zollie longer than he has, and apart from his encylopaedic knowledge, he is fairly useless. For starters Bilbo hates him, and Bilbo likes everyone. Anyway, we have a rock encyclopaedia and it has a better personality.

My chance comes out of the blue. Rick and Zollie have a knock down, drag out row about money, and as quickly as he arrives, Rick is out. Within two days he is on the air at the competition. It seems like he had already been talking to Dream 103 and had accepted a job from them. The row was only a pretext.

After a bit of wrangling, Zollie agrees to me taking over as Music Director. He will have to pay someone else to do it otherwise. This is my chance and I go for it with a vengeance. I call all the trades and turn on the charm, with the accent. I nearly make myself sick. I give them the low-down on the station, talking it up a storm, and two of them eventually say we can report weekly. They are two of the less prestigious trades, but all stations and record companies buy them anyway, and any publicity is good. At least now we get the name about, and it means the record companies will take an interest in us. I establish a contact at two of the main record stores and set about finding out what Chattanooga likes to listen to. Then I have a stroke of luck. Well, that's an understatement really. I add a record that no one else is playing. I don't think this is a big deal, but I don't quite understand the rules yet, you see.

Sinead has sent it to me from home. She loves it, and naturally when she heard I was back on the air as a DJ she wrote and asked me if I played it. I wrote back saying I'd never heard of it, so she sent it to me. It's different from all the other stuff the girls have sent, less punky, so I put it on the air on a heavy rotation, which means it gets played every two hours. People start to request it. We generally ignore requests as it's too much like hard work. Besides, people are so predictable. If you play a record a lot they begin to think it's their favourite. Over exposure is what it's called. If a record is played every couple of hours, chances are people will think it's because they have asked for it, even if it's on the playlist anyway.

The record I add to the playlist is called 'Dogs in the Moonlight' and it's by a singer I have never heard of called Jimmy Farrell. It has been number one in the charts in Britain for ages. This in itself is an achievement, because it is 1977 and the Brits are mainly into punk and all that shit. This song isn't cursing the Queen and there isn't one swear word in it. It's just a brilliant love song. Americans are so different, they are still enthralled with the Eagles, Fleetwood Mac and the soft West Coast sound, with the odd stadium bands like Supertramp and REO Speedwagon thrown in. Oh, and they love the Bee Gees.

'Dogs in the Moonlight' is special though, and it genuinely gets requested a lot more than anything else we are playing. It has a madly wonderful sax solo and I love it. So does Nate. It becomes 'our song' and he tries to buy it, but it isn't available. Not in Chattanooga. Not anywhere. This worries me. I phone in my second weekly report to *Golden Ears*, one of the two trades we report to. '"Dogs in the Moonlight" is my most requested single and it isn't stocked in town,' I tell them.

'Come again?'

'"Dogs in the Moonlight".'

'Never heard of it. What label's it on?'

'Shine Records.'

'Nope.' The person on the other end of the phone pauses. 'Hang on, I'll let you talk to the boss.'

Abe Goodman, 'the boss' (his favourite line, I am to find out, is that he was called 'the boss' way before Springsteen), is fascinated by my news, and also that I'd added a record not yet released. Apparently it is not the done thing. But he is also interested in me. I can tell that at once. He likes my accent and the fact I am a woman. There are very few women in the business.

'I suppose I should call Shine Records and tell them to send stock,' I suggest, trying to sound more knowledgeable than I am.

'Hang on, I'll give you the VP of promotion's direct line, you tell him I'm featuring it on the "Soaring to the Top" section this week. And,' he adds, in that way only Americans can without sounding like eejits, 'I like you, Maggie. You call me direct each week, don't talk to anyone else. This is my number. Okay, baby?'

I am delighted. I even let it pass that he called me baby. I don't know then that Abe Goodman is one of the 'heavyweights' in the music business, I am just pleased that I won't have to wait on terminal hold for a researcher to take my weekly report next time, and fight with Zollie about the phone bills. So I do what he says and I call Rolly Young at Shine. It takes me a while to explain about the record, and even longer to explain myself. He isn't too friendly. *He* certainly doesn't say 'I like you, Maggie'. He more or less wants to know who the hell I am, how I got his direct number, and why I am wasting his time talking about a record he's never heard of. He seems to have a major problem with the fact that I am in a 'small market' (not LA or New York), don't report to *R&R*, *Gavin*, *Billboard* or various other prestigious trades. A bit up himself, I think. I don't get too far. I let it go. He does give me the name of his local (Atlanta) promotion guy and suggests I call him. I do, he is not there, but he calls me back and mentions other records I should be on – they all make it sound like a drug – and says he will come to see me in the New Year. His name is Tom.

The following week I again report 'Dogs in the Moonlight' as our top song to Abe at *Golden Ears*. I speak to him personally and tell him that when I mentioned his name Rolly Young didn't seem remotely impressed, didn't seem to believe someone like me would know Abe, oh, and that he's mad at Abe for giving out his phone number. It is like lighting a touch paper!

'Leave it to me, babe, just don't miss next week's *Golden Ears*.'

As Abe hangs up I can hear the snarl in his voice as he orders his assistant to 'Get me Rolly Young now!'.

I don't think about it much as I am still totally involved in the Seduction of Nate.

Nate Gilmore is wooing me like a real Southern gentleman. He takes me to dinner, twice, at the most expensive restaurant in town, and we have long, sensual moonlight cuddles at his place on the lake. Yes, cuddles! Much to my chagrin, that was as far as we'd gone. Jaysus, am I becoming a sex fiend or what?

I ask myself. Less than a year ago I was struggling to stop at cuddles. Well, a bit of a poke and grope, too, I suppose, but I certainly didn't want to bonk the bejasus out of every man I met. Losing my virginity has turned my head. I am mistaking lust for love. I am mad for it. I am almost beginning to think of masturbation. I've never tried it, it hasn't really occurred to me, don't ask me why. Sharla has been on to it for years. Maybe it's the hot weather in America, or the fact of wearing so few clothes. Anyhow, the way Sharla explains it to me, masturbation could wear you out. It sounds like I'd need a waterbed for it too, to get the motion right. There is no point in trying it if I am going to end up disappointing myself.

The brilliant thing is, though, that Nate has invited me for Christmas, and maybe the Christmas spirit will turn him on. Sharla has invited me as well, but she will understand if I want to spend it with Nate. Besides, with only a day off, going to visit Sharla will mean my spending most of the holiday driving. The Gilmore Christmas is to be staged in his parents' house. They live in a huge house on Lookout Mountain. Like I said, they are SUPER RICH. The day after Nate invites me, I tell Zollie.

'Nate has invited me to spend Christmas Day at his parents' house,' I say, trying to sound casual. Zollie is disappointed. He looks at me pityingly.

'Spend Christmas with old Nathan Gilmore and his old tight-ass wife Bitsy? Maggie, you cannot be serious! Momma's already knitting you a Christmas stocking. She'll be real, real sorry to hear that you aren't coming to us. My brother and his wife and my nephews are coming from Arkansas.'

'But Zollie, I had no idea. You didn't say.' I love Annie Mae and I know in my heart I would be more comfortable there, but Christmas without Nate? 'I'm sorry. I've told him yes – you didn't ask me.'

'Well hell, Maggie, I just thought you'd know you were

invited. You didn't think I'd let you spend Christmas on your own, miles from your momma and poppa?'

I would have preferred to be back in Belfast, sitting in a smoke-filled bar with my sisters and our friends, even with the iron security gates, but at least here I won't be allowed to be alone. People are so friendly. I decide I'll wait and see about Nate, see if he mentions it again. Zollie wants me to work right up until Christmas Day anyway. A lot can happen before then. A lot does.

9

We are going to launch the station to the public with the give-away to beat all giveaways. We are running a competition, SKI ALABAMA. This is some deal Zollie has struck with Lee, Bilbo's old wheeler-dealer brother. We are giving away fifty free weekends in Alabama at the new ski resort, Alpine South, which is located just south of Birmingham off the Interstate. All people have to do to win is call the station when they hear sleigh bells ring. Corny but effective. Most of them think it is a joke and I don't blame them. Here we are, mid-December, yet the weather is nowhere near freezing in Tennessee, and Alabama is further south again. Besides, who the hell would want to go to Alabama except a Lynyrd Skynyrd fan? 'Sweet Home Alabama' is one of our top three requests, and I always follow it with Neil Young's 'Southern Man' just to be balanced, though I expect only the real fans notice. You can play Lynyrd Skynyrd all day in the South, people never tire of it, especially now, after the tragic deaths of Ronnie Van Zant and Steve and Cassie Gaines. Then, unexpectedly, it snows. Snows and snows and snows. Seven inches fall overnight and the town grinds to a halt. The nearest snowplough is in Chicago, people haven't a notion how to cope and cars are stuck on the highway. Next morning I am terrified driving to work. There are cars skidding everywhere, lots of 'fender benders'. Half the population stay off work, just stay in all day and listen to the radio. The request line lights up like crazy and the competition phones go mad. In one day we give away all forty-eight remaining SKI ALABAMA weekends. They are all up for grabs but no one at the station wants one, and the old Christian lady who is called Miz Zillah Ruth Knightly has already won the first one. I am worried about her because, according to Zollie, she really is seventy-six, and her proposed companion is her eighty-one-year-old sister, Miz Beulah May Knightly. He has called out to visit her, hoping maybe she would change her mind on account of the insurance liability and accept a gift voucher for Mamie's Modes, but she is heart set on it. She is crocheting a ski sweater and a matching bobble hat in lime green.

The resort is due to open over the New Year. I have never been skiing, it seems so exotic. Sharla has suggested that we have a weekend skiing in Gatlinburg sometime, which allegedly becomes a ski resort in winter. Gatlinburg is in the Smoky Mountains and is possibly one of the tackiest places I have ever been in my life. I was there with Sharla and two of her friends while I was staying in Johnson City. It is unspeakable, a cross between Lourdes and Hollywood, set to a country music soundtrack.

Nate is horrified when I tell him I might be going to Gatlinburg to ski. He tells me that if I want to try skiing, the Gilmores have a lodge in Aspen and he usually manages a couple of trips between now and Easter. He'd love me to come with him. A ski lodge in Aspen! Well, I suppose it fits in with everything else. I mean, I still find it hard to get used to a twenty-four-year-old guy who owns his own house, let alone one the size of Nate's.

Even Zollie, who is thirty-seven, can't afford one half that size, or any size for that matter. He is renting an apartment in the same building as me and is looking at property, but he is limited financially, he told me, because he is paying alimony to Sherilee the witch. She still drives him crazy calling him collect from Florida just to tell him what a bastard he is. It happens every time she has taken drink, or is smashed on dope. But I am not too concerned about Zollie's house problems, I fully expect him to come in one day and announce he has traded one out. I tell this to Nate. He has some funny opinions of Zollie. You can tell they are from such different backgrounds and despite money being the great equaliser, the snobbery is still there. It isn't obvious on the surface, you can't even go by the accent like at home, it takes some scraping away to figure out social mores in the Southern states, but I am learning fast. Old money is definitely better than new, but being nouveau is better than not being 'reech' at all. The Gilmores are most definitely old money. They own half the town; their money came originally from steel and then from property. Nate is Nathan Gilmore the fifth! Zollie says leastways they are not Yanks, that is the only thing they have in their favour.

Nate likes Zollie, but I can also tell he thinks Zollie is crazy. I agree, but I don't tell him. I still have loyalty to Zollie. When I tell Nate about the SKI ALABAMA contest he laughs so hard he cries, says it is the most insane thing he's ever heard. But that was before the snow started. It is still snowing steadily and now there is so much snow that even Nate begins to think it might work. We all hope he is right. This is the giveaway that will establish us.

Christmas week I have a mild distraction in the form of Tom, the local Shine guy, who drives up from Atlanta to take me out to lunch. According to Tom, I am 'happening' because of 'Dogs in the Moonlight', and should capitalise on this by going to a radio and record convention in LA in the new year. I mention this to Zollie, but he is not keen on the idea. For starters, you have to pay your own fare and registration money.

88

We are in a bit of a pickle – it would be one way to raise the profile of the station, but beyond our budget. The idea is dropped, maybe the next one, there are loads of them apparently. I don't mind, but I am sufficiently intrigued.

Meanwhile, Christmas approaches relentlessly. Nothing in my life has ever prepared me for Christmas in America. For a start it is actually going to be a white one. I have discovered that weather forecasts in America are accurate. I can't understand this. I have never taken weather forecasts as anything but a hopeful estimation of what weather should be like. No matter what was predicted at home it usually rained. Here they say things like: 'Today's high will be ninety-six degrees with some precipitation at seven o'clock,' and it is right. Maybe the government have discovered how to control the weather. They can certainly make the sun shine more often. So, when they say the snow is expected to stay for Christmas, well, we all go out and buy fur gloves and toboggans. Actually Zollie trades us out the toboggans and the fur gloves. We spend the Sunday before Christmas sledging up and down the golf course and then Nate takes me home to his place for hot punch, and in front of a big log fire we finally do it.

He is so gentle and sweet. I can't get used to it. I have nothing to compare him with except Jay, the surfer, who was sort of eager and puppy-like. Not that I have direct experience of puppies, but Jay was sort of vigorous. He bounced around a lot and whooped and yelled things like 'Help me, baby!', and, 'I'm on the Stairway to Heaven now!' (He loved Led Zeppelin.) This was usually followed by a loud scream of delight. He always satisfied himself, and if I got any pleasure out of it, well, that was grand, he was delighted and encouraged me to whoop as well, which I have to say I don't do instinctively. But I had loved making love to Jay. He made it feel so natural and basic. He had been a good one to deflower me as it were.

Nate is different. He is intent on satisfying me, which I find very touching, but I also find it harder to come. He is a slow, deliberate lover. I am longing for him, but he kisses me for about two hours before we get undressed. I am wet, soaked with desire. In Florida, Jay and I never had much on, so getting naked took seconds. Maybe, I think after the first time with Nate, I'll have another chat with Sharla about the masturbation lark. Somehow, for all his tenderness and attention to detail, Nate leaves me vaguely dissatisfied. No, make that totally dissatisfied. I wasn't even sure if we had done it or not. I couldn't feel much, although he very definitely has a big penis. I have a good look at it, touch it even. That is when we are having the foreplay bit. It seems to diminish rapidly after penetration. Not a promising start, but I know things can only get better. He seems to be interested in me as a person, not just for sex, and that is the important thing. The sex will improve. I have read that in a book, and at last, the deed is done. We are officially in love. After we finish he seems so happy I don't say anything, that's when he asks me again if I would like to have Christmas dinner with his family. I accept at once. I call Annie Mae and explain the situation. She says of course she understands and I am right to accept: 'But honey you make sure and be here for dinner next day. And,' she adds, 'don't go opening your heart too much to that Gilmore boy. Those Gilmores are trouble.' I put this down to a sort of mild jealousy, a bit out of character for Annie Mae, but understandable. The Gilmores do own half the town after all, and that doesn't usually spell popularity.

I am more than happy to go to Annie Mae for Boxing Day. I will have no chance to feel homesick, being invited out two days in a row. Boxing Day is usually a very lazy one at home, spent in front of the television. They don't call it Boxing Day here, just the day after Christmas, the day the sales start. We have lots of sales advertising lined up at the station, and now I am not going to see Sharla, Zollie has me working that afternoon doing a live shift. The plan is that I will finish work at three and then Zollie will pick me up and take me to Nickajack. Annie Mae will doubtless have a grand feast laid on and I will spend the night there. I am looking forward to it. No effort for me, and best of all, no driving. I don't fancy driving there in this snow. No way.

Meantime, I need a dress for Christmas day, something a step up from Mamie's Modes, and I also need to go see 'Herman the Hair man', as Zollie calls him. I am starting to say need. Everybody needs everything in America. I think they are afraid to say want, in case it looks as if they actually need it. I call in to Mamie's Modes anyway – there is still a lot of trade-out left, no one can use it up. They are thrilled to see me and rush to make me coffee and show me the array of Christmas clothes. There is Mamie and two assistants, Jolene and Luanne, who all have big hair, bright smiles and are incredibly friendly. They think I am a celebrity and are permanently tuned to Q92. The clothes for Christmas are, not surprisingly, red and green, or green and red. Many of the sweaters feature fancy embroidery, mostly of Santa, or reindeers or baubles. A feeling of despair creeps over me. How will I get out without buying anything? I give in and model a few numbers for them but feel totally absurd in all of them. Just as I have run out of excuses for not taking a bright red dress with green stripes and large leg-of-mutton sleeves, which they assure me 'Looks darlin' on you honey, jest' darlin',' I notice a few plain sweaters sitting on the counter. There is one which is pale grey cashmere, and one of plain red wool. I pull the grey out and take it to try on. It fits perfectly and feels wonderful. Reluctantly they allow me to buy it, although I have to take a silk red and green scarf which I promise I will drape round my neck to cheer it up. They insist on wrapping it for Christmas, even though I tell them it is a waste of gift paper. 'Nonsense, honey, you are worth it,' Mamie says. 'You're our little Christmas star.' I wish them all Merry Christmas, promise to play some requests for them tomorrow, and make my escape.

10

I don't know how we make it up to Christmas. The town is chaotic. The station is insane. Every five minutes it seems Zollie is rushing in with copy and I have to cut yet another commercial. I am almost starting to speak in tongues to change the sound of my voice. He really needs another DJ, a fresh voice. I am on the air virtually every commercial break, and add to this the fact that he has programmed in everything Bob Seger has ever recorded, which means virtually every second song is a Bob Seger song, means the station sounds demented. He is doing this purely to impress Sue Lynne who has a thing about the Silver Bullet Band, and Zollie wants to screw her. He sort of sees himself as the embodiment of a silver bullet, he tells me. 'Lean, mean, fast and precious. A killer!' It is so bloody Freudian and I think he actually means it. What a joke.

Sue Lynne has some sort of a boyfriend though. His name is Clarence Lee Dunne and he hangs about the station a bit when Zollie isn't around. He is a total moron, dresses from head to toe in polyester, and wears an aftershave that smells like cheap carpet freshener. He has little piggy eyes, pointy, sharp little teeth like a pterodactyl, a wispy little goatee beard,

92

and a huge Afro, which adds about eight inches to his height. Just as well, he is only about five feet tall. He hasn't really got a body, just a sort of bone structure with loose wrapping over it, leaving no room for any internal organs. The opposite applies with his large head, for he obviously has no brain.

He really gets on my nerves. He thinks he is witty, makes constant funny remarks about my accent, and leers at me. I plan to poison him. Well I don't, but it would be a good idea if someone did. Zollie has met him a few times and loathes him. I feed his loathing. I enjoy saying horrible things about Clarence Lee Dunne. Clarence Le Dumb is one of the things we call him. Not too imaginative, I admit, but it works in an insidious way. Clarence Lee works in the nearby nuclear power plant that dominates the landscape not far from the station. This is a truly terrifying thought, both the fact that it is there and that Clarence is employed by them. We get lots of calls for requests from the workers, most of whom sound not right in the head. The radioactive stuff must be corroding their brains even as they are on the phone to us. They wear wellies, or gumboots as Americans call them, full, I'm sure, of radioactive water. I think if I ever form a rock group that would be a good name for it. Radioactive Wellies.

In the meantime, Clarence Lee and his like stand between us all and the total end of mankind as we know it. What a thought! It is one of the things I worry about when I am homesick in the middle of the night. Clarence Lee makes me feel that Ireland is the only viable alternative. Sue Lynne appears to love him. She pats him a lot. This is a very American thing, I feel, patting. Their routine goes something like this. Clarence Lee sits there looking like the insignificant slime bag he is. Sue Lynne then addresses everyone, usually Bilbo, and me, 'Isn't he just adorable?' she'll say, patting his Afro. We say nothing and try not to choke. 'He's so darlin',' she says, and then she pats his knee. Clarence Lee just sits there with a shit-eatin' grin on his excuse for a face and replies, 'Hey baby, you're giving me active love'. At this point I gag and leave, Bilbo turns bright red, coughs and starts tidying the LPs. The funny thing is, she never does this in Zollie's presence, she is too sly – sleekit, we would call her at home. She needs the fix of Zollie's devotion so she downplays the relationship to him, two-faced cow that she is, and Zollie lives in hope, set to the soundtrack of Bob Seger's 'Stranger in Town' and 'Night Moves'.

On Christmas Eve, Sue Lynne and Clarence Lee almost ruin my Christmas. Sue Lynne is working late, we all are. Zollie had done a trawl for lots of last-minute advertising and had come up with a ton of commercials for me to cut. I am furious – my voice is already wall to wall on the stupid station, advertising everything from white wall tyres to a protein drink that tastes like roast turkey and makes you lose twenty pounds by being in the same room as it, or something like that! The ad starts with the immortal line 'Why not drink your Christmas Dinner?'.

Clarence Lee comes in to pick Sue Lynne up. The very look of him makes me want to spit. 'Ah'm here for my little baby doll,' he says. 'Ah'm going to buy her the biggest, bestest ole Christmas gift in the world.'

Sue Lynne comes simpering out of the office and straight into his spindly arms. Seeing them there together, I feel a wave of revulsion. I want to be back at home going out for a drink with the gang. I want to be with my lovely close family. What on earth am I doing here?

Yesterday I got a card from Maureen. She is getting engaged to Dermot Brady – one of 'our' gang from university. They have been going out since fresher's day, and her absence this summer made him realise what a treasure she was. I am happy for them. She says in her card that no one at home knows yet, but she thought she'd tell me since I was far away. I feel a stab when I read the words. They are getting married next summer when she has been teaching a year. Well, I suppose I wouldn't want that either. Why am I such a malcontent? Mammy was nearly crying last week when I said I definitely won't be home for Christmas. 'I wish we had the money to send you a ticket,' she said. 'It won't be the same without you.'

I am in lousy form. I look over at Clarence and Sue Lynne. Is this what Christmas in America is going to be, full of idiots and numbskulls? Nate Gilmore might be my 'boyfriend', but I feel appallingly alone. I can't wait to get out of the station and go home to feel sorry for myself in peace.

It is really late by the time I get all the commercials cut and finally leave. Bilbo is spending the night at the station and then driving down to Alabama in the morning. We swap presents. I kiss him and thank him, but I am not remotely full of Christmas spirit. Snow or no snow, I just want to get home and crawl into bed. Nate is coming to get me after church tomorrow. I have decided I will go to mass as it is hard to think of Christmas without any sort of religious aspect to it, and my apartment is near a Catholic church – ironically it's about the only place I can walk to.

I wish Bilbo a Merry Christmas, leave the station and walk out into the night. The cold air virtually takes my breath away. The light is glinting off the branches of the trees, which are coated in a thin film of ice, and if I wasn't in such lousy form I might think it beautiful. It is freezing cold. I scrape the ice from the windshield and wait for about ten minutes running the engine until the car seems warm enough to sit in. I am fearful of the drive home. This will be a challenge for me.

I drive as carefully as I can, but I am simply petrified of the ice. It has barely been any time since I passed my driving test and I've never experienced anything like this, even as a passenger. It seems that any pressure at all on the brakes sends the car into a waltz. I slither along as far behind the driver in front as possible. There isn't a whole lot of traffic on the road up to the Interstate, but everyone is driving like me, very gingerly. My armpits are beginning to smell like Bilbo's. Brake lights flash on and off. The temperature has dropped dramatically and the snow has frozen. It sits by the roadside in stiff meringue-like peaks, and occasional flurries drift in the headlights. It may well look like a winter wonderland, but driving in it is the scariest thing I've ever done. It is an almost unearthly quiet, like someone has turned down the sound. I turn the radio off to concentrate – there are only so many times one can listen to John Lennon singing 'So this is Christmas' anyway. The windshield wipers thrum, swishing the snowflakes from side to side and I concentrate hard on my driving.

Just as I am indicating to get on to the highway, a car comes racing up behind me flashing its lights and dazzling me in the process. I brake instinctively and hear a sort of shush and crink-ling sound, and then BANG! My car is spinning round and nothing I do seems to stop it. I am in some crazy ice waltz in the glare of oncoming traffic. I hold on to the steering wheel. My mouth is open, I think I am screaming, then there is another loud bang, then a thud. Then silence. The car has stopped. I can taste blood on my lips. At least I'm not dead. Paralysed? I wiggle my toes. I can feel them. Is that a good sign? I move my hand up towards my face and press it into it. It comes away covered in blood.

Just then the car door is wrenched open and there stands Sue Lynne with the ghastly Clarence Lee behind her, peering intently at me. Jesus! I am dead and in hell already!

'Maggie? Are you all right? Honey, I am so sorry, but Clarence was just trying to be cute, and beep hi to you. I guess he didn't realise it was so icy.' (She actually pronounces it assy.)

I leap in a rage from the car. Thoughts of paralysis vanish at once. I want to choke him. I am screaming abuse. He backs away with a look of terror on his face and as he does I notice another car on the left-hand side of the road. A tall, well-built man wearing a cowboy hat gets out and walks towards us.

'I've seen it all and I've radioed on my CB to the police. They'll be right along. I hope y'all weren't drinking?' He looks directly at Clarence who shakes his crazy Afro at him. I notice it has a layer of snow on it. ''Cos that sure was some mighty stupid driving, buddy.' He turns to me. 'Are you all right, young lady?'

'I'm not sure. I feel a bit faint,' I say, and I do, suddenly. I am also shaking quite violently, not just with rage at Clarence.

'Well, I guess the paramedics will be along as well. Hey, why don't you get back in the car, it's freezin' out. Hold on, I have an emergency sign.'

He goes over to his car and pulls out a triangle on a sort of easel, and props it by the roadside. It glows in the snow and the cars silently curve out to pass us, making sweeping tracks as they do. A few stop to offer help, but Buford, that's how he's introduced himself, thanks them graciously and says everything has been taken care of. He comes back over, and hands me a cup of something hot.

'Ma'am,' he says, 'I just bought this coffee and I haven't started to drink it, waiting for it to cool a bit. Maybe you should have it.'

I do think for a moment of throwing it at Clarence, but I get into the car and sip it gratefully. It hasn't cooled. Clarence and Sue Lynne shuffle uneasily outside in the snow. Clarence rubs his slimy hands together and clears his throat from time to time. I wish they would get in their own car, but they seem rooted to mine. The snow is piling on top of Clarence's hair and he looks absurd.

'Listen, Maggie, it was jest a kinda joke that backfired on me. I swear I didn't mean no harm. Look on the braaght saad, Maggie, leastways nobody done got kilt.'

'Done got kilt,' I mimic. Not yet you stupid moron, I think. Some bloody joke.

By the time the police come and take statements I have calmed down. Buford takes control and everything is sorted. I have only a small cut on my lip, no other injuries. Buford lends me a clean, white real hanky and I press it against my lip until the blood stops. Somehow the police manage to get a call to the station and Zollie comes for me. He has called his momma and told her that he is taking me home with him, so Annie Mae will have a bed ready. Zollie is unusually solicitous for a change.

'Why Maggie, baby, you pore ole thing,' he says when he arrives, whereupon I burst into tears. 'Hey, baby, don't fret. Momma is just thrilled to have you stay over.'

'I have to go to mass tomorrow, it's Christmas.'

'I'll take you, I ain't ever bin to mass, that'd be fun.'

'I have to call my mammy and daddy tonight.' I am regressing to pet names.

'You can call 'em from my place.'

'But Nate, he's picking me up tomorrow.'

'That's fine. What time?'

'About one.'

'Ain't a problem, Maggie. We'll have you there.'

Clarence Lee and Sue Lynne are dispatched home. Unfortunately they don't go directly to jail. I get into Zollie's car and wait while the good samaritan, whose full name is Buford Dewayne McConnell, nickname 'Big Boy' (yes, I think it is weird too, but this is Tennessee), has a long chat with Zollie and I hear Zollie promise to call him and keep him up to date on my progress. Then he wishes me a Merry Christmas and leaves. Zollie and I drive off in the snow, passing the tow truck with its eerily revolving red light, on its way to get my car just a mile or so down the road.

'Well, Maggie,' said Zollie, as he fires up a joint. 'You need a lil' toke to help you relax. This has been a pretty damm dramatic Christmas Eve now, hasn't it?' He sounds delighted, as if he'd staged the whole thing for my entertainment. He takes a deep draw off the joint and hands it to me. 'You know who your good samaritan was, Maggie?'

I shake my head.

'He's a country and western singer from round here. Used to be big, real big.' Zollie starts to sing (My God he has an awful voice) 'Let your love pour down on me like maple syrup.'

'Oh? I've never heard of him?' The dope has kicked in and I feel more relaxed.

'Nice guy. "Maple Syrup" was a huge hit. Yep, humongous hit, sold millions.' Zollie pronounces it *miiyons*, drawing the word out with a satisfied sigh. 'I guess he's still living on the proceeds.'

We have reached Annie Mae's by now. The snow is unlike any I've ever seen at home. Outside the town it is thick, white, and soft. Huge drifts of it blanket everything. The Americans do everything on a grander scale, weather included. We crunch our way through into a warm glowing house, which smells of Christmas: spicy and comforting. A bath is ready for me, with hot, fluffy towels piled beside it and a clean cotton nightie several sizes too big. About a half an hour later I am in bed, exhausted. And a minute after that, fast asleep.

11

'Merry Christmas, honey,' Annie Mae's big friendly face smiles down on me as I open my eyes. It is nearly ten o'clock, and there is a strong smell of bacon permeating the house. I shake myself fully awake. My first Christmas away from home. I push any feelings of that out of my mind for I am among friends. The house is warm and snug and, best of all, there are presents at the bottom of the bed. I push them with my toes.

'Looks like Santy came while you slept.'

'Oh Annie Mae, yours are all in my apartment. I was going to bring them tomorrow.'

'Honey, don't fuss. We just wanted you to have something to wake up to.'

She watches, beaming, while I rip them open. There is a gold chain with a Tennessee River pearl from Zollie, and another little box with instructions to open much later, alone. Intriguing. And absolutely the most perfect patchwork quilt from Annie Mae, which she's made herself. I can't believe my luck. And finally, all Springsteen's LPs that Zollie has somehow lurked from Columbia records. I am so chuffed.

'Well, Maggie, you're in the good ole U S of A for Christmas! What's it feel like?'

'Not bad at all,' I say, and it doesn't. Zollie is as good as his word and takes me to mass. He even goes to communion, which I let pass – the Foleys must have been Catholic at some stage – and then he takes me home. I will see him tomorrow.

Nate picks me up at one-thirty exactly. He listens sympathetically as I describe my ordeal of the previous evening. I guess Zollie has told him some of it on the phone already. He seems somewhat uncomfortable when I burst into tears, and pats me on the back limply. I would prefer a bear hug, but I am a bit over-emotional, realising perhaps for the first time what a really rotten experience it had been and what a dumb-ass jerk Clarence Lee really is. God knows how long my car will be out of action. What if Buford, whatever his name is, hadn't happened along in time and seen it all? I'd probably still be at the side of the Interstate, frozen to death. I stop crying and dry my eyes, I am being self-indulgent, and suggest we exchange presents. Nate kisses me, smiles, and tells me it is a Gilmore family tradition to exchange presents just before dinner, after they have had their eggnog, whatever that is. I have got him expensive cufflinks from a jeweller's shop at the Chattanooga Choo Choo that Zollie had traded me instead of my Christmas bonus, and I have got his mother a present, a 'hostess' gift. I am not too keen on handing them over in front of an audience, but if it's a tradition then I guess I'll have to live with it.

We leave in the Porsche and set off for Lookout Mountain. Am I presentable enough? I am wearing black velvet trousers, a cream silk blouse, and my grey cashmere cardigan, my last-minute 'find' from Mamie's. Boring but tasteful. But that's what I am aiming for today. Zollie had pushed a small vial of coke into my palm as he left my apartment. 'Last part of your present, Maggie, you might need this honey,' he said meaningfully. I am puzzled. I had figured that the mystery present was coke. What is this? I am too dumbstruck to argue. It is in my handbag – it feels radioactive to me.

Ochs highway goes right up Lookout Mountain, and about halfway up we turn into a long, winding gravel driveway and stop outside a largish, two-storey brick house. A wide veranda wraps the house and the front porch is supported by columns. It is an old home, obviously built some time in the last century, but then you could never be sure in America as they have this knack of building a house in a month that looks like it has been there for ever. Tasteful white Christmas lights twinkle on two of the large fir trees nearest the front porch, the snow sitting heavily on their branches, and the front door is decorated with a Christmas wreath, a muted green arrangement with a large red bow.

Nate rings the doorbell. That surprises me. Doesn't he have a key? A black woman answers so quickly that you would think she had been standing behind the door. That surprises me too. Do people still have black servants? Even in the South? It is, after all, the last week of 1977. Nate positively whoops with delight when he sees her.

'Hey, Miss Cora, how are you doin'?' Big as she is, he picks her up and swings her round. She seems chuffed to bits, and is chuckling but she pretends to slap him away. He ducks. 'Hey, Cora, Merry Christmas, you look just pretty as a picture.'

'Why, Mr Nate, you behave now, yo heah me? Yo ole flirt you.' After she has smoothed herself down she hugs him warmly. She looks to me like a different coloured version of Annie Mae. 'Now,' she says, turning to me and eyeing me up and down, 'you must be little Maggie, why honey, you are just a little doll.' She grins at me, a wide ear-splitting grin. 'Here, give me your coat and y'all go into the library and get yourselves by that big old fire, get yoursels warmed up.'

She scuttles off with my coat while I stand in the large hall with its high ceiling and minstrel gallery, looking at several portraits of rather severe, older versions of Nate. Although it didn't appear overwhelmingly large from the outside, it is deceptive. The house is enormous inside. This is another building trick perfected by Americans. In Belfast, we specialise in small outsides and minuscule insides. We both do as Cora tells us and go into the long, gracious, and exquisitely appointed drawing room. It looks like a scene from *House & Garden*.

I gaze around the room. It is furnished with four large, comfortable sofas in muted tones of honey and cream, occasional cushions in tapestries of reds, blues, and ochre, and polished mahogany end tables with large, gleaming ceramic lamps with Chinese patterns. They look very expensive. It is all absolutely tasteful, nothing in the room jars. It doesn't exactly say money, it whispers it softly with total confidence. The walls are covered in paintings, the one above the fireplace is a Wyeth print I am fairly sure. It features a solitary barn at the end of a wide field with a figure of a boy in the distance.

'Is that a Wyeth?' I am pleased with myself for spotting it.

'Hell, Maggie, I guess it is. I know we have two or three by him, my daddy likes art. He collects American painters. He has a couple of Hoppers as well.'

'You mean it's real?'

'Hell yes, it's worth a lot of dollars I think.'

He says this as if it was the most matter of fact thing in the world to have a real painting. I think of our house with the block mounts of Van Gogh's *The Yellow Chair* and *Starry Night*, Turner's *The Fighting Téméraire* and the picture of the Sacred Heart with the eternal lamp below. God, I could just imagine bringing Nate home to meet the folks and see our art collection. I reappraise the Chinese lamps. I ease away from them in case they fall on me and break. It is the sort of thing that happens to me.

The most beautiful Christmas tree I have ever seen is placed

103

exactly centre in front of the French windows. I walk over to inspect it. It is perfect. Each ornament seems to have been placed on exactly the right branch, and they are all pointing in the right direction. Little stripy candy canes, angels, trumpets, drums, rocking horses, all in shades of red, green and gold hang from the branches. There is no sign of the vulgar gold tinsel I am used to. The fairy lights are shaped like candles, and although they are electric, they look real. There is one placed exactly at the end of each branch, and another halfway up, they must have used a measuring tape. It is a real tree too, the heady smell of pine hit me the minute I entered the room. The little flames on each candle twinkle at me but my eye is drawn to the top of the tree where it is crowned with a large, confident star. It isn't even crooked like ours at home always is. Our tree at home is usually bought a few days before Christmas and bedecked with the remains of the ornaments that haven't been broken the previous year, plus a few new cheap ones if anyone has bothered to buy some. Unlike this masterpiece, the ornaments on the Lennon tree persist in turning the wrong way, and all our attempts to make them face out end in either another breakage or a dent in the ornament. But tacky or not, each Christmas we have such fun putting it up, with all five of us girls giggling like idiots and mammy fretting about whether the lights will work again this year. We always seem to have to get a new set or go out at the last minute for spare bulbs. We usually fill in all the bare bits of the tree with horrible tacky tinsel, and the crap ornaments we had all made in school every year. My mother, for reasons best known to herself, has always kept these faded bits of coloured paper with glitter stuck to them. They are wild looking.

'Well,' I say to Nate, 'I see your mum hasn't kept your school ornaments.'

'She hasn't kept my what?'

I explain about the school ornaments. Nate thinks it sweet.

He obviously hasn't seen them, plus rich people can like all the tacky shit they want and people think they're starting a new trend.

'The tree. It's so beautiful!'

Nate smiles indulgently at me. 'Yes, baby, it is real pretty isn't it? But not the prettiest thing in the house, that's you.'

'Who decorated it?' I ask. 'It must have taken ages.'

'Oh, my mother has someone come in and do it. Bitsy, well she takes Christmas real serious. Least it's coloured this year. Last year she had it done all white, and I think she had it blue one year. Daddy didn't like it, so we're back to colour. It's more traditional. There's a smaller one in the dining room.' He indicates an open door.

I am dying to get a good look around before the horde arrives, as it were, so I go in. Yet another spacious room, several more paintings, of course – one of the Hoppers is in here, a Rauschenberg, and another version of Nate on one of the walls. A long mahogany table almost the length of the room is laid to perfection. Twelve places are set, the distances between place settings precise. Three crystal glasses in ascending size sparkle at each place, and each beautifully starched, white linen napkin is embroidered with a discreet little Christmas tree on the corner. An impressive row of silver cutlery gleams. I am glad the nuns have drummed into us the 'work from the outside in' rule. And then, the only touch of frivolity, an enormous cracker placed at each setting. Shit! I am starting to feel just a bit unsettled now. Who will be coming, and when?

Not one member of the Gilmore clan has shown up yet. Where the hell is everyone? I want to get this over with. After all, I am the 'object on view' today and Zollie hasn't exactly made me feel relaxed about meeting this lot.

'Isn't there anyone at home?' I venture. 'The place is so quiet.'

'No, baby, they all went to church. They should be back any time soon.'

Cora bustles back in. 'Let me get y'all something to drink. Y'all go cosy up by the fire in the library, get yoursels warm. It's real cold out.'

She returns in minutes with two eggnogs sprinkled with nutmeg, and we take them and settle luxuriously into a large comfy sofa beside the huge log fire. The logs are about six feet long and the fireplace is enormous. I snuggle up to Nate and let him stroke my hair and nuzzle my ears. He begins to fill me in on just who I will be meeting: three sisters, all older than him, two husbands, and three grandbabies, his grand-mother Gilmore, known as Mimi, and her sister, his aunt Belle. Quite a clan. I hope I'll fit in, and not find it too intimidating. I'd have preferred Nate to myself for Christmas though. He is truly gorgeous. I snuggle closer to him, I feel cosy and in love. No one I know at home has a house like this, it is so perfect. There is something very seductive about the comfort and ease of this vast wealth. I could get used to this much luxury in no time at all. I wish the Lennon clan could see me now.

There is a crunch of tyres in the snow outside. They are back. We hear the front door open so we untangle ourselves, get up and walk into the hall. Bitsy, Nate's mother, is first in the door. She has bright blue, glittering eyes, perfectly coiffed frosted-mink coloured hair and a wide, tense painted smile. She has smooth, well made up skin, but I can't quite decide on her age – she is oddly expressionless, sort of young-old looking, no wrinkles at all. In fact a few wrinkles might loosen her up. She is tall and exceedingly thin. I know she and Nate's father have just returned from St Lucia, and she is tanned to perfection. I notice the diamond dazzlers on her fingers, it would be hard not to, and two the size of snowballs in her ears, quite masking her earlobes. Nathan Five, or Faave as the family calls him, pushes me forward with the alarming sentence 'Mama, I know y'all have been dying to get a look at Maggie, well here she is.' I think it a rather gauche introduction from such a cool guy, but Bitsy pauses and again smiles her wide, tense smile. I stand there being inspected while she shrugs off her coat to a waiting pair of hands (Cora's), and smoothes the front of her navy wool dress, which is hanging perfectly on her coat hanger body. There is not one single crease in it, and I wonder briefly if she has travelled in the car standing up. I am never to discover how she did this. She is the only person I ever met who can sit in *linen* and not crease it. Maybe the car has a built-in steamer, or she has.

We remain standing in the hall as she eyes me up and down, air kisses somewhere about a foot above my left shoulder and, touching my cardigan, says semi-approvingly, 'Cashmere'. The 'eer' lingers. I find it a constant source of fascination, this ability some Southern women have that allows them to drawl the last breath of a word out, making it sound sexy or disapproving or whatever they happen to feel at the time. Bitsy obviously approves of the cash*meeer*.

'Why, how do you do, Maggie?' she exclaims. 'We are so privileged to have you join us for dinnah. Nathan has told us so much about you.' She then turns abruptly from me, hugs her only son, and plants a bright red kiss on his cheek. She strokes his sweater. 'I just love blue on you, honey,' she says approvingly. 'Doesn't it suit him, Maggie? He looks adorable. You need a hayer cut though,' she adds. 'You look like a hippie.'

She glides into the library and we follow, as other members of the family enter from outside, kicking snow from their shoes and making little squeaks at being back indoors. Bitsy had had no snow clinging to her shoes of course. Maybe she walks an inch above the ground as well, she is light enough. I am familiar with her story, thanks to Zollie. Bitsy Lee Shames is a former Miss Tennessee, who married Nathan Gilmore IV for his money, and to her eternal regret had fallen deeply in love with him.

107

Every fibre of her being suggests this patent adoration. I soon come to realise that it makes everyone else in the room feel slightly superfluous and uncomfortable, and Nathan, her husband, perpetually irritated. It is hard being in their company. Her eyes rarely leave him, yet she manages with little furtive darting movements to take in every little detail of everything else going on around her while still gazing adoringly into his bored face. From the moment I first meet her I only see about three expressions on her face, and two of these are undying adoration for Nathan and for Nate. I guess the other is indifference.

Once Bitsy has checked that the room is up to scratch she then excuses herself profusely while she checks on 'the progress of our dinnah'. Nathan, who has been standing behind her smiling quietly, visibly relaxes and shakes hands warmly with me. No air kisses for him. I have obviously read the word patrician before, but rarely use it. Nathan Gilmore the fourth is the embodiment of it, and Nate is a clone. This is what he'll look like in thirty years, I think, still handsome as hell. Perhaps it is the familiarity of his looks, but I am instantly relaxed in his presence.

'Well ma'am,' he says with a broad smile on his face. 'I believe you are Irish?'

'Yes, from Northern Ireland.'

'My family originate from there.'

'Oh, do they? Gilmore is quite a common name in Northern Ireland. My cousin is married to someone called Gilmore.'

'Is that right? Well, maybe we are kin. We might have some relations in common.' He gestures towards my glass of eggnog. 'Nate, take that away.'

Nate obediently takes it from me. I had been struggling with it anyway.

'Now,' Nathan says, steering me to the seat by the fire, 'let's get you a real drink. I sure as hell need one after listening to that lil' creepin' Jesus rant on about charity at Christmas for ovah an hour.' He pauses. 'I know all he wants is more of my money. I say charity begins at home, right, Maggie? Now, what's your poison?'

Nate interrupts. 'Maggie just drinks wine or beer, Daddy.'

'Wine? Beer? Nonsense, Nate, she'll have plenty of wine with dinner. Let's get her a real drink. Now, Miss Maggie, what about some Jack Daniel's with ice? Or a bourbon?'

I nod. Either. He pours me a Jack Daniel's. It looks roughly about a half-pint. I sip it. It is smoky, sharp, like whisky. I am not sure if I like the taste.

'Good,' he says 'now you come with me.' He guides me gently out the door. 'I'd like to introduce you to all my girls, and my little grandbabies.'

None of them have yet appeared in the library though I had heard people go upstairs, no doubt to ready themselves. Just as well, one at a time introductions are fine by me. Nate's three sisters, the Gilmore girls, Beth Anne, Eveline, and Priscilla, are really friendly too. Priscilla in particular, who is just two years older than Nate, treats me like her new best friend, promises me we'll meet without Nate and do 'girlie things', whatever they are. I agree of course. I would have agreed to most things after the Jack Daniel's Nathan Four has poured me. I gulp it in record time and am flying.

Jeb and Cameron, the two husbands, are polite, rich, Southern boys. I have met a few of them before now. These two are clean-shaven, tall, dark-haired, with symmetrical features and, of course, the obligatory even white teeth. One of them is maybe a little bit tubbier than the other, but on first meeting, they are confusingly alike. Maybe they have a template for Gilmore husbands. They are wearing button-down shirts under smart patterned sweaters with little alligator logos, chinos, and loafers. They laugh respectfully at Nathan Four's jokes and flirt mildly with Bitsy before drinks, and more pronouncedly after a few. She appears to thrive on this and twinkles shamelessly to the 'boyahs' – she pronounces it as if it had three syllables.

The children are cute too, three little girls and a boy. Christopher joins the grown-ups for dinner for the first time. He is seven. The girls are paraded in a haze of expensive red and green velvet outfits with various appliquéd Christmas motifs, and after various cooing noises have been made they are whisked off by Cora to get dinner in the kitchen. Cora seems to fall into the role of nanny pretty quickly. I wonder, does she live here permanently? She'd need to. She doesn't stop throughout dinner. There doesn't appear to be any other help, though there might well be two dozen slaves tied up in the kitchen for all I know.

Before dinner we have the present giving and they give me wonderfully generous presents: suede driving gloves, a silk scarf, which actually matches my cash*meeer* sweater, a leather-bound diary and, best of all, Nate gives me a watch. I don't have one so I am really pleased. It is a nice one too, and looks real gold, with a snakeskin strap and a little blue stone in the winder. He tells me he just loves his cufflinks, and the Waterford rosebud vase I have brought for his mother seems to meet with her approval. Finally we all assemble and go into dinner. I am seated beside Nathan and Mimi.

The meal is just splendid, and of course the drink continues its job on me as well. It is flowing freely and, fuelled by it, I have my predictable bout of verbal diarrhoea. A captive audience listen enthralled as I answer all their misconceived questions about Northern Ireland. The entire family are agog with the idea that I have escaped from the 'War' in Ireland and are delighted I can have a peaceful Christmas courtesy of them, so it would be churlish of me to dissuade them of this fact. After all, what harm is it doing? It makes them feel like the March family, taking in poor war orphans for Christmas. During dinner they all listen, apparently fascinated, as I tell them all

110

about my family, and with amusement when I tell them about my job. A visit to the loo and a little pop of Zollie's 'present' gives me a boost of false energy. Dinner passes in a whirl of food and drink and general goodwill. I finally begin to relax. Zollie has put the fear of God into me, but they all seem determined to put me at ease. Nate is at his charming best. His granny and Aunt Belle are two classy Southern ladies straight out of Eudora Welty who seem impressed by the fact I have 'foah sistahs'. 'There were faave of us girls too and it is such fun to grow up like that,' Mimi confides in me. I feel we have bonded. She leaves me in no doubt that as long as I stand by Nate I'll be fine with her. She gazes at him fondly.

'Nate here is the dearest boy imaginable, any gal is lucky to have him, and why, he just loves his old Mimi.'

'We all do, Mimi, we just love you to bits,' Priscilla nods enthusiastically.

'Why, I do believe he needs a waafe, and to settle down soon, he's too pretty by fáh foh a man,' Aunt Belle chirps.

Mimi snaps at Belle instantly. 'He's not pretty, Belle, he's plain handsome, entirely different thing.'

Nate, half hearing from his part of the table, calls to me, 'Don't you heed them, Maggie, whatever they're saying.'

'We are merely remarking that Maggie here would make you a real darling wife.' Belle is not to be silenced. Bitsy raises her eyebrow but says nothing. I change the subject.

It is well after midnight when Nate and I leave and drive back to the lake. We do some more coke, listen to music and fall into bed. Life is good. Nate is adorable. I am in love and happy. I finally open Zollie's surprise present. It is two Quaaludes with a note saying 'Just in case y'all want to sleep'. We each take one. I am still a bit bowled over by the extent of my drug taking, but the Quaalude does its job. I am soon sleepy. I have survived my first Christmas away from home.

12

I go into work grudgingly the next day. Christmas is over fast in America — in Ireland by this time they are just getting the feel for it. They take the 'Twelve Days' seriously there. The station has a worn out, after-Christmas feel to it. The decorations already look jaded and tired. Bilbo isn't in the best of form. His brief excursion to Alabama has left him deflated. His mom was in mourning for Elvis and was in black from head to toe, and all the Christmas wreaths were tied with black ribbons. Since Elvis's death in August she has been behaving strangely, and has been in consultation with a medium to help her connect with 'The King' even though, Bilbo tells me with a look of despair, she doesn't really believe Elvis is dead. I find this intriguing. Mamie from Mamie's Modes doesn't think Elvis is dead either.

Apparently Bilbo's mum spent most of Christmas day playing 'Crying in the Chapel'. Bilbo shows me his Christmas present from her. It is a perfectly ghastly white polyester jump suit with gold braid trim, similar to Elvis's Las Vegas costume. It has the name 'Bill' monogrammed on the pockets. He hates the name Bill more than he hates the costume. I guess Bill makes him feel ordinary – Bilbo is his alter ego, his more exotic self. He says his weaselly brother, Lee, had been there too, and he got one with 'Lee' on it, but he didn't seem to care. His mind is on other things. Bilbo says he is full of delight that the SKI ALABAMA venture is going so well.

Sue Lynne is back at work too, at her desk with her head down. She has the grace to look shamefaced when she asks how my Christmas has been, a look that quickly turns to a scowl when I show her my watch. One thing that cheers me up is the fact that Tom from Shine Records has been on the phone about 'Dogs in the Moonlight', which is number one and looks like it is going to go platinum. Tom is absolutely delighted. He tells me Rolly Young sounds like the cat that got the cream. There is also a message from two of the trades asking for interviews with me. I am chuffed to bits. 'Mull of Kintyre' is number one in Ireland, my sister Sinead told me when I talked to them all on Christmas morning. She has sent me a copy for Christmas. It is the fastest-selling single of all time, though not in America. They hate it. Zollie hates it, but it is, after all, Paul McCartney and Wings, so he only protests mildly when I add it to the playlist. I play it a couple of times and am surprised to get a few calls from irate listeners complaining about the bagpipes.

Bilbo takes a call from some eejit of a guy who claims the sound of the bagpipes has sent his dog 'right clean into some sort of fit'. Allegedly it is foaming at the mouth. Bilbo worries all morning after taking the call, but Zollie's hunch is that the dog had probably eaten the guy's dope and he is looking for an excuse to sue the station if the dog dies. So Zollie calls him back and tells him the station's lawyer and a photographer would be along to take statements from witnesses. We will play the record at two o'clock sharp, directly after the news, especially for the dog, and observe the dog's behaviour at close range. He doesn't suggest the guy change stations because he never wants to lose a listener. Anyway, the guy suddenly changes his tune. Says it doesn't matter, go right ahead and play the record as much as we like, on second thoughts he hates the crazy goddamm mutt anyway. Maybe if it foams at the mouth again he can get the thing put down for free. Zollie is pleased his ploy worked. He promises to send the guy a free Q92 T-shirt. He confides in me that he thinks the guy has actually invented the dog, there was no tell-tale barking in the background, for example, but the call indicates an unhealthy attitude towards the song so we cut down the rotation of 'Mull of Kintyre' and eventually take it off the playlist.

I have talked of going to Aspen with Nate towards the end of March even though it will have to be unpaid leave – I haven't exactly worked long enough to get a holiday – and before I met Nate I was vaguely thinking at the back of my mind that when I did, I would be going home to Ireland. Little fits of homesickness have been hitting me a bit when I least expect them, and the idea of spending New Year as well as Christmas in Tennessee is a bit much. I won't even have Nate's loving embrace since he is spending New Year in Aspen with some college friends. It had been arranged long before we met. He hasn't invited me, which hurts my feelings a bit even though I know I can't go. I hate the idea of being away from him for a week. I hope he'll be faithful to me and several times am on the point of asking him that when I manage to bite my tongue. I feel instinctively that Nate wouldn't like me to be clingy.

Sharla has said she might come down to visit me from school, but that is dependent on her current squeeze. He is coming on hot and cold and she is keen on him and doesn't want to just abandon him, not till she has him firmly in her grasp. I understand this, after all I had forgone the pleasure of Christmas with her for love of Nate, so I can hardly complain. The prospect of dinner with Annie Mae and Zollie is cheering and I have decided to accept their invitation to spend the night, so I am going to drive with Zollie. I have no car anyway, since it is still in the body shop, and this morning I had to come in with Nate. Zollie is going to run us past our apartment block so I can pick up my presents for them.

'Well, Maggie, don't you just love Christmas in America?' Zollie is grinning widely as he steers the Cruzer up the I-24. I don't answer at first as I am tired and hungry and just a wee bit sad. I still can't believe we had to work today. I want to be at home in Ireland tucking into the big box of Quality Street we get from our Auntie Martha every year, and fighting with my sisters for stealing all the purple melty caramel ones with the nut inside. We always just sit around the house on Boxing Day watching naff things on TV, eating leftovers and opening any unclaimed presents.

'I miss home,' I say, 'it's weird being away at Christmas.'

'My home is your home, Maggie, my momma is just thrilled we're having a homesick lil' Irish girl to eat with us, she has been cooking up a storm.' I can't help smiling at his enthusiasm. 'And you can bet your ass you'll have you a better time than at ole Nathan and Bitsy Gilmore's.' He pauses. 'How was that? Y'all like my presents?'

'Yes,' I say wishing I had a little pop now to brighten me up actually. I hope they like my presents. They are in my bag. There are to be four of us for dinner as Bilbo is joining us. Zollie's brother Sam and his family have gone back to Arkansas already.

We make it safely through the snow and I notice several of the houses on the way have the most fantastical Christmas decorations: huge, lavish light displays, more like something you'd expect to see in a department store than on a normal house. Each house seems to be vying with the next one for displaying the most lights. I can't make up my mind whether it is ghastly or jolly, or jolly ghastly. Annie Mae has outdoor lights on the trees and the house is sort of edged in fairy lights, which makes

115

it seem very welcoming. The minute we go in the door she is clucking round me and hugging me, taking my coat and telling me to cosy right up to the fire. Zollie hugs and kisses her and she pretends to swat him off. The house is snug and warm and smelling blissfully of food. Zollie 'fixes' us both a drink, and Annie Mae doesn't drink liquor so she is having ginger cordial, 'On account of his pappy, lord rest him, being just a touch too fond of it'. She nods towards Zollie and exits to the kitchen again. Seconds later she bustles back in.

'Here you go, Maggie,' she says, 'take those cold boots off and get your feet into these.'

She hands me a toasty pair of knitted socks and I oblige. I am starting to thaw and I suddenly feel at home. I am happy. We will eat dinner as soon as Bilbo arrives, if he can tear himself away from the station. Annie Mae scolds Zollie when Bilbo doesn't appear by six-thirty.

'You work that poor boy too hard; he needs to get him a life.'

Zollie protests. 'He loves to work, Momma.'

'Yes, but he needs to eat as well.'

Zollie rolls his eyes at me; we both know that this is not one of Bilbo's problems. Annie Mae is also fretting that I am not warm enough on account of Jimmy Carter asking everyone to keep their thermostats at sixty-eight degrees. She offers me an Afghan, which I discover is a crocheted woollen blanket. I don't need it. It is stifling in this little house.

Finally Bilbo arrives, puffing and panting. Annie Mae claps her hands in delight, he has brought her two large poinsettias. She already has four, but obviously more is better. Bilbo refuses a drink, he is just ready for dinner, and now that he's here we move quickly into the dining room to begin the feast. The table is dominated by a simply enormous ham. It is criss-crossed with honey and cloves, and there is also a plate of sliced turkey from yesterday, sweet potato puffs, which I have never tasted before, and endless vegetables and muffins. We heap our plates and begin. I think at first that we are going to have iced tea with it, but that is just for Annie Mae and Bilbo, Zollie has come prepared. He has brought some Cabernet Sauvignon for us.

'Here you go, Maggie, this is real fine Californian wine,' and he pours me an enormous glass. I know that there will be pie so I try to go easy, but the boys seem to be competing to see who can pile in the most. We have crackers and hats and our napkins are rolled in little knitted Santas, and I have brought my camera so I can take some photos to send home. I didn't dare do that yesterday, somehow I don't think the Gilmores would have liked it. When I feel as if my stomach will burst from eating, we sit by the fire and swap presents. I have bought Zollie some Celtic design cufflinks from an Irish shop in Atlanta, but for Annie Mae I have an Aran sweater knitted and sent by my Aunt Martha. She is thrilled with it and thankfully it fits her.

Zollie insists on calling Maybellyne and singing 'Maybellyne why can't you be good', and we have a great chat – she has lost more weight and counting the days with the pounds. Then Annie Mae and Zollie extract every single detail about yesterday out of me and I tell all, wondering at the end of it if Nate is the guy for me, but he'll do for now. By the time I curl up in the little guest room under the patchwork quilt I feel I have had a real Christmas.

Over the next few days, I have to contend with SKI ALABAMA. Our first major giveaway is coming up fast. Work on the resort is almost complete and the first lot of prize-winners are due to go the weekend after next, the first after New Year. We have agreed before Christmas that Bilbo will organise the weekend. After all, slimy Lee is his brother, and surely family loyalty will ensure the whole thing isn't a fuck up. Zollie has been banging on to Bilbo about it non-stop.

'This has got to work, Buddy!' Zollie declares as we have our coffee back at the station. 'Our reputation will be made on this giveaway. You better believe it.'

Bilbo shifts uneasily and assures Zollie that he will do his very best. I feel sorry for Bilbo, the prize-winners are becoming a pain in the ass, calling a few times a day to check about accommodation, ski passes, meals and even what the weather will be like. But sorry as I feel for Bilbo, I still wish I hadn't agreed to go along for the weekend. It is a moronic idea, one of my worst decisions. It is all because I have acquired a new ski suit. Bilbo and I were in the studio cutting yet another commercial for a local ski shop when Zollie comes in looking excited and waving a large bag with the legend 'Southern Skiers' on the side.

'Maggie, honey, you have got yourself the ski outfit of a lifetime. It is real real classy and drop dead sexy. I was just in the door of the store and I spotted it and thought it would be real perfect on you. Here it is, all two hundred dollars' worth.'

He pulls open the bag and takes out a grey, red, and black ski suit. Right enough it is really gorgeous, but I don't exactly need it just yet. I have decided I am not going to Alabama. However, I appraise the suit. It is my size.

'Try it on, Maggie, you'll look real good in it, I promise you.'

'If I take it will I still get paid this week?' Trade-outs are a curse when they come instead of wages, and they are a favourite ploy of Zollie's when the cash dries up, which it does, frequently. Zollie does his totally aghast look.

'Maggie, honey, why you know I wouldn't do that to you.'

Yeah right, I think, but I take the suit from him, go into the loo and squeeze into it. It feels good.

'Hell, honey, that looks real purdy on you,' Zollie says as I emerge from the bathroom. Bilbo nods enthusiastically.

'How much is it?' I am not exactly well off.

'Well, it costs two hundred, but to you, Maggie, just half that. Special discount – the owner just loves your voice in the ad, says you sound real sexy. I told him you were Swiss.' Zollie beams, delighted with himself.

'Swiss? Swiss? Why on earth did you do that?'

'Well, think about it, Maggie, I told him that on account of the Swiss being so into skiing and used to snow, I told him we try to find the right nationality for every spot we cut. He really likes that attention to detail. Says that's why he is going to keep running commercials with us.'

'Great! I expect you'll want me to yodel in the next one!'

Zollie cackles loudly. 'Maybe, Maggie, maybe so. I'll suggest that. Now are you having the suit or aren't you?'

'I don't know. It's still a lot of money.'

'Well then,' says Zollie, 'maybe Sue Lynne would like to have it.'

At this point, emboldened by the fact that the spotlight has moved on to her, Sue Lynne begins to simper at Zollie. I haven't exactly been too friendly to her since the Christmas Eve crash, and she hasn't been doing her usual 'available slut' acting around Zollie – she is trying to stay in with me in case I sue Clarence, which I intend to do if his insurance doesn't pay for a new car for me. She forgets herself for a minute though, momentarily blinded by her own vanity.

'Why, I do believe those are my colours,' she says, smiling sickeningly at Zollie. 'And maybe closer to ma siaaze,' she simpers again. 'The red would pick out the haaalaaghts in ma hayer.'

'How can *you* afford it?' I snap, wanting to smack her hard in the mouth.

'Well,' she drawls, 'I do have some Christmas money from ma daddy. Maybe you can go get you a cheaper one in the sales, Maggie.'

She smiles at me, a trifle too triumphantly I think. Suddenly

I want it. 'No, forget it. I'll just take it,' I say. 'I am going to Aspen later this year and I'll need one then, possibly two.'

'Way to go, Maggie. You get you two suits. Get you three even. You're gonna be a skiing mother. This here is the first of many. Yes ma'am!'

Zollie cackles again loudly. Yes, he is fired up, he loves these sorts of scenes. He thrives on them. Poor Bilbo, on the other hand, has slunk off to stand at the door and fan himself in case his nerves get the better of him and he needs a spray of deodorant. Sue Lynne scowls and goes back to her filing, and I suddenly have a ski suit and only the vaguest prospects of a ski trip ahead.

I like the idea of owning a ski suit – I feel it adds a new dimension to my personality, and it gives me access to a hobby I have only dreamed of having. I like the feeling more than that of being a car owner – that is commonplace. All Americans own cars, not all Americans ski. I have joined the elite. Or so I think at the time. Before I am properly initiated in Aspen, there is the prospect of a weekend's skiing in the alpine state of Alabama.

About an hour after I get the suit Bilbo asks me plaintively, 'Maggie, honey, why don't you come to Alabama? I'd sure appreciate it, and you have you a ski suit now. Lee will rent you some skis, free of charge, and I would sure appreciate your company. Please? Pretty Please?'

I give in and agree to go. Bilbo is touchingly thrilled. Perhaps I do need a break from Nate as I have seen him every day since Christmas. I am besotted with him and I could look at him all day long. He is so handsome, such good fun and so perfect that part of me is constantly afraid he'll evaporate, disappear, and all those letters home to my sisters about the perfect man with money and movie star good looks will turn into some ephemera I have conjured up to stave off my homesickness, for the truth is that when I am with him I have

120

few thoughts of home. I am in a perpetual state of arousal. On the other hand, when I am alone I have time to dwell on the distance between here and Belfast. And it can be painful. My mother was so upset about my missing Christmas and the girls said it wasn't the same without me. Daddy only said, gruffly, 'I don't know what in God's name you're doing out there playing records anyway, when you could be building up your teaching pension,' which, translated, means he misses me too. I am torn. Politically things are at a stalemate at home, and drab grey Irish winters hold no appeal.

Tennessee looks wonderful right now. The snow is lying white and cool on the ground, the trees laden with it, the stalactite-like icicles hanging from the side of the mountain roads are set off to perfection by a bright blue sky and crisp cold air. No, I have little need for the relentless damp cold of a Belfast winter.

13

The SKI ALABAMA weekend has run into a spot of bother. First of all the long range weather forecast predicts a thaw. It comes through on the machine we use to get our news. I break the bad tidings to Bilbo and he gets on the phone to Lee straight away. I am in the habit of reading news headlines and weather at the top of the hour – we aren't quite flush enough to get a network news bulletin or, like some of the competition have, our own dedicated newsreader. About a half minute after I have finished the news, Zollie is on the phone. He sounds quite deranged. I tell him to hang on and line up 'Hey Jude', which I know will give me seven and a half minutes to try to talk him down.

'What's wrong, Zollie?'

'What's wrong? What's WRONG? Godammit, Maggie, did you *hear* that weather report?'

'Of course I did, I just read it.'

'Precisely, and you should not have done that. No ma'am, Maggie, you should NOT HAVE DONE THAT TODAY OF ALL DAYS!'

'Why on earth not? It's accurate. It came down the wire.'

'Because, Maggie, that is dangerous information, we don't need to give it out over the aayer when our prize-winners are listening.'

'But Lee told us he had a contingency plan, a snow machine.'

'Yep, he did, but when it snowed, he decided not to get it.'

'Not to get it?'

'Precisely, Maggie. You heard me right.'

'But how can he run a ski resort in Alabama without one? It hardly ever snows this far south.' I know this because all I have heard since it snowed before Christmas is that it never snows this far south and that the last ice storm they had was legendary.

'Well, they cost a lot, and use a lot of water, and he figured since there was so much snow he'd be better putting the money into the Alpine Lodge until it was a going concern.' Zollie pauses.

'He's crazy!'

Zollie sounds sheepish. 'It was my idea, Maggie, I thought the lodge could be a bit smarter, more Swiss-like, it looked real tacky before. Oh hell, Maggie. Listen here, forgit that last report, just read last week's weather report on the next bulletin and let me talk to Bilbo.'

Poor Bilbo, he has been listening to my half of the conversation anyway and is a sickly green colour. I hand him the phone and rummage till I find last week's weather. It predicts further freezing and more snow. Oh well, at least the competition winners will be happy, even if all the other listeners end up totally confused. I certainly am. Do all radio stations in America do things like this? I couldn't imagine the BBC behaving this way.

Despite all our hopes and wishes to the contrary, the weather forecast as usual proves correct. By the end of the week the thaw has begun. The stalactites slowly turn to puddles, patches of wet appear in all the fields of snow, and the roads are clear.

There is little doubt that one hundred miles further south in Alabama it's a similar story. We are about to cut our losses and offer alternative prizes (which Zollie is frantically trying to trade) when Bilbo comes in and tells us that Lee has hired two snow machines and that Alpine Peaks is thickly carpeted with the false snow. We are saved. Hallelujah!

The dreaded Saturday morning arrives, unfortunately. As planned, Nate leaves for Aspen. The weather for Colorado predicts several feet of snow. They are going to have blizzards and snowstorms, mounds of the stuff. We are predicted a high of forty-seven degrees. It isn't fair.

Nate flies out on the Gilmore jet on Friday afternoon. We have spent the night before in a torrent of passion and I am hoping the glow will last all week. He tells me several times he loves me and promises to call. I have managed to go the whole week without uttering one clingy word and am proud of myself. The next morning, Bilbo, Zollie and I drive to SKI ALABAMA, followed by forty-eight prize-winners. We are two short because Miz Zillah Knightly and her eighty-one-year-old sister Beulah have finally seen the wisdom of Zollie's advice (not to mention the obvious change in the weather), and have settled after all for a complete new wardrobe from Mamie's Modes and a new hairstyle from Herman. They are deliriously happy, and lucky! We have left Sue Lynne and a weekend guy called Bonzo in charge of the station. I think Zollie traded him out from central casting, but apparently he's a great engineer. It is a two-hour drive. Zollie is in manic form, elated one minute and extolling the virtues of snow machines, and down in the dumps the next predicting all kinds of horrors in store for us if the weekend is a disaster and, to quote him, 'we lose our goddamm asses'. Every few minutes he quizzes Bilbo about Lee.

'Well, Bilbo, you think your brother can pull it off? Or is he gonna make us look like fools! Can we trust him?'

'Gee, Zollie, I don't rightly know. He's done real good up until now, don't forgit his ass is on the line as well.'

This is hard talk indeed from poor old Bilbo. He is obviously under severe stress. He is getting redder and redder and tugging at his underarms. My heart goes out to him.

'Leave him alone, Zollie, it was all your bloody idea.'

'I'm telling you, Maggie, we'll be looking for another licence if this fails.'

'It'll be fine. Sure, hasn't he two stupid snow machines?'

'I hope they ain't *stupid* machines, Maggie, they got a lot of snow to produce.'

He is certainly right there, the sun is burning my arm through the window as he speaks. We are zooming down the I-24. The temperature outside the American National Bank had read forty-four degrees as we left Chattanooga. Zollie saw it, but at the time he didn't say a word. Bilbo and I had exchanged looks of desperation.

The ski lodge is hard to miss. Lee has fifty-foot-high posters every ten yards from the Interstate exit to the location. All of them show snow-laden slopes with happy skiers and depictions of mountains roughly on the scale of the Himalayas. SKI ALABAMA, they proclaim in large letters and several exclamation marks!!!!!!!!!!!!!!! Spend your days on the slopes!!!!!!! !!!!!!!!!!!!!!! AND your après ski moments at ALPINE PEAKS!!!! !!!!!!!!!!!!!!!!!! Alabama's answer to the SWISS ALPES!!!!!!!!! !!!!!!!!!!!!!!!!!! No, I haven't made it up, it is spelled that way.

The lodge itself looks fine, suitably faux Swiss, apart from the inflatable fifty-foot-high Santa and sleigh anchored precariously on the top. Though there isn't a peak in sight, I wonder briefly does Alabama even have any mountains. Still I don't suppose he could call it Alpine Humps, doesn't have quite the same ring to it.

It is eleven when we check in. I am already in my ski suit and feeling uncomfortably warm. The prize-winners too are mostly checked in and there is an orientation talk at noon followed by a free eggnog promotion. Lee meets us at the door with the reassuring words that the machines are operating at full throttle and the slopes are looking good. We relax somewhat, trying not to remember that tomorrow's high is predicted at 48 degrees.

We fix our grins, helped by a small toke to settle our nerves, and get ready to meet the 'fifty luckiest listeners in the whole of Tennessee' (well, forty-eight as I have already explained, but we haven't corrected the ad). Ten minutes later we enter the fray. The lobby is a riot of would-be skiers, and Lee is dashing to and fro like a little tornado handing out eggnogs. He is wearing a pair of lederhosen and a pointed hat, and he looks utterly preposterous. He seems unaware of this, and indeed maybe I am just a sour bitch because some of the prize-winners tell him he looks real cute, like a proper Swiss gentleman. He has tried to get Bilbo to don lederhosen too, but Bilbo has his principles and refuses. There are four waitresses charging about in short little Swiss maid outfits of red and green, smiling brightly and telling everyone they all are real, real happy to welcome everyone to Alpine Peaks. All have their hair braided, and they look like cocktail waitresses from a mildly seedy nightclub as they hand out the drinks. Sue Lynne would fit in perfectly. After tasting one of the proffered eggnogs, which are being served from a large glass bowl in the lobby, Zollie vanishes, only to reappear minutes later with a huge flagon of liquor which he proceeds to empty into the bowl. Bilbo looks at me and rolls his eyes. The fun is just beginning.

It is time to hit the slopes. I have never skied, therefore I see nothing too unusual about the ski lift that consists of a cable with little t-bars which you either grab with your hand or hook your ski pole on to. You are then dragged up a slope covered in snow, rather slushy snow, and patchy, but snow nonetheless. There are no cable cars and no chair lifts. A procession of people line up in their gear to get to the top of the only hill. Most of them have never skied before either and that is fortunate. Many of them are wearing denim and sweaters, and several people have discarded their jackets since by now the sun is shining brightly and the drink has kicked in.

Bilbo, dressed in denims and a bright yellow ski jacket with matching bobble hat, is taking tickets at the bottom. A guy in a dirty white jump suit with *De Wayne* woven above the left hand pocket is hooking people on to the t-bar as it passes at about forty miles an hour. Every second person misses it and is hurled to the side, but De Wayne ignores them and concentrates on catching the next hook by hand. I am not taking any chances. I place my poles firmly under my left arm and lunge for it, grab it, and I am yanked so hard I think my arm has been dislocated. I have no feeling in my right hand, just a numb tingling sensation but, clinging on like grim death, I make it to the top and am promptly flung sideways on to my arse. I right myself and take a deep breath.

There are two signs, *Beginners – Green runs only*, and *Experienced skiers – Black runs only*. This is all very well, but the second arrow points the same way as the first. It is like something out of *Alice Through the Looking Glass*.

I launch myself downhill gingerly. Skiers are passing me at varying speeds, most of them totally out of control. Some of them are roaring loud Rebel Yells. I reach the bottom in one piece in time to see a guy fly past me at about ninety and go splat! He zooms straight past the bales of hay at the bottom (the crash barrier) and falls into a pool of melted snow. From the pandemonium going on about me it's evident he isn't the first to do this.

Total chaos reigns for the entire afternoon. As the sun warms things up relentlessly, Lee cranks up the snow machines, and at one point a virtual avalanche of machine snow is shooting over the heads of the skiers on top of the hill. Some alpine peak this is, it is really a humpy field as far as I can make out. Several of the skiers have serious co-ordination problems due to the alcohol content of the complimentary eggnog. Most of them belong to the 'last to the bottom is stinking' school of skiing, and even though the number of hay bales at the bottom have been increased, several people still land splat in the mud, or go headlong into the 'Swiss Souvenir' stand which is to the left of the crash barrier. The best buy of the day is a cuckoo clock with SKI ALABAMA painted on it and a rebel flag decal above the door where the bird comes out. This appealing touch is Zollie's idea. Unfortunately I told him it was a traditional Swiss souvenir, but they are selling like crazy.

De Wayne is covered in mud from head to foot but he doesn't seem to mind, he is grinning broadly and still hooking people absentmindedly onto the ski lift. He is probably on some class of drug that anaesthetises him. Luckily there are no broken limbs – another by-product of the alcohol level no doubt. There is one dubious moment when one of the skiers, over-come by the exuberance of the experience, hurls his ski pole in the air as he hits the hay bales. He really should consider a career as a javelin thrower, because it sails over the roof of the motel and bursts the fifty-foot blow-up Santa and sleigh on the top. The loud bang causes yet more pandemonium on the 'slope', but fortunately several people take it as a signal that the day's skiing has come to an end. The light is starting to go anyway, and people peel off looking like a pack of hippos after a mud bath, to prepare for the 'Ski Hoedown with guest Yodellers'.

I prepare myself for the barrage of complaints. Surprisingly we only have one or two, and these Zollie and Lee deal with skilfully. Free albums are promised and a good meal, and allegedly after the Swiss yodellers (from Birmingham, Alabama), there is to be a well-known country and western singer making a sur-prise visit. I hear Willie Nelson mentioned. Even I like Willie.

We finish quite an appetising supper of hamburgers with Swiss cheese and Swiss fries and settle down for the entertainment.

The yodellers are execrable, and they look truly comical in their lederhosen and alpine hats, but they get a standing ovation; I think perhaps Americans have a highly developed sense of irony after all. I start to relax and am looking forward to the mystery guest. Zollie has refused to tell Bilbo and me who it is. Suddenly, I hear the immortal line 'Let your love pour down on me like maple syrup'. It is my good samaritan, Buford, aka Big Boy McConnell. The crowd go through the roof. Gosh, I think, he must be popular.

Buford McConnell isn't bad actually. He puts on a tight show. We all feel enormously grateful to him, because he certainly saves our bacon. Although Q92 is strictly 'Balls to the wall rock 'n' roll' and NOT country and western, many of our listeners can't shake the old c&w out of their blood, and they respond to it with yells and whoops and hollers. The room rocks. Buford makes a good attempt at what we call crossover. He's brought a couple of the session musicians with him and they are dynamite. It is great fun – we have a little bit of polypharmacology to brighten us up even more though. Zollie seems temporarily to have forgotten his 'only organic' pledge, but I figure we need it, we are emotional wrecks.

Buford does a few Van Morrison covers and sings the blues as well, and he even does a tribute to The King, and finishes with a rather impressive rendition of 'Your Cheatin' Heart'. The audience love it and I even find myself singing along. The beer and liquor is flying, everyone seems to be wearing Q92 T-shirts and Zollie is working the room giving out mugs with the station's logo on and chatting up the crowd as only he can do.

It seems Buford had been in Muscle Shoals, Alabama, cutting a new record, and Zollie had found that out and booked him (after the doomed weather forecast). They've kept in touch since my Christmas Eve fiasco. He's rung once or twice to enquire about my health, which I think is thoughtful of him. Buford joins us after his set and I am instructed by Zollie to be 'real nice' to him because he has saved our asses. I oblige. I am so sweet I nearly make myself sick. Maple syrup has nothing on me. I am, I hope, sexless, nun-like, pure, and virginal, because although Buford Big Boy seems a decent enough sort, he is not remotely my type on account of the large gut, wispy beard, and general good ole boy demeanour, not to mention the series of crowns, one of them gold. Plus he is old, at least thirty-five, and looks it. And also I have my lovely, lovely Nate, skiing down real snow fifteen hundred miles away, and hopefully thinking of me. But I am very nice to Buford. I am a good-mannered girl, and besides, Zollie has pushed a lot of coke up my nose. This helps. I am even nice to Lee the ferret.

Sadly, Buford seems *very* interested in me, and I haven't the energy for a sparring match. At about eleven, despite the fact that Zollie's eyebrows are through the roof and his smile is fixed and rigid, I excuse myself and go to my room, where I lock the door very firmly and try to sleep. I can't sleep. At one-thirty I am still twitching. I call Bilbo in his room. I am scared now. I will never do drugs again. God is punishing me. God says NO. He must be from Ulster. Bilbo surprises me by suggesting further drug abuse, namely that I should immediately take one of the famous Quaaludes, so beloved and abused by Vance and Chance Prince, and my Christmas surprise from Zollie. Apparently it is a legal sleeping pill. He drops one by my room. Soon my limbs stop twitching and I fall asleep with a smile upon my face and dream blissfully of Nate. Not for long. At about three a.m. my phone rings. It is Zollie, who is obviously still laying out the white lines. He has Buford with him in his room, two down from mine, and a selection of musicians. They are in party mode. The background din is deafening.

'Goddammit, Maggie, you party pooper, whut the hell you doin' in bed?'

I groan, 'Zollie, please go away. I am fast asleep.'

'Well, we have lots of stuff to wake you baby.'

'No,' I say, 'let me take a rain check.'

Zollie starts. 'Maggie, goddammit, here I am with one of the finest—'

'Please, Zollie, I've got my period. I feel awful.'

That shuts him up immediately. Bilbo has told me that Sherilee the witch was a monster when she had her period. She used to beat Zollie with kitchen utensils of enormous proportions and several times had tried to run them both off the road to their deaths. One time she filled all the pockets of his three best suits with scrambled eggs. You only have to mention 'monthly' and Zollie starts to quake. The gambit works.

'You get you some beauty sleep, Maggie. Buford and I will join you for breakfast.'

Oh goody, I am reprieved. I snuggle up and drift away back to my dreams of pretty boy. I am so horny. I think I have several erotic dreams, before I get back to sleep. Perhaps I am getting the hang of the masturbation thing. Personally, I blame the Quaalude.

14

It takes me a couple of days to recover from the Alabama caper, but we are back at work on Monday morning, cutting commercials and spinning discs. I don't hear from Nate at all while he is in Colorado. I don't really expect to until about halfway through the week, then I find my heart stopping every time the phone rings, and a little pulse of expectation rising in me, until it is confirmed that IT WAS NOT NATE. By Thursday I am starting to feel wounded, gouged, ripped apart. I run through several excuses for his lack of contact in my head; there is no phone at the lodge; there are no phone booths in Aspen; there is a time difference of one, two hours?

He has rung home when I am at work.

He has rung work when I am at home.

He has met someone else.

He has someone there.

He has fallen down a crevasse.

He has forgotten I exist.

He doesn't love me any more.

Finally I phone his parents' house. Bitsy picks up the phone. 'Hello, Mrs Gilmore,' I stammer, 'it's Maggie.'

'Maggie? Ah'm sorry?'

'Yes, you know, Maggie, the Irish girl, I'm a friend of Nate's, I had Christmas dinner with you . . .' I trail off.

'Why of course, Maggie, how are you doin'?'

'Oh fine . . . Eh, I just wondered if there was a phone at your home in Aspen?'

'A phone in Aspen?' She echoes me.

'Yes, you see Nate has called me and I wasn't there', this could be true. *It is true*, 'so I thought I'd call him back, but I don't have the number.'

'The numbah?' Long pause.

Is there an echo in my head? 'Yes, the number of the phone in Aspen, if there is one?'

'Why, yes, I believe there is a phone. Howevah, I am not sure I recall the numbah off hand.' Longer pause. 'But,' she brightens, 'I am quite sure he will call you back if it is important.'

I am not important, I think bitterly. Not enough. 'Well thanks, I'm sorry to bother you, thanks again for Christmas.'

Another long pause. Is she still alive? 'Oh, well yes, we did enjoy meeting you so much at Christmas.'

'Yes, thank you very much. I had a wonderful time.'

'I am so glad.'

The conversation is finished. I hang up. I feel worse. I call Sharla for a long dissection of the possible reasons Nate hasn't called. My heart is sore. I want him. I want to see him. I want to hear his voice. I want to touch him. Oh God! I am obsessed. Nothing else breaks through. I have a calendar from Alpine Peaks, an eight by ten copy of an awful photo of Lee, and I stare at it fixedly while Sharla tries to reassure me. He will be back on Sunday night, I think. Only three days to go. How will I survive?

At work I am a zombie. Bilbo empathises. Cups of coffee appear, BLTs at lunchtime (Zollie has arranged a trade-out at

133

Delroy's Diner, a nearby restaurant, and this is the only edible thing they do. Everything else is 'Fried or Smothered', including Delroy himself.) I feel smothered too. My heart has taken over my body, my whole being is receding. Every chance I get I play a love song. Paul Simon, Neil Young, James Taylor, slow Beatles. Zollie doesn't like this pining version of Maggie.

'Goddammit, Maggie, you still got your period? You oughta see someone.'

'I am fine,' I lie.

'Fine? You call this fine? You cain't hear yourself. Playing all that goddamm *dirge music*. You are dismal, honey, real dismal. I'd sure hate to see you in a badass mood if this is you being fine.'

'I just haven't been sleeping well. The bed is too hard.'

'Oh, you need me to trade you out a soft one?' Zollie pauses and eyes me up and down. I feel my soul is visible. There is a window in my heart. 'You wouldn't be lovesick, would you?'

'I don't know what you're talking about.'

'When does Nate get back?'

I try to sound vague, 'Saturday, I think.'

'Has he bin callin' you, honey?'

'He's only away a week,' I snap. 'Hardly any need for him to call!'

'But honey, your lil' heart is lonely, right?' Zollie breaks into song. 'I'm so lonesome I could cry.' Oddly enough the words seem appropriate. Maybe country and western singers have a point.

I call Maybellyne in Florida that night and she has news for me. She has lost 50 pounds and has bought a truck. She is moving to Tennessee next week! I am overjoyed. I have really missed her. She listens patiently as I bore her to death about Nate, and go over the myriad possible reasons why he hasn't called me. She tells me men don't think about such things, so don't attach as much importance to it, but deep down I know this is significant, something is up. He mustn't love me. I replay all the moments of our last night in my head frame by frame to poor Maybellyne. She listens calmly, allows me to pour out my demented rantings. Eventually she excuses herself and hangs up. I go to bed and toss and turn. I am wretched. At eleven-thirty the phone rings. I grab it eagerly. It is Buford McConnell. I am not even gracious. 'How did you get my number?' I snarl. He apologises for calling so late. Then I instantly feel sorry I was rude and am now toe curlingly nice to him. I guess he has had a drink or two. He has rung for a chat and suggests we might have a meal sometime. I say maybe, just as friends of course. He tells me he knows I have a boyfriend and I am glad he knows I do. I sure as hell don't. I hang up and finally fall asleep.

I go into work the next Monday feeling ragged. However, one moment of sheer insanity that lifts me out of the gloom is the visit to the station of Miz Zillah and Miz Beulah. They have availed themselves of both the trade-outs in lieu of the ski trip. Zollie has picked them up in the 'Big Black Box' and promised them a tour of Q92. I am on the air when they arrive and I don't know whether to laugh or cry when they come in. In both cases their aging, wispy hair has been coaxed by Herman into Stevie Nicks perms, a sort of ripped out wool look. Miz Beulah, the elder of the two, though they look like twins, is wearing a hot pink trouser suit with sequined beading on the jacket. She has a fluffy lemon scarf tied round her neck which she tells me she had knitted for the ski trip. Miz Zillah is wearing a similar number in a lurid shade of tangerine, and perched on her head, atop the Stevie Nicks perm, is her lime green bobble hat.

'Don't we just look like the last of peatime!' Miz Zillah exclaims. It sounds about right, whatever it means. I think they look like opal fruits, but they are so sweet and so pleased to be at the station, they never stop smiling. It is hard not to smile back. They are both totally smitten with Zollie and have been across the way with him for smothered chicken in Delroy's Diner. I am introduced to them and they assure me they never miss my show. They are in rhapsodies over Herman. He has treated them with niacin. I hope briefly that is all. They love their hairstyles.

'Whaa, we have bin given a whole new lease of laafe,' they tell me in unison. It's hard to feel down in the dumps all the time. I forget about Nate for at least an hour. When I get off air I drive by his house, even though it is miles out of the way. I am by now a gibbering wreck and I have lost weight. Part of me is thrilled to have such classy hip bones and to have my jeans so loose, but the sane part of me knows I am moronic. I can't help it, I am a woman possessed.

The Porsche is outside. He is back. I feel faint. Should I go in? Maybe there is another woman with him. I drive out to Nickajack, to Annie Mae. She opens the door to a sobbing wretch. I blurt it all out to her. She listens without comment. Then she hugs me, goes into the kitchen and brings me some hot chocolate. I can barely swallow.

'Honey, you look like a lil' wisp, you need to eat some. Now can I fix you dinner? I'd sure like the company,' she says. I nod, but I'm not very hungry.

A feast is laid out nonetheless, and I do my best. My appetite picks up. It is hard to resist Annie Mae's home cooking. Despite her pleas for me to spend the night, I drive home. As I go into the flat the phone is ringing. I have just missed the call, and though I wait, it doesn't ring again. Once more I go to bed with a heavy heart. I am wrung out. I don't call Sharla or Maybellyne. I still have a Quaalude that Bilbo has given me so I take it. It is only nine o'clock. I take the phone off the hook in case Sharla calls. In minutes, I am fast asleep, a numb, dreamless sleep.

*

Nate has been back for a week now and still no word. I have phoned his number and hung up several times. While it rings I rehearse the speech I am going to make when he picks up. The 'Well, I know it was all a bit fast and intense and maybe you're scared, but is that any reason to quit cold turkey?' speech. But the few times he picks up the phone my voice dies in my throat. I am constricted by a large lump of emotion, and I know that if I speak I will dislodge it and everything will pour out: the hurt, the pain, and worse, the tears. I didn't think I could cry this much, but I am a walking bundle of damp tissue.

Even Zollie starts to get sympathetic. 'You're hurtin', Maggie, ain't you?' he asks me one day after I have finished my show. I had tried like mad to sound 'up' but I expect he can see through it. 'Maggie, I told you, honey, those Gilmores are trouble. He is acting like a grade A asshole. Forget him and get yourself a nice boy. Rich people are spoiled and mean.'

I have no appetite, and I have begun to enjoy the little pop of coke Zollie gives me before I go on the air. It gives me a sort of false courage. It numbs my sinuses and numbs my brain. I am disquieted underneath, but I keep excusing myself to myself. It's just for now, till I get over Nate.

Then, unexpectedly, I meet him on my way to work. I stop by Hits For Less Records and there he is, in the flesh, in an aisle beside the 'B' records, 'B' for Beatles that is, although in his case it should be 'B' for Bastard. He looks tanned. He looks like he has eaten my heart and is feeding on it. I feel sick. We stare at each other. I recover first.

'Hello, how are you? Did you have a good ski trip?'

'Maggie, I was going to call you, I'm sorry, things have been kinda crazy since I got back, I guess I left things—'

I interrupt. 'It's okay, I was just surprised not to hear. If you don't want to go out with me that's fine, but I always thought we could at least have stayed friends . . .' I trail off. I am trembling, and I don't want to look weak in front of him. I want to kill him and hug him simultaneously.

'Could we maybe have coffee?' He indicates towards the mall.

'Yes, but not now. I'm on the air in thirty minutes.'

'Of course, well I guess I'll call you this evening. You home?'

'I'm not sure. You can always get me at the station.'

'I did call the station yesterday.'

'Oh?' I must sound sceptical.

'Yes, I talked to the girl, what's her name? Sue Lynne?'

The girl! The *bitch*! I feel like killing her. I will check as soon as I get there. We both start to leave.

'Sure, well I'll call you then, it's good to see you. I'll be in touch.'

Is it my imagination or does he look more miserable than I feel? In the parking lot I see the Porsche. I feel like ramming it as I drive past. I have gone over every possible reason for his lack of communication and exhausted every theory, and now I am mad as well as hurt and shamed. I go to work. Zollie isn't there. Sue Lynne is. I am a mad seething lunatic. Taking a deep breath I ask her as calmly as I can manage, 'Did Nate call looking for me yesterday?'

'What, I believe he did, you was gone.'

'Were gone!' I snap at her. 'Were gone.'

'Yes, you were.'

'Why didn't you give me the message?'

'I figured he'd git you at home?' She looks at me, sudden realisation flooding her stupid face. 'Wha Maggie, is everythin' okay?'

'Yes. Everything is fine, just fine.'

'Are you sure? I hope he's treatin' you good.' She manages to suggest she means exactly the opposite.

I go into the studio. Now the silly bitch knows something is up. A wave of tiredness washes over me. I go on air and I put on some upbeat stuff. Some Bee Gees, 'Staying Alive', but it's too impossibly cheerful. I play 'Running on Empty' by Jackson Browne. It fits my mood better. Maybe I will meet Jackson Browne and run off with him.

In our last late-night chat, Sharla diagnosed Nate as a commitment phobic. It's a new term in one of her textbooks. 'Hell, honey, he probably is scared just how much he cares, I guess he missed you so much it frightened him.' Yes, it is an interesting but completely unconsoling philosophy. He loves me so much he can't bear to be in touch, or spend time with me. Fucking great! Nate doesn't call that night, though I have been on the phone to both Sharla and Maybellyne for an awfully long time, so perhaps he has. I toy with the idea of calling him, but decide against it. I put some music on and write letters home. Then suddenly I can't wait until they get the letters so I phone them. I speak to all of my sisters in turn, and then Mammy comes on the phone and I am talking to her about the station and basically how wonderful everything is when she says, 'What's up? Are you missing us?'

She sounds so concerned that I burst into tears and tell her all about Nate.

'Look, love, no man is worth all that, anyway it sounds as if you're a wee bit out of your depth. All that money couldn't be good for anyone. Why don't you come home? You know your daddy and I were talking about you last night. He has a wee insurance policy which will pay out when he's fifty. That's next month. We'll send you the fare.'

'No, Mammy, honestly, don't worry. I promise I'll have enough saved to come home soon. Really, I'm okay.'

'It's far from okay you sound to me.'

'I am, I feel better now I've talked to you.'

'Sinead is thinking of coming out to see you.'

'When?'

'Soon I think, maybe over Easter, during her holidays.' Sinead has just started teaching. 'She has almost two weeks then, and sure, maybe you'll get home in the summer.'

I suddenly feel a lift of optimism, but then I remember that's when I was supposed to be going skiing. Well, there's not much chance of that happening now. There's only thirteen months between myself and Sinead so we are close.

'That's great news, Mammy, I can help her with her ticket and she doesn't need any money while she's here.'

'Well look after yourself, pet. I'll get your Auntie Martha to light a candle for you.'

My Auntie Martha's candles always work. She is a master candle lighter. On Tuesdays her house looks like Lourdes (Tuesday is St Martha's day). Several times she has had incidents with the candles and once nearly burned her house down. She also lights candles in churches all over Belfast. Touch of pyromania, I think, but of course I don't say this to my mother. I hang up feeling cheerier. Nate can go to hell. I don't need him. I soothe myself to sleep with this mantra. It doesn't work.

15

Next day Buford calls yet again and I agree to meet him for a beer; a reward, I suppose, for his persistence. He takes me to a trendy new restaurant/bar in the centre of town and offers to buy me dinner. I have no appetite, but I have a beer. We have an amiable time. I don't let him know that I am single again. I can barely let myself know. I talk too much, but he seems to like it.

'You are some woman,' he tells me as he gazes admiringly at me. I am unmoved by his obvious admiration. Why do we only want admiration from those we admire? He tells me he has been married three times. He is thirty-five but looks ancient. His face has a lived-in look to it, it looks as if someone has chewed it. I notice a few of the people in the bar looking over at him. I guess he is famous in a sort of way. I am unimpressed. He tells me that he lives mostly in Nashville, but is originally from near Chattanooga and that he is thinking of moving back here – to escape a few ex-wives, he jokes.

'Just like Zollie,' I say laughing; I don't mention the Colombian mafia. It would seem excessive. Anyhow, Zollie *is* more frightened of Sherilee the witch.

I promise him we will have a few beers again soon. He is kind and sweet, and I expect it can't do any harm and anyway, secretly in one half of my frazzled brain I am still fantasising about the great reunion with Nate, even though in the other half I am getting on with life alone. I reason that I may as well not get a proper boyfriend yet, just in case Nate and I get back together, but I am not admitting this out loud to myself, or to anyone. Well, maybe to Sharla. The one cheering thing is that Maybellyne is back, and she *has* lost weight, rather a lot in fact. Admittedly she still classifies as fat, but she is so cuddly and it is so good to see her. She is still on her special diet – all liquids, absolutely ghastly milkshake things which expand in your stomach and fill you up. We are all banned from bringing fries and burgers to the station, and Zollie hasn't included her in the Burger Barn trade-out. He does ask me, I think in all seriousness, if we should get her on the toot, on account of it being an appetite suppressant, but I have always been a bit coy about drug-taking in front of her, and I tell him he should be too. In fact, I am determined to stop. It seems to make me do all kinds of things I don't normally. I have not yet worked out if this is a good or bad thing.

Zollie has traded us out a meal at the upmarket restaurant Bistro. We are all going, Bilbo, Sue Lynne, and me, to celebrate Maybellyne's return. The one thing she can eat is a steak, one a week. She can have a steak and salad with no dressing, and she will have one glass of champagne since it is liquid. She can now fit in the Cruzer, which is handy, though she can't drive because her arms are too fat, or maybe her legs. I don't like to question her too closely about this.

The mood is up and there are no drugs on board. Then, disaster for me, Nate is in the restaurant with his sister Priscilla. I nod frigidly and go to our table, but Zollie goes into overdrive and stops to greet Nate like a long lost brother. Nate looks over at me in a funny way and I think I might cry, except Maybellyne is holding my hand tightly under the table and talking me down. I hardly taste the food, then finally before we order dessert I go to the bathroom. Priscilla follows.

'I have tried to call you,' she says, 'but your phone is constantly busy and I guess I haven't been persistent enough.'

'That's okay, it's nice to see you.' I feel like crying.

'Maggie, I know it's not my business, but Nate seems real unhappy to me. I don't know what has gone on between you but he has talked about you all evening, won't you come and say hello?'

'I don't think so.'

'Please, for me? I know he cares for you.'

'If he cares for me he would have called me when he got back from Aspen.'

'Oh?'

'Yes. Look, Priscilla, I appreciate your trying to help, but I didn't break up the relationship, Nate did.'

She looks embarrassed. 'I'm sorry for butting in. I thought y'all had just had a row.'

I go back to the table and as I sit down I catch Nate's eye. He looks miserable. I feel miserable. Zollie leaps up as soon as Priscilla comes back from the ladies.

'Hey, if y'all are done eatin',' he says to the Gilmores, 'why don't you join us?'

My protests are drowned out by the shuffling of chairs to make room, and within minutes Nate is beside me, despite Sue Lynne having moved to make a space beside her.

'We are gathered here,' Zollie declares solemnly to the assembled group, 'to welcome to Tennessee our wonderful Maybellyne all the way from the Sunshine State.' He gestures to the waiter. 'I think we need us some champagne, ain't that right Bilbo?'

Nate interrupts quickly. 'Let me get it, Zollie, I insist.'

143

A list is produced, Nate looks at it. Zollie relaxes and sits back smiling.

'Maggie here tells us she had her some very fine French champagne in Atlanta, what was it, Maggie? Don Periyawn?' He deliberately mispronounces both words. I nod dumbly.

Nate looks again at the list and grins. He knows what Zollie is up to, but he seems happy to go along with it. Priscilla nods her approval.

'Well,' Nate says to the waiter, 'looks like we'll have some of that. I think you'd better chill a second bottle. Lucky we are in about the only restaurant in town that serves it.'

Zollie beams, satisfied, I can read his mind: the Gilmores can afford it. Everyone relaxes after that and between the seven of us we have three bottles. The awkwardness between Nate and me evaporates with the bubbles in the champagne. He is a very charming and handsome man and Sue Lynne is practically salivating over him from the other side of the table. I find myself telling amusing stories about Ireland, and by the time we leave I have almost forgotten Nate is no longer my boyfriend, he has been so attentive all night.

I remember he isn't as soon as I arrive back at my apartment. The drink is dying in me and I feel desolate. I still want him, there is no getting away from it. I call Sharla. Her line is busy so I call Maybellyne for her 'view'. She tries her best.

'Anyone can see he still loves you, honey, why don't you wait, see if he calls.' She sounds tired, and why not? She has had one small filet mignon, one glass of champagne and nothing else all day and it is now almost midnight. I find a Quaalude and go to bed.

I am dreaming, someone is calling my name, I am floating. I hear a noise, a loud crack and I wake up, startled. My chest is tight with fear, I am being burgled. Christ! I sit up in bed, fumble for the phone, but can't remember the American number for 999. I find the phone and call Bilbo as I know he has gone

144

back into the station after the meal, he virtually lives there. I am deranged.

'Bilbo, oh Bilbo, oh God Bilbo! I am being burgled. He's out there now. Please, what will I do?'

'Call nine-one-one, Maggie, and keep your bedroom door locked. Just calm down now, I'll be right over.'

There's no lock on the bedroom door so I pull over a heavyish chair and wedge it against the handle. I dial 911, give my address and wait. I am terrified. People have guns here. The effects of the Quaalude are long gone and now I am wide awake, trembling. But very soon, almost immediately in fact, I hear the wah-wah sound, the police are here. The doorbell rings. A deep voice growls 'Police'.

I leave the bedroom, go to the front door and open it, very slowly, keeping the chain on. I should explain, my apartment is on the first floor, though Americans call it the second floor. The front door opens on to a veranda. A very large policeman is standing outside on the veranda.

'Ma'am, I believe you called us, you have a problem?'

'Yes, I heard someone at my door. I think they were trying to break in. You got here very quickly.'

'Yes ma'am, we sure did. Lucky we were just nearby at the 7-Eleven. I believe Officer Goodrich has apprehended someone down below in the parking lot.'

I look over the railings and down to the car park where another policeman is talking to someone in a car, which looks like a Porsche – it *is* a Porsche. Oh God, no, it can't be. It is freezing outside. I have no dressing gown so I throw a coat over my nightie and run down leaving the policeman standing at the door. It is Nate and he is showing his driving licence to the other policeman.

'Nate? Oh Nate! I thought you were a burglar.'

The policeman looks at me suspiciously. 'You know this guy?'

'Yes, yes, he's my boy—' I trail off, uncertain.

'Her boyfriend, officer,' Nate finishes for me. He lifts an eyebrow and looks at me quizzically.

The ice-water that has been coursing through my veins for almost a month starts to thaw. Suddenly I am fizzling with joy, just about to burst. Bilbo drives up then, and gets out of his truck, a sweating heap of worry, his face anxious.

'Hey, Maggie, you okay? Hey Nate, she call you too?'

The other policeman has come down. They are starting to realise it's all been a waste of their time. They are annoyed at first and then the radio crackles and I hear Officer Goodrich say, 'Yessir, yessir, I sure will.' He comes over and mutters to the other guy, and suddenly they start acting real sweet to us and saying we should go indoors as it was fixing to freeze.

'Next time, Mr Gilmore, you be sure and call the lady first.'

They drive off and I notice I am shivering. We all go in, but Bilbo refuses my offer of tea, coffee, drink of juice, anything. He needs to get back to the station. He leaves and Nate and I are alone. I can't think of anything to say.

'I sure am lucky the police knew who my daddy is. I figured I was gonna need him to post some bail bonds.'

'I'm sorry,' I say.

'No, Maggie, I'm sorry, I have behaved like an asshole. I've missed you. I owe you an apology. I guess I just couldn't cope, after Aspen I just left things . . .' He trails off. He puts his arm around me and pulls me to him. 'Mmm, Maggie, you are freezin', why don't we get you back into bed.'

'Yes, but . . .'

'It's okay, I'll just sit and talk to you.'

I want him though. I just want him. I know I'm not doing a good job of hiding it.

'How about I warm you up?' he says.

'We should talk first,' I say, shaking my head.

'Why don't we talk afterwards?'

146

His blue eyes regard me with what looks to me like love. I nod. 'Okay then.'

He gets in beside me and I inhale his smell. I have certainly missed that. He always smells of fresh laundry and love, and his skin is soft. I'd like to nuzzle the back of his neck right now, but I lie there completely still, thawing out. He snuggles up to me and murmurs, 'I couldn't settle down after the restaurant, so I figured I'd drive over and burgle you. Oh Maggie, I've missed you so much. I think I might have to marry you.'

I say nothing but my heart is thumping and I am scared and excited. I excuse it as the champagne talking. I think over my weeks of hell. It doesn't matter now. He cups my face in his hands and meets my gaze.

'Did you miss me even a little bit?'

'I missed you, just a bit.' I measure a little bit of space between my index finger and thumb. 'I missed you this much,' I tell him.

He laughs and pulls me back down on top of him. 'I don't think I'm gonna let you outa my sight again, you hear?'

'Yes, I hear.' And that seems to be it.

16

I have a little niggle at the back of my head – am I letting Nate off too lightly? He has told me that he had a bad case of cold feet, he felt we were getting too serious too fast. Then, about a week after his return from Aspen, he realised that actually that was the way he wanted it, but he had let things drift and felt afraid to call in case I told him to go away. He seems sincere and we have spent every night together this week in a state of intense passion. Our lovemaking is getting better all the time. I bounce into work every morning and Zollie can't believe my good mood.

'Looks like you're really getting yourself loved up, Maggie.'

I smile and say nothing. Sue Lynne scowls behind my back. Her scowls are penetrating things. I loathe her. Clarence Lee's insurance has paid up for my car, and she is madder than hell because, as she whinges to Bilbo about every five minutes (when she knows I can hear), his premium will rocket. Good, I think, serves him right, the stupid bastard could have killed me.

On Sunday we have family lunch at the Gilmores again. They are so nice to me, and seem only delighted that Nate and I are together, not that anyone but Priscilla knew we weren't. This time it's just Mimi, Aunt Belle, Nathan, Bitsy and Priscilla. Nate is all over me and they are tickled when I describe SKI ALABAMA. They insist I must go to Aspen at Easter. I say my sister might be coming then and they extend the invitation. 'We are taking the plane, of course, and there will be room.' Aspen, and by private jet too. I am dying to phone Sinead and tell her.

The next few weeks pass in a haze of music and lovemaking. I am happy. Nate asks me to marry him about a hundred times. Priscilla takes me to lunch and tells me the family just love me to bits. 'My daddy just adores you,' Priscilla says, 'and I can't think of a nicer sister-in-law.' I am bowled over, so on Valentine's Day when Nate asks me for the thousandth time, I say yes. The next week Nathan takes us all out to the Mountain City Club, which is ultra posh, and they toast our future. I am both thrilled and scared.

The following week, Nate asks me to come to Atlanta with him for the weekend. He would like me to meet a jeweller friend of his father's who will fix us up with an engagement ring. There is a selection of family ones, and I am to pick one and have it altered to fit me. We have been through the family 'dinnah' again, and lunch at the country club, and although I will never get totally used to it all I promise myself I will try. Bitsy is emotional at losing her 'baby boy', but Nathan is gruff and tells her it might make a man of him and he is lucky to get such a pretty and intelligent girl, so she is complying. I like his Dad, there's no nonsense about him. Bitsy makes me nervous but Nathan has charm and strength. I can't help noticing he doesn't seem totally relaxed with Nate. I can tell he likes it when I am there.

We haven't set a date for the wedding and I am not in any rush, I'm still a bit freaked out that I've agreed to get married. Anyway, the Gilmores do so much travelling, what with the

Kentucky Derby, the Masters at Augusta and God knows what else, we will be lucky if they can manage to come to the wedding at all.

In Atlanta we stay in the Gilmore apartment off West Paces Ferry Road. It is bigger than most houses and they have a live-in help there as well, also black and lovely. She is called Esther. She cooks us a huge breakfast that I can barely eat I am so worked up about the ring. Nate seems relaxed. He makes lots of jokes about choosing the most expensive. I haven't told my family yet, I am waiting till tonight when the ring is on my finger. Sharla and Maybellyne know, and I am spitefully imagining the look on Sue Lynne's face when I walk in on Monday. We go to Saks in Phipps Plaza first and Nate insists on buying me some new clothes. I try on various things and, unlike Mamie's Modes, most of the clothes look good, so I end up with four new outfits. I feel like Pollyanna. We pass Tiffany's where I linger outside looking at rings in the window. There are no prices on any of them, but we are not getting the ring there anyway. Part of me wishes we were: *Breakfast at Tiffany's* is one of my favourite movies.

We go to the offices of the Gilmores' family solicitors. Mr Jackson is the senior partner and he greets Nate as if he were the Messiah. He is waiting for Mr Loew who is the family jeweller. We have coffee from china cups and some awful biscuits, then Mr Loew arrives, apologising profusely for being five minutes late. The men beam at me and at Nate, they both seem to think it is a very good idea that Nate is getting married. Mr Jackson opens a safe and brings out seven rings on a tray. I have to pick one. They all look as if they are worth a fortune, but they don't look like anything I would ever wear. They seem the sort of thing the Queen would wear, or even worse the Queen Mother. Although nearly all the stones are huge, the settings are all twiddly and old-looking. I wish one would just fit me, then like Cinderella I could rush off with my prince.

But it's not to be. I try them all on in order, and then try them on again. I take ages. Nate senses my discomfort and says, 'Shoot, Maggie, let's just go back to Tiffany's and get you something you'd like.'

This does not go down well with Mr Jackson. He smiles ingratiatingly at me. I notice he has a rubbery mouth. 'With respect, Mr Nate, your father would specifically like the young lady, Maggie that is, to choose one of your great-grandmother's rings. You are the only male, it's a tradition.'

What can I do? I finally settle on a square cut emerald with a diamond each side. It is enormous. It is so big it looks like a fake. Mr Loew gets a little measure thing and I poke my finger in it and he makes calculations. He says he will drop the ring by the apartment in the morning. I feel curiously flat. Mr Jackson produces a pair of earrings to match it.

'I haven't any holes in my ears.'

'I'm sure that's easily remedied.'

For a moment I expect a person to jump out of another door, hold me down and bore holes in my ears. We say our goodbyes and leave. Everyone is smiling but me. When we get to the car Nate turns to me.

'Let's go back to Tiffany's. You can have two engagement rings. I want to buy you one myself.'

I am suddenly happy again. I just love him for understanding, but I can't believe I am marrying someone this rich. It is terrifying. I pick a heart-shaped diamond in a very plain setting. It fits me perfectly, which means I was meant to have it. I can't stop looking at my finger.

After lunch, two engagement rings richer, we phone my parents. It is Saturday night; all the girls are out except my sister Maeve, who is a cheeky wee shite. I tell her Nate and I are engaged.

'I thought Sinead said he left you.'

'Well, he came back and we're getting married.'

'Can I be a bridesmaid?'

'Maybe, if you're nice. Can you get Mammy for me?'

My mother comes on the phone. She always sounds hesitant.

'Is everything all right?'

'I'm engaged, Mammy, to Nate.'

'Oh Maggie love, how could you get engaged to someone we've never met? I think you've lost the run of yourself entirely. You should come home. You could get a job teaching. I hear they're looking for people.'

'Mammy, Nate wants to talk to Daddy.'

We had agreed Nate would formally ask for my hand. I had tried to dissuade him, but he was adamant it is the Southern way. I am in a state of trepidation, Daddy hates talking on the phone. I wait till he comes to the phone.

'Well?' he says, 'what's wrong?'

'There's nothing wrong, Daddy, I've just got engaged to Nate, and he'd like to talk to you, I think he wants to ask your permission.'

'Sure, what's the point of that if you're already engaged?'

I hand the phone to Nate. I listen while Nate speaks to my father. He calls him Sir and although I only hear one side I can tell that Daddy is actually being nice. Nate is saying things like 'Yessir', and 'I sure will', and finally he hands the phone back to me. It's my mother again. Mammy is rushing me off the phone; she's started to worry about the bill. I tell her it's okay, but I can't exactly say he's a millionaire in front of him so I give in and promise to write. I put down the phone.

'Well,' Nate says, 'looks like we're going to Ireland for the honeymoon.'

About a week after I am officially Nate's fiancée, Buford McConnell calls and asks me to dinner. Bolstered by my flashy engagement ring, I feel there is no harm in going. I call Nate

152

and tell him I am having lunch with my Good Samaritan. He seems 'cool' (his word) with it. I meet Buford in town at the beer and burger place. When I walk in I see him sitting in the corner by a window with his hat on the table and his lank hair tied back in a meagre little ponytail. I think of Nate's thick chestnut hair and feel sorry for Buford. I go over and his face lights up when he sees me. I show him my ring and he congratulates me, but without enthusiasm. During the meal he seems quite dejected that I am engaged.

'How I wish I had met you sooner,' he tells me, 'and then nobody, not even rich old Nate Gilmore, would have gotten their hands on you.'

I laugh it off, but I can tell he is serious, I swear to God his eyes are moist. I tell him I am flattered and that I'm not really that big a catch. He almost chokes on his reply.

'You are a truly wonderful person, Maggie, a warm, lovely, exceptional human being.'

To my utter horror, he sings a line of the song 'You light up my life'. I hate that song so much, it makes me puke. It's puerile shite. I have banned it from the playlist. Sue Lynne loves it, of course. I check quickly to see if anyone is watching. If they are, they have turned away quickly. I am trying not to laugh because he is making me feel quite hysterical and I can tell he means every word, or thinks he does.

'If ever things' — he says thangs — 'don't work out between y'all and Nate, I will marry you, Maggie. I would be real proud to spend my life bah your side.'

Oh shit, I think, please don't let him break into song again. I thank him profusely, but I tell him things are perfect right now, just perfect. Nate and I are in love. I reckon next time I see Buford I will at least smoke a joint first or get some kind of pill from Zollie. You would need to be on some form of drugs to be with him. He is hard to take straight. I am touched by his devotion though, and his seemingly true desire, despite his thwarted hopes, to remain friends with me. I can always use another friend; after all, I am a poor little Irish girl far from home.

It is going to be awkward going to Ireland and getting back into America unless I am already married. Something to do with the fact I will need a visa and I have overstayed on my J1. I am alarmed, but Nate seems thrilled. He is using this for a reason to get married sooner rather than later. I am unsure if I want to rush things. As long as I don't go home in the meantime it'll be okay. But it has been so long since I saw them all. After several phone calls home it is agreed my sister Sinead will definitely come here for a visit. She can give the family seal of approval. I would prefer Mammy to come, I miss her, and honestly she would be more fun than Sinead who is a bit on the serious side, but Mammy won't hear of it. She thinks it will be a great thing for Sinead. So Sinead will come in two weeks. I am paying half her fare, but I can only do this because since I have been going out with Nate I don't seem to spend any money. I have my car payment and my rent and utilities and that's it. I have been saving a bit and Nate wants me to move in and give up my apartment, but I don't want to do that, not yet. I am not there very much but I like having a place of my own. I have always shared a bedroom and here I have a whole flat to myself. I am expanding my record collection and I have even begun to get back catalogues of all my favourite groups and singers, everything from Atlanta Rhythm Section to ZZ Top. I love it. I have put them in special crates in alphabetical order and I get a real kick out of owning them. The record companies give me lots of giveaways since Abe Goodman gives me so much press and I have broken a few more records 'wide open'. They send me records early and ask for my opinion, and when I add the song it gets splashed over the trades. I have become a 'flavour', as Tom from Shine tells me, mainly 'cos I 'give good phone'.

Maureen and Patricia have both sent engagement cards and seem genuinely delighted I am to marry a millionaire. I expect our ones have told the entire neighbourhood. They are all just dying to meet him. Everyone would like to marry a millionaire, wouldn't they? The only thing about Sinead's visit that I don't like is that she is bound and determined that she doesn't want to spend one of the weeks in Aspen. She doesn't like the idea of skiing. I can't go off and leave her, but Nate promises me we have forever to ski and it will give me a chance to spend time with her. I feel somewhat cheated, but I suppose he is right. So Nate goes off to Aspen, he'll be back next week. I don't feel as threatened by his departure this time. There's Sinead's coming, plus I have my insurance policy in the form of my ring, well my two rings.

The night before Sinead arrives I go to an ELO concert in Atlanta. It is a record do and the record company pay for the hotel, but Nate offers me the use of the Paces Ferry apartment. I am reluctant to stay there without him, but he insists, so I do. I can't understand why this annoys me a little, but it does. The concert is great, absolutely spectacular. The ELO rise up 'Out of the Blue' in a large trippy spaceship and the audience at the Omni goes berserk. Bob, another Shine record promotion man, had taken me and a few other radio people to dinner beforehand. We had partaken liberally of various polypharmacological substances. At one stage during the concert I think Jeff Lynne is levitating, or maybe it's me. Concerts are so much better in this altered state. Bob and a few radio hangers-on drop me off at the apartment, well the limo does. Bob is impressed with the location, he is dying to come in and have a snoop around, but I have calmed down now and Esther would be nosy, so I say I have to get to bed because my sister is arriving from Ireland tomorrow and I am meeting her at Atlanta airport. He immediately suggests he organise a limo for her. I think this is a brilliant idea. She will be impressed,

I bet. We don't have limos in Belfast, except for funerals and weddings.

When I get back to the apartment at one a.m. the phone is ringing. It is Nate calling from Colorado to check I am back safely. I am still somewhat stoned so we have a very smoochy conversation. I am horny and wish he was here. Being horny is drug-related, I think. Next time I'm away I won't smoke any dope unless Nate is with me. Well I mightn't.

Next morning Esther makes me breakfast, about six dozen pancakes and bacon and eggs. I nearly get ill finishing it. We chat while I eat. She says she is so happy Nate is getting married, and to such a sweet girl. I don't feel too sweet, but I smile anyway.

'His Daddy was just real worried about him not finding the right gal.'

I am not sure why, he is not exactly over the hill. I'm sure people would be queuing up to marry him. Maybe they just want him to have a family, although I don't want kids just yet.

Esther tells me all about herself, she has had a sad life. Her only son has died from something called 'smilin' mighty Jesus', and her abusive husband has left her. Later, on the phone Nate tells me her son died from spinal meningitis. I suppose it sounds the same the way Esther says it and smilin' mighty Jesus is a happier sort of death, I think.

The Gilmores treat her real good, she tells me, although she implies rather than says that Bitsy can be difficult at times. That doesn't surprise me, although she hasn't been difficult to me. I do find myself puzzled from time to time at how quickly Bitsy and the whole family have accepted me. I am not rich and you would think they'd be looking for an heiress for Nate, but they don't need the money. I suppose I am a blank canvas of sorts. I don't fit the white trash definition, and no one here will ever find out too much about my family background. Maybe they've told all their friends I am Irish aristocracy, or arse-a-crockery as my Auntie Martha says. I dismiss the thought at once and concentrate on the next twenty-four hours. I want everything to go well for Sinead. Perhaps I am being too cynical? Maybe they just want Nate to be happy. I hope he will be. I do love him.

Sinead is arriving at lunchtime. Bob and I will pick her up in the limo and take her to a launch party for a new album from a hot group called Acid Drops, and then afterwards I will drive her to Tennessee. I can't believe she is arriving, it seems just yesterday since we discussed her trip. I am apprehensive. It is nearly a year since I last saw her, although she's been great at writing. Bob wants to pick me up in the limo, but I decide that I'd rather Esther didn't know all that was going on as she asks such a lot of questions, so I pack up the car, thank her profusely, and leave.

As I drive into town, my brain is teeming. I sort of assess what has happened to me since I last saw Sinead. A lot, really. I am driving my own car for a start, I have my own apartment, I am on the air, I am Music Director and, of course, I am Nate's fiancée. Fuck! It's scary. Bob Seger's 'Still the Same' is playing on the radio. Am I still the same?

I park my car at the hotel where the launch is to take place. Bob arrives in the limo to pick me up. He is smoking a joint and he is buzzing. He offers me some. I refuse; I have a drive to Tennessee ahead of me, not to mention picking up Sinead who misses nothing. Bob also has some toot, so he offers me that as well. I haven't had any for ages. I think what the hell and do a few lines. I am ready for Sinead. Bob is lying back in the limo, legs splayed. He is totally off his face and he is singing 'Born to Run'.

The limo drops us at the terminal and we go in and race to the gate. I am in turmoil, I hope Sinead will like it all. Does it matter? How could she not? Then suddenly she is here, looking ridiculously non-American and ill at ease in too warm clothes. I rush towards her. She is exhausted, hence exhausting; she was always a grumpy kid when she was tired. She is full of complaints about how long the flight was, how big the airport is, and how long she had to wait at immigration. I listen and smile and hug her, I can see through this, she is feeling overwhelmed. She suddenly collects herself and grabs my hand and oohs over my ring.

'God, Maggie, it's huge. It must have cost a fortune. It's gorgeous.'

We get her case. I introduce her to Bob, who has been waiting for me to get my hellos over, and we go outside to wait for the limo to pick us up. It is circling.

'Who on earth is he?' Sinead asks me when Bob is flagging it down.

'He's a friend, he works for a record company.'

'Where's Nate?'

'In Colorado, skiing. I told you. He'll be back on Friday. I thought you might like to meet Acid Drops, they're a really good group, from New York, a bit like Talking Heads.'

'Who are Talking Heads?' Sinead sounds puzzled.

'An American group, they're hot.'

'What do you mean, they're hot?'

'Never mind, I'll explain later.'

'Do you play The Clash?' she asks. 'The Jam? The Stranglers?'

'No, we don't play punk much. It's more a rock 'n' roll station.'

'Well, they don't exactly sing ballads.'

'The music is different here.'

'Not all of it.'

'I know, but punk just hasn't caught on, I suppose people like to be happy all the time, or romantically sad. They don't like to hear about anarchy and stuff. It's all love or broken hearts and flowers.'

Sinead has brought me the new Clash LP. 'I can't believe,' she says with some contempt, 'that you could be a DJ and not play The Clash. I can't wait to hear this radio station.'

Yes, she sounds as if she can't wait. The limo arrives and we get in. Despite herself, Sinead is impressed.

'Gosh,' she says, 'I've often wondered what these were like inside.' She sinks back gratefully into the seat and then I realise what a bad idea it is to bring her to this do. Poor thing, she looks wrecked.

'You're tired, maybe we should just head home.'

'No way José,' Bob says. He takes out his little travelling coke kit. 'Why don't y'all just do a few lines.'

He proceeds to lay some out on a small mirror. I look towards the driver, but he has his eyes very firmly on the road. He's probably inured to this sort of thing anyway. Sinead follows my eye.

'Don't you think it's a bit rude to keep the window closed? He might think we're talking about him.'

'Hell no,' Bob says, 'he's probably sick of listening to all the bullshit.'

Sinead is staring now at the cocaine. Bob has pulled a little tray out of the seat and has his mirror placed there. Sinead seems mesmerised.

'What *is* this?' she asks Bob archly.

'It's toot.'

'Is that a drug?'

'Yes, it sure is.'

'Is it not illegal?'

'I guess.'

Sinead turns to me. 'I hope you haven't been doing any of this, Maggie,' she says.

I shrug. 'Occasionally,' I say. 'Everybody does.'

'Well, I don't want to try it. I'd be frightened something would happen to me. I mean,' she continues, with a stern expression on her face, 'are you not afraid you might jump out of the car when you're on it?'

Bob rolls his eyes at this, but says nothing, and then snorts two lines hastily as we curve round a corner. He doesn't offer me any and we change the subject. He is trying to persuade us to spend the night in Atlanta and go to the concert at the Fox, but I can see that Sinead is not in the mood so when we get to the hotel I say I will pop in for a short time and then Sinead and I will head off. Bob offers us a room in case Sinead wants a shower. I guess it was a bad idea trying to impress Sinead. I have been here too long and have forgotten that people at home are normal. I have grown too used to crazies.

Sinead showers and we go in to meet the group, but maybe because it's a daytime bash, it doesn't seem any fun, although the drummer latches on to Sinead and spends most of the time telling her how the rivalry between the two lead singers depresses him and how he's the only true talent in the group. She tells me this later, adding that the lead singer had asked her if she wanted to 'suck a stick'.

'What did you tell him?' I ask, feeling slightly panicky.

'I said *certainly not*,' and she looks at me with her eyebrow raised. 'I suppose that's another drug.'

I say nothing. The explanation would upset her. I'm just bloody glad he was so out of it that he was slurring his words, though Sinead wouldn't have heard of dicks anyway; everyone in Ireland has willies.

'That drummer,' she says, once we are on the road, 'he's very friendly, but he was obviously getting a cold, his nose was run-ning and his eyes were red.'

I decide not to explain that either, it will only make her paranoid. I change the subject. Sinead loves my car, and she likes what I am wearing, jeans and a silk shirt. We fall into our old, comfortable, easy chat. I tell her all about going to the lawyer's office and getting the 'family' ring, and all the little

160

details about Nate that it is hard to fit in on the brief phone calls or even the rambling letters. She asks endless questions and gives me all the craic from home. My other sisters are dead jealous that they didn't get to come with her, so Sinead is already worrying about what she will buy them and if her money will last.

'Look, you don't need money. You can spend all you've brought on presents.'

'How can I? I can't stay with you for two weeks and let you pay for everything.'

'Sinead, you *can*, Nate is a millionaire; he won't let me pay for anything.'

'I hope that's not why you're marrying him.' Finally, on the home straight, she falls asleep. I turn the station to a classical one and drive carefully. I feel protective of my big sister. I can't wait for her to meet Nate.

We arrive at my apartment and find about ten buckets full of flowers outside the door and a large piece of cardboard with 'Welcome Sinead'. At first I think Nate must have lost it, but the note says *Please call Zollie at the station.* I might have known it was something to do with him. It turns out Zollie has fixed a trade-out with a florist who is moving premises. There is some mix-up and they got three times their daily delivery so Zollie took all the flowers in lieu of advertising. I try to explain this to Sinead, I'm not sure I make much sense, but she is touched at the welcome, overwhelmed in fact. We bring them indoors and arrange them as best we can. I have only one vase, so we have to leave most of them in the buckets. When we finish the place looks like a funeral parlour.

Next day, after a good night's sleep and a meal at home, the 'grand tour' begins. Everyone is so hospitable and friendly to her. She meets and adores Annie Mae, and thinks Zollie is a hoot. Bilbo and Maybellyne are both given the seal of approval and she even makes valiant attempts with Sue Lynne. I decide

161

a visit to Herman's Hair Haven is a must, so we drive off to Racoon Mountain. She leaves with streaks, or 'sun-kissed highlights' as Herman prefers. She suits it. She passes on the perm, even though she likes mine. All the Lennon girls have straight hair. When we were small my mother spent hours coaxing our hair into ringlets. Every Saturday night we were all lined up for bed with foam curlers in, only for the precious ringlets to fall out on the way back from mass if it rained, which it did, a lot.

Sharla comes down for Sinead's first weekend. Sinead takes to Sharla immediately, of course, everyone does, although she has some trouble understanding Sharla's east Tennessee twang as I once did. I increasingly feel like a tour guide, though everyone pitches in, and she has a selection of drivers and guides.

On the Saturday, Nate comes back. We are a bit awkward with each other at first, but Sinead appears to adore him. On Sunday he gives a party for her and invites the 'gang' and Priscilla. After some persuasion she has her first 'go' in a hot tub. We forgo the obligatory joint in her honour, and we are all wearing swimsuits, of course. I hope fervently that she is generally having a ball. I am exhausted with all the goings on. Back at work on Monday I come off my shift to find Zollie waiting.

'You know, Maggie, I sure do like Miss Shin-aid, but don't you think she needs to lighten up just a little itty bitty?'

'What do you mean?'

'Well, she's so serious, and she's just on holiday from a goddamm war zone, don't you think she needs to have her some fun?'

'She is having fun.' But unfortunately I do see his point. I am in manic entertainer mode and she has remained throughout somewhat unrelaxed. 'Listen, Zollie, I've been doing my best to entertain her considering I *am* on the air every day,' I explode at him.

'Hell, Maggie, just think about it. All she's done since she got here is eaten her some food, and visited some dumbass tourist things. She hasn't had any FUN. I am talking *real* fun, some *sex'n'drugs'n'rock'n'roll.*' He has started to say it as one word. He is losing it.

'She doesn't do drugs.'

'Hell, she needs to, Maggie, believe me, honey. She is one tense young girl. How old is she?'

'Twenty-three.'

'Is that all? She acts like she is thirty.'

'That's not true,' I protest, but he does have a point. 'I guess she is pretty straight. I never did drugs till I moved here. People aren't drug fiends in Ireland.'

'Hell, they oughta try some, it might cheer 'em up, then they wouldn't need to bomb the fuck outa each other.'

Zollie isn't too informed about the Irish question. He seems to think it's a bit like the Wild West. I guess he has a point. He pauses mid-rant and beams at me. I can almost see the light going on in his head.

'What now?' I say crossly.

'Never mind, you leave this to me.'

Next day, Zollie asks Nate, Sinead, myself, Bilbo and Priscilla out to the Steak House. Poor Maybellyne refuses. She's doing so well with her diet she can't place herself in an occasion of sin. She thinks the steak fries there are 'to die for'. Although I sympathise, I wish she could come. She has been wonderful at showing Sinead round while I am on air, and Sinead seems to have really hit it off with her, and why wouldn't she? She has made Maybellyne promise that when she reaches her target weight she will start saving for a trip to Ireland. Maybellyne has always wanted to go there. Her great great grandparents were from Wexford. She has confided in me her touching but surreal notion of Ireland, one where the South is green and pleasant, full of leprechauns, pots of gold and cosy pubs teeming

163

with fiddlers and happy people drinking Guinness. But, on the other hand, the bit where I hail from, the top right hand corner of the country, she believes to be teeming with murderers, bombers and bigots. Actually, she might have a point there. She often asks me things like why we don't all escape 'down South'. She is worried I might go back and come to a bad end. I think I'm managing that here, actually.

Zollie says he will pick us up in the Cruzer so that we can relax and drink more. Priscilla is pleased to be included. She is my new best friend and is trying to assimilate me into the family. I can tell by the smell of the van that Zollie has had a joint, and as soon as we're on the road he cranks up the radio, lights another, and offers it to Nate and me. I still can't really smoke, and I feel self-conscious in front of Sinead, but I take a puff and Nate does too. Sinead refuses, though the smell is so strong she must be getting stoned anyway. Suddenly there is a loud bang like a gunshot. Everyone screams, except Zollie who starts to cackle like a madman. He has burst a large balloon filled with nitrous oxide, laughing gas. He has been to the dentist today – he probably traded it out, or robbed it. Within minutes we are all shaking and laughing uncontrollably. I am crying with laughter and feeling very out of control. Sinead is a bit dazed but is cackling away. I think I am about to burst a blood vessel. Nate is bright red and crying. None of us are in any condition to get mad at Zollie. He stops the car for what seems like an age and allows us to laugh it off, and fortunately it wears off quite quickly.

Finally our laughter subsides and we calm down. We are all somewhat confused. I am weak from laughing. I feel as if I have been tickled mercilessly, this is all I can compare it to, and I need to go to the bathroom soon, very soon. I may have wet the seat. I am glad it is not my car.

'What time is it?' I ask, thinking of Priscilla waiting at the restaurant.

Zollie pauses dramatically and grins at me. 'Early summer, baby, early summer.'

It is a demented thing for him to have done but it has certainly lightened Sinead up, probably killed off millions of her brain cells in the process. I expect her to be furious and start giving out to us all, but she doesn't say a word, just sits there smiling like an idiot, and when we get to the Steak House she is the liveliest I have seen her in years. It would not be an understatement to say she has fun, even if she does flirt with Nate all evening.

The rest of Sinead's visit just flies past. We are getting to know each other again. As far as possible she is having a good time. She thinks Nate is wonderful and she is just as gobsmacked as I am with all the trappings of wealth. We have been up to the big house, since Priscilla insisted on cooking dinner for us one night, and Sinead can't believe the paintings. She writes down all the names and titles. She finds a Kandinsky on the upstairs landing and is thrilled by it. I wish Nathan had been here for her, he would have loved to natter on about his art collection. Before they went on holiday he had just bought another Rothko, but it hasn't been hung yet.

Before Sinead is due to leave we decide to have dinner alone and talk about the wedding. It looks like Nate and I will get married in September, mainly because I would like us to go home for Christmas. It'll mean an awful lot of planning, but I'll have plenty of help. Priscilla has a sort of job in the family business – it isn't too demanding and she seems to have appointed herself as the wedding organiser. I am pleased, I can't be doing with lists and all that shit. She and Sinead have had loads of chats about it this past week. I hope I'm allowed to voice my opinion, or at least pick the dress, or maybe the lawyer has a load of old wedding dresses in another closet.

A few days later I help Sinead to pack. Her case is awful, so Zollie has got her a new one from Lenny's Luggage – I had to cut the commercial. She is delighted; it's a Samsonite, red plastic, and huge, just as well since she seems to have bought a present for everyone in Ireland. We talk a lot about Nate while she is packing. Sinead thinks it is a flaw in me that I am so impressed by looks. I can't help it though. She says she can't understand why I think it is so important that Nate is handsome, as long as he is a nice person. But I get pleasure from looking at him. He's tall, that makes me feel secure – I am small, or short, as they say here. I love the limpid blue of his eyes, and the whiteness of his teeth, and the way he dimples on one of his cheeks when he laughs. I don't think there's anything wrong with that. Sinead can marry some ugly bastard if she wants, I am certainly not going to. Sinead looks at me earnestly.

'You do love Nate, don't you, Maggie?'

'Of course, why are you asking?'

'No reason, just that you both seem very unpassionate.'

'Unpassionate? I'm not sure if that's a word.'

'You know what I mean, you're sort of calm when you're with him.'

'Isn't that good? That's how you know you want to marry someone.'

'Really?' She sounds unconvinced. I am not sure I like this conversation. I do want to marry Nate. I think back to the painful time without him, I think about the nuzzly bit at the back of his neck, I think of kissing him. He is such a good kisser. He has a melty mouth.

'I couldn't imagine life without him.'

'Good, Maggie, I hope he'll make you a good husband.' She pauses. 'Are you going to have babies?'

'Of course, but not till I'm about thirty.'

'Oh?'

'What do you mean, oh?'

'Just something Priscilla said about her daddy hoping you

two will start a family right away,' and she adds, 'are you leaving work?'

'Why would I leave work?'

'Well, you'll hardly need the money.'

'It's got nothing to do with money, I love my job, it's great fun, and I get to travel.' I tell her about all the rock concerts I've been to, and about the record conventions I will be going to. She appears unimpressed.

'Won't Nate be jealous of you going off to things like that?'

'How do you know what they're like?'

'I don't, but that launch party, I mean I know I was jet-lagged, but apart from Dave the drummer, they all seemed so . . .' She searches for the word, 'sordid.'

My heart sinks at her answer, but what did I expect? I thought they were fun, and the bloody party was dull compared to some rock parties. She hadn't liked Bob, probably because of the cocaine. She thought he was relentlessly repulsive.

'Well, I am not quitting my job, and that's it.'

'You should talk to Nate about it.'

'Maybe I will.'

I don't like this conversation. We finish our dinner and talk about home. Safer territory. Much safer.

17

I am utterly lost after Sinead leaves, and have a bad bout of homesickness. Nate tries to cheer me up by taking me to Atlanta for the weekend, where we have lots of stoned sex, which is consoling. We are getting good at it, the sex, yes we are definitely improving. I have discovered that you can sort of train men up to do what you enjoy by making the right sounds, sort of reinforcement grunts, and then next time you work on another bit. The cumulative effect is great fun.

Miz Beulah has crocheted me a bright pink bobble hat. It looks like a tea cosy. I wear it on the air and thank her. There is no way in hell I would wear it out, I'd get sectioned. She and Miz Zillah listen to my show every day, and have really got into Bob Seger, and a new group called Tom Petty and the Heartbreakers. Every Friday they come out to Delroy's Diner and have the smothered chicken, which they declare is as good as their own. Bilbo usually joins them and then they have the weekly tour of the station. Herman is still doing their hair. I expect he'll have them on the weed next, nothing surprises me any more.

Out of the blue, the Goodman Report call and ask me to appear on one of the women programmers panels at a record convention in Seattle as someone has dropped out. They are obviously desperate for people – there aren't too many of us women DJs. It is one of the smaller meetings. They will pay my fare and I will be there from Friday until Sunday night. I am unsure about going, but it would be good to see what these things are like, and for me to get to meet some of the record people I talk to several times a week. I have met the local guys at some of the rock concerts in Atlanta, but I speak to people from all over the country, and of course I have never been to Seattle. I ask Nate what he thinks and to my surprise he says I should go. He had been thinking of snatching another weekend's skiing, the last of the season, and there won't be much snow on the lower slopes so he is going to powder ski by helicopter. It sounds very impressive. He will be back Monday, same as me, so I call Goodman and agree. It's exciting.

Sue Lynne informs me that Buford has dropped by the station to leave some tickets for his next show. He gave her two. She thinks he is wonderful, so does ghastly Clarence Lee. They never miss a show. I hope we are not sitting beside them.

'I just love his voice,' she tells me with a sycophantic grin on her face. 'And my Lord! Have you heard his Elvis Tribute? It makes me cry my heart out.'

If you have one, I think, but I smile anyway and thank her for taking them for me. I have promised Buford we will go to hear him next time he is in town. I genuinely liked his show at the ski weekend in Alabama, even allowing for the gratitude we all felt at him saving our asses, but it isn't really my type of music.

While I'm away, Zollie is to split my shift with Steve, our new morning man. I leave for Seattle on the Thursday morning. It is quite far away and I have to change planes in Atlanta. I finally get there and check in, feeling somewhat awkward. It shouldn't be too intimidating as this is not one of the big ones, and I am only here because I am on a panel.

Record conventions are sheer babble. The noise level rarely

169

drops, especially in the lobby. I am issued with my badge and I put it on, *Maggie Lennon Q92*, and I blithely launch myself into the middle of the sea of faces. There are lots of thin smiling people who appear to know each other really well, though I suspect they really don't. I watch as people exclaim, hug each other in an unrealistic, over the top way, and give high fives and repeatedly ask each other 'Whenjageddin? Whennyaleavin?'

Several people look pointedly at my badge and ask me 'Which Q92?' I say 'Chattanooga, Tennessee,' and they say things like 'Not with that accent', or they mimic my voice. They are relentlessly friendly. Several of them seem to have heard of me. I guess Abe's tip sheet has quite a following. I wander about saying hello here and there, and before long I feel as if I have heard of all of them as well. They like my accent, they like that I'm a woman, but they seem confident and forward so it takes me a while to relax.

Rolly Young is here briefly. He looks like I expected a record guy to look – golden and confident. I run into him in the CBS suite and he acknowledges me with, 'Hey, the single is nearly platinum, way to go, babe!'

I am unsure what this means but I smile anyway.

'I'll be in touch. Before LA.'

Before LA? What's happening in LA? But he's gone before I can ask. Then there are meetings, and various forums on Arbitron ratings and demographics, which is all about finding out precisely who listens to your station so you can boost your ratings and make more money. Me, I think it should all be about the music.

I am sitting in one of these meetings, watching a panel of big-name jocks talk about their station and how they came to dominate the market, wondering vaguely if indeed it might all be, as we would put it in Belfast, a load of wank, when I hear the woman next to me mutter under her breath, 'Assholes, every last one of them'.

I turn around and she grins at me. I notice her teeth are very white. She has thick, black curly hair, freckles, and she wears little round granny glasses which make her blue eyes look huge. She is trim. She wears a T-shirt which says *Who do I fuck to get off this label?*. She grins at me again.

'Hey! I'm Lindy Konnig, I work for . . .' She mentions a well known VP of promotion. I introduce myself.

'Wow! I've heard of you, you broke "Dogs in the Moonlight" right under Rolly's nose job, didn't you? Boy, did you make him look like a dumb piece of shit.' She shrieks with laughter.

'I did? How?'

'You mean you don't know?'

'No, I don't. I thought it helped him. They told me last week it looks set to go platinum.' I toss the words out like I've always known what they meant. Lindy looks at me and laughs.

'You wanna get a sandwich?'

'Yes, I'd like that.'

We go to the lobby restaurant and order, and before I have finished lunch I have made a new friend and had my first real lesson on the business of rock 'n' roll from Lindy. I learn a lot. And she picks up the check. She insists.

'Always let the record person pick up the check.' She waves an American Express card at me. 'But never act grateful, it's a killer.'

I am grateful to Lindy though. I feel I know a bit more about what is 'coming down'. She is a New Yorker, a sharp, funny Jewish woman with a wicked sense of humour and a visible contempt for most of the men present. Rolly Young seems to feature high on her hit parade of assholes. I expect she is good at her job. We talk a lot about music and she says she will call me each week and send me stuff. She likes the idea that I listen to the songs before I add them and only add what I like. I am surprised that this is not the norm. Apparently some Music or Program Directors add what certain promotion men or 'Indies' tell them. She is amused when I describe Zollie and Bilbo and the station, and promises she will come in some time soon. She is so easy to talk to I tell her all about Nate. She is impressed but asks me my age. I tell her twenty-two and she says 'I guess that's okay for a first marriage.' I must look stricken because she immediately laughs and says 'Just kiddin', he sounds amazing.'

Seattle is a wonderful city; there is an amazing energy about it. Although we are mainly confined to the conference hotel, we do leave on the Saturday night to visit a wonderful fish restaurant. Bob has come and tries to 'hit on' me, twice, but in a sort of nice, affectionate way. I have just picked this expression up from Lindy. It means he fancies me. I am not interested though, well if I am even a little bit, I am not supposed to be, so I'm not. If I talk to a man for too long Lindy walks up and asks them if they have seen my *second best* engagement ring and sings 'Who wants to be a millionaire?'. I quite enjoy the attention from the men, though I know it is because of my accent mainly.

The Women in Radio and Records panel is the last one on Saturday, and I think I do okay. There are bigger names and bigger egos than mine, so on the strength of my accent I get away with a few interjections. I am glad when it is over. And then it's back to the station, and to Nate of course. He tells me the skiing was great and he certainly looks tanned and healthy. I feel awkward though, vulnerable, because he seems to be in a funny kind of mood again, and almost pulls his photos out of my hand when I look at them. I think there might be some girl in them, but it's mainly Nate and a buddy of his called Tommy on the slopes. But he cheers up quickly, and in a few days it appears we are back to our routine.

I am giving up my apartment and moving in with Nate. I won't do this until the end of July because I have paid the rent until then. I suppose it's practical, but I know I will feel sad leaving it. I have enjoyed my short bout of independence.

The wedding is going to be an awful lot of fuss, I can't really believe how much. We have decided on September 20th. It is settled that it will be at the Country Club, and not the Gilmore house. This, unfortunately, is because they are inviting half of America. This is my list:

Sinead, Aileen, Anna and Maeve – my four sisters

Mammy and Daddy

Sheila – my cousin from Canada who has loads of money and wants to come

Annie Mae, Zollie, Maybellyne, Bilbo and Sharla

Connie and Angelina – my two ex flatmates from Johnson City

Lindy

And that's it. We shall be outnumbered by the Gilmores' guests by about twenty to one. I am beginning to panic. We are now in the habit of having Sunday lunch on the mountain and Bitsy is on overdrive. She says I should have a wedding list, it is a list of things you would need to set up home. It makes no sense to me at all because Nate has everything that I could possibly want for a home in terms of 'things'. He has two TVs, food mixers, plates and salad bowls and endless towels and bed linen. But of course I agree, what else can I do?

Bitsy tells me where the 'lists' should be. One at Saks Fifth Avenue in Atlanta, and one at Millers in town. She twitters on endlessly about which pattern we will have on our dinner service, which silverware, and which crystal. Waterford is fine, she says, but Baccarat, which I thought was a card game until now, is better; not so tacky. Well thanks a lot, Bitsy. I'm sure I will never use crystal anyway. And here's the mental bit, I am having six bridesmaids. Jaysus! You'd think it was a royal wedding. I can't take it in. Six! I wanted just Sharla, but I got a strong hint from Nate that I should ask Priscilla as well. I am

173

happy to have Priscilla, she is sweet to me, and she is pretty, but I think they just want her to be bridesmaid so she can catch the bouquet and increase her chances of being the next bride. Bitsy is in a perpetual panic that Priscilla hasn't found a man, though Priscilla seems to be in no rush.

'Maggie, I presume you would like to ask your sistahs.' This is Bitsy at lunch last Sunday.

'Well, it might be awkward . . . I mean them not being here and that.'

'Nonsense, you can't possibly leave all those pretty babies out, they can send ovah the measurements and we'll have the dresses made.'

Numbly I agree and hope fervently none of the girls gain any weight at the last minute. I have to go to Atlanta again to get my dress and pick the material for the bridesmaids. My dress is to be bought, and Bitsy has a dressmaker there who can do alterations. Priscilla is to take me and we will stay at the apartment. Nate says I am to have whatever dress I want, he'll buy it, but I think it is unlucky to let the groom pay, isn't it? I have this insane recurring thought that I should send the whole thing up and get my dress traded-out from Mamie's Modes. I am sure they have some little number covered in sequins. Or maybe Miz Beulah can crochet me one, in acid lemon. But this is a passing insanity. Nonetheless, I am starting to feel queasy at the thought of it all. I wish we could just live together for a while first. If I hadn't screwed up my stupid visa all would be well – I know I definitely want to marry Nate, but it's all going too fast for me.

I try to remember what that theory from the Bible is about one moment changing your life, something about a mouse I think, or a leaf falling. It's something to do with fate. Well, it seems my fate is to be Mrs Nate Gilmore or, as I can be called here, Maggie Lennon Gilmore – I only know that because today Bitsy asks me if I want the towels monogrammed MLG in red or navy. I noticed Nathan roll his eyes and pour himself a large bourbon when she said this. I think he finds the whole thing as ridiculous as I do.

'Does your Daddy enjoy a drink, Maggie?'

'I think that is a distinct possibility,' I say, 'and not just one.'

Nathan laughs out loud, and his eyes crinkle like Nate's. 'I like you, Miz Maggie,' he says, 'Nate is a lucky man.'

Oh God, I hope he's right. Later I tell Nate that it all freaks me out.

'Baby, you can have the linen monogrammed with a marijuana leaf for all I care.'

I snuggle up to him, pleased he understands. 'I'd prefer that. At least it would be funny.'

'Just agree with her, baby, this is her project. It gives her something to do and keeps her from nagging Daddy.'

But wedding arrangements aside, I enjoy living here. Tennessee is beautiful in late spring. The trees are a froth of pink and white, a profusion of blossoms: magnolia, cherry and dogwood. Magnolia is my favourite; I have seen small ornamental magnolias at home in Ireland, but here they are full and blowsy, voluptuous, and the scent is intoxicating. Daffodils too seem to grow all over in Wordsworthian quantities. They call them jonquils here. The gardens in front of my apartment building are full of them, and Nate's parents' house is choked with them. They have a gardener who sees that the house is full of flowers, though Bitsy arranges them – she says it relaxes her. I expect it's the most energetic thing she does. I feel guilty that I haven't quite warmed to Bitsy, or she to me for that matter. I expect she would find it hard to be warm towards anyone who was going to take her only son from her. Maybe I am not trying hard enough, but she intimidates me, she makes me feel just that little bit too opportunistic, and that is wrong. But maybe she recognises something of herself in me, perhaps the fact that she wasn't exactly an heiress herself.

18

The station has settled down to a routine that is less manic than WA1A. Zollie is still trading-out like crazy, but he's selling some advertising too. I'm supposed to sell as well, but I've become complacent. I hate that bit of the job anyway, and I have slowly started to think of myself as rich by default. I can't help this, and underneath I feel uneasy about it. I wouldn't think of stopping working though, I love my job, it's great. I do the afternoon shift from twelve till three and am supposed to sell advertising in the afternoons when I come off air. I talk to the record companies and the trades in the mornings. We are heading into high summer now and I have lived in America almost a whole year. The skies here are blue and big and airy, not grey, heavy and sitting on my shoulders like they are at home. I tell myself this when I am feeling homesick. I have a theory that people are in good form all the time here because of the weather. Sunny skies must make for sunny personalities, because I do think that on the whole the people here couldn't be friendlier or nicer. It doesn't annoy me when people say 'Y'all come back', and 'Have a nice day', I don't care whether they mean it or not. And I love getting my groceries packed.

Sinead couldn't believe that bit. She's used to bunging everything into a carrier bag while the person behind's groceries are hurled on top of yours at ninety miles an hour.

Zollie comes in at the middle of my shift and wants to know if I would like a fish tank as a belated engagement present. He has one traded out from Aquatic Attic. It isn't an attic – I know this, because I have been there to pick up fish food for him – it's a modern, plain old store in a small development of shops. I guess the owner thought the name sounded good, but you'd expect it to at least have a pointy roof. I have given up on names of all kinds here. They specialise in weird. The other thing I can't quite get used to is the habit of spelling everything literally, like Krispy Kreme and Dunkin' Donuts, so you'd think everyone illiterate morons. My father would go crazy, he hates things like that.

The aquarium, do I want one? Apparently fish are very calming, and Zollie says they are amazing to look at when you're out of your head. I've seen him just sitting there spaced out, staring at the fish going round and round or up and down, whatever little multicoloured fish do. Maybellyne thinks it's a cute idea, and I am tempted. My apartment is sparse so an aquarium would look good. Aquatic Attic is out near the lake. I call Nate before I leave the station but he isn't there. I am not seeing him tonight since we were together all weekend and I usually have Monday nights at home.

Leroy, the guy at the fish shop, is very laid-back, really into fish. I want to pick them for colour and prettiness, but he explains that I have to choose compatible ones in case they eat each other. I am to have twelve to start with in the aquarium, and I choose some plants as well. It is big, about five feet across, and it has a stand. He will deliver it for me because it won't fit in my car, and he will set it up, all part of the service. I am delighted with it. Afterwards I think I may as well just call in and say hi to Nate if he is home as I am just a five-minute drive away. People don't tend to drop in here, it's different from Ireland that way, mainly because it's such a drive everywhere.

Nate is home because the Porsche is in the driveway. I don't have keys to his house so I go round the back. I call his name; no answer. I walk in through the kitchen to the living room, and then I hear something upstairs. I go up quietly, I don't know what makes me do that, but I suddenly feel uneasy. I don't know what I expected to see, but I certainly wasn't prepared for the sight of Nate and another man in bed together in an embrace. I recognise him as the guy from the ski photos, Tommy. They are both naked, it is warm, and the covers are pushed aside. As I enter Nate wheels round towards the door. I stand there rooted to the spot, unable to avert my eyes. The look on Nate's face is one of pure horror. Tommy, on the other hand, looks almost triumphant. I feel sick, my head is spinning, I can't speak. Finally I manage to say 'I was at Aquatic Attic, picking out the fish,' and then I turn on my heel and leave.

I hear Nate calling after me, 'Maggie, oh please, Maggie.' He sounds as if he is in pain. I don't care. I am in torment. I want to die.

I drive like a madwoman. I pay no attention to traffic lights or speed, but somehow I make it home alive, and without a speeding ticket. Once I get into the apartment I run to the bathroom and throw up. I wipe my face and go into the kitchen and pour a glass of water. I sit down on the settee. I can't stop trembling. What I am going to do? I can't think straight. Who can I talk to about this? Nate is homosexual, he must be, but he makes love to me, and he has had other women. And Tommy, I didn't even know he was in town. I thought he lived in Aspen. He must be Nate's boyfriend. It doesn't make any sense. I don't know very many homosexuals, it's not something I know a lot about.

Sharla will know about it, won't she? I dial her number. She is out. It is six o'clock. It's lunchtime in Ireland. Should I call Sinead? I can't. There's no one. No one at all. I can't face Zollie. I suppose I should have a drink, but I don't keep drink in the apartment, I suppose I really don't entertain much. I don't need any mind-altering drugs, my mind is altered enough. I can't even cry, I try to but it feels like I am faking it. I sob and heave and go through the motions but no tears come out. I have frozen. I try to clear my thoughts. What did I see? Two men, naked, in bed, in the middle of the day. There couldn't be any other explanation. They had to be doing it, having sex. I refuse to call it making love.

The doorbell rings. Unthinkingly I go to answer it. Nate is standing on the doorstep and I take one look at him and start to cry. My mind is split, I need someone to hold me so much, but he is the person who has caused my pain. Nonetheless, he is all I have right now. I fall into his arms, and we both cry together as if our hearts have broken. Eventually I stop, I can hardly see out of my eyes, but the cry has helped. Nate excuses himself and goes to the car. He comes back with a bottle of whisky.

'Did you bring that specially?' I can feel the acid thoughts curdling inside me. Hate and love are so close.

'No, I didn't bring it specially. I just remembered it was in the car.'

He gets two glasses and pours us each a large tumbler full. I am reminded of his father pouring me the drink at Christmas. I wait for him to speak. I am afraid that all my thoughts are too jumbled up and whatever I say will be the worst thing to say.

'Maggie, I am sorry. I am so very sorry. I hate that you saw us, and I hate that I did this to you.'

'Why is he in town?'

'He came to see me.'

'How long have you been lovers?'

'We aren't lovers.'

'Yes you are, I saw you.' I sound like a child.

He tells his story slowly, as if to understand it himself. He and Tommy had gone to college together and had been friends since day one. They dated girls who were best friends and played football for the college team. There are photos of this all over the place, I have seen them. At New Year in Aspen they were in the hot tub smoking a joint after everyone else had gone to bed when Tommy reached for Nate and kissed him on the mouth. Nate responded and felt confused and ashamed afterwards, but he had been stoned and excused it to himself as drug-fuelled craziness. I don't ask him what 'responded' means, I am hoping it just means he kissed him back.

'And did it happen again?'

'Yes, the night before I was due to come home.'

'Is that why you didn't call me?'

Of course it was. He had been confused and scared by the whole business. By the time he had put some distance between himself and Tommy, when his head cleared, he realised the episodes with Tommy had been madness. He missed me, he truly loved me.

I am shivering as I listen to this. He tells his story in a humble, wanting to be forgiven way. He looks dejected and he sounds wretched, but I can't feel it in me to console him. Tommy had arrived in town today unexpectedly because Nate refused to see him when he had been powder skiing and hadn't returned any of his calls since.

'But the photos?'

'They were from last time.'

I don't know if he's telling me the truth, but I let him talk. He tells me Tommy is really messed up on drugs and is threatening to kill himself. When he arrived today he was totally distraught. Nate tried to talk him down but somehow they had ended up in bed. He shrugs helplessly. But Nate wasn't

180

drunk or stoned or anything. He knew what he was doing. I can't begin to fathom it. Why bed? 'Couldn't you have just told him to go?'

'I should have, but he's my oldest friend and I feel guilty, and worse I feel ashamed, he keeps reminding me of the other times, and I am afraid to refuse him now. He has threatened to tell my daddy. It would kill my mother to hear I had been to bed with another man. Nathan would disinherit me.'

I am scared, really scared. My heart is pounding. What will happen now? All the stuff about the wedding. It is like a whirl-wind, out of control, unstoppable. I am mentally thinking of all the things we will have to undo. Due to Bitsy's grim deter-mination, there has been an engagement picture in *The Times*, and of course I have the two rings. There is little point in saying all of this because Nate knows it anyway, but I do: I say it all, over and over until I am exhausted, and to use a local phrase, all cried out.

'What are we going to do?'

'I love you, Maggie. I still want to marry you.'

'What about Tommy?'

'Tommy has gone.'

'For now.'

'No, I have told him I don't want to see him again.'

'Just say he does tell your parents? What if he does kill him-self?' Nate doesn't say anything. He just looks abject. 'Oh Nate, you have been to bed with him,' this is the scary bit, actually saying that out loud, 'I'm not sure I can marry someone who likes men like that.'

'I don't like men like that. I promise you, Maggie. It was just Tommy. I have never been with another man, just him, and only those times.'

I am not sure I believe him. I want to. But it is hard. I have no frame of reference for this. I guess I haven't been around enough.

'Are you going to tell anyone?' Nate's face is contorted with anxiety.

'Is that all that is worrying you?'

'No . . .'

'I have to talk to someone.'

'I saw someone when I got back in January.'

'What do you mean, someone?'

'I guess you could call her a counsellor.'

'I'd rather talk to a friend.'

'Will you tell Sinead?'

'No, I won't. Does Priscilla know?'

'I couldn't tell her, no way.'

He wants to spend the night, but I can't cope with it. It is now nine o'clock and all I have had since lunchtime is a large whisky. Ridiculous as it seems, I am starving. We phone for a pizza. We eat, and then he leaves. I look after the car as he drives off and I feel profound sadness. I can't handle all this alone. I try Sharla's number again. I get her roommate and leave a message to call me urgently, and I go to bed and lie awake unable to still my racing brain. I am still awake when Sharla phones at midnight. Calmly, I tell her the whole story. I hear my voice coming out flat and expressionless, like I was talking about someone I didn't know.

'You poor baby, this is just awful, I just wish I was there to give you a hug.'

Then I start to cry again.

'Honey, I can't believe it. Have you given him back the ring, I mean rings?'

'No. It didn't seem the right moment.'

'I'll be down tomorrow. This isn't something to talk about on the phone.'

'Are you sure?'

'Yep, I'll see you about six.'

I try to sleep after that, but when I get into work the next morning about an hour after my usual time, I look and feel like a ghost. Sue Lynne gives me a pile of pink message slips. I don't feel like returning a single call. I get through the day somehow, though Zollie calls once and sings the first line of 'Maggie May'. He always does that when I sound dismal. It certainly doesn't make me laugh today. Nate calls me twice. I ask him to leave me alone for a few days. I am still wearing my ring, the Tiffany one. Sue Lynne would spot immediately if I took it off. Maybellyne expresses concern that I look so bad but I tell her I'm having a bad period. She understands this; she has a condition called pre-menstrual tension and takes things for it. She offers me a pill. I take it, maybe it'll work for pre-possibly-cancelled-wedding tension.

Sharla and I are sitting in the Steak House at a window table. I watch my reflection pretending to eat a steak. Sharla thinks a meal will help, but all the pieces seem to stick in my throat and taste like paper. I chew slowly till it feels like pulp. I am drinking beer though. I have gone over everything that happened yesterday about twenty times. She has listened patiently. Sharla thinks Nate must be homosexual and repressing it. She thinks that is the reason he wants to marry so fast, so he can be 'cured'.

'But of course you can't cure 'em, honey. Some guys are just like that. They like to get it on with other guys.'

'I expect it isn't too popular in the South.'

'Hell no, homosexuals are more unpopular than black people. I tell you, they scare the shit out of all those rednecks.'

'Sharla, what do they do?'

'What do they do? Honey, what do you mean what do they do?'

'I mean, how do they have sex?'

Sharla looks at me as if my head is cut. 'Honey, I am not rightly sure, but I guess they might . . . are you sure you want to hear this?'

'Yes. I am. I feel stupid that I don't know. I suppose I've never thought about it before.'

So she explains. I can't really take it in. Sharla says Nate may be bisexual, and like to have sex with both boys and girls.

'He says it was only Tommy.'

'Honey, get real, maybe it *was* only Tommy until now, but later on he might meet another guy he would like to get it on with.'

'He says he won't.'

'Are you going to call off the wedding?'

'I'm not sure. I suppose I am, except it frightens me, y'know, telling everyone.'

'Well, honey, take ma word for it, you oughta. Just say you marry him and it doesn't work out? Think about it, a divorce if all of y'all have babies will be a whole bunch scarier.'

I know she's right but I am feeling overwhelmed thinking of all the people who will have to be told the wedding isn't going to happen. It would be easier to go ahead with it. Sharla leans on both elbows and faces me, looking concerned. I shrug.

'Listen, you don't have to give anyone a reason, you can just say you changed your mind, decided you were too young, whatever,' she continues. She finishes her steak and baked potato, and starts to pick at mine. I sit as if in a trance and watch her. I still don't know what I am going to do.

I don't notice then when Buford McConnell comes up behind me and bellows, 'Well if it ain't the purtiest Irish girl in Tennessee.'

Sharla lifts an eyebrow and I introduce them. She has heard about him from me, of course, but they have never met.

'What is that fiancé of yours doing letting you out on the town like this?'

'Girls' night out,' Sharla tells him.

'Well then, I'll go leave you two in peace. Real nice to meet you, Sharla, maybe we can have lunch some time soon, Maggie?'

184

'Yes,' I hear myself say. 'I'd like that. Call me tomorrow.'

'He's nice really,' I tell Sharla, 'even if he looks like a red-neck.'

'Hell, honey, I know rednecks can be nice. He has the hots for you though.'

'Pity he's not my type.'

'Yes, it is a pity, 'cos *then* you could . . .' Sharla strums an air guitar and sings in a mock country and western voice, 'let your love pour down on him like maple syrup.'

We both laugh, and for the first time I think that maybe I will survive the whole bloody mess.

It's hard to hold on to that thought the next day though. Sharla has gone back to Johnson City as she has a term paper to write, and I have an air shift to do. We talked last night till the early hours and I think I decided that I would call things off. But now I feel frightened again, as well as having a sore head from all the beer we drank. I don't want to shock the hell out of my family by telling them Nate is bisexual, because that's what Sharla and I have decided he is, or alternatively that he is queer and won't admit it. My father is always scathing, in that Irish homophobic way of his, about men who are 'light on their hooves'. He has accused both of my previous English boyfriends of this, mainly because they talked posh and he equates posh with effeminate. I can guess what his reaction to Nate would be and I was already worrying about my parents being intimidated by all the wealth. I am going to see Nate after work. It has occurred to me to call Priscilla, but I don't. I'm not sure just how close Nate and she are.

Before work this morning I went up to see Herman for a long-standing hair appointment and I felt such a fraud when he admired my ring. He has cut my hair and streaked it and restored my keratin with something that smelled of strawberries. He has bought two tiny dogs, little Yorkshire terriers called Rupert and Ringo. They are utterly ghastly. They sit on a blue

185

fur pouch thing and yap all the time. They look like long-haired rats. Herman says he intends to 'quaff' them himself.

I start giggling hysterically. He nods approvingly. 'Good dope?' I say yes, although I haven't had any. I don't want him to think I am laughing at him. He offers me a puff of his joint and for once I take it. I sit laughing non-stop while he does my hair. I laugh like a maniac. I am glad Herman thinks this is normal behaviour. He keeps saying things like 'Well, Maggie, you sure are in sunny form today,' and 'Boy you are one happy woman,' and finally when the tears are streaming down my face, he comes out with, 'That's right, laughter is the best medicine'.

It occurs to me that I might be losing my mind. This whole deal with Nate has pushed me over the edge. I haven't laughed this frantically since the time Zollie let the nitrous oxide out on Sinead. Herman gives me some shampoo samples and promises he will do my hair for free for the wedding. I hug him and leave, I am glad I didn't cancel the appointment, it sure makes a change from all the weeping and wailing.

I am wearing a really lovely blue silk shirt, which Nate bought me in Atlanta, and my new jeans and I have taken extra care over my eye make-up – I want to look good when I see Nate. I want him to know what he has thrown away. I have the other ring in my handbag. It probably would have fitted Tommy if it hadn't been altered for me. Tommy has long, thin fingers. I noticed them. He's not as pretty as Nate though. Sadly I can't think of anyone more beautiful right now. It is a disadvantage. I wish he repulsed me, but it's hard to hate someone on demand, at least when you're in love with them it is.

Nate seems sad, he compliments me on how I look and then almost starts to cry. I have said I will stay for dinner, but not for the night. He has the barbecue lit, and because I have told him I had steak last night he has bought some spare ribs, and silver queen corn, which he knows I love. I don't love it enough to make me happy though. I want it to be last week and erase everything.

I am glad spare ribs are nibbly things and no one checks how much of the actual meat you finish. I am desperately trying to eat, but I've got that awful block of unhappiness that sort of settles somewhere at the base of your throat and nothing can push it down, not even food. I am hungry, I know that because my tummy is rumbling, but I also feel hungry in a different way, for love I suppose. Christ, my thoughts are starting to sound like the lyrics to a bad country and western song.

Somehow Nate and I get through the evening. We postpone the wedding, or agree to. I expect that is easier than full on cancellation, it can become that when the great Bitsy wedding train has slowed down. I will allow him to say it was a mutual decision. In the meantime, the emerald ring will go back to the lawyer and I will continue to wear the Tiffany diamond. It has started to feel part of my finger anyway. Nate thinks he is on probation and if he keeps away from Tommy it will be okay, but both of us know that this is just a 'let me down easy' strategy, because he also tells me he wants me to keep the diamond as a present anyway and he's so glad he bought it for me, and then he cries again.

I am not used to seeing a man cry. It seems so heartrending. He looks too big and manly to be sobbing. His tears seem wetter than any tears I've seen. I want really everything to be okay, I want to kiss it better. I feel like his mammy. I gently refuse his request that I spend the night. 'Please, Maggie, please, just this once? I beg you. I promise I won't ask you again.' I am a sucker, I know. I am too far from home. I am in a foreign country and my boyfriend prefers men. But I stay and go to bed with him and have the best sex of our entire relationship. So when I leave next morning I am even more confused than ever. I want my mammy, although she would be utterly useless with this little 'problem'.

19

The station has a visitor, a surprise visitor for me. Sue Lynne hasn't fluffed up her hair and she has forgotten to prop up her little pointy tits, so it must be a woman. It is Lindy. Hallelujah, I believe in God!

'What are you doing here?'

'What a welcome! What am I, chopped liver?'

'I can't believe it!'

'I was in Nashville, and on my way by car to Atlanta so I thought, how about I give little Miss Maggie a call and surprise her. Bilbo here has been so kind and taken me over to Delroy's Diner for breakfast. He is such a doll.'

The doll looks enthralled at the compliment and says, sheepishly, 'It was a real pleasure to be able to do something for such a nice lady.'

To his embarrassment Lindy hugs him, then she turns to me. 'So, what time is this to get into work? We rang your apartment over an hour ago and you had left.'

'I stayed at Nate's.'

'Told you,' Sue Lynne nods satisfied. 'I done got it raaght. She cain't stay away from him.'

I smile grimly and motion to Lindy to come into the office. 'Can you spend the night?'

'Yes ma'am, I intend to. I've booked into the Hilton and you and I are going for dinner. I want to meet Mr Two Rings, your friendly millionaire.'

I say nothing. I feel as if Sue Lynne has the place bugged, but Lindy has to go visit the other stations in town and we arrange that she will meet me after my shift. I am so happy she is here. She is sophisticated and will know what to do. It had occurred to me to call her before now but I was unsure, but fate meant her to know, otherwise why would she land on my doorstep without warning?

Lindy is unequivocal when I recount it all to her over some amazing wine in the restaurant, later. 'Honey, you need to get out, and fast. He sounds mixed up as hell.'

'But I love him.'

'Hell, I love him, who wouldn't love a young, good-looking millionaire?' She has seen photos of him.

'It's going to be crazy cancelling everything.'

'That's an excuse and you know it.'

'I'll have to leave the States. I haven't a visa to get back in, except on holiday, and I want to see my parents and my sisters.'

'So you were only marrying him for a Green Card?'

'A Green Card?'

'Yes, isn't that what you need to stay here? You know, some sharp lawyer can get you one for a couple of thousand dollars. Cheaper than a divorce later on.'

'No, I love him. Do you think he might be queer?'

'Well, having sex with another guy is a bit of a giveaway.'

I tell her about last night and she hears me out, but she thinks that even if he is bisexual I may not be able to cope with it, I haven't lived enough. She says that she had already figured I am not ready to settle down yet.

189

'Face it, honey, you were dying to screw Bob Templeman at the Seattle gig.'

'I didn't though.'

'I know you didn't, but you two were hanging out of each other like you were gagging for it.'

I feel slightly miffed at this. I thought I had been friendly but not overtly so. People here frequently mistake Irish friendliness for sexual interest. It can be off-putting. The whole country, or at least all the guys in the record business, think everyone is permanently ready for sex. It pisses me off. But maybe Lindy has a point about Bob. I tell her it's just because I know him better than any of the others and therefore I feel more at ease with him.

'Well, it looked like steam was coming out of his ears when you were together. You might need to see a bit of life before you settle down. Marriage USA-style can be a tough business.'

She could be right. I had indeed flirted with Bob, but I was a secure engaged woman then. Not a poor jilted immigrant.

Before Lindy leaves for Atlanta she talks me into taking off my ring. She says it will be more honest, and give me time to clear my head, sort out my feelings. I know Nate will refuse to take it back, so I bring the ring to the bank and they keep it for me. They give me a key to a little box in the back, just like in the movies. It looks lonely sitting in its little box on its own, but I have nothing else of value to put in with it.

Now that I'm not getting married and not seeing Nate I need to earn more money. I suppose I will have to start to sell advertising. I never feel more Irish than when I have to go into a shop and start expounding about the benefits of advertising on Q92. Americans are so good at that sort of thing, they don't seem to have the squirm factor. They are so openly enthusiastic about things and love selling. Leroy, the fish guy, is a fine example of American enthusiasm. He has delivered and installed my fish tank. Even though Leroy wasn't making a sale, he spent the hour or so it took to set it up raving on about how fish would change my life. They have already. If it hadn't been for the bloody fish I'd still be engaged.

And I love them, a tank full of lovely little darting rainbows, little angel fish, tiger-fish guppies. It is soporific but calming, better than a TV. Still, I might get one of those next, even though apart from *Saturday Night Live* I think American TV is awful. It would give me something to do in the evenings. I am desperately trying to fill the emptiness in my life, but every day I wake up and I haven't died of a broken heart.

It has been two weeks now, and though I've talked to Nate on the phone, I haven't seen him. I haven't been out much, otherwise I probably would have bumped into him. Priscilla phones and asks if I will go for lunch. I say I will, but we haven't fixed a date yet. I am dreading it really. What will I tell her? More to the point, what has Nate told them? I expect they think I'm some kind of awful bitch.

My parents are surprisingly calm when I tell them I am postponing the wedding. I think they felt we were rushing things. My sisters are merely pissed off that they aren't getting a trip to the USA. My mother wants me to come straight home, but I tell her I want to fix up a visa before I do. I don't want to give up the possibility of staying here, not yet. There's something about the place, for all its flaws, that quite seduces me. I don't feel so circumscribed, and I feel like I've been given absolution to reinvent myself, to act out impulses I've always sat on, and I like being relatively unknown. Sometimes people recognise my voice – at the gas station, they'll say something like 'You're her, ain't you? The girl who talks funny on the radio?'. But mostly I have a sort of blissful anonymity. And I don't have to wake up to the news of some ghastly sectarian atrocity each day. Sometimes these make the front page of the newspaper here, but mostly they are consigned to a small paragraph down the side of one of the inside pages. I like that. It may be cowardly of me, but it means I don't have to face it all.

20

We're going to Buford's concert, the Maple Syrup Tour. We are promoting it on air even though it's a country gig; God knows what sort of deal Zollie has done with Buford, they seem to have become very pally. I am going to be Bilbo's date. Zollie has some lady friend we are all to meet for the first time. Her name is Shirley, he calls her squirrelly Shirley. Steve, the new DJ, is coming, and of course Sue Lynne and Clarence Lee.

We meet at Zollie's apartment, which is in the same building as mine, and have beer and dips 'n' chips before we go. Zollie also has several drugs to hand. I smoke some dope and pass on the others. Bilbo is driving the Black Box so the rest of us can partake. Shirley is lovely and seems quite taken with Zollie. For some reason, Sue Lynne seems pissed off about this. Clarence is sitting clamped to her, she a vision in pale green polyester, he in light tan. Each time he moves I can hear the crackle of the static, but the dope has made me relaxed and I can cope. I must have been too friendly to her, because when we go to the loo on the way into the concert, she confides in me that Clarence is saving some money so he can buy her a boob job for her birthday. She has to explain what this means. It appears he doesn't think her breasts are big enough – he thinks Dolly Parton the ideal woman – and so she will have silicon implants inserted and end up with a super-large chest. I almost feel sorry for her.

When we worked in Daytona there was a waitress in the next door restaurant who had simply enormous boobs. She used to win the wet T-shirt contest at the Pink Pussycat night-club every week. Maureen and Patricia were horrified when they heard this, and so was I. It seemed a bit cheap to us. I expect we all felt morally superior. I was in the loo one night when she came in, and I must have been staring at her in the mirror, when she came over to me.

'Hi, my name is Estelle.'

'Hello, I'm Maggie Lennon, I work next door.'

'I know. I can see you're staring at my boobs.'

'No,' I stammered, 'I'm not.'

'It's okay, I don't mind, I'm used to it. But I've been entering the wet T-shirt contest every week and winning, did you know that?'

'Yes, I did.'

'Well, I have almost saved enough to get a breast reduction when I go home to Cleveland. It's been tough, it isn't easy being a freak. I just want to be like everyone else.'

I looked at her and she seemed on the verge of tears. I felt ashamed that we had all been so quick to judge her. She and I always waved at each other and said hello after that. I am thinking about Estelle when Sue Lynne confides in me. Well, whatever gets you through the night, I think. But I sort of feel sorry for Sue Lynne that she feels it is necessary, and to keep Clarence of all people?

There's a completely different feel to a country and western concert, I find. The crowd seems much more good-natured. It doesn't have the same raw sexual energy about it that a rock concert does. I'd guess quite a few of the audience have smoked a bit of dope, but beer is the drug of choice. They also know all the words to all the songs, and Buford is their main man. They are beside themselves when he sings 'Maple Syrup'. I reappraise him, perhaps I have been a bit harsh on him, he has been kind to me and he most certainly has presence and a way with the crowd – he seems totally different on a big stage with an appreciative audience. When he sings 'Your Cheatin' Heart' I find myself singing along lustily and imagine I am serenading Nate. It is cathartic.

We have backstage passes with *access all areas*, which means we can watch the concert from the wings. We decide to do this. I am getting used to these passes, having had them for Bob Seger, Fleetwood Mac, and a few of the bigger rock groups. It's bullshit, but it gives one a feeling of self-importance, even if in reality the show is best viewed from the auditorium. The truth is that backstage most of the rock groups are burned out from meeting fans, and only say hello and pose for photos out of obligation to the record companies.

Buford is different. He virtually ignores everyone backstage, true fans included, to make a fuss of me, and despite myself I am flattered. Sue Lynne is trying hard to get his attention, pushing her big hair back and wittering on about how he has just 'blown her clean away'. I wish he would.

'Why, Clarence Lee remarked on the tears running down my cheeks during your tribute to the King, didn't you, baby doll?'

Clarence nods dutifully. 'You done broke her heart. I wiped her eyes throughout.'

But old Buford virtually ignores her and persists in raving on about this wonderful Irish woman, and hugging me like we're the best of chums. 'Isn't she a honey?' he says happily, with his arm round me. I try to free myself from his grasp since he is just a bit sweaty from his performance, but I continue to smile moronically, after all I am fairly stoned. Poor Sue Lynne, I bet she feels like puking and I couldn't blame her, so do I. On the other hand it is nice to be appreciated. It's a distraction and I couldn't have enough of these at the moment.

We all go back to the band's hotel, even Bilbo who is the only one who hasn't been chemically altered. Zollie and Shirley are flying, God only knows what they are on, but she is certainly behaving like squirrelly Shirley. Since I need to ride home with Zollie later I hope they come down off the cloud soon, because Americans aren't into taxis outside New York, and I don't want to be stranded in town. I tell Zollie this and regret it, since he breaks into a chorus of 'Stranded in a Limousine', which he keeps up till we arrive at the Hilton. Sometimes I could choke him, but he has been sweet about my 'postponed' engagement and offered to pay for my family to come out to see me regardless, or as he puts it, 'irregardless'. I have refused, of course, but I appreciate the offer all the same.

The 'down home' country and western guys are not too down home to appreciate their drugs. An ounce of coke is tipped out on the glass coffee table in the suite in the hotel room. I certainly don't want to give Sue Lynne any ammunition, so even though I wouldn't mind a little pop I refuse to do any. She and Clarence refuse piously. I am glad about that too, the idea of Clarence on a coke high going into his shift at the nuclear power plant is not a relaxing one. Zollie and Shirley have no such qualms. The bass guitarist is busy chopping it up to spell *sex and drugs and rock'n'roll*. I suppose sex 'n' drugs 'n' country doesn't have quite the same ring to it. The mood is one of reckless hilarity; I think Zollie and Buford bring out the worst in each other. They are competing line for line. Buford orders champagne and then, to cheers and catcalls, a razor blade from room service as, apparently the coke is too lumpy. I think everyone is flabbergasted when it arrives.

Pretty soon the decibel level has risen dramatically and

everyone is talking at each other animatedly about nothing in particular. They all look like characters in a Hieronymus Bosch painting. The three girls in the room, I am unsure who they are with, are giggling like fools; they eventually siphon off to nearby rooms with various band members. I'd love to go home, but it looks unlikely for a while. I am tempted to call Nate, I miss him so much. The dreaded throat lump is back, it won't shift.

What does it matter that he made love to Tommy? I want him now. Finally, Sue Lynne and Clarence can't take any more of the madness and make their excuses. Soon there are only Shirley, Zollie, Bilbo, Buford and me. I give in and do a few lines and get an energy rush. I feel churned up inside still but I start chatting to Buford and he is really quite sweet. He seems really interested in Ireland and my family. Eventually in an effort to slow down we smoke a joint and I find myself telling him about my engagement being off. I don't tell him the reason, in fact I unintentionally give him the impression that Nate has another woman. Zollie and Shirley are not driving me home. They are totally wasted and poor old Bilbo has fallen asleep. We talk for hours, and somehow by the end of the night I find myself agreeing to think over Buford's proposal to marry me so I can get a Green Card.

'Way I see it is this,' he tells me, 'I'd just be helping out a friend. You could go home for a vacation, and you'd have no problems getting back into the country and staying.'

I point out that he has been married three times already. My parents would die. They are strict Catholics.

'Why would you feel the need to tell them? It can be our secret. It can be simply a favour for a friend.'

'It's really sweet of you, but I couldn't let you do that.'

'It would be an honour for me to help out, and then if Nate and you get back together, you guys won't feel no need to rush things. I guess that's what fucked things up for y'all.'

If only he knew the real reason. It's hard for me to keep up the front, but I have promised Nate I will. The truth is I'm too embarrassed to explain it to people anyway. I'm sure his parents just think it's all my fault. I still haven't had lunch with Priscilla, I've been unable to face her.

This idea of having an arranged marriage to get a Green Card sort of sticks in my brain, apparently it's common enough. I do nothing about it, of course, except talk it over with both Sharla and Lindy, who think why not? As Lindy says, 'Make sure it's just a business deal, pay him something, a token.'

Nate and I meet for lunch again and I still can't swallow a bite. He remarks on how thin I am. He's right, I am too thin, there's nothing like pining to take off the pounds. I still love him. I always had a fantasy of what my husband would look like and sound like, and I always had a thing about men with crinkles at the side of their eyes from laughing. He still has those, but his eyes are haunted. I want to rush out of the restaurant and straight out to his house and fall into bed beside him. I want the warmth and closeness of another human being. But there is a stiffness between us, a sort of new formality. I wish I could be sure that I will fall for someone else sometime, but right now it seems impossible. I tell him about Buford's offer.

'I'll marry you,' he says immediately. 'We can go to Las Vegas and do it, we needn't tell my folks.'

'I couldn't marry you, that would mean something. It has to be meaningless.'

'I still love you, Maggie.'

I say nothing, I want to cry. I gulp my water – I have no show on Saturday but I am driving. I wish I had let him pick me up as he had suggested, so I could numb myself with drink. We talk in circles about nothing. What is there left to say?

'Oh Maggie,' he says at one point, 'what will become of us?'

'Have you talked to Tommy?' He is silent. I feel stung. 'You have, haven't you?'

'He's been calling a lot and I guess I got fed up hanging up on him.'

'Are you seeing him again?'

'I have no plans.'

'That's not what I asked you.' I stand up, almost knocking over the chair. 'I need to go,' I tell him. Suddenly I am white with rage. I have to get out of the restaurant before I throw something at him. I hate this passive side of Nate. He's going to let it all just happen to him. He'll let Tommy have him, make him like that all the time, ruin his life. I hate Tommy. I hate Nate Gilmore. I wish I'd never met him.

21

I go into work earlier each day now because it is something to do. It stops me brooding. I am slightly worried that taking a Quaalude every night is not ideal, but I have a prescription for them from a really lovely doctor friend of Zollie's who thinks that if they are not abused they are a good aid to sleeping – he does warn me not to get dependent and to take a half instead of a whole one. I do wish I had enough 'backbone', as the nuns used to say, to get through this emotional mael-strom without the props, but I seem to be on some sort of treadmill, and haven't found the stop button.

Monday morning, I am just in the door when Bilbo tells me there is a call for me, someone from Shine Records is on the line. I rush into the office and grab the phone. It is Rolly Young. I try to sound casual.

'Hey babe, Rolly Young here, just wanted to let you know that "Dogs in the Moonlight" has just gone platinum, and Shine would like to present you with your platinum disc in LA the weekend after next. Jimmy Farrell will be over from London. Okay?'

'Oh, that's brilliant,' I say. 'I am really delighted.' God why do I sound so gauche! He doesn't seem to notice though.

'Cool. Glad you can make it. I'll have my assistant book a hotel and flights for you and there'll be a limo to meet you. I'll be there myself. We'll party, okay? Oh, my assistant is Jude, she'll call you. Later, babe.' He hangs up.

All thoughts of Nate recede, slightly, I am ecstatic. Zollie is thrilled too, not so much for me as for the station.

'Sheeeit, Maggie, this could put us on the map, we could get reporting status with *Gavin*, *Billboard* . . . and we could get us some bigass publicity outa this.' He thinks for a moment. 'Wait, let me call Ed, he needs to do another feature on you.'

'No, Zollie, he doesn't. Besides, I haven't had the platinum record yet.'

'You do know, Maggie, that the record will belong to the station.'

'What do you mean?'

'Well, the station played the record. It gits the reward.'

'I played the record. My sister sent it to me. You didn't want me to add it to the playlist, remember?'

'I don't recall stopping you, Maggie.'

'No, but you tried to.'

'Listen, Maggie, stations get gold and platinum records, people don't.'

'Fine, let's wait till it happens.' I am not in the mood to argue with him. But my jollity is ebbing away.

Somehow the rest of the week passes. Rolly's assistant, Jude, calls and takes all the details, apparently this presentation will take place the last night of a radio and records convention. She asks me if I am coming early for that. I say I am not sure, I will speak to Zollie. Zollie is thrilled for me to go for the convention, and seeing as my fare to LA and accommodation is being paid he will fork out for the registration fee. He thinks it will do me good, get me a high profile and above all help Q92. He is eloquent about all the possible giveaways we can scam from the record companies.

Maybellyne is also encouraging. 'This is just what y'all need, honey. You go and meet you a nice boy. I plan to visit LA sometime, I bet it's real glamorous.' Poor Maybellyne. I have her tortured with all my stuff about Nate, and I still haven't told her the real reason. I form the words sometimes but the sound doesn't catch up with them. Nate is homosexual. It makes me feel I am lacking something somehow. Surely I could have done something to fix him? What is wrong with me? Say I had been better in bed? If I was sexier? If I had known more 'things'. Would that have helped?

Next day I call Jude and tell her I will be there for the full four days. She says my tickets will be at the airport. I can't really feel any sense of anticipation. I play 'Ob-la-di Ob-la-da' on the air. I hope Nate is listening. I play Bob Seger 'Still the Same', I play 'You're so Vain', twice. Then I call and register for the record convention. In spite of myself I am beginning to feel excited. I am happening, I tell myself. I am happening.

And then it is time to go. I have spoken to several of my local guys from different labels and they will all be there, and Bob will of course, and Tom and all my new best friends from Seattle. LA, just imagine. Hollywood. I have always wanted to go to California.

I'm booked on an early morning flight and so I will be in LA by lunchtime. I get on the plane and can't find my seat. My ticket says row two, but there is no row two. I am just attempting to eject a fat woman in the second row which is inexplicably called row six, when the stewardess comes to my rescue. 'Ya'll are in first class honey,' she tells me, and leads me out of the economy section, through the curtain, sits me down, and serves me a glass of champagne. The seat is leather, wide and comfortable. I sit back and look out the window. I am happy.

I am met at LAX the other end, by a man with a big sign

on a stick saying *MAGGIE LENNON*. He takes my luggage tickets from me and I am whisked away to a waiting limo, which I roll around in, it seems so over the top and unnecessary but I guess by now I'm sort of expecting the weekend to be like this. It is warm and balmy in LA and I gaze in awe through the darkened windows of the limo at the brightness outside as we cruise along the wide streets with familiar names like La Cienaga, and Sunset. There are tall, soaring palm trees, the cover of *Hotel California* made flesh. Finally we stop outside a large, plush hotel in Beverly Hills. The limo driver ushers me into the lobby and puts my bags down. He indicates that I should check in, says goodbye, and leaves.

I feel completely overwhelmed, and slightly nervous that there may be some mistake and I'll be asked for money. I have got some dollars with me, but I don't have a credit card. Then I see Lindy in the lobby talking to a few guys. She breaks away immediately, rushes over and hugs me.

'Hey babe, you look great! It's so good to see you.'

She is completely at home. She marches me up to reception with a wide smile and her insouciance is infectious. I take my lead from her and tell the girl on the desk, as instructed, that I am Maggie Lennon and I am a guest of Shine Records. I am rewarded with a large 'Welcome to LA,' accompanied by an even larger sycophantic beam. Money isn't mentioned, and within seconds a bell hop takes my bags and brings me to a room on the top floor. Lindy tips him a five-dollar bill. There is the slightest hesitation as he checks the denomination, then he closes the door and leaves.

'You look fantastic,' Lindy tells me.

'I feel awful.'

'Hey? Stop that, Maggie May. You're in la-la land now and you're gonna have fun. Okay?'

I nod. 'I hope so.'

'Look, he's a schmuck. Get over him, you're gorgeous. Do

you need to shower?' I nod again. 'Right, I'll see you in the lobby bar in twenty minutes.' And she leaves.

I look at the room. It is like being in the movies, it is so posh. I have never stayed in a five-star hotel before. The room in Seattle was nothing like this; there are two sofas, occasional tables and a bed the size of a football pitch. On the table near the window there are flowers and beside them, chilling in an ice bucket, a bottle of Dom Perignon champagne. I suddenly notice a card that has my name on it. *Welcome to LA, Maggie. Rolly Young, Shine Records.* Life is sweet.

I push all thoughts of Nate to the back of my mind as I pull out a change of jeans and a clean T-shirt and throw them on the bed. Then I take a shower. I am just finishing dressing when the phone rings and it is Rolly Young. He is in a suite on the same floor as me and asks if I would like to join him for drinks about six. A limo will be picking us up at seven; we are going to dinner first and then catching Jimmy Farrell in concert at the Roxy. I am feeling a bit tired now, but I guess the excitement will help me keep going. But first I go down to meet Lindy. I need a cup of coffee.

Promptly at six I arrive in Rolly Young's suite. I feel somewhat overawed. It is massive, and full of record people, local DJs, promotion men, and West Coast types. I am introduced to all of them but I barely recall one name. I see Tom, my local guy, and greet him like we are best friends. He seems as ill at ease here as I do. He comes and joins me on one of the many settees. Tom is from South Carolina, quite a down home type, and he seems in awe of Rolly Young, who is smiling and grinning like a fool, looking cool and Hollywood. I sit beside Tom and pretend to be part of the party. I notice they all go in and out of the bathroom a lot. They talk and chatter a lot, but no one seems to be listening to anyone else. We drink Dom Perignon, which reminds me of Nate. Eventually I need to pee. I move to go into the bathroom.

Rolly notices me going in. 'Be sure and powder your nose, baby,' he says.

I am slightly embarrassed; is my nose red or what? Then, while washing my hands, I notice a little glass dish, like my Auntie Martha's salt dish, sitting on top of the vanity. It is full of white powder. There is a tiny little silver spoon in it. It surely couldn't be coke? There is far too much. I know coke comes in grammes. I dip my finger in it and lick it. It makes my tongue numb at once. Yes, it is coke. Oh! I suddenly get it. This is what he means by powdering my nose. I forget that I have told myself I am giving up drugs. I take a spoonful, and snort it. I am not sure if this is okay, but this is what Rolly meant, isn't it? How could anyone notice a spoonful gone anyway, I reason, so I take another. Immediately, it seems, my tiredness goes. I feel cool, part of the jet set. I am flying. I come out and Rolly nods towards me.

'You get some, babe?'

'Yes, thank you. I got some.' I am not sure what to call it. Zollie's term, Colombian marching powder, doesn't seem appropriate – do they refer to it as 'tootski'?

'Good, anytime, babe, feel free.'

Lindy comes in, she is with her boss who is obviously a buddy of Rolly's, but she leaves him and comes and sits beside me. I feel better at once. I whisper to her about the coke.

'I'll take a rain check.'

'Oh?'

'Yeah, maybe before we leave. It freaks me out doll, makes me run my mouth.'

The whole deal of being in Los Angeles, and in such a hotel, is what freaks me out. Emboldened now by the coke I look around the room. Apart from two bored-looking model types, there are mostly men in the room. One of them is nice though, his name is Mark. He is quiet and asks me lots of intelligent questions about Ireland. He finds my accent cute. He also, I

205

notice, doesn't 'need to pee' every ten minutes. He is a promotion man for Shine. He works out of Chicago, and like most of the others he has 'come in' for the convention. He doesn't say as much, but I can tell he isn't really a fan of Rolly's. I tell him who I am, and surprisingly he has heard of me and he is extremely complimentary about 'Dogs in the Moonlight', and the fact that I added it without being asked. He asks me how that came about and seems impressed when I explain about Sinead sending it and tell him I talk directly to Abe Goodman, the boss, each week. He says Goodman gives an Ear of the Year award at the convention and that I am nominated, and maybe I will win. He gets me a copy of the convention special of *Sounds Around*, Goodman's tip sheet, and there is my name plain as can be. I can hardly contain my delight. I notice all the other nominees are from places like Minneapolis, Atlanta and Chicago, but at least my name is there.

We don't get the chance to talk much more as a flurry of limos pick us all up to go to dinner. We end up in some impossibly chic restaurant, but no one has any appetite, except Mark. I know by now that this is a side effect of the coke. It seems so wasteful though, all that expensive food ordered and not eaten; my mother would have a fit. I try to push all thoughts of home out of my head and copy the others while they all rearrange the contents of their plates and drink more champagne. Rolly presses a vial into my hand at one stage, and asks me if I want to freshen up. I do. Everyone else does. It seems most people spend more time going to the loo than eating. Eventually we are herded once more into limos and we arrive at the Roxy. The Roxy! I think of all the groups that played here, The Byrds, The Eagles, Jackson Browne.

I am high, flying, I feel like a rock star. I stay as close to Mark as I can. The concert passes in a mad buzz of music and a haze of champagne and cocaine. Afterwards, we are lined up like school kids and given sticky patches to wear that will enable us to go backstage to meet Jimmy Farrell. He is from Glasgow and seems either shy or bored. Rolly is effusive with him and when it is my turn to meet him he keeps telling him I was the person 'who broke the record wide open'. I nod as if I know what this means. Jimmy doesn't seem to know what it means either. I start to tell him my sister Sinead sent it to me from Belfast when Rolly stops me and tells Jimmy he was 'blown away' by it the very second he heard it, and my enthusiasm only made him work it all the harder. I am appalled that poor Sinead's amazing effort at spotting hits is so cruelly swept away, but before I can utter a word of protest, I am moved along the reception line and Rolly is gushing on about something else to Jimmy. Mark is behind me, I whisper to him 'That's not true, Rolly hadn't even heard of "Dogs in the Moonlight" when I called him.'

Mark smiles at me and tells me I will soon learn that the truth has nothing to do with anything in this business. 'And Rolly is *always* the star, baby, you'd better get used to it.'

I don't really care; I can now see that Jimmy Farrell is regarding them all with something close to contempt on his face. Despite their pleading, he is unapologetic; he won't be coming back to the hotel tonight. He will see us tomorrow night. The crowd disperses. Outside, the line of limos await, but I have other lines in mind. I am feeling tired now, and I want to get back to the suite for some more toot. I sit in a daze in the back of the limo on the way home to the hotel.

I feel lonely. Mark has been attentive, and pleasant, but in that almost imperceptible way I think we have both worked out there is no sexual chemistry. He says he is tired and goes to his room, so I go up to the suite alone. The noise level has been jacked up a few notches and there are several more girls, sullen, louche, confident-looking women. I look for Lindy but she has gone. Back at the room my phone is blinking; there is a message from her saying she will see me for breakfast. Paranoia

207

sets in – here I am, my first visit to California, and I am high, alone, and lonely. I think of calling Ireland but I am unsure how much this will cost and decide not to. I would only start blubbing anyway, and then they would think I wasn't having a good time, and I am, am I not?

22

All this chat of Mark's about my possible win has made me self-conscious about my outfit, that it is maybe too Mamie's Modes and not Rodeo Drive enough. The uniform throughout the convention has been jeans and whatever promotional T-shirt you fancy, but apparently this bit is dressy. Lindy comes to the rescue. She thinks we should go to Rodeo Drive to Neiman Marcus and search there. She also suggests that the station should pay for it. I somehow can't imagine Zollie doing a trade-out with Neiman Marcus, but to my surprise when I call him (collect) he agrees to pay half, and says that if I do win, he will pay all, just keep the receipt. I choose a black silk strappy thing with tiny outlines of coloured squares. It is impossibly expensive but it looks the best so I buy it, on Lindy's card. I can't believe Lindy trusts me this much.

In the lobby of the hotel we meet Bob, my smooth-talking, good-looking friend from Atlanta. He is all smiles when he hears we have been shopping. He tells me I am at his table and I am surprised at how relaxed I feel with him after our last meeting in Seattle. I go to my room to get into my gear for the evening. Bob calls and asks if I want him to stop by with some toot, I say yes. It is like fuel for these things, you feel so out of kilter with everyone else without it. I hope I am not getting dependent.

The room is buzzing. We have just watched a new 'hot' group called Sammy and the Mainliners perform their latest offering. Each conference, one or other of the record labels takes it in turn to introduce some new act, hoping of course to break them wide open. Shine is hosting tonight's entertainment. Rolly Young is sitting at the table next to mine looking satisfied with himself. I am beside Tom, Bob and some people I don't know. Afterwards, Jimmy Farrell is to sing 'Dogs in the Moonlight', and then I am to get my platinum disc presented, of course, by Jimmy. I am very nervous. I hope I don't have to speak in case my voice goes weird. Being on the radio is different, you can fool yourself into thinking you are alone, or that no one is really listening. Then suddenly I am up on stage, everyone is clapping and cheering and Jimmy is giving me the disc. It is framed like a picture, it says *Presented to Maggie Lennon for sales of over 1,000,000 records.*

Bob and I sneak out up to his room and do more toot, he wants to do more than toot but I am wearing an expensive dress.

'You're funny,' he says. 'Everyone loved you. You're hot, baby.'

I think it is probably good to be hot, for now anyway. We get back down just as the nominations for my award start. I want to win now, badly. It seems crazy really because two days ago I didn't even know I was nominated. I am certainly getting competitive. I catch Lindy's eye, she is seated at the table next to us. She winks broadly and crosses her fingers.

'And the winner is from Q92 Chattanooga via Ireland, Miss Maggie Lennon.'

I think I am going to faint, but I get up and smile and wobble my way up through a sea of hands to the stage. It feels like the Oscars, and I suppose it is in a way. Abe Goodman, who is surprisingly not much taller than me and like a little leprechaun, hugs me and tells the audience how I was a girl with attitude, I was the sort of programmer they needed in the business, then he hands me the mike. Oh God I feel sick, but I smile even wider and open my mouth.

'Thank you all for voting for me. I can't believe I've won this. Thank you, Abe, for your support.' Abe beams from the front row. 'And I'd like to thank Lindy Konnig for lending me the money to buy this dress. It's such a pity Neiman's don't do trade-outs, because now I'll have to pay you back, or my boss will.'

The audience cheer and laugh at this. They all know about trade-outs. So I get thunderous applause. I make my way back to my seat and plonk the trophy on the table. Everyone hugs me and tells me how wonderful I am. I love it. The trophy is actually a golden ear, it is totally tacky, but I don't care.

Afterwards the suites are really hopping, the music is blasting and everybody seems to love me. I am floating. Bob is marching possessively at my side. I think of 'Hotel California' and realise how on the ball the words are.

In the Shine suite I finally get to talk to Jimmy Farrell. 'This beer is pure piss,' he tells me.

'There's champagne,' I say brightly.

'Ah can't stand it, it's just fizzy piss.' He gestures round the room. 'How can you stick aw' o' this, a wee Irish lassie like you?'

I smile inanely and he shakes his head dolefully. 'Didya ever in yer life think ye would meet so many wankers at once?'

I agree wholeheartedly because I want him to like me, but my words have a hollow ring because I am enjoying the adulation of the wankers very much.

Bob sticks to me like a plaster, all evening. I am trying not to think of Nate, but the buzz is wearing off. Perhaps I will go

211

to bed. I say this to Bob and he smiles at me.

'Want me to escort you to your room?'

'No thanks, I'm really tired, I'll be fine.' And I leave.

My feet are sore anyway as I am wearing my new, very high-heeled shoes, which have wooden soles and a sort of perspex slip-on bit. Lindy has assured me they are 'very LA'. I am walking down the long corridor towards my room when I hear the ping of the other elevator.

'Hey, Maggie baby, gimme some lovin'.' It is Bob.

'You followed me.'

'Well, Maggie, that's what happens if you wear those lil' "follow me, fuck me" shoes.'

'What did you call my new shoes?'

'I believe you heard.' Despite myself, I smile. He takes it as encouragement.

'Shoot, Maggie, you're the star of the show, you can't go to bed early, can you? Why don't we find something to waken you up a little bit?'

I feign ignorance. 'Such as?'

He winks knowingly, and blocks one nostril. 'C'mon,' he says, 'let's go to my room, it's only one floor down, and Miss Sinead ain't here.'

I mean to say no, but somehow I don't, I follow him. His room is not as big as mine. He goes to the little fridge, or mini bar as I have learned it is called, and gets out two beers. We sit at the table. He has a little kit just like Zollie's. I wonder, are they standard issue for record people? He goes through the little chopping thing and lays out lines. We snort a few lines. It is strong. After a few minutes I start to feel a bit shaky. I tell him this and he lights a joint.

'Here, this will help calm you down, hon.'

It doesn't. There is a fast pulse beating in my neck. I am scared. I am going to die of a drug overdose in a strange hotel room in LA with a man I hardly know. My mother will die

212

from the embarrassment of it all. I am about to cry. I tell him I want to go back to my own room. Bob puts his arms round me.

'Maggie, honey, you're just a bit spooked. Look, take this.' He gives me a Quaalude. 'This will work, but let's go back up to your suite and I promise you you'll feel better soon.'

I am so grateful when Bob gently guides me back up to my room, opens the door and says he will put me to bed. I don't even mind that he seems to feel that he is invited too.

He is intent on making love. I tell him I have just broken up with my boyfriend and don't feel ready to be with anyone else, although I am, strangely enough, very attracted to him.

'Never mind,' he says, 'we don't need to have sex, I'll just eat your pussy.'

'But that is sex,' I say in horror, no, make that mild horror, I can't seem to articulate my resistance very well. I should really be screaming, very loudly.

'No, hon,' he tells me, 'I promise you, *eatin' ain't cheatin'*.' He says this with such fervour, almost like it was part of the constitution of the United States, that I give in and have my first experience of oral sex. I am aware that it is extremely intimate and I certainly don't return the favour, but Bob doesn't seem to mind, and it is pleasurable in the extreme. I'm sure it is a double mortal sin, far worse than drugs. I shudder to think what my immortal soul will look like now.

23

Bob and I and a whole posse of Southern record promotion men are on the same flight home, the red eye. The cabin lights are dimmed but we are all wide awake, the steady chopping of coke followed by noisy snorts from the first class loo, can be heard clearly throughout the cabin. The mood is one of hilarity, though everyone looks wrecked. In Atlanta, I say goodbye to Bob. He tells me he will be in touch, but fortunately he is not expecting our 'romance' to continue because, as he confessed when we were on the plane, he actually has a girlfriend in Atlanta. I am surprised at how shallow this makes me feel.

I call Sharla from Atlanta while I am waiting for my next flight and give her the low-down on the convention. I rehash the whole trip. I express misgivings about Bob, and she tells me I have got to stop thinking I need to be in love with every guy I sleep with. I agree with her, although in my gut I don't really believe it. Still, I can live with that philosophy for now. Maybe I have grown up just a bit over the last five days.

Zollie is thrilled to bits with both the platinum disc and the Golden Ear. He is keen for both to remain at the station. I am happy to oblige. In the cold light of day the ear is perfectly ghastly – a large golden ear on a stick. He points out, in his demented way, that I wouldn't have won anyway if he hadn't paid for the dress, so I agree and we are all happy. He gets Ed to do another full page article about me. It is cringingly awful. I sound like a mad leprechaun with golden ears, and the picture of me is vile. The photographer has shot it from below so I look like I have a massive hump on my back and huge nostrils. I send it home anyway; I know my parents will be delighted no matter how I look.

Zollie takes the ear to help with his selling. It is a talisman for him. He brandishes it at possible accounts and tells everyone I am 'flavour of the month'. This means everyone thinks I am wonderful, or says I am even if they don't think it, because other people do and they don't want to look as if they don't know who's happening. I have also made some friends at the convention; Mark calls me all the time now, as does Bob – our little 'escapade' has forged a bond between us. He comes to town to take me for dinner and to work his latest release. He checks into the Hilton. I go to meet him and we do lots of coke and smoke some weed and then we end up in bed. I go into work next morning feeling slightly jittery. I haven't had much sleep. Then, when I am on the air, I suddenly have a massive nosebleed. I put three in a row records on and go outside. Maybellyne follows me into the loo. She presses a cold cloth to my nose and holds it till the bleeding stops. Then she shakes her head and looks me straight in the eye. I am embarrassed at the fierceness of her gaze.

'Maggie, honey, this has got to stop.'

'What has?'

'You know what. You look like shit.'

God, this is strong stuff coming from Maybellyne. 'What do you mean?'

'I mean we are all real worried about you, well, certainly

215

Bilbo and me. How much do you weigh? About ninety pounds?'

'No, about a hundred.'

'It's not enough, and I may be a big ole fat girl, but I'm not dumb. I know what gives people nosebleeds.'

'Maybellyne, I'm sorry, I don't do it very much.'

'Once is too much.'

'I know, but it just helps me forget Nate and besides, everybody in the business does it all the time.'

'You are too intelligent to believe that makes it okay, and last night? Maggie honey, you need to value yourself more.'

I feel ashamed. She is referring to Bob I think. 'I'm sorry,' I mumble.

She strokes my hand. 'You know, baby, you'll be fine, you're already getting over Nate, but you need to ease up on the drugs or you'll forget who you are.'

She's right, of course, but how can I explain how messed up I feel?

'Listen to the words of the song playing right now,' Maybellyne says suddenly. I do, it is Billy Joel singing 'Just The Way You Are'. 'Now that might be real corny but that's how we feel about you.'

I start to cry then and she comforts me. I want my mammy. I want to go home. As Lindy would put it, I need a reality check. But it's impossible. I can't afford a ticket. Maybellyne's words have hit hard though, I have to stop the coke, and I really need to stop obsessing about Nate. But it's not that easy.

Then life intervenes. Sinead rings to tell me my favourite auntie, my Auntie Martha, has cancer and only three months to live. She is our spinster aunt and has been so good to us girls all her life. She also cared for our grandparents till they died, and she is only fifty-eight, it is not fair. I will never forgive myself if she dies and I haven't said goodbye, so I need to get back to Ireland fast. Zollie and Maybellyne agree to loan me the money. I book a flight home, but I want to be sure I can get back into the country, so I call Buford and ask him if he will still agree to marry me. He accepts my proposal with alacrity; I suppose he is an old hand at the marriage game anyway. It is all relatively quick here. You post banns and you can do it in three weeks.

My parents and sisters are thrilled I am coming; mind you, I wouldn't dream of telling my parents how I am suddenly able to sort things out. I have told them my boss has paid for the ticket, and I guess I'll make up a white lie, a sort of venial story about a lawyer getting me a permit. It is far better than admitting the real sin, which by my reckoning my parents would consider major mortal, at least. Hardly an ideal husband, our man Buford. They'd pass out if they knew the truth: a three times married and divorced, overweight country and western singer with one gold tooth, and not even a Catholic. Hell is waiting for me. Well, purgatory, as long as I don't have sex with him, and this certainly is not an option. I'd more or less said that I could only cope with platonic during our chat on the phone, and he'd told me that was cool for now. I suppressed the feeling of alarm at the use of 'for now'.

I am in town at lunch with Buford in Bistro working out some of the details. He seems inordinately happy for a man who is about to be used for visa purposes. Maybe he enjoys the marriage ceremony or something, he obviously isn't too good at the bit after the actual vows are made, but hopefully that won't apply with fake marriages. As I get up to go to the loo I spot Nathan Gilmore in the restaurant. I smile at him and on the way back to my table I stop and talk to him.

'How nice to see you, Maggie, we have missed you so much.'

His words seem so kind and so genuine, I feel touched. He also looks so much like Nate I feel disproportionately familiar. I am about to reply when, to my horror, I burst into tears. He guides me quietly but firmly to the door and out into the sunshine.

'My Lord, I didn't mean to upset you, you poor baby, is everything okay?'

'Yes, it is, I mean it's not really. It's just my Auntie Martha is dying and I have to go home and I am marrying Buford so I can get back into America – it's not a real marriage like it would have been with Nate, just a sort of business deal. I loved Nate, you see, I loved him. Oh, I'm so sorry.' I fall into his big strong hug and sob my heart out. After I wise up and stop, he suggests I come and see him at his office tomorrow.

When I go back in Buford is in a state. He has some poor waitress pinned to the wall accusing her of body-snatching. He didn't see me go outside and consequently he thought I'd collapsed in the loo. When the hapless waitress said I wasn't there he was about to burst in and break down a door. I manage to calm everything down and when Buford introduces me as his fiancée I grimace and don't contradict him. The waitress gets a huge tip by way of apology and Buford and I part amicably with a list of weddingy things for me to do of the form-filling variety. I hope I don't screw up. I guess Buford knows them off by heart.

Lindy is coming down for the mock wedding and then I am returning with her to New York and then home. Zollie is unsure about letting me off the air that long, but I shall only be gone six days, and Maybellyne, Annie Mae and Shirley have all pitched in on my side. I have also just been responsible for 'breaking' a few more hits, and the giveaways are coming thick and fast from the record companies. We are getting free tickets for every major rock concert in Atlanta and Nashville, and we have even been up to Memphis for the Stones' 'Miss You' tour. Zollie loves this high profile and since a lot of it is down to my bullshit and being Irish, I'm still a viable commodity. Anyway, he's a friend now, he is to act as best man at the fake wedding. You need two witnesses even for pretend ones.

I am intrigued by Nathan Gilmore's offer of lunch. He has always made me feel welcome – Bitsy could think what she wanted, but having Nathan on my side meant she toed the line. I also want him not to think less of me. I had given Nate my word that I would not shop him, but something in me wanted to check that I hadn't been painted as the baddie. So during a break at work next morning I phone his office and his secretary puts me straight through. He asks if I have plans for Saturday evening. I say not really, so he says to be prepared for a long day as he would like to introduce me to his favourite restaurant and it might take some time. He offers to send a car, and I am about to say no and then I figure, why not? I might as well have my last dose of luxury.

And luxury it is. I think we are on our way to the golf club, but we only stop there to pick Nathan up and head off to the airport.

'Well, Maggie,' he says as we drive off, 'my favourite restaurant is in Kentucky, my mama was from there. I have a soft spot for the Bluegrass State.'

We drive right to the runway beside the plane. You don't even have to go inside the airport. My God. I try to act nonchalant, but we are flying to Kentucky for lunch. I can't quite take it in, but I have a feeling we're not going there for Kentucky Fried Chicken.

And so I get my first flight in a private jet. It seems incredibly roomy with just the two of us. I am worried that I mightn't be dressed well enough, although I am wearing a nice dress – one of the dresses Nate bought me in Atlanta – and I am thin. Too thin. Then I start to worry that he might be a dirty old man and I may be sending out the wrong signals. My fears are groundless, he is my dream date – affectionate and paternal, and flirtatious in enough measure to make me feel feminine.

Another car is waiting for us in Louisville and we are whisked off to a really fancy restaurant. It is obviously a Michelin one, or whatever America's equivalent is. Either Nathan owns it or they think he is God, because I have never been treated so well in my life. The waiters (there seem to be dozens of them) are busy pulling chairs back and anticipating our every whim. My appetite suddenly returns as dish after dish appears before me. Nathan is really good company. I can see why some women prefer older men. He doesn't ask any questions about Nate, just makes a few little remarks that I can nod to, or not. First of all we agree that the lunch will be our secret. Then he says, 'I guess you're upset things didn't work out between you two?'

I nod.

'I know you loved my boy.'

Again I nod. I am not sure how to respond to this. 'Yes, I love him a lot. I mean, I did . . . I know it all seemed to happen really fast and I'm only twenty-two . . . well, I'm twenty-three now, but—'

'It's not my business, but I'm guessing he screwed up. Now, can things be fixed?'

'I don't think so.'

'Maggie, you know you could have a very comfortable life as Mrs Nate Gilmore?'

'Yes, of course I do, but that's not why I liked him.'

'I know that, but you still have feelings for him?'

'I'm getting over him.'

'You know, not all marriages are made in heaven. If you and Nate like each other and could have a family, make a go of things, well I guess you could both be allowed your "free time" occasionally. You'd have plenty of domestic help.'

I look at him and say nothing. His face is relaxed, but it registers with me then that he *knows* about Nate being queer. They all must guess, even Priscilla. No wonder they were keen on the marriage. Nathan regards me intently.

220

'I would like you to reconsider. I know Nate wants to marry you. I'm sure he would behave. I think it'd settle him down.'

'I don't think it would work if it wasn't quite real.' I am close to tears.

Nathan is gracious, he knows not to push. Then he says quietly, 'But you are going to marry this singer fella, Buford. Tell me, Maggie, can you trust him?'

'I think so, I mean it's not real either, I won't really be married . . . We aren't going out . . . I won't, eh . . . you know . . .' I am not sure how to put this.

'You mean you won't consummate it?' he says gently.

'No, we won't. He's just doing me a favour. You see, I just don't think I'm ready to leave America for good yet and it's too expensive to get a Green Card from a lawyer.'

'I would be happy to arrange that for you.'

'No, I couldn't let you, but thank you.'

'Okay, here's my final word. If anything goes wrong, I want you to promise me you'll call me and tell me. You hear?'

I promise him I will. And then we have the best lunch of my whole life and the most amazing wine, and I tell him all about Ireland and my mammy and daddy and my sisters and the Christmas tree, and how I felt seeing theirs at Christmas, and he laughs and says Bitsy is just crazy and he'd love to see a higgledy-piggledy tree. He says he's sure I could start a fashion for them.

'I'll bet it's a proper tree, it sure sounds fun with all your little school ornaments hanging on it, not some fancy expensive nonsense. Why, we had a blue tree a year back. I had to put my foot down.' He tells me about growing up with Cora's mammy looking after him and his parents always being away and how he played with Cora's brother because he was the only boy, just like Nate. Then he went away to school and was very lonely. He tells me about taking over the company when his daddy died and how he loves being a granddaddy. We chat endlessly and effortlessly, and he gives me such confidence because he laughs at all my jokes. He also makes me feel important and deserving of all the various people in attendance.

And then, too suddenly, it is five o'clock and it's time for us to leave. The car has waited outside. We fly back and have brandies on the plane. Glenn Gould is playing Bach on the sound system. Nathan says he is the best pianist ever for Bach, and he will send me a recording of him playing the Goldberg variations. I am drunk but happy, and as I get into bed that night I lie awake for a while and think about the unusual day I have just had. Probably one of the best I will have in my whole life, and sadly I realise that I would have done very well as a Gilmore.

But it seems instead I am to be the fourth Mrs Buford McConnell.

'I can't believe I'm going to wear this. I look demented!' I am looking in the mirror at the cowgirl outfit Lindy and Sharla have talked me into wearing.

'Honey, we need to send this up. There has not gotta be one serious moment today. Right, Lindy?'

'Absolutely. Look, doll, it's a *fake* wedding; anyway this is my only chance to go country without losing all my friends.'

Lindy is tying her dark curls with a bandanna, and wriggling into a fringed, suede cowgirl jacket. Sharla and Lindy are my 'bridesmaids'. I am wearing blue jeans, a red and blue checked shirt, cowboy boots and a fringed leather jacket. I also have a cowgirl hat, which I may or not wear. I expect it's the right idea, turning it all into a total farce. Even Buford seems to be playing along, but then he's a cowboy anyway.

The 'ceremony' takes only slightly longer than the driving test, and is easier. At the ring bit Sharla gets a fit of the giggles because the guy who is marrying us is wearing a red wig and Buford's hat brushes it accidentally and knocks it to one side. We are all wasted. Before we came into the 'office', Zollie produced a killer joint. 'Wonderful Wedding Weed' he called it. I need to be stoned to handle this.

We swap rings, kiss and leave with what seems to the poor bewigged notary indecent haste. He just about manages to tell us to 'Hev a reall reall heppy laafe together. Ya heah?' before we leave for Ho Lo's Chinese restaurant in the Big Black Box, which now has a Pink Floyd *Dark Side of the Moon* prism on the side. Bilbo drives us, of course, I can't believe he doesn't mind chauffeuring loonies around so much. Lindy and Sharla are in the back singing, 'Mama don't let your babies grow up to be cowboys'.

The lunch is, of course, a trade-out. We make our way through a vast menu for eight. The dope has given us the munchies. Zollie is away with the fairies. He keeps saying 'Hullo Ho Lo'. It gets annoying after the twentieth time. Mr Ho Lo, if indeed that is his name, smiles serenely. Personally I think a karate chop in the balls would be a more understandable response. When we get to the fortune cookies – there is unsurprisingly no cake – Zollie stands up.

'I want you all to be the first to know that Shirley and myself have just got ourselves engaged, so the next wedding will be a real one. This here is just a dress rehearsal.'

We all cheer and toast them with Chinese beer. I am genuinely delighted for them. Zollie seems like a different person since he met Shirley. I look around the table: Zollie, Shirley, Bilbo, Maybellyne, Sharla, and Lindy, and Buford of course. I have made some good friends here. I smile to myself. Buford sees me smile and squeezes my arm affectionately.

'Well Mrs Buford McConnell, are you a happy bunny?'

I hear the words out loud and my blood chills. I very nearly throw up the lunch on the spot. What the fuck have I done? Everyone watches as Buford hands me a package, smiles, and declares solemnly, 'I got you something as a memento of the day.'

Shit! I didn't get him anything. I smile, thank him, and take it.

'Go on ahead and open it, baby.'

I open the package slowly and can't believe my eyes. It is a gun, a fucking gun. Is he crazy or what? But no, everyone is nodding approval. Well, except Lindy, who is trying not to laugh. These people are insane. I know America has a gun culture, I know this is a mock wedding, but how black a sense of humour has he got?

'It's a special ladies thirty-eight; y'all can keep it in your purse. I figured it was the only way you was gonna git your gun in this marriage.'

Oh, so he *has* a sense of humour. I know this is a colloquialism for having an orgasm. Everyone laughs and Zollie pipes up that I was probably missing mine, having to leave it back in gun-toting Ireland.

'Thanks so much, Buford, you shouldn't have.'

I can probably sell it or give it back later. I don't know a thing about guns, even if I am from Northern Ireland. I take a quick look at it and shiver. It looks like a toy. I find it impossible to believe that something this small can end a life. I look at Lindy, her right eyebrow is just passing the top of her forehead. She winks at me and I relax and put it in my bag. I must remember to take it to the safety deposit box tomorrow.

Bilbo has brought a Polaroid camera, which I think is appropriate considering it's an instant wedding. We pose for photos outside in the parking lot. I think we all look absurd but then that's how it should look, and it has been fun. But I have to get home, straighten up my act and get ready for Ireland.

Next morning Lindy and I are on a flight to New York, me with my masses of documentation so that I will be readmitted. I have left my new 'husband' behind without a pang of regret. I hope when I really get married it will be a lot better than this.

★

On the Aer Lingus flight to Dublin, via Shannon, I am sitting beside a priest. It all feels a bit surreal. Maybe the old confessional urge is still in me, because I have to bite my tongue several times to stop myself from confiding in him about my crazy wedding. Now that I am away from the loonies I am starting to come to my senses somewhat. Never mind, I console myself with the fact that we just have to stay married for six months.

The weather is crap the entire six days I am home, but I am not here for the weather. My family are overjoyed to have me back, and I am so happy to see them. There are lots of remarks about my mid-Atlantic accent, which stops after the first day or so when my Belfast nasal has been reabsorbed. My thinness is exclaimed over and worried over by every single family member. Sinead has primed them by implying that it is because of my broken engagement, and I let everyone think that. It is partly the truth – I obviously can't talk about coke. I am managing very well without it though, so I resolve to stay that way. I was getting too dependent, and if I am honest, I don't even enjoy the way it makes me feel. Unfortunately, Sinead has filled their heads full of Nate's wealth and they have seen pictures of him and his house so therefore mingled with all the sympathy is the sense of regret that I won't be elevating the family to millionaire status.

There is a party for me. I have had more to drink in a week here than I would in a month in Tennessee, but of course there are absolutely no drugs. I forgot my birth control pill as well, so I think I might as well stop that for good, or at least till I am in a steady relationship again. My mother seems relieved that I am not getting married yet. She thinks I am not ready for marriage. She is probably right, and she was having awful trouble talking Daddy into going over to that 'godforshaken' country for the wedding.

The day after I arrive I go round to spend a few hours with Auntie Martha. She has a nurse coming twice a day but mostly my mother and her other sisters are taking turns to look after her. She doesn't want to die in hospital if at all possible. She is in the front bedroom propped up with lots of pillows in my granny's big bed. She looks so small and old, I have to stop myself gasping. But she knows I am shocked. After I have hugged her and settled myself on the bed beside her she says, 'Now darlin', I have cancer, so that's my excuse for losing all this weight, what's yours?'

'Well, I expect I didn't feel like eating for a while after I broke up with Nate.'

'But that's been a couple of months now, are you still not over him?'

'I'm not sure. I know it probably wouldn't have worked.'

'Well, with the help of God you'll come home eventually and meet a nice boy here and settle down.'

I am about to say I don't want to when she interrupts. 'I don't mean right away. I know your mammy and daddy would like you home, but this place is in a terrible state now. It's no life for young ones. You have your fun first and get a bit of experience, see a bit more of America. You know you have cousins in Detroit, don't you? You can always visit them.'

'Yes, maybe next year if I'm still there.'

She takes my hand; it's as if she knows everything. She is so wise. 'But don't sell yourself short, and above all don't lose your self-respect. I'll be praying for you.'

Over the next hour I tell her all about my new life, and then I tell her the real reason Nate and I broke up. She doesn't seem shocked.

'Don't tell Mammy, please.'

'Sure, why would I? She doesn't need to know, she wouldn't understand. But believe me, love, you did the wise thing. Marriage is hard enough, and them boys are built like that, they can't change. It's very sad.'

I leave feeling heartbroken. Although I say goodbye reluctantly to my family, I leave more certain than ever that I am not yet ready to re-enter the humdrum of this life. I have progressed, I am changed; not necessarily in a better way, but for me in a more dynamic and truthful way. This other Maggie is maybe not so nice a person but is closer to how I feel I really want to be. It is, more importantly, closer to who I am – for now anyway.

24

Back to my crazy life then, but I am not looking forward to getting down to the reality of my bogus marriage to Buford. It makes me uneasy. He spooks me by calling my parents' house twice while I am there. I don't know why on earth I gave him the number, there was absolutely no need. I catch myself laughing to myself about the effect my new marital status would have on all of them if I were to tell. I have had to bite my tongue each time I am alone with either Maeve or Sinead. I hate having this secret, but I have to keep my counsel. My parents would simply freak out. Come to think of it, I am freaking out myself at the idea of what I have done. I am looking forward to my impending divorce which we have agreed will be in six months' time in case we arouse suspicion. Buford had suggested we live together to really fool them, but I'll take my chances, there aren't too many immigration people in Tennessee. I suggest we have a weekly meal together instead, and he settles for that.

The trip back is a pain, delayed flights and storms down the eastern seaboard, and God knows how many changes of plane. I don't know how I manage the drive from the airport, and I am hallucinating by the time I get back. Therefore imagine the shock of opening my apartment door and smelling food cooking and seeing Buford wearing a large plaid apron and wielding a spatula. He immediately calls to mind the nine check teddies from Daytona, except they were a lot prettier.

'Welcome home, baby doll!'

'What are you doing here?'

His face falls when I say this. But I am genuinely puzzled. I remember that I had given him keys because he offered to keep an eye on my apartment during my absence. I had given them to him on our wedding day when I was much the worse for wear and not thinking straight.

'Why, I thought I would surprise you by fixing some dinner. I cook a mean shrimp Creole.'

'I'm not hungry.'

'You will be when you see this meal.'

He gives me a sort of awkward bear hug. I try not to push him away. I expect he's just trying to be sweet, but I have a growing sense of alarm. This is not part of the agreement.

'I've missed you, baby,' he sighs.

'I've only been away a week, why would you miss me?' He ignores this remark. I tell him I need a shower and bed as soon as possible, but then I see the look of disappointment on his face. 'Maybe I'll feel better after a shower. I probably should eat something.'

He accepts this and goes off delightedly to 'fix' rice. Southerners fix everything, nobody here cooks.

I stay in the shower for about thirty minutes. It is blissful. I have missed this water-wasting way to wash while at home. In Ireland our shower is a hand-held rubber tube and barely enough water comes out to wet your hair. Every time you work up a lather, it trickles out and you have to shove your head under the tap to get the soap off. I had to bite my tongue when I was home in case they all thought I had got too jumped-up, but the truth is Americans are spoiled. Life is so much easier here, at least as far as creature comforts are concerned.

Buford is right, he is a good cook. The shrimp Creole is delicious. We have an amicable meal. I tell him all about my trip and about seeing Auntie Martha, and all about my sisters. He has been to Ireland on tour, but never to the North. He says he would like to go with me next time. I say nothing. I can't think of anything I would hate more. I think of how much I was longing to show Nate around Ireland and introduce him to all my friends and I start to feel full of self-pity and begin to cry.

'Why, honey, you're exhausted. C'mon, you get yourself to bed. I'll clear up. Would you like me to spend the night here?'

'No, I'm fine, Buford. And thanks so much for dinner, that was really thoughtful of you. You're so sweet.'

I'd never talk like this in Ireland. It seems so phoney. But I have a split personality now. Buford smiles with pleasure at my words, and I feel like a villain. I can't wait for him to leave. I get into bed and I listen to him thrash around the kitchen for a bit, clearing up. He sticks his head around my bedroom door eventually and says goodbye. It is still early, just about eight-thirty, but I have work tomorrow and I can't wait to be alone. He has left before I remember that I should have asked for my keys back. I fall asleep wishing I was still in Ireland after all, crap showers or not.

I go into the station next day, and nothing has changed, it's like the song says, 'It feels like I've never been gone'. Zollie is on overdrive and delighted to have me back, we have a lot of work on. Nothing cheers him up more than the prospect of money, and while I was away he has done a deal with one of the largest beer distributors in town. They have bought a huge amount of airtime with us and we are going to be the sponsors of the Roaring River Rafting Trip. We will be sending ten lucky winners and their partners to North Carolina to the Nantahala River for an all-expenses-paid weekend of white water rafting. I have never tried this, but it sounds like it would be fun. There are places for four people from the station as well. I have to cut the commercial and I find the details in my in tray on top of an enormous pile. I am obviously going to have to crowd the airwaves with my voice to make up for lost time.

About two hours after it airs, the phone rings. It is Zollie. I can't make out whether he is laughing or crying.

'Maggie, you have any calls on the giveaway?'

'No, we haven't, it's odd really, isn't it? I thought the phones would be jammed.'

'I 'spect they would be if anybody understood it.'

'What do you mean?'

'Goddammit, Maggie, what kinda language are you speaking? Did you forget all of your American when you were home?'

'I don't know what you're talking about.'

'Hell what does a "wee ring" mean?'

'It means phone us!'

'Not in Tennessee it don't. A wee ring is a small bitty ring, like a pinky ring, Maggie. If you want somebody to phone you, you say CALL US, you got that?'

'Okay, I'll change it.'

'Right, and what in the hell is a crate of beer?'

'You said we had fifty crates of beer to give away.'

'Hell no, I did not! I said CASES of beer; a crate is what you shift furniture in or put a dead body in. Here in America, beer does not come in crates.'

So I change it. I must have picked up all my old habits of speaking while I was home. I preferred the first one though, it sounded less demented.

Priscilla calls just before I am ready to leave the station. I am somewhat jet-lagged, but I've been putting off meeting her for too long. It's sort of now or never, I have run out of excuses. We arrange to meet at the Japanese restaurant near my apartment.

She asks me about my trip home. I am surprised that she knew. I think at first that her father has told her, and I feel betrayed, but she explains that she called the station while I was away. I don't mention the Kentucky lunch, and neither does she. I guess Nathan has kept his word and has not said anything. I still can't quite believe it happened, I have thought about it a lot. I loved that day, it was so unexpected and so grand somehow. I told everyone at home but I juggled the dates and made it before the break up, they were all suitably impressed. It actually made me think at one point that I might have been unbearable if I were rich. I got so much pleasure out of boasting about it. I suppose I had too much hubris. Well, I'm paying for it now.

It takes Priscilla ages to get round to the broken engagement, she is obviously so well brought up. I don't help her; I'm not sure what tack to take on it. She finally shocks the hell out of me by coming out with, 'Did Tommy have anything to do with your break up?'

I can't believe she said that. I practically choke on the rubbery shrimp I am chewing. 'Tommy? What do you mean? Why did you say that?' I squeak.

'Well, I saw him at the airport a few days before you guys split and when I asked Nate why he was here, he couldn't give me a straight answer. In fact, he seemed downright embarrassed. I was puzzled.' I say nothing. 'You know, he's always been totally obsessed with Nate, right from the first day of college. He was like his slave.'

I am not sure how to respond, but she's obviously no fool. So I say, 'Do you think Tommy is a queer?' There, I've said it out loud.

She goes white at once, and for a second I think she will

pass out, but she takes a gulp of Perrier and looks directly at me.

'That's not what I meant at all,' she says cautiously. 'He might well be, but he's just real pally with Nate and I guess he prefers him to be a bachelor. I thought maybe he had talked Nate into waiting for a while.'

I look at her and say nothing. I am afraid I might give it all away, but also, I know that in her heart she knows.

'You know, I simply hate the way he is fixated on my brother.' She scowls.

I pause and then say, 'It *was* something to do with Tommy.'

'Oh?'

But I can't bear to tell her what it was so I chicken out. 'I suppose in a way he made things difficult for both of us.'

'You know, Maggie, that is so sad. I know Nate really loves you. He's just plain silly to let Tommy get in the way of that. Maybe in a while y'all can get back together again and I'll get to be your sister-in-law after all.'

Her optimism is touching, but sadly, I fear, unfounded. 'It'd have to be after my divorce,' I say, and I tell her the whole saga about Buford. I ham it up for her benefit. I realise I am laughing without faking it for the first time in ages. I tell her about 'getting my gun', and the absurd wedding lunch at Ho Lo's. We decide to live dangerously and order a pitcher of margaritas. I haven't that far to drive and she says she will spend the night with me. I would nearly marry Nate just to have her in my family, she's just brilliant. She leaves next morning with a thumping hangover and a promise to stay in touch. I hope she means it.

Bloody Buford is seriously getting on my nerves. Three times he has 'dropped by' to see how I am. On the day of our 'month anniversary', he arrives with a bunch of flowers. I thank him profusely and go to the Japanese restaurant with him. Once more I finish a plate of rubbery shrimp. I expect he means well when he comes on all possessive like this, but his behaviour makes me feel powerless and trapped, and deeply beholden to him. On the one hand I can't be rude to him because I have used him shamelessly for my purposes, but he is actually starting to harass me, and I don't like it. He's supposed to be cutting a new album in Muscle Shoals, so why is he in town so much? And I hate the way he touches me all the time, sort of rubs my arm and chucks me under the chin, calls me sugar and lots of irritating stuff like that. Sharla says just to grin and bear it till it's time for the divorce. Only four months to go.

I can't believe I am back from Ireland nearly two months. I haven't talked to Nate or seen him, I am trying my best to dismiss all last traces of love for him, to purge all my soft feelings, to stop my constant longing, but it is really hard. One day, in a fit of abject sentimentality, I go to the bank and take out my ring. I think I will go and throw it at him, and then suddenly I can't bear the thought of losing it. I put it back and decide I have to make an effort to get out more. So I agree to join the gang on Friday night. They have got into the habit of going to La Cantina, one of the downtown bars. Tonight there is a great group on, and one of my record guys, Rick from Warner Brothers, has come into town to hear them. Warner has just signed them. Rick is fun, he knows Bob, and they are buddies. It's a beer and tacos place, but the atmosphere is good and we are in fine form. Zollie and Shirley and Steve have joined us. Little brown bottles are passing from hand to hand, visits to the loo abound, but I am sticking strictly to the frozen margaritas. I am off the coke, I have promised Maybellyne, and anyway I love margaritas, I get such a buzz from them. Then, on my way back from the loo, I notice Nate. He is standing beside a really good-looking girl. They look as if they are together. Another girl? I can't believe it. But what did I expect? He'd hardly start swanning round town hand in hand with a guy. I am distraught. I go back to the table and within about the next half hour I down an entire pitcher of margaritas.

Sometime later Buford joins us. I look at him smiling and talking bullshit, being really familiar and even worse, groping all over me, and I feel sick. Every few minutes I peer through the crowd to check out Nate and the girl. Who is she? She is looking at him as if the sun shines out of his arse. He is chatting away to her. I hate her. I hate him. Sue Lynne and Clarence arrive and for some reason this puts me over the edge. Next time I go to the loo I take a little brown bottle. Surely Maybellyne would understand, just this once? I need to look bright and breezy, not dull and jaded. I come back and notice that Sue Lynne is flirting outrageously with Buford. He is simpering like an eejit. Good. I am glad she is distracting him from me. She doesn't know about the 'wedding', or if she does she hasn't said. Clarence Lee is sitting nursing a beer and looking dejected.

Sue Lynne manages to get a jibe at me. Obviously the flirting wasn't pissing me off enough. 'I see Nate Gilmore is with Betsy Anne Roberts,' she announces to the table.

I pretend not to hear. She blabbers on. 'You know Roberts, they own the steel company, big time rich, live on Lookout?'

I chat madly away to Rick. My heart rate must be two hundred and forty, but I don't care. I refuse to listen to it. I want it to burst. When will I start feeling normal again? I feel like going over to Nate and asking him about Tommy in front of this Betsy Anne person, but I control myself. There is talk of going to the Hilton where Rick is staying, presumably to do more coke, but I am in a state now and announce I have to go home.

'Maggie honey, there's no way you can drive.' Shirley is concerned.

'I'll take her,' Buford says. 'I need to get an early night anyways. Got to get to Muscle Shoals before ten tomorrow.'

So it is settled. Buford will take me home. Not ideal, but the idea of bed and getting away from here is suddenly appealing, and wasted as I am, I can't help noticing a little moue of disappointment on Sue Lynne's pretty lip-glossed mouth. We push our way to the door past Nate and the girl. He is talking so animatedly to her he doesn't even see me. I am bereft.

I can't remember getting home, but my head is reeling and Buford is 'fixing' me a cup of coffee. I don't want it. I want to be sick. I actually feel as if I want to die, but I am sort of glad he is here. I have done too much bloody coke and my pulse is too fast, after I had meant to give it up for good too. Maybe I will have a heart attack and then Nate will be sorry.

I decide I will take a shower. I stand there crying with the water running down my face and then I get the urge to throw up. I suppose it is practical if you are going to throw up over yourself to get in the shower first. So here I am, wasted, drunk, vomiting, crying, deeply ashamed at myself, and miles from home. If I was any good, I'd sit down and write myself a country and western song.

Buford is in the living room singing to himself and drinking coffee. I pop my head in – there is no door to pop it around – and announce drunkenly that I am going to bed.

'Go right ahead. I'll just stay here till you settle down, honey.' I don't care. I just want oblivion. I take a Quaalude, I adjust the air conditioning unit and get into bed, it used to keep me awake at first but now it sends me to sleep.

I don't know how long I am asleep, or passed out, when I am aware there is someone on top of me, someone heavy and smelling of cigarette smoke and beer. It is Buford. I try to push him off, but the 'lude has knocked me out.

'What are you doing?'

'Honey, I want you so much. I guess despite my heartfelt desire for you we never did consummate that marriage of ours, did we?' He has a wheedling tone in his voice.

'That wasn't part of the deal. Please get off me.'

'Maggie, please let me make love to you, baby. You must know how I feel about you. I thought if I was patient you would come around to me. You don't know how it feels to be me, hopelessly in love with you from the moment I saw you.'

I am pinned beneath him, helpless, and he is naked and aroused. I am afraid, and not afraid. 'Buford, I like you a lot, but as a friend, a good, dear friend,' I stammer. My head is reeling from the margaritas, and the drugs.

'But I lurve you. I want you, baby, just feel.' He whimpers at me, and takes my hand and tries clumsily to make me touch him.

In the end I surrender, and passively allow him to have me. I feel like an empty vessel. It is horrible, but he calms down afterwards, and tries to kiss me. But he doesn't use anything, so if I don't get some god-awful disease I'll get pregnant anyway. I am still off the contraceptives. I tell him I am going to be sick again and I get in the shower for a second time, feeling humiliated and loathing myself. Somehow I get back to sleep in the guest bed. He is snoring loudly in mine.

Next morning I play possum and refuse to wake until he is gone. I lie there listening to him whistle and shower and I feel appalled. I have no control over my life. I seem to have cut the guidelines. My insides churn. I am glad it is Saturday, no work. I call Sharla, no reply. I try Lindy, she answers at once.

'Hey doll, what's up?'

I tell her what happened.

'That's rape!'

'I sort of let him in the end.'

'Well, it was a pity fuck at best. Never mind, Maggie baby, we've all done it, if men only knew. I suppose it's their desperation gets us.'

'Just say I got pregnant?'

'Jesus! You mean he didn't use anything?'

So now I have that to worry about. Plus I have a thumping hangover. Despite the sunshine I stay in the house all day listening to music and feeling sorry for myself. I wish I could lose my memory.

I haven't answered my home phone for a week. I have a service, call forwarding, which lets my home number ring at the station where Sue Lynne answers it. The pile of pink message slips grows, Buford is my main caller. She hands me a bunch when I come into the station about a week after my encounter with him.

'Why, Maggie, you lil' teaser you! Pore ole Buford has called from Muscle Shoals again. He is just dying to have you return his call,' she simpers at me.

'I am busy, I'll get round to it eventually,' I say tersely.

'He is such a doll, why if I didn't have Clarence Lee for my baby, I would be in lurve with him myself.'

She smiles like a lizard. She has developed this outrageous way of sitting since she got her new boobs; she sort of lies back in the swivel chair and points her nipples at the ceiling. I watch her through the studio window when I am on the air and she is forever tweaking her nipples and rubbing her breasts and rearranging them. They are simply huge now, at least 38DD. She could give Dolly Parton a run for her money. They make her waist seem tiny, and sometimes when I see her mince around the station I get the feeling she will topple over. But she and Clarence Lee are thrilled with them. Zollie finds them a constant source of amusement and butt for his jokes, and poor Bilbo virtually closes his eyes when she passes, so overwhelmed is he by the sheer enormity of them. Yes, Sue Lynne's tits have certainly added a new dimension to life at Q92.

About a week later I am on the air when I see her point to the phone and mouth 'Buford'. I shake my head and she doesn't put it through. I watch her and I see she doesn't hang up, but is pouting and preening and chatting away to him. She can have him. They deserve each other; they both pronounce 'lurve' the same way.

The episode with Buford is haunting me. I can't help blaming myself for being so foolish and getting so wasted, and wondering if I have learned anything at all in my year in the States. I have not had a drink since and I have no intention of touching cocaine again. I must be acting too serious though, 'cos after about a week of brooding Maybellyne stops me as I take my coffee break.

'Maggie, honey, what's up?'

'Nothing, nothing.'

'Y'all aren't still fretting over Nate?'

'No, not that, not that at all.'

'You aren't doing that old snorting again?'

'No, I've stopped, for ever.'

'What then?'

I can't say it out loud to Maybellyne, it seems so sordid, and I don't want her to think badly of me, but she teases it out in a sort of yes no quiz, and I tell her all. I can almost feel my body blush as I speak. I want her to absolve me: I have toyed with the idea of going to confession and communion and cleansing my soul, but then I decided it would be hypocritical for me to crave absolution for my misdeeds. I am a grown-up. I need to live with the consequences. Maybellyne is sweet and understanding, and indignant at Buford, but also, she gently reminds me that these things are more likely to happen when our defences are down; in other words when I am wasted.

'He's calling me all the time,' I tell her. 'I won't take his calls.'

'You need to, and tell him he'll have me to deal with if he won't leave you alone. But stay calm, don't get emotional.'

So I finally take Buford's call – we are running out of

message slips – and tell him over the phone that I want to go ahead with the divorce. I tell him quietly that I am not in love with him. I say I am scared about being pregnant and he tells me he has had a vasectomy. At least that's one less worry. I tell him I appreciate the fact that he has helped me get a Green Card, but I would not be doing him any favours by encouraging him. I refuse to discuss our 'night of passion' as he calls it, despite his entreaties, and I hope fervently he will get the message. But I am wrong. I think he is living on a different level of consciousness to me. He has talked himself into thinking that if I was to make the effort we could really make a go of our marriage. What fucking marriage? It is like talking to a lunatic. I try to keep calm and talk to him without sounding too desperate – this is Lindy's advice too – but despite my efforts I can't get him to see sense. He is a persistent bastard, and for some reason he has decided that he won't go easily.

25

Fortunately, Buford becomes heavily involved in cutting his new album and is spending most of his time in the studios in Alabama. I am in a sort of routine now. Work is suddenly the most important thing in my life, and I have some good news, Sharla is moving to town. She has got a job here, she is going to sell real estate for Happy Havens. The company builds new developments – a small cluster of houses – and starts up new 'family friendly communities'. I think a job selling real estate would be nightmarish, but the money is good and Sharla is so positive about it all. She thinks she will do well, be a success and own her own home before long. She's probably right. She is charming, and people here like to listen to bullshit. She also looks good and I know that helps in selling, at least Zollie swears it does and he should know. I am just glad she'll be near me, I can use a good friend. One thing I won't do though, even for my closest friend, is move into a Happy Haven development. I have my principles.

The whole thing is dragging on too long. I can't count how many times Sharla and I have analysed Buford's behaviour – it seems so unreasonable. Basically, if I had balls, he would have me by them. Lindy is quite sure it's because I had reacted so badly to his pathetic attempt at lurve-making. It obviously offended his masculine susceptibilities that I didn't swoon with gratitude and desire him intensely for ever more, but what the hell did he expect? I mean you can't just jump the bones of some poor drunken drugged-up female when she has no means to defend herself and call it love, even if you are legally married, can you? I don't think so, especially if the marriage has simply been a dodgy deal in the first place. I don't know. I am going crazy at the idea of having to sue him for divorce. It means I will need a lawyer and they don't come cheap here. Where will I get the money?

I spend a lot of my time now pondering my dilemma, so when Priscilla calls me unexpectedly I am caught off guard and I blurt it all out to her. She is appalled. She is such a kindly soul, but too protected I think, too rich to know what life is all about. At least Nate got out of the house, away from crazy old Bitsy. I am tempted to ask about Nate and the Roberts girl, but I don't. I still think about him all the time. I miss kissing him most of all. He has such a warm friendly mouth. He once told me it hadn't really fitted any mouth but mine so well, and I knew exactly what he meant. These thoughts are flitting through my mind as Priscilla repeats that she thinks I should call Mr Jackson, their family lawyer. Is she out of her mind?

'He's very well regarded, Maggie. Hot Shot Jackson is his nickname,' she says.

'Priscilla, I've only met him once, when I got the engagement ring, and it doesn't seem a good idea to call him now that Nate and I aren't getting married any more. He'll hardly know who I am.'

I pause and before I can stop myself I ask her if Nate is engaged again.

'No, he most certainly is not.'

242

'Oh? I heard he was dating someone, Betsy Anne Roberts.'

'Betsy Anne?'

'Yes, is he not?' My heart is thumping, I am sorry I asked. What is wrong with me? Why can't I keep my bloody mouth shut?

'No, they are really just friends. Why, she got engaged to Jake Moss, a close friend of Nate's, just last week. I believe Nate took her out for a meal while Jake was away on a business trip just recently.'

For some reason I am flooded with relief. I am so happy I ask her out to dinner next week. My treat, well actually the station's treat. I suggest the Steak House and she agrees. I am glad I have stayed friends with her, it's the last thing I would have expected, but it is consoling in some way.

I am just coming off the air when Nathan Gilmore calls. I am shaking when I answer.

'Hey, Maggie, how're you doing?'

'I'm fine, just fine, I just finished my show, and I am going to go home and have a swim.' I hope I sound scintillating enough.

'Good, well I'll tell you why I'm calling. Cilla told me you were having problems getting yourself extricated from this here marriage of yours. Now don't be mad at her, I quizzed her a bit when she told me y'all had talked and I'd like to help.'

'I don't know what to say.'

'Well, let me suggest you say nothing and I have Mr Jackson send him a little letter on your behalf. I think that should take care of things.'

'It's very good of you, but I'm sure he'll agree in the end.'

'Maggie, let me do this for you, please.' And he hangs up. I feel completely overwhelmed.

I get a copy of the letter two days later. It seems fairly straightforward, just informs Buford that Jackson, Buchanan and Jackson will be representing me in our forthcoming divorce which they understand will be a mere formality. I show it to Sharla. She is delighted.

'Honey, you will not see him for dust after this, unless I am greatly mistaken: according to this letter you appear to be a client of the most prestigious law firm in the Southern United States.'

Sharla is not greatly mistaken. Four weeks later and after filling out a lot of forms, and one court appearance lasting five minutes, I am no longer the fourth Mrs Buford McConnell, and he is free to start the hunt for number five.

I enjoy being free. In some way the whole business of going through a fake marriage so soon after I had intended to go through a real one had unsettled me more than I realised it would. And the last few months have virtually pushed me over the edge. I have never even mentioned the episode to my family, they would have gone berserk. So now I won't have to tell them, that's a relief for a start. And the good news is that I have a Green Card. I am now a registered alien. I can move on, I can become a citizen in five years' time if I want. I can't think five years ahead, I am learning to live life as it comes. One thing I do know, I hope I never set eyes on Buford again. I hate the stupid bastard. Zollie is still mates with him, but they haven't been spending too much time together these days. Shirley is taking up a lot of Zollie's time; to Annie Mae's eternal delight, and Zollie's, Shirley is pregnant, and we are all off the drugs. It's official station policy. Buford is still in Alabama trying to record another hit. I hope he misses. Still, maybe I'll get over that eventually too. Lindy says in time I'll see the whole thing as a huge joke. I hope she's right.

26

We are divorced almost six months when Buford finds wife number five. It is Sue Lynne. She has gone and left Clarence Lee, who is allegedly losing his mind with grief. He has just made the last payment on her new boobs. Bad investment. But undoubtedly this is a match made in heaven, she and Buford deserve each other. She is leaving the station and I will suffer through her going away party just to please Zollie. It means I have to see Buford, but I am a big girl now. I have booked a holiday with Lindy and Sharla to the Virgin Islands this fall – I am saying fall instead of autumn. I have reached my twenty-fourth birthday and am still single. I am going to be bridesmaid in September for Zollie and Shirley. I am happy for them, she is so good for Zollie. I think in some way I have found equilibrium.

So this new, mature Maggie goes to Sue Lynne's farewell party. I am feeling cool about it. I know once he is married again I can awaken from the bad dream. I don't even get wound up watching Sue Lynne and Buford eating the faces off each other throughout, I simply wish them well in their new life. She and Buford are moving to Nashville, he is hoping to regain some fame and fortune with the release of this new album. I will be glad to have them out of town. Somehow the conversation gets around to guns – not unusual here. Sue Lynne wants a new one. Why? Did she wear out her old one? I suddenly remember my 'wedding gun'. I say to Buford that I would like to give it back to him, she can have that.

'It was far too generous of you, and I could never use it.' The truth was I had put it into a cupboard in the apartment and forgotten all about it.

'It's a lil' ole lady's gun,' he says, 'too purdy for me to pack, but if you're sure, sugar babe.' He looks at Sue Lynne.

'Oh Buford baby,' she simpers, 'I'd just love to have me a little bitty gun. I could carry it in my purse, for protection. I know just how much you want me to be safe.'

Yes, that's all very well, but how safe are we with idiots like her toting guns about the place?

She nods enthusiastically at the group. 'I just love guns. Whaa', ma daddy has about two dozen. Our family have always had guns.'

'Well,' I say to her, 'you'd better call and pick it up then. I don't want to carry it in the car. I hate the thing. I haven't even touched it ever.'

And tonight, on their way to Nashville, they call to pick it up. They arrive just as I finish my take-away meal. I go to get the gun. I want them all out of here as soon as possible, Sharla is coming round later. Buford looks particularly repulsive tonight and I swear Sue Lynne's tits are getting bigger each time I see her. They sway when she moves. I wonder briefly if they are inflatable. I go to the cupboard to get the thing. I open the box to check it's there and to look, out of curiosity I suppose. It's shiny. I suppose as guns go it is 'pretty' – pretty deadly that is. Then Sue Lynne opens her stupid mouth.

'I guess, Maggie, you're lucky Buford here didn't turn it on you.'

'What are you talking about?'

'Why, the way you was so mean to him, begging him to marry you after Nate Gilmore jilted you, and then two-timing him like that.'

'Two-timing him! What are you talking about?'

'Yes, after all he'd done for y'all.'

I count to ten and grimace. God, give me patience. I feel like screaming. Buford is looking uncomfortable and wants to leave. I don't know what he has told her about us, but I am obviously cast in the role of baddie. I suppose I have to live with that but what in the name of God has he been filling her head with? She is wound up, stoked, she can't stop herself, she is on a roll. All the distaste she has felt for me over the year or so I have known her spills forth like bile. Her lip is quivering with indignation.

'Yew always was a taker, Maggie, not a giver like me. Whaa', I don't know how yew have fooled so many people up till now, yew and that cute aarish accent of yours. Still, I guess they all learn in the end, don't they?' She pauses and smiles her scaly lizard smile. 'Well, Buford and me had better get our asses outa here.'

Go, I think, just get the hell out and leave me alone. But she isn't done yet.

'Oh, and I have some news for you, we're gonna have a lil' baby, what do you think of that? That's all he ast from you and yew couldn't even give him that. Well now he's gonna be real happy and I'm gonna lurve him like he deserves.'

The bastard! He could have got me pregnant, the bloody lying bastard. What a thought! Vasectomy my arse! The gun is in my hand. I suddenly find myself pointing it at her. I pull the trigger. Partly to see what it feels like – it is unloaded of course. There is an enormous bang and Sue Lynne falls down. I guess it wasn't unloaded after all. Then in walks Sharla.

★

So here I am, waiting for them to come and take me away. What an ignominious end to a blossoming career. I hear the doorbell ring and as if in a trance I buzz them up. Sharla puts a comforting arm round me. 'Don't worry, honey, remember you were preevoked.'

It is like a scene out of a movie. Everything here is in a way. Two paramedics rush in, and with them two policemen. I recognise one of them from the night Nate 'burgled' me. He says hi and smiles in recognition. They seem very friendly for people who have come to incarcerate me.

'I believe y'all have had an incident with a gun?'

I am dumbfounded. I have suddenly lost the power of speech. It all seems to be happening in slow motion. Sharla is explaining something about the gun going off by accident. Buford hasn't said a word yet. It is as if the appearance of the police has rendered him dumb too. The paramedics and the police, in synch, move over to Sue Lynne's body, stretcher at the ready. The paramedic puts a stethoscope to her chest.

'I can't hear a heartbeat,' he declares solemnly.

I feel the room start to spin. I am going, about to lose my grip, when suddenly Sue Lynne sits bolt upright. I scream. I have become a banshee. I scream louder than I have ever screamed in my life. All attention turns to me, I point a shaky finger at Sue Lynne, all eyes follow it. She gets to her feet very slowly. She is clutching herself round the bosom. Her chest is curiously flat. Buford waddles sobbing to her side.

'Oh baby, baby, ma purdy baby I thought yew was a goner.'

Sue Lynne looks dazed. 'Ma boobs seem to have burst or something. Did y'all hear a big ole bang?'

I guess her silicone implants have imploded, and the shock momentarily stunned her. I knew no good could come of those tits. I try to concentrate. One of the policemen is pointing to a hole above the door. There is actually a hole. The bullet has gone into the wall. I sit down, shaking, and finally allow myself the luxury of tears.

Sharla tells them apologetically that it was all just a terrible mistake, we shouldn't have called them at all. I was showing them the gun and it went off by accident. The policeman turns to me and asks if I have a licence for the gun. Buford suddenly finds his voice and tells them he has it and can drop it by the station. They recognise Buford then and spend about ten minutes discussing the merits of country and western music and ask him for his autograph. I wish they would all just go. The bizarre nature of the whole business is too much for me, I just want to sit down and recover. Fortunately, one of the police radios crackles into life and they make to leave. As he is going out the door one of the policemen turns to me and says to me, 'I sure enjoy all of those British groups you play, ma'am. I never miss your show.'

'Thank you,' I manage to croak. I am weak with relief. 'You'll have to drop by the station and I'll give you some albums.'

'Why, that would be real kind of you.'

'No, I'd be happy to, we like to keep our listeners happy.'

'And how's Mr Nate, Mr Gilmore, ma'am?' His tone is respectful.

Of course, my engagement to Nate had been in all the papers, and needless to say we didn't put an announcement in to say we had split. Well this isn't quite the moment to explain the changes.

'He's just fine,' I manage. 'He's doing real good.' I am starting to sound like I am from here.

'You give him my best, ya heah?'

'I certainly will.'

I wonder to myself if that connection had anything to do with how understanding they had been about the whole situation. If it had been Belfast we'd all be in jail by now, or interned.

Buford and Sue Lynne follow them out the door. She is clutching her poor collapsed bosom and weeping quietly. Sharla and I listen as Buford reassures her that he'll pay for the biggest pair of tits in Tennessee. Sue Lynne and Buford *are* the biggest pair of tits in Tennessee. But they are out of my life now, I can move on. Sharla comes in with a pitcher of margaritas and pours us each one. On the radio Joe Walsh is singing 'Life's Been Good To Me So Far'. We drink to that.